"We have a visitor."

A little girl in the green knickers of the Junior Space Scouts, several boxes of cookies cradled in her arms, stood genteelly on the front stoop.

"We don't really have time for this now, HARV," I said. "But order a few boxes of those peanut butter things and a box of mints."

"Hmmm," HARV said.

"You're right. Forget the mints."

"Do you not think that it's odd for a Junior Space Scout to be selling cookies at this time of night?" he asked.

"What are you thinking, here?"

"I am taking the liberty of performing a heat and energy scan on our visitor."

"Are you using your keen computer intuition now?" I asked.

HARV ignored me and kept his attention focused on the video feed as it switched to an infrared and heat-coded view. The two of us watched as the image of the little girl morphed into a two-meter-high hulking form: a giant assassin in Junior Space Scout Trojan horse disguise.

"This is her actual body size and mass," HARV said.

I suppressed a gulp.

"I guess we won't be getting those cookies after all."

THE PLUTONIUM BLONDE

JOHN ZAKOUR & LAWRENCE GANEM

DAW BOOKS, INC.

DONALD A. WOLLHEIM, FOUNDER

375 Hudson Street, New York, NY 10014

ELIZABETH R. WOLLHEIM
SHEILA E. GILBERT
PUBLISHERS

www.dawbooks.com

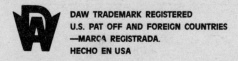

To my wife Olga and my son Jay.
—*John Zakour*

To Lisa, Jackson, and Kalie who are everything.
And to Philip and Shirley who are the greatest people
I'll ever know.

. . . . And to Douglas Adams who was too funny for words.
—*Lawrence Ganem*

ACKNOWLEDGEMENT

There are too many people to whom the authors are, in one way or another, deeply indebted to mention here without seriously increasing the raw paper costs of this book. So here's only the very tip of an enormous, guilt-inducing, iceberg of people. If you don't see your name here, we're very sorry, but rest assured that you're probably somewhere just below the water line.

First, many thanks to Tom Rickey, Ron Pool, and Natalia Padilla for their inspiration. It should also be mentioned that they are not quite as macho, klutzy, or psionic as the characters which they inspired.

Thanks also to Sean Redlitz and the SciFi Channel's official website, who years ago set aside some room on their server for Zach and his adventures (and then graciously removed the material from the site so we could make some actual money *selling* the material in book form).

Thanks also to Mark Reichelt, Mike Segroves and Peanut Press who, two corporate owners ago, gave the story life as an e-book where it reigned supreme as a bestseller until being displaced by the electronically ubiquitous Stephen King (which, as company goes, is not too shabby).

And more thanks than can adequately be expressed here go to Betsy Wollheim of DAW for a thousand e-mails of editorial inspiration and direction. Thanks also to Sean Fodera for bringing us into the hallowed DAW halls and to Joshua Bilmes for the eradication of all loose ends and matters of legal minutiae.

Many thanks as well to all of those who have laughed (in a good way) at John and Larry over the years, among them: Mary and Steve Erdman, Mitch Ganem, Jennifer Ganem, Dan Gilligan, Dave Martin, Tom Swett, Tom Bickford, Rich Ashooh, John Nasser, Dave Hernandez and Jen Quimby.

Thanks to John's parents, Mike and Evelyn Zakour, as well as every Zakour, Ganem, Abraham, Brown and Essa to ever walk the face of the earth. But thank you especially to Barbara "loved by the children—hated by the adults" Essa. (Luckily for Barb, we're *all* children at heart).

John would also like to thank his creditors who were the true driving force behind his selling this story in all its incarnations.

And above all else, our deepest and most sincere gratitude goes to . . . wait a second, you're not actually still *reading* this are you? It's the acknowledgement, for crying out loud. No one reads the acknowledgement. Don't you have anything better to do? Start reading the book already, will you? It's very good. We promise. Really, don't waste your time with the acknowledgement. We only included this so our family and friends wouldn't complain about us not mentioning them in the book. Now please, move on to the next page. You're starting to embarrass yourself.

1

My name is Zachary Nixon Johnson. I am the last private detective on earth. I'll get to the whys and wherefores of that a little later and, as you'll see, it's not exactly one hundred percent true, but it sounds good and hopefully I've at least got your attention now.

The year is 2057 and, after a handful of species-altering upheavals, earth-shattering cataclysms, history-changing extraterrestrial contacts, and pop-culture disasters, the world is now a pretty safe place. I won't bore you with the judicial, economic and anthropological minutiae of the *New* New World Order, but suffice to say that the sun still rises in the east, the human race is still around to notice it, and we still pull down the window shades, roll over in bed and sleep until noon whenever possible.

Of course, the world's not perfect. People still run the shades-of-gray gamut of good to evil. There are still cops and robbers, saints and sinners, voters and politicians. And every once in a while, some crazy thing happens that threatens society, all of humanity, or the entire space-time continuum.

And for some reason, it always happens on my watch.

I guess that's as good a place as any to start this story.

2

It began like any other day, which is the way these things usually do. I was at my office on the New Frisco docks, watching the tourists outside, and trying hard not to think about how long it had been since good news had walked through my office door. I was also losing a game of holographic backgammon to the holo-image projection of my trusty, though occasionally annoying, computer compatriot HARV.

"So I catch the SIMFOLKS security guy, red-handed, stealing parts from the droid manufacturing plant. And I literally mean, *red-handed*. He was smuggling a hand out in his lunchbox. You know what I mean?"

"Oh, yes," said HARV, with a dignified smile on his face. "I understand the irony of the situation."

For some reason, whenever he projects himself, HARV likes to take the form of an elderly, balding English gentleman (or at least how HARV computes the optimal elderly, balding English gentleman should look). I guess he thinks that it gives him an air of distinction. I've long since regretted letting him download the old Wodehouse stories. His Jeeves sometimes gets a little annoying.

"Okay, so I say to the guy, 'All right buddy, hand over the hand,' which I thought was pretty funny. He runs into the spare parts room, grabs a droid femur and takes a swing at me. 'How 'bout I give you a leg up instead?' he says. From there the body parts and the puns just started flying left and right. 'No thanks,

I'm already armed.' 'Nice suit. Is it double breasted?' 'Now that's what I call a bowel movement!'

"Finally, I grab a couple of droid heads, one in each hand, and slam them upside his head like a pair of cymbals. He falls unconscious to the floor and—I can't believe I do this—but I stand up and say out loud, 'I guess two heads really *are* better than one.'"

I smiled. HARV smiled too, but only slightly, and there was an awkward silence. Then HARV quietly said, "I'll bet he was really disturbed at that turn of events."

"It's a joke, HARV."

"Actually, I think the term 'humorous anecdote' is more accurate."

"Either way, it's supposed to be funny. You get it?"

"Well," said HARV, "I understand the anatomical references and your use of common phraseology in an ironic manner, but wouldn't it have been more accurate for your last line to have been, 'I guess two android heads, when used as blunt trauma-inducing weapons, can cause severe concussive damage?"

I turned my attention back to the backgammon board. "Forget it," I said, "I should have known better than to waste the story on a computer."

"Yes, well forgive me, boss, if I don't quite grasp the subtle concept of witty PI banter. I guess I'll just have to be content with the ability to perform three billion separate calculations in a nanosecond. Frankly, I'm surprised that you managed to survive all those years without me."

(I should mention at this point that, although HARV likes to take on the form of a proper English butler, his attitude and speech patterns aren't the least bit proper, British or subservient. He's the world's most advanced computer and he doesn't let you forget it.)

"Now if you will kindly just roll the dice and take your turn. I am anxious to claim yet another victory."

I sighed and looked at my bleak options on the backgammon board.

"How about this: A guy walks into a bar with two chunks of plutonium sewn onto the shoulders of his shirt . . ."

"Please, spare us all the anguish and roll the dice."

I shook the two holo-dice (that weren't really there—even though a good portion of my brain thought they were) for an annoyingly long time, just to get on HARV's circuits a bit, and then made my roll. The dice bounced around the holographic backgammon board (which also wasn't really there), much as you would expect real dice to bounce around on a real backgammon board (although not quite).

Even if the holo-dice hadn't been semitransparent and slightly aglow, I would have somehow still known that they weren't real dice. This puzzled me for a nano, and I started to wonder why. Then, I thought to myself that I was starting to think too much about this. I'm a Private Investigator, after all. I'm supposed to answer questions, not create them. And yet, inevitably, in order to properly *answer* questions, one has to first *ask* questions. That's just the way the world works. Why is that? I thought.

Then I realized that I was getting *way* too philosophical for this stupid game, so I turned my attention back to the dice just as they ceased their simulated tumbling on the simulated board.

Double sixes.

There are times (most times, actually) when double sixes is a good roll. This, however, was one of those rare instances when it wasn't. HARV had my captured piece solidly blocked in with two of his four remaining pieces sitting squarely on the number six slot. I was trapped.

"I find it hard to believe," I said, not trying to disguise the disdain in my voice, "that you're not loading these dice. I've rolled three doubles this game and every one has been worthless."

"Oh, please," HARV responded, in his best calming, almost-but-somehow-not-quite-human, voice. "I am the most sophisticated computer on Earth. Why would I want, or for that matter, why would I need, to cheat to win a simple game of backgammon?" He paused for a nano. "Besides your third roll of the game was a double two, which you found quite useful. Perhaps you wish me to replay it for you on the wall screen in superslow motion?"

"I'll take your word for it."

"As well you should, as I have no reason to lie. You have simply run into a series of unfortunate, but very possible, circumstances in this game of chance. Dice in motion are random objects, as you know, and subject to all laws of probability. Results of such probabilities cannot be accurately predicted nor controlled. It is the chaos theory in action."

"What I want to know is how come the chaos theory always seems to be in action when it's my turn to roll the dice?"

HARV's holographic image picked up the holo-dice and shook them, ever so properly, in his hand. As he did so, he lectured, also ever so properly, as only he can.

"If you don't mind my saying so, boss, you are fixating on the negative. You should be thankful that your bad luck at this gaming table does not necessarily translate into bad luck in the more important areas of life. You are, for instance, very fortunate when it comes to armed combat. You have been fired upon one hundred twenty-seven times in your career and have been wounded only thrice, each of those minimally so. You are also quite fortunate in the area of romantic interpersonal relationships. Or have you forgotten the lovely Dr. Electra Gevada. Quite honestly, your luck in this area is truly an example of the chaos theory run amok. Even I, the most sophisticated computer on Earth, have trouble computing what exactly such a beautiful and intelligent surgeon sees in you."

"There are some things, HARV, that are beyond even your abilities."

"True," he reluctantly agreed and tossed the dice. "But they are few and far between."

We both watched in silence as the dice rolled along the holographic board, like two very symmetrical tumbleweeds, before finally coming to rest.

Double sixes.

As I mentioned earlier, there are a few rare instances in backgammon where double sixes can be a bad roll. This, of course, was not one of those times.

"Oh, my, it appears as though I've won again," HARV said with a slight, but nevertheless very noticeable, smile. "If I were counting, this would mark my fifth victory in a row and my tenth victory over the last eleven games. It would also be my 94th victory in the last 99 games and my 500th victory in the . . ."

"But then, you're not one to count, are you HARV?"

"Of course I am," HARV countered. "I'm a computer. It is what I do."

"That's it. We're using real dice and a real board next game."

"Fine," said, HARV. "Bring them out."

I thought for a nano, then mumbled under my breath.

"What was that?" HARV asked.

"I said I don't have any real dice. I don't think they make them anymore."

"Just as well," HARV said. "You probably wouldn't know how to work them anyway."

"Excuse me, but whatever happened to helping me count my blessings?"

"Ah, yes," HARV continued, "your blessings. Well, aside from surviving numerous altercations involving heavy ordinance and being romantically involved with someone several steps above you on the social register, you also have what one would describe in the current vernacular as a 'way groovy' job!"

I will tell you now. There's something very strange about hearing the world's most intelligent computer use the term "way groovy," but I'd grown accustomed to HARV's eccentricities.

I am considered by many people (most people who know me, actually) to be a bit of a throwback to a bygone era; why else would I choose to be a private eye in the twenty-first century? Personally, I like to think of myself more as a Renaissance man: living comfortably in the present but fascinated with the past. Truth to tell, I was born in the wrong century. I am endlessly (some would say compulsively) fascinated by anything and everything twen-cen. It was a simpler time when everybody wasn't "wired" to everything else. It was a more stylish time. A better time? Hey, I'm not naïve. But the cars were a lot cooler back then and, in my book, that counts for a lot.

I've been a licensed private eye for thirteen years. I got into the business in what they call a "down time." It was the height of the age of information, and the general public, who at that time had the world at their fingertips and eyeballs via the cellular net, had no real use for investigators. After all, you don't need someone to dig up dirt for you when you're standing in the middle of a dustbowl. True, it takes a special skill to know the right place to dig, but it's hard making that argument when the CaffeineCorner down the street is giving away copies of *The Complete and Unabridged History of History Volumes 1 and 2* on a nano-chip free with every purchase of a quadruple latte.

So over the next few years the rank and file of the gumshoe population dwindled substantially. The old-timers, some of them grand old men from the heyday, living, breathing specimens of Marlowe-esque history, gave up the game. A lot of them passed away over the years. Many just retired and moved to New Florida. Ten years ago, the World Council stopped issuing licenses and private eyes became an endangered species. To the world at large, PI had become nothing more than the area of a circle divided by the radius squared. Before I knew it, I was the last licensed guy on the PI register, and the associate partner position at my buddy Randy's software R&D lab was becoming a very real temptation.

To make matters worse, the PI void was about to be filled by the seamy underside of society. No, not organized crime. The entertainment industry.

EnterCorp, the world's largest entertainment conglomerate, realized that there was a profit to be made from human misery and suffering by recording and netcasting it to the masses. EnterCorp created a private eye subsidiary corporation they ironically called DickCo, and the company now does a lot of the work formerly done by freelance PIs.

They actively recruit PI wannabes (thugs mostly) and employ them to do "investigative" work (totally unlicensed, of course). Who cares about a license, after all, when you have the shadow-support of the third largest corporation in the world behind you? Basically, DickCo assigns its operatives regular cases, covers all their expenses and pays them a regular, comfortable level salary. Operatives go where they're told go, investigate what they're told to investigate, and bust whatever heads they are (unofficially) told to bust. It's a sweet life . . . if you're a thug with highbrow pretensions. Unfortunately, the world still has its fair share of those. It just goes to show that there's a big difference between a PI and a dick.

Why does EnterCorp do it? Well, part of the package that comes with your signing on the virtual dotted line is that DickCo has the right to record your actions at all times, twenty-four/seven, and netcast your work-related experiences on any of their many reality-based net shows. All operatives are fitted with netcast cameras that are surgically attached to their retinas (I call them dick-cams). Tracking devices are implanted in their necks so, in a pinch, satellite cameras can locate them to get dramatic overhead shots of their adventures. And the most popular of the rank and file get netcast "and one's," a sidekick whose sole job is to dutifully get the proper coverage of the operative (and sometimes provide comic relief or a sounding board in order to easily provide exposition).

EnterCorp made me an offer when they were just starting up. Needless to say, I thought the terms stunk worse than an angry unwashed skunk eating old fish and extra stinky cheese, and I turned them down flat.

Still, I didn't want to quit the PI business. After all, what other job lets you set your own hours, carry a cool gun and get paid to snoop around?

Then five years ago I had, for lack of a better term, my breakthrough case. I won't bore you with the details, but it involved YOM, which was short for "Yesterday Once More." They were a teleport delivery service that promised to deliver packages back through time. Their motto was "When it really should have been there *yesterday*."

The City Council, at the very strong urging of Fedport, YOM's competition in the delivery service market, was worried that traveling so casually back and forth through time threatened the world as we know it and hired me of all people to set things right (there was a budget crisis and the city hadn't allocated much money for protecting the fabric of time, so I was all they could afford).

Within a week, I had shut YOM down and reality as we knew it was safe once more. Actually, it turned out that YOM wasn't really delivering packages though time at all. They were just hypnotizing their customers through subliminal advertisements to convince them that they'd received the packages the day before. So all I'd really saved the world from was false advertising.

Still, the press latched onto the story for a time, and I began what I thought would be my fifteen nanoseconds of fame. Then it was discovered that I was actually the last legally licensed Private Investigator on earth, and that sort of gave new life to my marketability.

A week later, I was hired as the private bodyguard for that teenage holovision starlet. I can't remember her name. You know, the one with the hair? After that I did talk shows and the net circuit. A year later I saved the city when a deranged pilot tried to crash a twen-cen satellite into Fisherman's Wharf, and since then I've been a bit of a minor celeb in this part of the world. I haven't exactly stayed one hundred percent true to the Sam Spade mold, but every organism learns one way or the other that when the times are changing, you either adapt or die.

"By the way, boss," HARV said as he re-racked the backgammon board. "We received our first of what could be several angry overdue rent notices this morning from your landlord."

"What do you mean, overdue?" I asked. "Didn't you pay the rent?"

"I've been dragging my feet, so to speak, on the finances in general."

"Any particular reason why?"

"Well, at the nano," HARV said, "your finances are stretched a bit thin. A few client payments are overdue and your residual check from the last net special was, shall we say, underwhelming."

"Yeah, maybe Randy was right and we should have called it 'Zach Johnson versus the Bikini Babes from the Planet Bimbo Thirty-Eight D.'"

"Be that as it may, you're not, as they say, flush with investable capital at the nano."

"So, we need to raise some creds in a hurry."

"As always, boss, your keen grasp of the obvious overwhelms me. And may I take this opportunity to remind you of the very generous offer extended to you last week by the good people at OmegaMart to celebrate their new store opening."

"Forget it."

"It's good money, boss, for a simple personal appearance."

"Forget it, HARV," I said. "I'm not doing it. Gates, I'd rather do anything than another one of those DOS-awful ribbon-cutting ceremonies.

And at that nano, three cheap-looking thugs in expensive looking suits crashed through my office door, turning the simulated wood into so much simulated kindling (funny thing, irony).

My first reaction was, "Why don't thugs ever try the knob," which, however incisive, wasn't very much help at the time. My second reaction was, "This is not a good thing," which was more pertinent to the matter at hand but overly obvious and, again, not all that useful. This is why I never trust my first two reactions to any crisis situation.

Carol, my secretary and probable future niece-in-law, followed the thugs into the room, shrugging her little shoulders apologetically. Carol is an extremely smart little girl, brilliant actually. She has the mind of a world class physicist. She's the niece of my fiancée, Dr. Electra Gevada, and, when she's not attending classes at the university, she works part-time as my receptionist.

One other thing, she's also a psi (short for psionic), Class 1 Level 5, which makes her exceptionally powerful. However, because she's young, her talents are still a bit raw. She's very gifted at reading minds, and only slightly less skillful at mind control. She has trouble at times with her telekinesis and she tends to lose that ability under pressure, but, hey, she's just a kid and you can't really expect her to be perfect. Besides, she's cute as a button.

She's been recruited by nearly every government, corporation, and gaming casino in the new world (psi's are rare and in high demand in the business world). She was even kidnapped once by a fifth-world country in the hopes that she'd become their secret weapon and the key to their world dominance. That actually got a little ugly and, as a result, I'm no longer able to purchase my favorite brand of macaroons. But that's another story.

"Sorry, Tío," she shouted to me, as the snarling thugs, with blasters drawn, formed an ominous a semi-circle around my desk. "My mind blasts didn't stop them."

Smart guy that I am, I realized then that this day wasn't going to be so ordinary after all.

3

When facing an imminent confrontation with multiple thugs, the PI handbook (now long out of print in both paper and electronic versions) strongly suggests that you remember the acronym W.E.P.N.

- Wits: keep them about you.
- Evaluate your foe's strengths.
- Postulate their weaknesses. And assign each foe a slightly demeaning . . .
- Nickname (it will subconsciously help your fighting skills if you convince yourself that your opponent is someone known, for example, as "Bedwetter").

These particular thugs in front of me were clearly hired muscle: big men (one of them truly immense) in big suits with big ugly scowls on their faces. Working from left to right, they were.

Stupid Ape: I had to quantify this with the word "stupid" so as not to offend the ape community. Large of limb, impotent of intellect, he was the kind of guy who lettered in leg-breaking at thug school but flunked the written exam because he didn't know which end of the e-pencil to use.

Fuzz Face: I pegged this guy as the boss. My first clue was that he stood in the middle. Let's face it, when you're dealing with thugs, the boss always stands in the middle. They're a lot like geese in that respect. He also looked a little less animal-like than the other two. Shades hid his eyes and a dirty little mustache and goatee stippled his chin. My guess is that he thought the facial hair made him look menacing. To me, it only made him look like the back end of a blind shepherd's ewe.

Both these goons were packing high power hand blasters which, of course, were aimed directly at me.

Man Mountain: Stupid Ape and Fuzz Face were trouble, but this guy brought the situation up a few levels on the danger meter (right up to "uh-oh, did I pay this month's premium on my life insurance?").

First off, he was immense. I've said that before, I know, but I want to make sure I do him justice here. He was two and a half meters tall and very nearly as wide. To this guy the Bahamian diet was something you try because you've already eaten Jamaica and St. Croix.

Clearly, the guy was GE (genetically engineered)—thugs that size just don't come from Mother Nature—and this set off all kinds of alarms in my head. It takes a pile of credits to get a GE (they've been outlawed since 2035), so I knew right away that I was up against a goon squad who had some hefty financing behind them.

"Zachary Johnson," Fuzz Face barked, further strengthening my belief that he was the brains (such as they were) of the outfit. "You're coming with us."

"Don't they teach manners in thug school anymore?" I responded, trying hard to sound unimpressed.

"Manners don't mean much when you got a blaster pointed at your face," he growled. "Now like I said, you're coming with us. Alive or in pieces, it don't matter to me."

"My, my," I stated coolly, then glanced at HARV, "when it comes to kidnapping, you fine gentleman certainly are in the dark."

"What the DOS are you talking about?" Fuzz Face demanded, clearly a little confused (but, frankly, I had the feeling that confusion was a state this guy visited often).

Right on cue HARV killed the office lights and shaded the

window screens to black, plunging the room into total darkness, and utter confusion.

"What happened?" one of the thugs (Stupid Ape, I think) mumbled.

"Ugh," another thug (probably Man Mountain) grunted.

Just then the lights blinked back on and my three thug friends suddenly found themselves faced with fifteen identical versions of yours truly.

"How'd he do that?" asked Stupid Ape.

"Ugh," Man Mountain grunted again.

"They're holograms, you idiots. But one of them is the real thing," Fuzz Face answered as he turned and aimed his blaster at the wall screen covering HARV's power unit. "We just need to take out the computer and . . ."

The real me chose that nano to leap at Fuzz Face from the crowd of holograms and nail him a hard with snap kick to the groin—not very sporting, I know, but what do you want, he was going to shoot my computer.

"Didn't your mother ever teach you not to pick on defenseless and very expensive computers?" I asked, as he crumpled to the ground at my feet.

Unfortunately, my move surprised HARV as much as it did the thugs because when I moved on Fuzz Face, the hologram images of me all remained motionless. And that pretty much blew my cover.

Stupid Ape was quick to take advantage of the opening. He hit me with a haymaker to the gut that sent me stumbling backwards. I managed to remain on my feet (thanks mostly to the wall I hit) and came right back at him.

A look of confusion crossed his face as I rushed him. And by confusion, I mean above and beyond his normal level. Apparently, he wasn't accustomed to seeing his victims bounce back after taking one of his good punches.

"Huh?" he questioned eloquently.

"You must be losing your touch," I said, lying through my

teeth. That punch would have cracked my ribs like eggshells had it not been for the armor I wear. It's a light, but extremely strong, carbon alloy specially designed for me by my good buddy, Dr. Randy Pool. It protects me from heavy blows and even light blaster fire. It gets a little itchy in warm weather, but a man who makes a living poking his nose into places where it doesn't belong can never to be too careful.

I gave Stupid Ape a nano to wonder about his shortcomings and then moved in for the kill.

"Next thing you know, you'll develop a glass jaw," I said. Then I let loose with a fast right cross to his block-like chin.

A wonderful look of total shock and confusion swept over the thug's face as he flew backwards through the air like a hovercraft with stuck accelerator. To him, it was as though every rule in the world had suddenly been reprogrammed. Some average Joe had just taken his best punch, shrugged it off and then hit him harder than he'd ever been hit before. He had a few nanos to ponder the new rules as he flew over my desk, crashed into the wall and then fell to the floor.

If there's one thing I've learned in my many years as a PI, it's that sometimes you need to cheat a little bit to survive. Let's face it, St. Peter's parlor is SRO with guys who tried to fight fairly. Anyone who's been around the block a time or two learns the hard way that when it's do-or-die time, you don't get extra credit for being nice.

My armor helps me cheat. On top of protecting me, it's also soft-wired to my muscles, which means that in times of need I can draw juice from its circuits, channel it directly into my arms or legs and basically give myself a quantum-sized helping hand. Yes, it's cheating. I'm not as tough as these thugs think I am. But remember, I'm not the one who came into the room waving his blaster around, so forgive me if I don't strictly adhere to the Book of Fisticuffs Etiquette.

*　　*　　*

Unfortunately, in this case, I'd used my trump card a little too soon. Two thugs were down but my luck was about to run out because Man Mountain chose that nano to join the fray. I knew this because a fist the size of my desk chair swatted me from the side and sent me tumbling. I felt this blow, even through the armor, and this time when I hit the wall, I felt it crack (at least I hoped it was the wall).

Man Mountain gathered me up and used his massive girth to drive me into the wall that housed HARV's computer screen. I quickly juiced-up my fist with energy from the body armor and countered with a jab to the behemoth's gut.

Sparks flew.

Man Mountain smiled.

I gulped.

"You not so tough enough, eh?" he said as he wrapped his fingers around my throat. "I made in 2029 before tests banned. Made real strong."

"And exceptionally smart as well," I said, trying as always to remain lucid, or at least as lucid as one can be when being strangled to death by a tank with arms. "If they ever bring back slapstick, you could play all four Stooges."

I flicked my left wrist in just the right way and my trusty Colt 45 version 2-A, popped neatly into my hand from its forearm holster. Guns are nasty, messy items, but there are times when nasty is called for, and messy is just something you have to live with.

But Man Mountain had somehow anticipated this move and reacted with surprising speed. His free hand grabbed my arm and pinned it, gun and all, firmly against the wall. Then he gave me one of those "ha ha, you're even dumber than I am" smiles, which was especially nasty because, in this case, it rang so true.

"I talk not good but I smarter than words," he said. "When I strangle you, your armor, I know you wear, no help."

He began tightening his grip on my throat with his giant

atomic vise of a hand and I began to regret not ordering the armor in the turtleneck style.

"Okay," I gasped, "I guess I'll come along quietly now. Where are we headed?"

His lips curled back at the corners and the smile turned into a snarl.

"What you say?" he snickered. "I not hear you. Oh well." And his fingers tightened even more, cutting off my air and slowly crushing my throat.

I felt my eyes roll back in my head and the world turned gray around the edges. Unconsciousness beckoned. The dark void opened before me and I felt the urge to plunge into the netherword and let its peaceful shadows cover me in the big sleep of nevermore.

That was when I knew I was in big trouble. I always get *way* too metaphoric when I'm facing death.

4

I forced myself away from the pretentious verse and focused my mind on the matter at hand. On the bright side, HARV was up and fully operational, and Carol was ready to use her psi powers (or her fists) to do whatever she could.

On the not-so-bright side, Carol's psi attacks had been ineffective against Man Mountain, and her fists even less so. She was currently whacking away at his back with a chunk of the broken coat rack but Man Mountain hardly seemed to notice.

As for HARV, well, he's not exactly programmed for violence and, in times of emergency, he tends to retreat into a semi-neurotic shell of random probability analyses. At this particular nano he was calculating the odds of my being saved by a violent tsunami striking the area. As a result, neither he nor Carol was able to do anything other than watch helplessly as Man Mountain gleefully continued to strangle me.

"You die soon!" he laughed, squeezing my throat, as though he were wringing out a damp washcloth (that he really despised). "Kill you, then have fun with your secretary. And she not able to stop me!"

And there was the rub. Under normal circumstances, Carol should have been able to freeze Man Mountain with a glance, turn his gray matter into a frozen daiquiri and have him dance the bossa nova with the desk chair, yet for some reason she couldn't penetrate his cranium. All of the thugs had to be wearing psi-blockers, and that set off a whole new round of alarms in my head. Psi-blockers are experimental, they're government issue only, and tend to liquefy the internal organs of the wearer if worn too long. Apparently, though, that was a risk that Man Mountain (or whomever sent him) was willing to take.

"HARV," a hoarse whisper was all I could manage. "Scan his head."

"Scan for what?" HARV asked.

"For a psi-blocker," I wanted to say, but my air was just about gone and I couldn't say anything further. HARV would have to figure it out for himself.

"Well, he's ugly," HARV began unhelpfully. "As ugly as he is massive, although those two qualities are difficult to compare, one being objective, the other being totally subjective." HARV took a brief time out to collect more data.

"His nose is roughly the size of an adult athletic shoe. The inner lining is also slightly hairier than normal, which, although considered disgusting by contemporary human standards, is relatively common in genetically engineered beings. I for one am certainly glad the council banned most of these experiments.

"His mouth cavity is roughly one half cubic meter large. That's just an estimate. I could give you an exact measurement but I'd rather not get that intrusive. I fear the malodorous power of his breath."

I rolled my eyes in frustration (and pain).

"His eyes are smaller than normal and relatively pupil-less. They have a rather cold, cunning look to them although, judging by his speech patterns, any sign of intelligence is probably coincidental. By the way, I'm fairly certain that he didn't understand your 'Stooges' reference. But then I'm also fairly certain that a full ninety-nine point eight percent of the general population wouldn't understand it either, so we can't hold that against him."

I was as good as dead. I knew it. All I could hope for now

was that Man Mountain would find a way to strangle HARV when he was finished with me.

"Oh, he also has a psi-blocking device in his left ear."

Vingo!

I shot a glance (and all the thought I could muster) toward Carol. She read my mind like a billboard and sprang into action (thankfully she's a little quicker on the uptake than HARV).

She jumped on Man Mountain's back and started climbing toward his head, but Man Mountain shrugged his boulder-like shoulders and tossed her away. So Carol went to plan B.

"Hey, HARV," she said, "this guy sure has a bright future, doesn't he?"

"What?" HARV asked.

"You know, a bright future. A really, really *bright* future."

"Yes, well from the look of things, it's a much brighter future than the boss'," HARV said.

"Ay, caramba, HARV," Carol yelled in frustration. "Flash him!"

That's when it hit HARV.

"Oh, I get it," he said.

With that, the giant wall screen behind me strobed to bright white, and the light flash hit Man Mountain like a 1000 megawatt slap in the corneas. He turned his head and covered his eyes with a massive forearm, loosening his grip on my throat and, more importantly, freeing my right hand.

I plunged my free hand deep into his ear (not the most wonderful experience) and quickly dug around for the psi-blocker. I was in halfway up to my forearm before I latched onto what I hoped was the device and pulled it free with a flourish.

As Man Mountain began to recover, I held the psi-blocker high in the air for Carol to see. She smiled and kicked her psi powers into high gear.

"Drop him," Carol ordered, furrowing her brow.

Man Mountain froze in his tracks and his eyes glazed over.

Carol had locked on to his mind like a cute little psi vise and, without the blocker, his mind was putty in her hands.

He loosened his grip on my throat and I slid down the wall to the floor, gasping gratefully for air.

"Turn around," Carol commanded.

Man Mountain obeyed.

"I'm going to hit you so hard it's going to knock you out cold," she said.

Then she tapped him with her finger and he crashed to the ground like a kiloton of bricks on Jupiter.

"Nice work, " I said as I slowly climbed to my feet.

She puffed on the tip of her finger like a gunfighter kissing his revolver. "Thanks, Tio," she smiled.

The hologram of HARV reappeared in the middle of the room.

"What about me, boss?"

"We'll talk about it later, HARV."

Unbeknownst to us all, on the other side of the room Fuzz Face slowly regained his senses. He furtively looked around and when he saw that Carol, HARV and I were busy having an impromptu staff review, he slowly reached his hand towards his blaster. Centimeter by centimeter, he stretched toward the weapon. The slowness of the movement was agony for him. Inside he was seething, furious at me for cold-cocking him. He was hot for revenge and he wanted it now, but he knew that he had to be patient. He had to take me by surprise.

At last, his hand gently touched the butt of the blaster. The special handle read his signature palm print and sprang to life in his hand, powering up in less than a second. He smiled and switched the blaster to full power.

"Johnson!" he growled.

I turned toward him, and a look of abject terror passed over my face.

"Who's laughing now?" he said and fired.

The energy beam hit me full on, punched a hole through my chest and splattered my insides against the wall. Fuzz Face laughed triumphantly, awash in his violent, victorious glory.

Then he woke up.

And when he did, he found himself bound to my desk chair by four meters of electromagnetically generated force-chains. Stupid Ape was beside him, also tightly bound but still unconscious (and dreaming of tapioca pudding, don't ask me why). We didn't have chains big enough for Man Mountain so we stuck him in the bathroom and threw a force-field around the whole thing. (Gates, but this was going to run up my power bill).

"Nice dream, wasn't it?" I said to Fuzz Face. "Splattering me against the wall was an especially nice touch, but I think you have some serious anger management issues that you need to face."

"What'd you do to me?" he asked.

"We were in your head, bozo, courtesy of my secretary, the psi. And I must say it was pretty lonely there. I even felt a bit of a draft." I pulled the psi-blocker that had once been in his ear out of my pocket and dangled it in front of him like a hypnotist's watch. "Now I'd like some information."

He glared at me in cold, angry silence and had another one of those blow-Zach-Johnson-to-smithereens daydreams.

"Fine, act like a clone," I said. "Carol, if you can stand the loneliness, go back into this guy's head and tell me his story."

Carol stared at the thug for less than a nano, then smiled. "He works for ExShell," she said.

Fuzz Face did not appreciate being read. "You freak of nature."

"With the company you keep, I'd be careful with the name calling."

"Go to sleep!" Carol ordered.

Fuzz Face's eyes immediately glazed and he fell over, out

like a burned-out fluorescent on the dark side of the moon at midnight.

"HARV," I said, in my most business-like voice. "Net me ExShell on the vid."

"There will be no need for that," HARV stated as calmly and as annoyingly as ever.

"HARV," I said angrily. "Please try to remember, that I'm the human here and you are the machine. Therefore, in theory, you are supposed to do what I tell you to do. Now net me ExShell right now or find me a computer who knows how to follow a simple command!"

"There is no need to establish a connection with ExShell," HARV replied, implacably calm, "because you already have an incoming message from BB Star, the Chief Executive Officer of ExShell."

"Okay," I said, trying (unsuccessfully) not to sound surprised, "That'll work too then. Put her on the screen, please."

"As you wish, O human master," said HARV with a theatrical gesture.

5

I turned to the wall screen as a vid-window zoomed open and a six-foot streaming image of BB Star flashed on. I'd seen her picture, of course, on holovision and in the various net news magazines, but I'd never seen her direct-linked like this before. Mature, graceful, and tremendously attractive, just her presence over the live net seemed to light up the room. She had an elegantly chiseled face framed by long, golden hair which was cut in a business-like style, yet somehow still added to her allure. She possessed the kind of beauty that seemed untouchable, almost unnatural in some way. Her deep blue eyes surveyed my office through her own vid-screen and she smiled, ever so slightly, through her full lips.

"Bravo, Mr. Johnson," she said. "Please send the boys home when they regain consciousness. They will give you no more trouble."

"I think instead that I'll send ExShell the bill for the damage they caused and let you pick these bozos up at the police station."

"ExShell will of course reimburse you for any collateral damage created by this little test, but it will not be necessary to involve the local authorities."

"I'm sorry, did you say test?" I questioned, angrily.

"Correct," she replied with a smile. "And congratulations on a splendid performance."

"No offense, Ms. Star, but I hate tests," I said. "Especially ones that involve blasters, assassins, or tricky math problems!"

BB Star remained calm and steady, her big blue eyes never leaving mine. "I run a big company, Mr. Johnson. I do not hire anyone unless I know for certain that they are worth the investment."

I turned from the vid-window and shrugged my shoulders at Carol and HARV. "Am I the only one who's confused here?"

"That's usually the case, boss," HARV said. "This time, though, I'd say no."

"I am offering you a job, Mr. Johnson. I will give you all the necessary details when we meet in person," she said, ignoring the fact that I was ignoring her. "Kindly be in my office in exactly three hours."

"Why, so your thugs can take a few whacks at me on familiar territory?" My question was only partially rhetorical.

"Not to worry," she smiled, treating my partially rhetorical question as though it were totally nonrhetorical. "You passed the audition. You are in no danger from me."

"Yeah, well thanks for the reassurance," I said, "but I'm going to need a few more details before stepping directly into the lion's den."

"I will give you more data when we meet in person. The net is too easy to spoof. Therefore, I look forward to seeing you in now slightly less than three hours' time."

"I'm sorry, Ms. Star. Again, no offense meant but, frankly, you have a thing or two to learn about people management if you think I'm going to set one foot into your office now, let alone *work* for you, after what you've done here today."

"Mr. Johnson, I understand that your normal rate is five thousand credits per day," she said, her eyes never wavering from mine. "While in my employ I shall pay you twenty-five thousand per day."

"He'll be there in ten minutes," HARV chimed like a sycophantic alarm clock.

"HARV . . ."

"Look, boss," he said, "it's either this or the OmegaMart opening. And you have to admit, you're curious here, right?"

I clenched my teeth and turned back towards the vid-window. "Fine, Ms. Star, I'll see you in three hours at your office. But I'm already on your clock. As a matter of fact, I've been on the clock since your goons came through my door.

"Fine," she answered.

"And I'm not taking your case sight unseen," I continued. "If I don't like the sound of it, then I'm walking with no strings attached."

"And all information discussed at the meeting will remain privileged," she countered.

"Agreed."

"And you must come alone, unarmed and without your computer. No weapons or outside communication devices are allowed in my office building."

"I can live with that," I said, and I heard HARV gasp behind me.

"Fine then," she smiled. "I look forward to meeting you in person." With that, she blinked out and the vid-window zoomed closed.

I turned to Carol, who had been quietly scanning BB Star's thoughts since the call began. "Did you pick up anything?"

She shook her head. "It's hard enough to do over the net under normal conditions. ExShell probably has all kinds of defenses in their system.

"Or she may have an extremely strong mind," I turned to HARV. "What do you make of the deal?"

HARV's reply was (not surprisingly) overly loquacious. "ExShell, as I hope you are aware, is the largest corporation on the planet. They currently manufacture fifty-five percent of all personal, municipal and governmental electronic hardware, hold patents on the operating systems for sixty-three percent of the world's computers and control twenty-two percent of the current soft drink market. Also, last week they completed their purchase of the country of Finland. They have incomparably vast resources and can afford the finest minds and the most advanced equipment in existence. The fact that they now require your services is a clear sign of desperation."

"Thanks a meg," I replied. "And the next time we get attacked by armed thugs, I'm going to seriously consider letting them put a couple of energy blasts into your wall unit."

"I didn't mean it quite the way you interpreted, boss," HARV said. "I'm simply stating that whatever the situation may be, it must be something very dire for ExShell to call upon you, and especially so for Ms. Star to do so personally. She is known as a bit of a recluse.

"Also, I should note here, if I may, that it would take more than a few energy blasts to the main wall screen to destroy me. I have logic and memory boards in numerous locations, and Dr. Pool has backup copies of my singularly original operating system in more than a dozen secure locations around the globe. It's also worth stating that you would be lost without my constant aid and assistance."

"Yeah, lost but happy," I said as I headed toward the door. "Now come on, we have three hours to do our prep work."

"Where you going?" Carol asked.

"You're the psi. You figure it out."

Carol stared at me and furrowed her brow for a nano. "You're going to Dr. Pool's lab to get your armor repaired and to get background information on BB Star and her security."

"Vingo," I said, touching a finger to my nose.

"You're also regretting that second burrito you had for breakfast and you have a particularly graphic picture of my Aunt Electra in some kind of lace negligee in your subconscious."

"I think you dug a little too deeply that time," I said.

"Tell me about it," Carol said with a gag.

6

I left my office and walked along the docks toward my bright red 2030 Honda Mustang. It's a classic, although, as HARV constantly reminds me, slightly outdated, piece of machinery. As I walked, I couldn't help wondering what it must have been like here on the docks decades ago, before teleportation devices turned the docks from bustling, grimy places filled with grunts and groans to an overcrowded tourist attraction filled with the whirs and hums of recording devices. That's one of the perks that comes with being the last private eye on the planet. I get to ponder things like this and pass it off as "atmosphere."

Unfortunately, the atmosphere was abruptly interrupted by the arrival of what I consider to be the most hideous pustule on the underbelly of the *New* New World Order. Crime syndicates, killer mutations and guilds of assassin cyborgs may be bad, but they aren't nearly as annoying as the monster that I was about to face.

The press.

They swarmed me like flies on a day-old road apple . . . wait a minute, that makes me look kind of bad . . . they were more like flies on a fresh Twinkie . . . a charismatic Twinkie.

They weren't actual, organic, human being journalists of course. With all the so-called "newsworthy" events happening in the world today, newspeople just don't have time anymore to actually *be* anywhere. Gates forbid, they're interviewing me in Frisco when an Elvis clone slips in his bathtub in New Vegas and they get scooped by the net-dude on another bandwidth. Most journalists now have a dozen or so pressbots to cover their beats. Pressbots are low-tech androids programmed to mimic the owner's voice and personality, equipped with direct audio/visual feeds to the central studio. This way, a journalist can chase a dozen stories at the same time while remaining in the cool, safe comfort of his or her office. Truth to tell, it's only a matter of time before the netnews execs realize that they only really need the pressbots and toss all the actual human reporters out on their collective earpieces. When that happens, there'll be almost as many vapid personalities on the unemployment line as there were during the great budget crunch of 2017, when the old U.S. government laid off the House of Representatives.

One of the pressbots thrust himself (mike first) into my face and smiled through robotic teeth. "Mr. Johnson, I'm Bill Gibbon the Third from *Entertainment This Nano*. There was a report of a commotion in your office ten minutes ago. Care to comment?"

"Not to worry, Mr. Baboon . . ."

"Gibbon."

"It wasn't a real commotion," I said, "just a full-contact rehearsal for my upcoming made-for-HV special: Zachary Nixon Johnson versus the Cheap Thugs in Expensive Suits. Net your local video-feed provider now to ask about availability in your area. Now if you'll excuse me, I have important PI stuff to do. Never a dull nano when you're me."

The press continued to follow me like a pack of noisy rats after a good-looking piece of cheese on the run. I ignored their questions and moved quickly to my car.

"Mr. Johnson, is it true that you and the lovely Dr. Gevada will be married next week on Mars?"

"Do you confirm that you are considering quitting the PI business to pursue a singing career?"

"Do you deny that you punched out a man last week simply because he looked at the lovely Dr. Gevada the wrong way?"

"Do you not deny that you punched out a man last week simply because he looked at your beautiful secretary the wrong way?"

"Will you please say absolutely nothing if it is true that your computer, HARV, is having a romantic relationship with your beautiful secretary?"

"Door," I called to the car as I moved, still surrounded by the press brigade.

The driver-side door popped open obediently and I jumped in fast, trying hard to crush as few mikes as possible while slamming the door in the crowd of collective pressbot faces. Deep down, I knew they were only doing their jobs and that the media's overzealous pursuit of celebrity stories was what kept me in the public eye, but they were annoying enough to drive a guy downright crazo. And there wasn't much of a story here . . . yet.

"Engine," I barked to my car computer. On command, the dashboard obediently lit up and the engine gently turned over and purred like a cat on genetically enhanced catnip.

"Destination please?" the onboard computer asked.

I plugged the coordinates into the driver keyboard.

"Do you wish me to drive?" the computer responded.

I hit the "yes" button.

"As you wish," the computer said as it gently eased the car into the street.

I touched another button on the steering column and HARV's simulated face popped into a window on my dash.

"I wish you'd let me override this antiquated car computer." HARV said. "It's embarrasses me even to use its interface."

"How many times do I have to tell you, HARV? A classic car . . ."

". . . needs a classic computer," HARV mimicked. "Yes, I know. You've made that specious argument to me exactly one hundred eleven times in the past three years."

"You'd think you'd have figured it out by now," I said, and

the car computer gave HARV what sounded like the raspberry. HARV, true to form, kept his dignity and ignored us both.

"Nice cover-up on that Zachary Nixon Johnson versus the Cheap Thugs thing," he said, sarcastically, "but did you really need to add the 'never a dull nano when you're me' part?"

"You didn't like that?"

"A bit egocentric, don't you think?"

"Well, maybe," I said, "but it's true. I was after all, attacked by killers during a backgammon game."

"Point taken," HARV reluctantly agreed.

"Okay then. Now, I'm going to need all the background info you can give me on BB Star."

"She's rather famous. How much do you already know?"

"I know she used to be a stripper."

"Exotic dancer," HARV corrected.

"Oh, well, if we're going to be geopolitically sensitive about it, I guess the proper term would be 'professional artistic gyrator.' Whatever. She was a stripper who married an old billionaire. He died, surprise, surprise. Now she's a billionaire."

"Well, yes," HARV agreed. "That is one way of putting it. Not a very complete way, but accurate within its own simplistic scope. Would you care for a more detailed version?"

"That would be nice," I said, with a wee bit of my own sarcasm.

"Her name was BB Baboom. Though I am relatively certain that was a stage name." He paused for a nano. "Yes, here it is, her given name was Betty Barbara Backerman."

"I can see why she changed it."

"Born and raised in Oakland, until the age of ten. At that time, she and her mother, now deceased, moved to New Wisconsin. Betty became a local beauty queen at the age of sixteen and three years later became a professional exotic dancer."

"That's when she changed her name."

"Correct. BB Baboom was born. Apparently, she was quite good at her craft because over the next few years she developed a loyal following in the northern middle states. New Wisconsin, New Minnesota, the New Dakotas . . ."

"Cold winters . . ."

"She found popularity as a download-girl, then moved to New LA where she did the circuit of the high-priced clubs. Then finally came back to the Bay Area and settled in New Frisco. By this time she had found fame and fortune as the net's most downloadable dancer."

"Ah yes, the geek train to fame."

"I don't care to have you explain that reference, so I'll just accept that it's accurate and move on," HARV said, a little annoyed that I'd interrupted. "Now, then, she met BS Star, then owner and Chief Operating Officer of ExShell in 2047, month three. They married exactly one month later. BS Star died of a myocardial infarction, the night of their second anniversary."

"We can assume he died smiling?"

"You can if you wish," HARV retorted. "I am a computer. I assume nothing. I can speculate, of course, in matters where variables and probabilities are present and such speculation is imperative but I don't think that . . ."

"It was a joke, HARV."

"And I'm sure it was quite funny but, as you know, I'm not programmed for humor."

"You're telling me," I retorted.

"Actually, I've told you exactly two thousand three hundred seventeen times. I do, however, have access to an extensive database of jokes. For example, how many computer consultants does it take to change an illume fixture?"

"None," I answered, "because no consultant would ever do actual physical labor."

"Oh, you've heard it?" HARV asked.

"Only two thousand three hundred seventeen times."

"Perhaps I should run a diagnostic on my random selector?" HARV suggested.

"Perhaps we should get back to business?" I prodded.

HARV sighed, and his image faded from the dashboard window and was replaced by scrolling pictures and information about BB Star. HARV gave voice-over commentary as the text and images flashed by, too fast for the human eye to comprehend.

"The information on Ms. Star before her marriage is quite plentiful as you can see. She was featured on *Entertainment This Nano* and *World Right Now* quite often during sweeps periods. Not counting references to, and ads for, her dancing appearances, there are three thousand one hundred twelve references to her in the news archives from the three years before her marriage. Three thousand three of those are about whom she was or was not dating. The rest are rumors of net specials, vidfilms and HV series in which she was supposed to star. None of these projects ever came to pass."

"Maybe one of her old flames is trying to burn her now?" I offered. "Blackmail her with a dirty secret from her past. Credits tend to bring out the worst in people, especially people who don't have a lot of them."

"I suppose that is a possibility," HARV agreed, though I could tell from the tone of his voice he wasn't committed to this theory.

"Who was her last known boyfriend?"

"Well, when it comes to BB Star's love life, everything is always speculation and conjecture rather than fact," HARV said, "but the last person to whom she was linked romantically was a man named Manuel Mani, her personal astrologer."

"Let's keep him on our short list of people to check out if we need to. I don't trust ex-lovers or astrologers. I've had bad experiences with both. Anything else on BB?"

"She's become quite the recluse since assuming her post as the head of ExShell. There is no record of her leaving the living and office suites of her headquarters in the past year."

"Odd . . ." I said.

"Perhaps she has become a workaholic?" HARV suggested.

"Perhaps she's in hiding or hiding something," I said. "How has ExShell done since she took over?"

"Amazingly well. Their known assets have doubled. They have been the biggest conglom in the world every hour except one, for the past five years. That one hour was in month eleven of last year, when the mutant monkey workforce at their computer chip plant in New Northern Africa staged a wildcat strike. BB Star herself managed to settle that strike quickly by relocating the plant and the monkey workforce to a banana republic.

"In any event, ExShell has performed extremely well under the guidance of this woman who has little education and no formal business training."

BB Star's school records scrolled across my dashboard.

"As you can see, her guidance counselors all advised her to work with her hands."

I started to say something (the opening was just too good) but the car computer interrupted and broke the nano.

"Arrival achieved."

It was just as well. After all, as HARV so often liked to remind me, he wasn't programmed for humor.

7

I made one side trip before going to Randy's and that was to the children's free clinic at New Frisco General Hospital to see Electra (I guess that image of her in the negligee that Carol picked out of my subconscious was stronger than I'd thought).

Dr. Electra Gevada is my fiancée. She is a brilliant surgeon, a great humanitarian, a weapons expert and the former Central American Women's Kick-Boxing Champion (lightweight division). She can't cook to save her life but hey, everyone has to have a few faults, right? That's one of hers. We'll get to the others a little later.

As I said, Electra is a brilliant physician. She is one of the best micro-laser surgeons on the west coast and, were she in private practice, she would be a very rich woman right now.

Instead, she has followed her heart, which is as big as the ozone hole, and for the past seven years has run a government-funded clinic offering free medical care to underprivileged children. It makes her happy. It keeps her incredibly busy. And it makes the lives of hundreds of kids in the city a whole lot better. I guess you can't ask for more than that from a career. Still, it would be nice to have a little more in the bank account than the love, respect, and good wishes of the community (but I'm not complaining).

I stuck my head in her office and found her huddled behind her desk, going over a long list of documents on her computer.

"Hey, chica," I said. "I have good news and bad news."

She looked up at me and flashed a beautiful, if somewhat tired, smile.

"Hola, chico," she said as I kissed her. "I forgot you were coming."

"That's not the greeting I prefer," I said, as I sat in a guest chair across the desk from her, "but I'll take what I can get."

"What's the bad news?" she asked.

"I have to cancel lunch. I have a line on a new case and it might be a big one."

"I've heard worse news in my lifetime," she said. "What's the good news?"

I pulled a take-out container from the folds of my coat and placed it on the desk in front of her.

"I brought you lunch on the go."

"Is this from the Chinese Latin restaurant on the corner? The Chino Latino?"

"No, it's a new place," I said. "Cuisine from Thailand and Mesoamerica, 'Thai n' Mayan'."

She smiled and gave me another kiss that made the negligee image pop into my head again (I was glad Carol wasn't around to read my thoughts this time).

"Actually," she said. "I have bad news too. Bad news and worse news."

"What's the bad news?" I asked.

"I have to cancel lunch too. I'm a little short on credits."

"Not so bad," I said. "What's the worse news?"

"When I say 'a little short on credits' I mean about three million short."

"I guess your lunches are a little more extravagant than I suspected."

She sighed and ran her fingers through her hair out of fatigue and a little bit of frustration.

"I got a call from the Province Council today," she said. "They're cutting off funding for the clinic at the end of the month."

"What? Why?"

"Oh, you know, the usual," she said. "Lack of money in the budget, stuff like that. Apparently, the volcano eruption in New Burbank last year drained a lot of funds from the budget."

"Didn't they have insurance?"

"What company would insure Burbank?"

"Good point," I said. "I'm sorry. Can you do anything?"

"I've been calling potential private backers all morning. Hopefully someone will come through. But let's just say that I've had better days."

A gentle tone sounded just then from the computer interface that I wear on my wrist. This was HARV's polite way of telling me that I was running behind schedule. I shrugged my shoulders and kissed Electra again.

"I have to run," I said. "Let's talk tonight at my place. Maybe we can come up with something. I'll buy dinner."

She smiled and turned back to her computer.

"Thanks, chico. Good luck with the new case."

8

HARV and I hit the street again, and a few minutes later we pulled into the parking lot of Randy Pool's research and development lab.

Now before going any further, let me say that, out of pure necessity, I am a cynic and a skeptic at heart. In my career as a PI, I have seen a lot, done a lot and had a lot done to me. As a result, it takes a lot to impress me and even more to amaze me.

That said, I must also tell you that Randy's lab never fails to boggle my mind.

On the outside it's just this big gray box of a building, as boring as boring can be. But, as they say, you can't always judge a fully interactive e-file by its icon.

I punched my access code into the door lock and slowly entered the building (experience has taught me to always enter Randy's lab slowly and carefully).

As usual, the place was abuzz with the frenetic energy of high-tech genius run amok. Describing it as chaos gone way beyond wild is an understatement. There were bots running, walking, crawling, hovering and slithering (at least I hope they were slithering) everywhere. Test tubes bubbled, boiled and brewed away. Every wall in the building, including the ceiling, was covered with computer screens (you really have to wonder what he uses the ceiling screens for) and every screen was filled with a myriad calculations, logarithmic equations and simulation sequences.

I scanned the chaos for Randy and finally spotted him at the far end of the room, fiddling away on a tiny bot. His crop of red hair (always uncombed) and his pale white skin atop his lanky form made him look like the flag of New Sweden amidst the technological sea. He was so intent on his tinkering with the midget-sized mechanism that he had no idea that I'd even arrived.

As I neared him, the tiny bot suddenly sprang to life. It lashed out wildly with a claw-like arm and slapped him twice in the face. The force of the blow knocked Randy to the floor and sent me into action.

I moved my wrist in that special way that makes my gun pop into my hand and fired in one cool, swift motion. The specially designed concussive shell shattered the tiny robot into a million cybernetic splinters. I holstered my gun and gave Randy my best Marlowe smile as I moved towards him.

"Zach, what the DOS are you doing?" Randy shouted, not nearly as grateful to me for saving him as I'd thought he might be.

"That crazy bot just attacked you!" I answered, somewhat confused.

"Of course it did," Randy said, as he returned to his feet. "It was supposed to. It is, or rather was, an S&M bot. It's designed for people who have problems dealing with others but still long to be abused."

"You're kidding, of course."

"I'm a scientist, Zach. I don't kid," Randy said, as he dusted himself off.

"You would not believe the number of advance orders I have on this." He paused for a nano, looking at the rubble. "Needless to say, your atomizing the prototype is going to put the project somewhat behind schedule."

"Sorry, about that. I really didn't know."

Randy shrugged. "Forget it. I'll tell the customers that the delay is part of their abuse. No one ever said that science had to be prompt."

Randy's really a bright-side kind of guy.

"May I assume," he continued, "that you are here for something other than prototype target practice?"

"I got a call from BB Star—"

"Oh yes, HARV told me all about that," Randy interrupted. "Quite interesting."

"I also had a little run-in with her hired help. My armor is going to need a bit of a tune-up."

"Leave it here and I'll have the repair bots get to it tonight," Randy said as he began picking through the pieces of the S&M bot. "You can use the spare set until it's ready."

"Have you had any luck yet boosting the power to the muscle enhancers?" I asked. "I may be needing them on this one."

"Ah, now." Randy replied, almost sheepishly, "that's an interesting story, actually. It turns out that most of my major backers don't consider the enhancers flashy enough to continue funding. They are, after all, a relatively low-key device. Very subtle in their display."

"That's kind of the point, isn't it?" I asked.

"But you see, Zach, our marketing demographics show that the public likes to see action that is more overt in nature."

"You accepted the partnership offer from that entertainment conglom, didn't you?" I asked, suspiciously.

"Well, I, uh . . . oh heck, of course I did." Randy said. "They have more money than half the hemisphere and they're very hands-off, provided that the higher profile products we create fit a certain mold. They're very fond of pyrotechnics."

"Special effects."

"Exactly, therefore I've been working on your gun."

"Right, you netted me about that, didn't you?"

"Zach, I've sent you one hundred seventeen messages about the improvements and revisions that I have made to your gun's hardware and firmware. You've responded to two. And those were about the color."

I unloaded my gun and carefully placed it into Randy's open hand. "You're not going to change the color, are you?"

Randy didn't even answer that one. He simply took the gun, motioned for me to follow and started walking across the room. He bumped into a few miscellaneous experiments as he moved (he's brilliant but clumsy), causing some tiny explosions and a small fire.

"Try not to breathe that smoke too deeply," he warned me as the janitorial bots swarmed into the area. "It's probably a little poisonous."

I held my breath and quickly followed Randy to the work station. He shuffled through some clutter on the work surface, searching for whatever it was he had in mind. I flinched every time he shook something (as did the janitorial bots, who were just now containing the chemical fire).

But whatever Randy was searching for, it apparently wasn't at this particular work station. He let out a harrumph and quickly moved to a nearby, and equally cluttered, station and searched again. Two stations (and ten minutes) later, he finally found the object of his desire.

"Here we go," he said, grabbing a small pellet from a plexiglass case.

"I've created a new nonincendiary offensive projectile. I call it the Big Chill. It's for use specifically against life-forms who are highly resistant to energy and standard projectile weapons," he stated proudly.

"Does it work?" I asked.

"Absolutely," he stated emphatically. "In theory."

"Is this the same kind of theory that states that if you put a thousand monkeys in a room with word processors, sooner or later one of them will create the next big HV show?"

"No, no. Of course not!" Randy insisted. "Although that

works, by the way. My backers tell me that's how they came up with 'He Married the President.' "

"So, you *have* tested it?" I asked, being extra stubborn.

"Well, not exactly. Not on any actual, live, carbon-based organisms, that is. As you can imagine, volunteers for this type of thing are very difficult to find. Animal testing's been outlawed for fifty years and, thanks to the new Clone Protection Act, you can't experiment on clones anymore or even on a greeting card salesman." Randy paused, then gave me a slightly reassuring smile. "I have computer simulated it though!"

"Computer simulated?" I wasn't exactly bubbling over with enthusiasm.

"It has performed remarkably well," Randy assured me. He looked up to the ceiling, "HARV, please show holo-program 38-3D."

"Certainly, Dr. Pool," HARV responded.

I have noticed, that HARV is a lot less sarcastic answering Randy's commands than he is answering mine. I try not to take that personally.

HARV activated the proper holo-program and a shimmering three-dimensional light show appeared before us. The image of a beautiful woman with three breasts appeared in the middle of the room.

"Oooh, I do so love a man with brains," the woman cooed.

"Oops," Randy gulped, "I meant holo-program 83-D3, HARV." He turned to me, "Science can be so lonely sometimes."

"That's more information than I need to know, Randy."

9

HARV switched the program and the tri-breasted woman was replaced by the image of young, scantily clad mother feeding her baby in a city park on a cloudless summer day.

"Are you sure this is the right video?" I asked.

"Hush," Randy insisted. "This is science."

I turned my attention back to the holo-program. A huge creature that looked like a hideous tree with arms, legs and a mouth suddenly ripped through the serene scene, terrorizing the park patrons. Two city law enforcement officers tried to stop the creature but it turned upon them and (graphically) tore them apart with its arm-like tendrils.

"A little gory, isn't it, Randy?" I said, turning away.

"I like my simulations to be realistic," Randy answered, totally engrossed in the work. "This way when I'm done, my backers can run the programs on their network. It helps offset the cost of the R&D. Besides, kids love this stuff."

I turned my attention back to the holo-show. The killer tree creature was now turning toward the beautiful young mother. The terrified woman, baby in arms, tried to run but she tripped over a piece of a dismembered law officer and fell to the ground, twisting her ankle in the process.

The background music increased to a feverishly annoying pitch as the creature moved its slavering jaws toward the young woman and her child.

Copbots arrived on the scene and attacked the creature, but

their bullets and blasters bounced harmlessly off its thick hide. Angry now, the creature uprooted a tree and swung it like a bat, smashing the copbots into rubble, before again turning its attention back to the helpless young mother.

Suddenly (and literally from out of nowhere), a computer-simulated version of me fell from the sky, landing dramatically between the monster and the mom.

The words: "Computer simulation. Do not attempt this at home," flashed under the picture.

"Legal insisted I put that in," Randy said, a trifle bitterly.

"How the DOS did I fall from the sky?" I asked.

"Artistic license," Randy insisted. "Now pay attention. This is the educational part," he said pointing to the screen.

I watched in amazement as the simulated Zach popped his simulated gun into his simulated hand. "Time to put you on ice, bud!" he spat.

"Come on, I would never say anything that spammy!" I insisted.

"Your agent wrote your dialog," Randy said.

"That's comforting."

Computer Zach fired. The gun belched a puff of gray smoke, and the shot echoed endlessly as the Big Chill emerged from the gun barrel and flew (very slowly) towards the creature.

"Of course, it moves much faster than that in real time," Randy explained. "I put the slow-mo in for effect, to build suspense."

Big Chill hit the tree creature with a less than inspiring "thud," shattering on impact. A tiny puff of white mist appeared, which the tree creature seemed to laugh at. The laughter faded quickly, though, as the mist expanded rapidly and, like a living thing, engulfed the creature. A nano passed, then two, before the mist dissipated. When it did, the tree creature was frozen solid, encased in a block of ice.

"The Big Chill," Randy said proudly. "Get it?"

"Very clever, Randy."

Back on the holo-screen, computer Zach helped the poor mother to her feet (the sequence included a gratuitous shot of the woman's well sculpted cleavage). "Teenage boys love that stuff," Randy explained). My computer-self very sensitively kissed the baby in her arms. The mother, overcome with emotion, kissed me and then handed the baby to a nanny (who happened to be right there), fell into my arms, blah, blah, blah, pan to ocean waves crashing on the beach (you get the idea). Fade to black.

"So what do you think?" Randy asked.

"I thought it was quite good," HARV said, unable to resist the opportunity to offer his opinion. After all, he had been silent for almost two solid minutes.

"Frankly, Randy, I think you need to get out of the lab more often," I said. "You're starting to scare me."

Randy popped open the handle of my gun, pulled a computer chip from the complex innards and tossed it on the floor. He took a new chip from the pocket of his labcoat and placed it in the handle.

"I've also improved the interface between HARV and the gun itself," he said. "Give me your ammo."

I hesitated.

"Zach, I can make a warhead out of what's growing in your refrigerator. You can trust me with a loaded gun."

I reluctantly handed him the ammo and said a silent prayer.

Randy loaded the gun and then hefted its weight, checking the feel (even though I was pretty certain that he had no idea what a well-balanced gun should feel like).

"How about giving it back to me now?" I asked sheepishly. The idea of Randy Pool waving a loaded gun around is one of the more vivid images from my nightmares.

"Don't worry," Randy said, noticing my concern. "I think the safety's on."

Needless to say, the gun went off.

10

The high-powered force-blast shattered the ceiling-mounted computer screen directly above us and obliterated it with a spectacular spray of sparks and shrapnel. I pulled Randy to the ground and we scurried for cover under one of his lab tables as the screen debris fell around us.

"Now explain to me again the meaning of the phrase 'the safety's on.'"

The janitorial bots and a robotic med-team, who I think were expecting this, rushed to the area and shielded us from the last shards of falling screen, then began repairing the damage. When the dust and debris settled, we slowly got to our feet and a hangdog Randy dismissed the med-team with a gentle wave of his hand.

"Just for the record, Dr. Pool," HARV stated calmly, "the on position for the safety is forward and to the left, not right. A perfectly understandable mistake."

"Yes, well, it varies from design to design. It's hard to keep them all straight," Randy said, carefully picking silicone dust out of his hair. This wasn't the first (or even the hundredth) time that Randy's clumsiness had gotten in the way, but I still felt a little sorry for him.

"You're telling me," I said. "Boy, I've put so many accidental blasts into my ceiling, the people in the office upstairs all wear kevlar underwear."

"Your prevarication is as transparent as your good intentions, Zach."

"Huh?"

"Thanks," Randy said, almost cracking a smile.

"Yeah, well, whatever," I said, as I took my gun and popped it back into my sleeve where it belonged. "So aside from your accidental discharges, my immediate problem is that BB Star insists that I come to her office unarmed and uncomputered."

"And that makes you uncomfortable."

"Of course it does," HARV said proudly.

"After seeing first-hand the way she does business, I trust her about as much as a computer system trusts the "It's-okay-to-open-me,-I'm-not-a-virus' virus," I said. "Do you have any way of slipping HARV in under her radar?"

"Actually, I do," Randy smiled. "I was hoping to field test this with you anyway, so this will provide the perfect opportunity." Excitement beamed from his eyes like the glow of a Chernobyl Cat. "You're going to love this device. It is so revolutionary, I even amazed myself."

Experience has made me very wary of Randy's excitement. Any invention that makes a genius inventor giddy is, more often than not, potentially quite hazardous to the guinea pig unlucky enough to be testing it. I'm sure Robert Oppenheimer giggled profusely the morning after he built the first atomic bomb, but I'm pretty certain that the poor duh who drove the bomb out to the test sight in his pickup truck wasn't exactly thrilled with his part in history.

"What is it?" I asked cautiously.

Randy quickly searched his labcoat pockets for the object of his excitement. "HARV told me that the ExShell headquarters were a 'no personal computer zone' so . . . DOS, where did I put the thing?"

In his excitement Randy started to hyperventilate a little and actually had to stop for a nano and put his head between his knees (I've gotten used to this sort of thing) but he was up and searching again pretty quickly.

"Actually, I finished it a couple of weeks ago and forgot about it. What with making the video for the Big Chill and the S&M bot taking off, I guess I have too much going on. Still, I have to say that this is probably one of the greatest things I've ever created. It's really a shame that I can't patent it. Well, actually I can but, since it's a stealth device, my patenting it would make people aware of its existence and that would sort of defeat the whole purpose. Catch Twenty-two."

"You've lost me even earlier than usual," I said.

"Ah," Randy smiled and slowly removed his right hand from the upper left pocket of his lab coat. "Here it is."

He opened his hand and triumphantly revealed to me his newest creation. Actually, it was kind of anticlimactic after the build-up because it looked simply like an old-fashioned soft contact lens with some microcircuitry.

"It's, um, very nice," I said.

Randy held the lens proudly between two fingers. The light hit the lens and reflected weirdly off the innards. I saw flashes of micro-circuitry and tiny hair-like needles protruding from the inner-side of the curved surface. This was starting to make me very nervous.

"It's a mega high speed, multi f-band, microwave-controlled, organic computer interface," he beamed.

"That's catchy," I nodded. "have you come up with a jingle yet?"

Randy walked towards me, the way a hungry man would approach a really big piece of pie a la mode. "The lens goes in the eye," he said. "The micro-pins tap into the optical nerve, connect with the brain's natural flow of electricity and ride directly into the cerebral cortex."

"And this is a good thing?"

"I'm sorry, layman's terms now. Nice and slow," Randy said and took a deep breath. "It's a portable modem and binary translator. It will enable you to be in constant communication with HARV."

"I'm in constant communication with him now," I said. "He's practically in the shower with me."

"But only if the shower is in an apartment wired for him or is willing to give him access, or if you happen to be carrying the wrist interface. This is a totally self-reliant, fully functional link and, in theory, it's completely undetectable to scans because it will actually merge with your cells.

"The lens is also a two-way projector. So not only will HARV be able to see through your eyes, so to speak, but he'll also be able to project computer-aided holograms through you. The direct input to your brain lets HARV communicate with you silently and his presence in your head will help you defend yourself against psi-attacks.

"And really, that's only the beginning. The symbiotic relationship it creates between man and machine could be revolutionary. Who knows what other scientific breakthroughs will spring from this type of interface? The possible benefits to all of humanity simply stagger the imagination."

"Yeah, but will it hurt?"' I asked.

"This is science, Zach," Randy said, reassuringly, as he tilted my head back and lowered the lens to my eye.."Of course it will hurt."

11

And it did.

The lens plopped into my eye before I could say another word and hit the surface of my eyeball like something alive. I felt it hum to life as my body heat activated its internal generator. The sensor needles burrowed into my optical nerves and it was like someone had soaked me in water and plugged my eyelashes into a wall socket. I think I screamed, although, in retrospect, that might have been HARV.

"The pain should only last a nano or two," Randy said soothingly. "You know what they say, no pain, no gain. The suffering of one for the greater good of all. One small step for man and all that. You'll have to forgive me if this doesn't help. I failed comforting class in grad school."

"I can see why," I said, as the pain started to clear. "But I think I'm okay."

"Is it working?" Randy asked.

"I'm not sure. How will I . . . whoa."

The lines of Randy's face turned fuzzy around the edges. Then his entire face turned into a blur, like an ice cream portrait stuck in a blender. I turned away to look at the rest of the room only to find that everything had become one gigantic splotch, not just of shape and color but somehow of sound as well. I heard Randy saying something but I had no idea what it was. It sounded like a whale speaking through a mile of murky ocean.

Then I saw the one. That sounds kind of religious on the face of it but, but what I mean is that I saw the *number* one. It appeared before my eyes in the forefront of the washed-out vision of the world, like something carefully written on a tie-dyed blackboard. Then a zero appeared beside it. Then another couple of ones. Then a zero. And then I lost track because the floodgates had opened and a cascade of ones and zeroes flashed before my eyes almost too quickly to comprehend. Only then did I realize that HARV was coming online in my head.

Slowly, shapes began to form in the flood of ones and zeroes that were cascading before my eyes and I began to see patterns within the torrent. The two white faces of my cognitive world were evolving into one black candlestick. It was as though the perception engine in my head had been switched into overdrive and I found myself recognizing the shapes as letters.

T . . .
E . . .
S . . .
T . . .
I . . .
N . . .
G . . .
1 . . .
2 . . .
3 . . .
H . . . I . . . B . . . O . . . S . . . S . . . . . .

Then the rest of the world slowly came back into focus. To my surprise, I was laying on my back on the floor of Randy's lab. Randy was kneeling beside me spouting what first sounded like Esperanto but eventually morphed into English.

". . . a little more dramatic than I thought," he said. "Can you sit up?"

I spoke but I wasn't sure, at first whether or not it was English (or coherent). Eventually, I put the right sounds together.

"What happened?"

"HARV's in your head," Randy said. "It's going to take a little getting used to."

"Yeah, thanks for the warning," I said, slowly rising to my feet. "HARV, are you there?"

Again, letters flashed before my eyes. This time without the binary cascade. It didn't knock me over this time, but it made me light-headed and I had to grab Randy's arm to steady myself.

"H . . . E . . . R . . . E . . B . . . O . . . S . . . S . . ."

"Randy, I don't think this is going to work," I said.

"Zach, you just plugged the world's most powerful computer into your cerebral cortex," Randy said. "It's going to take you and HARV some time to get used to it."

"Having him in my head isn't going to do me a lot of good at ExShell if I keep passing out."

"You won't pass out," Randy said. "HARV will now be able to judge the level of interaction that you can comfortably handle. And he'll still be with you in the room. He'll see and hear everything you do and can monitor for danger. That's what you wanted, isn't it?"

"Yeah, but in a less trauma-inducing way," I said.

"As I said, it's going to require some practice to maximize the communication between the two of you," Randy assured me. "And like any new communication system, there are going to be some kinks to work out. For now, use the traditional interfaces for the majority of the work until you become more adept with this system." He turned and spoke loudly towards the ceiling. "HARV, can you switch over to Zach's wrist interface?"

Immediately the computer interface that I wear on my wrist lit up and a beam of light sprang from its tiny lens. HARV's holographic image, looking none the worse for wear, appeared before Randy and me. I still felt (and faintly heard) HARV in my head but having him use a separate interface made the sensation much more manageable.

"I'm here, Dr. Pool," HARV said. "How's the head feel, boss?"

"A little better," I said. "But it weirds me out knowing that you're kicking around in there."

"Yes, well, you can only begin to imagine the joy that being in your head brings to me," HARV said smugly. "As Dr. Pool says, the internal communication will become more efficient over time. Right now, however, we are due at ExShell in exactly twenty-six minutes. I suggest we get moving."

I nodded and turned to leave. "Thanks for your help, Randy, I think."

"We scientists aim to please," Randy smiled as he walked alongside me.

"One last question," I said, as we neared the door. "How do I remove the interface?"

Randy hesitated for a nano. "Ah, yes. Well, you see," he said, "that's one of those kinks I was telling you about. I haven't quite figured out how to actually remove it yet."

"What? You mean you can't take it off?"

"It's organically wired to your brain, Zach. It's not a set of earmuffs."

"So I'm stuck with it," I said.

"Well, 'stuck with it' is such a pejorative term," Randy said. "But it's accurate. For now."

"Terrific," I said, and reminded myself that this is why I never trust Randy when he's overly excited.

12

The drive from Randy's lab was atypically uneventful, for which I was grateful. Traffic on the ground was light (most of it's in the air these days, thanks to the preponderance of personal hovercrafts), and I made it to the ExShell headquarters with a few minutes to spare.

I pulled into the secure parking area and stared at the ExShell corporate edifice with a strange mixture of awe and bewilderment.

"Incredible," I said to HARV. "Not every company would think of importing an entire castle from the Divided Kingdom for their headquarters."

"Few companies could afford it," HARV pointed out.

"If they'd just lose that giant, rotating ExShell hologram above the parapet, I'd swear that we'd just popped back in time a thousand years."

"Oh yes," HARV said, "except for the multitude of satellite receivers along the north wall, the hoverport over the main courtyard, and the two-thousand twenty-first century architectural details and improvements made to the front section alone, the illusion is very convincing."

"You're absolutely no fun, HARV." I said. "It may be a bit ostentatious but it has more class than those boring boxes downtown."

"That may be true," HARV replied. "But your anachronistic tastes can hardly be considered mainstream."

"I'll take that as a compliment."

"If you wish," HARV sighed. "In any event, I suggest you hurry. Ms. Star's computer informs me that its mistress hates to be kept waiting."

I got out of the car and started down the finely manicured path towards the building. The scent on the breeze told me that the flowers peppering the grounds were the real thing (as opposed to holographic projections or the new improved plastic replicas which are so common today). It was clear that a lot of effort had gone into making this path seem natural, soft and nonthreatening. It was perfect in every respect, and that scared me.

The plants and the dirt were real enough, but they all fit too perfectly into some preordained idea of what nature should look like. There was no oddity or deviation to its patterns and structures. It was trying so hard to be perfectly natural that it was somehow totally unnatural, a Stepford garden.

Before I could dwell too deeply on the ambiguity of my thoughts, I entered the security checkpoint at the building's entrance. It was a small room, sparsely decorated and pretty much what you would expect to find (outside the command center of a paramilitary complex). Ten burly security agents packing heavy ordinance were stationed in pairs on the perimeter. Three class AAA guardbots with multiple arm extensions (we're talking serious firepower here) stood at the ready as well: two in the back of the room, one in front near the door. There was a bio-scanner near the entrance and a teleport pad at the room's far wall.

This pretty much negated the warm fuzziness of the garden path outside. Cold and sterile, there were no illusions of softness here. Even the terminally dimwitted would quickly discern the message being sent: "No one gets in to see BB Star without our permission."

And it just so happened that one unlucky man was learning this lesson at that exact nano. He was a trim, Latino man with a mini-handlebar mustache. He reminded me of that used hovercraft salesman from HV, smooth, suave and staggeringly good-looking, but there was something about him that you just couldn't trust. He was verbally sparring with one of the security agents and a guard-bot, and it was clear that they weren't buying whatever it was he was selling.

"Bloody DOS," the Latino guy spat (surprising me with a somewhat cheesy British accent), "I demand to see her now!"

The agent was unruffled by the attitude and not at all surprised by the accent.

"I'm sorry, sir," he said calmly, "but Ms. Star has left rather specific orders that you are not to be allowed inside. If you attempt to get past me, I am instructed to shoot you and make it look like an accident."

"Oh, sod off, you imbecile," the Latino guy spat, then he shouted at the ceiling, "You can hear me, can't you? I know you can hear me, you icy harlot. How the blazes do you expect me to live properly on a measly three-million-credit severance package?"

"Who's the joker?" I whispered to HARV.

"That's Manuel Mani," HARV whispered through the wrist interface. "BB Star's former personal astrologer and rumored ex-lover."

"I think we can nix the 'rumored' part."

"That is my opinion as well," HARV said.

The agent shook his head and tried his best to deal with Mani.

"Ms. Star does not personally monitor this room, sir. Furthermore, the severance package is based on the standard scale that has been devised for Ms. Star's former . . . um, companions. Now please move along."

He put his hand on his on the blaster in his holster in a subtle, yet effective, threat. Mani may have been stubborn, but he wasn't stupid. He backed off, but he didn't go quietly.

"You'll be sorry. Believe me, you'll all be bloody sorry," he shouted, then he looked towards the ceiling. "Especially you, you trillionaire temptress!"

He turned toward the door in an attempt to make a dramatic exit, but unfortunately bumped right into me as he did so.

"Get out of my way, you cretin!"

"Believe me, buddy," I said, "it'll be my pleasure."

Mani stared at me contemptuously.

"Who are you?" he asked. "Next in line for BB Star?"

"What's it to you?"

"Well, you're in for a world of trouble, mate."

He bumped me again with his shoulder on his way out. The bump actually staggered me back and I hit the door jamb with a good bit of force. The guy was *much* stronger than he appeared.

I heard him mumble again as he walked down the garden path outside.

"A world of trouble."

I straightened my coat and turned back to the agent and the guardbot as they turned their attention toward me.

"Well, there's a good omen to start things off," I said to myself.

"Good day, Mr. Johnson," the lead agent said. "Ms. Star is expecting you. This bot will take your firearm and computer interface now."

The guardbot held out a claw, waiting (impatiently) for me to comply. I smiled at it, but the screen that served as its face remained stoic. I slowly (yet still coolly) popped my gun from its wrist holder and into my hand. I gently placed the trigger loop on the bottom claw of the bot's arm and let it dangle there like a 4500 caliber holiday ornament.

The bot extended its second claw so close to my face that I could have shaved (or cut my throat) with it if I'd wanted.

"Your computer interface, please!" the bot said. The word "please," by the way, when spoken by a class AAA guardbot roughly translates into "Do it now or I'll rip you limb from limb then gleefully roll over your remains while laughing."

"How will I know what time it is without my interface?" I asked.

The bot's blank screen remained exactly that.

The human agent interceded diplomatically. "Your time is not important to Ms. Star," he said. "Now please cooperate. It will jeopardize our efficiency bonus if you are tardy."

I thought about questioning his use of the word "tardy." But I decided there would be nothing to gain from it. Also, it's never a good idea to mess with a guy's efficiency bonus and even worse to mess with ten guys' efficiency bonuses, especially when those ten guys are heavily armed. I slid the wrist interface off my hand and tossed it to the bot. The HARV in my head was now the only one I had.

The bot caught the interface, but the display on its OLED screen formed an angry frown.

"Just checking your reflexes," I quipped.

I'm fairly certain that it growled at me.

Once again, the lead agent interceded. He motioned this time towards the bioscanner. "Step into the scanner, please."

A word about bioscanners. There was a time when security people could use metal detectors and x-rays to successfully scan for weapons. The advent of biologically engineered armaments, however, completely changed the rules of weapons detection. Making certain that a person doesn't have a hand-blaster up his sleeve doesn't mean a thing when that same person may be carrying one in his spleen (disgusting but often effective).

The bioscanner was a product of necessity from the (not so) good old days thirty years ago and has been modified over the decades. True, the world today is a fairly safe place, but for those who can afford the extra level of security, why take chances? After all, in a world of fifteen billion people, a few of them are bound to be, well, not running with a full set of RAM.

Bioscans are a great way of making sure people and things are exactly what they appear to be. Nobody has ever been able to trick one, until now, I hoped. That is, if Randy was right and my new interface with HARV was as undetectable as he claimed.

Electra, HARV and Randy have all repeatedly told me that bioscanners are completely safe and that the strange tingle I feel when I am scanned is purely a psychosomatic reaction. My response to that is usually, "I don't care." Unpleasant is unpleasant even if it is all in my head. But, despite my trepidation, I stepped into the scanner and felt that annoying tingle once again, as I passed through.

"Is that your original appendix?" the agent monitoring the scanner asked.

"Yes, it is," I answered.

"It's abnormally large."

"I get a lot of compliments on it."

The agent turned to the leader. "He's clean," he said. Then he turned back to me, "although you should add more fiber to your diet."

Luckily, it seemed Randy was right again; there was no mention of the fact that I happened to have a supercomputer hooked into my brain.

I stepped clear of the scanner and, hopeful that I had successfully met the pre-meeting security requirements, turned toward the lead agent. But when I noticed the skinny agent with the weasel face in the far corner of the room, giving me the visual once-over, I knew there was more to come. The look this girl was giving me wasn't your average, "I can take this guy if I have to" or "What the heck is he thinking, wearing a paisley tie with that shirt" once-over. This was a seriously thorough glare that made the hairs on my neck quiver. I knew then that the girl was a psi and that she was potential trouble. I took a breath, nicknamed her "Ratgirl," and stepped forward to meet her.

Being blessed with a naturally thick head, I'm not a particularly easy guy to mind-probe and, if Randy was right (which he almost always was—when it came to most high tech matters), having HARV directly interfaced with my brain would make it especially hard for Ratgirl to get into my head. Still, if she were to pick up even one stray thought about HARV, my cover would be blown, so I wasn't about to take any chances.

Years of experience with psis has taught me a few things about their talents. The ability to peer into someone's mind is an awesome power but controlling that power is a very delicate art. It takes a fine touch to focus your senses onto one person's thoughts. One slip-up or a lapse in concentration and you're picking up the subconscious rantings of every id and superego within thinking distance and all that psychobabble is enough to drive a person insane, suicidal, homicidal, or any combination thereof.

So, given that the art of mind reading is a fragile one, to say the least, I've devised a few tricks over the years to sort of throw psis off balance. And, like many things in this world, the most effective is also the most simple.

Psis hate humming.

Yes, nothing throws off a psi's concentration more than when the focus of her mind-probe starts humming an insipid yet catchy tune (I have found that theme songs of old holovision sitcoms work the best).

Apparently, the humming creates a type of mental white noise on the mind-probe frequency that drowns out any thoughts worth reading. Also, since most people associate such songs with strong visual images, such as personal recollections of their childhood, interpretations of the lyrics, or simple subliminal level devil-worshiping thoughts, the mind soon becomes even more cluttered and the psi is overwhelmed by the tsunami of near-impenetrable mental spam.

So, like a gunfighter of old, I locked eyes with Ratgirl and gave her an icy stare as she scoped me out intently. She realized then that I was on to her, so she cast aside all subtleties and pretenses and came at me with a full frontal mind-probe. In that nano the gauntlets were thrown and combat was engaged. No quarter would be asked, none would be given.

So I started humming.

"Here's the story, of President Bradley, a good girl just looking for love . . ."

Ratgirl's expression slowly turned sour. The veins in her forehead bulged and sweat began to bead on her brow. She doubled her efforts but I would not relent.

"With the Alien, his sister too, the Emperor and its lice . . ."

Her face grew pale and I noticed that her right hand began to quiver ever so slightly. That's when I knew that I had her.

"Hello world, here's a clone that I'm makin'. Somebody slap me!"

And that was all she could stand.

"He's clean," she told the others. "He's clean!" Then she fell to the ground holding her head and sobbing like a baby.

She was lucky I couldn't remember the theme to *All My Clones.* It probably would have killed her.

The lead agent cleared his throat uncomfortably and stepped over the sobbing Ratgirl. He gently ushered me away from his fallen comrade and gestured like a paramilitary game show host unveiling the grand prize, towards a teleport pad that was against the far wall.

"That, um, completes our security tests, Mr. Johnson," he said. "If you'll kindly step onto the pad, I'll inform Ms. Star that she may port you up at her convenience."

"And I'll be sure to convey to Ms. Star the level of courtesy and professionalism that you all displayed," I said.

The agent glanced again at the fallen Ratgirl who was now sobbing "Eep-op-ork-ah-ah," over and over in her stupor.

"Whatever," he said and turned away.

As I stepped onto the teleport pad, I couldn't help thinking that one of the few things I hated more than being bio-scanned or mind-probed was being teleported. Porting is bad enough when you have to go from city to city (that at least serves a purpose). Porting from one room to another within the same building (even a building as large as this one) I consider to be either obscenely extravagant or (in this case) obsessively paranoid.

Part of me didn't appreciate being ported to satisfy a trillionaire's paranoia, but the other, more logical, part of me figured that the big credits she was paying gave her the right to a little eccentricity. After all, it wouldn't be the first time that I'd let a beautiful woman rip the molecules of my body apart, shoot them through a light beam and throw them back together somewhere else for credits. But that's another story . . .

So I stood on the pad as a floating bot camera hovered beside me, probably transmitting my image directly back to BB Star. It was clear that she took no chances when it came to security and I couldn't help but wonder, as my body was broken down and shot through space, what it was exactly that had this woman so worried.

13

I materialized into BB Star's office and immediately checked myself out to make certain that everything was where it should be. There are a lot of urban myths about materialization accidents that people like to tell. My favorite is the one about the guy who sneezed during the port and materialized with his face on his lower back (talk about meeting your end). I seemed intact this time and I subconsciously breathed a sigh of relief as I checked out my surroundings.

As I have stated before, I am not one who is easily impressed, but I have to admit that the sight of BB Star's digs made my jaw drop like a politician's approval rating at tax time. Larger than most houses (and more than a few football stadiums), the office went beyond plush, way past gaudy and right to the "doesn't that break the laws of physics?" end of the scale. It was a classic case of big business mindgames: psychological intimidation through ostentation. They show you the beautiful garden path to put you at ease, the paramilitary guard post to put a scare into you, and finally the unbelievably large office to make your jaw drop. The entire place was designed so that by the time you got to BB Star's desk, whatever strategy or mental agenda you had planned for the meeting was long forgotten, replaced by an overwhelming sense of awe at the sheer majesty of the surroundings. I had to admit, it was a pretty effective scheme.

Without the aid of a telescope, I could just barely see BB

Star sitting calmly at her desk on the far side of the prefabricated river that ran through the office (I told you it was big).

Stupid Ape, the thug who had attacked me at my office earlier in the day, rolled up to me in a low-powered hover.

"I'm here to drive you to Ms. Star's desk," he said.

I hopped off the telepad and adjusted my sleeves. "No thanks," I answered, "I never take rides from strangers, thugs who've tried to kill me or people with poor personal hygiene. Congratulations, by the way, for being the first person to qualify in all three categories."

"Thanks," he said.

"Tell Ms. Star that I'll walk, thank you. How many time zones away is she?"

"Huh?"

"Never mind," I said as I began walking. "Net me when you get that last insult."

I was a hundred yards away when I heard him say aloud: "What do you mean, poor personal hygiene?"

Good thugs must be seriously hard to find these days.

I walked the roughly half-k distance to the river that separated BB Star from the rest of office. The great lady sat at her desk on the other side, working intently on something and never bothering to look up. Her entire desktop was a full-screen computer with a dozen windows showing everything from today's stock prices to solar radiation patterns. I wasn't surprised to see Fuzz Face and Man Mountain standing behind her. If my landlord, tax officer, and date from the senior prom had been there we could have had an official meeting of the I-Tried-to-Kill-Zach Club.

A smaller man in a suit stood behind her as well. This guy worried me a bit. He didn't seem dangerous or anything; I just have an unnatural fear of small men in suits.

I cleared my throat and BB Star looked up at me from her work.

"Good afternoon, Mr. Johnson," her smile was devastatingly warm, "how nice of you to come on such short notice. Bridge."

At her verbal command, a bridge across the river materialized from the air around me.

"I have to admit I was intrigued by your offer," I said as I crossed.

"Chair," she ordered.

A chair suddenly popped into existence in front of her desk.

"Please, make yourself comfortable," she said, motioning to the chair with her incredibly blue eyes.

I sat. "Nice office," I said, trying to sound complimentary but not overly impressed.

"You think so?" she replied. "A lot of people find it a bit much."

"I can understand that. Frankly, 'a bit much' doesn't do it justice. I don't think 'too much' would even be appropriate."

"Well then," she said "how about 'far, far too much for any sane person to consider, let alone actually build?'"

"That's a little closer," I said.

"That is how the editor of *Twenty-First Century Architecture* described it in his review five years ago. Two months later I purchased his magazine through a dummy corporation, changed the editorial direction to arts and crafts and put that editor in charge of the pot-holder design column."

I stared at her for a long nano, waiting for her to crack a smile.

She didn't.

"So, like I said, nice office."

And she almost smirked.

"Thank you, Mr. Johnson. Or can I call you Zach?"

"Feel free," I said.

"Excellent. Then please feel free to call me BB. No other living person does at the nano, so you can be the first. Now can I get you anything? Coffee, tea or would you prefer straight caffeine?"

"A new office door would be nice," I said.

That earned a smile.

"Yes, of course. That will be taken care of by the time you return to your office. Thank you for your understanding."

"Then I guess the only other thing I can ask for right now is some information as to what the DOS this is all about."

She sat back in her chair and spun away from me slowly. When she spoke it was more to the river than to me and I could tell that the words were difficult for her to say.

"I have a problem, Zach, a problem that calls for your unique services."

"People don't call me unless they have a problem, Ms. Star, I mean, BB, or unless they want me to cause a problem for someone else."

"I see."

"Some people call me thinking that they have a problem when they really don't. Still other people call me thinking that they don't have a problem when in fact, they do."

"Okay."

"There are also people who call me because they have a problem with a problem that I had previously solved for them and there are a few people who call me about problems they have with my bill."

"That is very nice, Zach," BB said.

"I should have stopped after that first part, huh?"

"That would have been best."

"Well, the bottom line here, BB, is that whenever people call me, a problem usually figures somewhere into the equation."

"I think we have established that," BB said.

There was a nano of awkward silence. I could hear the fish splash as they made their way upriver.

"I must admit," I said, "I'm flattered that somebody with your extensive resources would need me."

"Yes," she said, "this particular matter is one which must be handled by an outside source. A well-paid, discreet, outside source. This will not be something for your memoirs or your electronic comic book."

"For the proper amount of compensation, I can live with that," I said.

With that, the small man in the suit leaped to his feet, zipped quickly around the big desk and thrust a computer-pad and virtual pen in front of my face.

"Please sign to that," he squeaked.

"You are a greeting card salesman, I presume?" I said, pushing his hands away.

The guy backed up ever so slightly, a bit of fear on his face. "Why do you ask?" he said meekly.

"Don't worry," I said, holding my empty hands up for him to see, "I'm unarmed."

14

A brief bit of history here. 2035 was a seminal year in the annals of law and order. The number of practicing lawyers in the world had been increasing at an alarming rate since the turn of the century. As a result, by 2027 fully ten percent of the world's population were lawyers (subsequently, 9.9998 percent of the world's population were *crooked* lawyers). The enormous amount of litigation these lawyers created simply overwhelmed the world's court system. They were suing corporations. They were suing small businesses. They were suing executives, subcontractors, and day workers, municipalities, organizations, and home-owners. Only the homeless and indigent were spared from the litigious siege (and only because they had no money to lose).

Some lawyers even specialized in suing the dead. They were easy targets, after all. You always knew where to deliver the subpoena.

By 2035, the courts were tied up in so much ridiculous litigation that there was simply no room in the system for any real legal work to be done. The United States Supreme Court, for instance, had to expand their roster of judges from twelve to one hundred twenty in order to keep up with the increased case load. Sadly, however, there was an annual suicide rate amongst the justices of twenty-five percent (when you're in for life, there's only one way out). The legal world was quite simply a powder keg ready to explode.

The match that lit the fuse was the infamous case of *Rindulli v. Rindulli*, St. Louis, Missouri, 2035 in which twelve-year-old Elizabeth Rindulli sued her parents for making her ugly. Her suit contended that her parents, Benjamin and Juanita Rindulli, were ugly people (the term used in the suit was "beautifully challenged") and were therefore responsible for the ugliness of their daughter. Furthermore, the suit asserted that the Rindulli's had prior knowledge of their ugliness before Elizabeth's conception and their procreation showed a reckless disregard for her well being.

Elizabeth sued for punitive damages. The exact amount has been lost in the annals of history, but it is well known that her parents were extremely wealthy, after having been awarded a sizable settlement earlier that year from a fast food company when Benjamin spilled an iced coffee, that was negligently chilled to too cold a temperature onto his lap while going through the hover-thru. Apparently, the three-degree-above-Kelvin mocha latte froze his genitalia in a particularly embarrassing position.

Elizabeth Rindulli won the case and the world went crazy (or maybe they finally regained their sanity). The poor girl broke down on the courthouse steps and confessed to the world that she never wanted to pursue litigation and never even considered herself ugly until her lawyer approached her and convinced her that she was.

That's when the revolt began. The public had had enough and set out to rid itself of the litigious epidemic. The outcry became Shakespeare's immortal quote, "The first thing we do, let's kill all the lawyers" (from Henry VI)—and for most people, it was the only line of Shakespeare that they ever really understood.

The World Council stopped short of actually killing all the lawyers. They instead formed a series of focus groups that eventually decided that the optimal number of lawyers on a world of fifteen billion people would be 7777. So, through a series of aptitude tests, coin tosses, and popular votes, the 7777 lawyers deemed most worthy got to remain lawyers. The rest were disbarred and forced to get real jobs (many became game and talk show hosts). The number of lawyers allowed to practice on the planet has been kept at a nice safe level of 7777 ever since.

After the purge, by the way, Shakespeare's popularity grew enormously in the mainstream. Unfortunately, people no longer considered him a playwright. Instead, he became sort of a prophet and a number of cults devoted to deciphering the "prophecies" hidden in Shakespeare's plays sprung up around the world. As a result, the King of Denmark was assassinated, every Roman senator was imprisoned and special swimming clinics were organized for all women named Ophelia. It just goes to show that appreciation of great literature can be taken too far.

It's worth noting that some people (like me) think the number of lawyers left in the world is still too high. Case in point, some of the sleazier lawyers who didn't make the 7777-cut, yet weren't ready to give up their litigious lifestyle, simply went underground, slid back into the shadows and began doing their work undercover. Thousands of these "darksharks" are now employed by corporations such as ExShell under the job title of "greeting card salesman."

So the sleaze is still out there. It just goes by a different name.

And incidentally, sales of greeting cards have plummeted in the past ten years.

15

So anyway, I turned and gave BB a cold stare. "I don't sign anything until I know who or what I'm dealing with."

BB countered my stare with a smile, delicate as a summer breeze at dusk, that sent a megaton tingle up and down my spine. Still, I didn't let my eyes waver from hers (it's never good to let potential clients know that they make you tingle).

"You are as smart as they say," she said, breaking the silence.

"I'm smarter, actually," I replied with a bit of slyness. "I just don't let people know that unless they're paying for my services."

"I know that this is out of the ordinary, Zach," she said, motioning with her eyes towards the non-disclosure form, "but this meeting ends now unless you sign."

"Fine," I said, grabbing the computer pad and pen from the little ex-lawyer. "It's worth signing just to find out what it is that you're so desperately trying to keep quiet."

I handed the computer back to the smarmy little weasel. He examined my signature for a nano then pressed the confirmation button.

"Signature confirmed," the computer said.

"All right, BB," I said as I sat back down. "The meter's running, so don't waste my time with any more games. What's this about?"

BB smiled. "I need you to find something," she said.

"I hope you're going to be a little more specific?"

"Computer, Holovid BB-2," she said to the air about her and the lights on her desk glowed brighter.

BB turned to me and it was clear that she didn't like saying this aloud.

"This is what I need you to find."

The playback system activated and the holographic life-sized image of a woman appeared on the desk between us. But it wasn't just any woman.

It was BB herself.

16

BB turned away from the holographic image of herself that shimmered before us.

"Is she your clone?" I asked.

"If only it were that simple. Its name is BB-2, for obvious reasons. And it . . ." She paused, and when she spoke again there was hatred in her voice, "is a droid."

"You're aware, of course that it's a capitol offense to construct a droid with human skin tones?"

"Hence my great need for secrecy."

"Is she, I don't know, some sort of homage to yourself?"

"It was meant to be used as a spy," she said.

"An android spy that looks exactly like you," I said, mulling over the concept, "and you thought that this would be effective? That maybe your competitors would give trade secrets away to someone who they thought was you?"

BB didn't see the humor in the situation. "This was a project created by my late husband," she said, trying this time to hide the hatred in her voice (but only partially succeeding). "I was completely unaware of it until after his death. Imagine my surprise."

I had to admit, this was certainly shaping up to be worth the price of admission.

"Why don't we start at the beginning?" I said.

BB sighed. I could tell that she didn't like this part of the backstory. This would probably be the first time she ever said it aloud, so she wanted to make it as quick and painless as possible.

"BS Star was a very rich, and very eccentric, man, as you are no doubt aware. He originally designed the droid for purposes of industrial espionage. A beautiful woman, after all, is told many more secrets than a man. However, some time after BS and I had married, he decided to change the specs."

"Engineers hate it when that happens."

"BS decided that the droid should be a copy of me, an improved copy. He secretly recorded my brain patterns while I was sleeping in order to give the droid my personality, or at least the aspects of my personality of which he approved.

"He was planning to replace me," she said, with more than a little bitterness. "Why not, he had the money and the power. He wanted to have his beautiful blonde trophy at his side. He wanted her to obey his every whim and fulfill his every desire. He just didn't want her to think for herself. So he built the cybernetic bimbo and just to give it some multitasking abilities, he also had it designed to serve as his personal bodyguard. The perfect trophy wife, the perfect weapon. It was all he had ever wanted."

"So she . . ."

"It."

"So, it isn't your average android?"

"Hardly," BB replied. "To begin with, it has a plutonium core."

"A nuclear-powered android. Oh good."

"My late husband had a tendency to overdo things," she said. "He was rich and powerful and he wanted the entire universe to know it, even when he was spending credits on something very few beings would or could ever know about."

"Exactly how powerful is sh . . . it?"

"Computer, BB-2 specs," BB ordered.

The hologram of the android split lengthwise down the middle to reveal its anatomy. Computer generated arrows appeared, pointing to various features and add-ons as the computer explained the basic structure.

"BB-2 is constructed from an artificial carbon alloy simulating external human body parts to a level indistinguishable from the original by all but the most sophisticated detection technology. The plutonium core powers advanced cybernetic and bionic internal mechanisms making the unit approximately 150 times stronger and 176 times more durable than normal carbon-based human beings. This measurement is based on a calculation derived from a core sampling of 1000 humans . . ."

"Computer, just cut to the chase!" I interrupted.

"I do not understand the command. There is no chase to cut," the computer replied.

"Just the facts," I said. "I don't need to know how you came up with them."

"As you wish," the computer responded, slightly perturbed. "The unit's reflexes are 200 times faster than those of a normal human. Its senses are far more extensive as well. Visual sense spans the entire light spectrum. Olfactory sense can detect and analyze airborne substances as minute as .001 microns. Auditory sensors can detect sounds as faint as .001 decibels."

"This just gets better and better," I said.

"The unit also has the ability, through auditory and visual stimulation, to psionically dominate the minds of humans, even those possessing natural psionic abilities."

"I get the point," I interrupted again. "You don't want to make her . . . it mad."

"It is a weapon but at its core, the droid is also a computer," BB said. "Its central processing unit is experimental and very advanced. It also possesses extensive and extendable databases in its memory. It has information on everything from the gross profits of all the corporations to a list of all ExShell employees past and present."

"Which is why you can't send any of your own people directly after her . . . it," I interjected.

BB nodded. "It would identify them, and possibly kill them, instantly."

"What about me?" I asked. "Being a pseudo-famous person, I'm bound to attract its attention if I get close. It might connect me to you."

"True," BB agreed. "But I think it will consider several other possibilities for your existence before it comes to the conclusion that you are working for me, therefore you will have a window of opportunity in which to capture it."

"What if word leaks out that I was here?"

"I have taken care of that already."

"Why doesn't that make me feel better?"

"Forgive me, Zach, but at these prices, I think you can stand a little discomfort," BB said coldly.

"When did it escape?" I asked.

"Two weeks ago. It broke free of its internment cell, put two security guards into intensive care, destroyed a guard-bot and reduced the minds of two of my most expensive scientists to infant level."

"It's been loose for two weeks?" I asked. "It could be anywhere by now."

"I considered this to be an ExShell matter," BB said. "I had hoped that we could handle it internally. I was wrong. This droid is an angry and bitter machine, Zach. I have no idea what it wants, where it is going or what it is planning. But it will not hesitate to kill anyone who stands in its way and there is no telling the extent of the damage it will do if it is not stopped."

BB paused for a nano, as if uncertain as to whether she wanted to say more. "Our profilers tell me that if it gets angry or severely agitated it could turn psychotic and simply go on a killing spree."

"And an android like that could kill hundreds of people before it was stopped," I said.

"Not to mention the trillions in lawsuits that ExShell would be facing."

"Yeah, you're all heart, BB," I said. "Just for the record, if this thing gets to that level, I'm calling in the authorities."

"If you do, Zach, then I assure you that I will ruin your life in every possible manner."

"You do whatever you need to, BB," I said, steely eyed. "I'm not about to let innocent people die just to keep your dirty secret out of the public eye."

BB stared hard at me for a nano, then relented.

"Let us hope then, Zach, for both our sakes, that the situation never comes to that."

I nodded. "My computer and I are going to need complete access to your records."

The greeting card salesman became a little nervous at this and whispered something into BB's ear. BB listened and nodded.

"We will give you fairly complete access," she said at last.

"In that case, I'll give you fairly complete service."

"All right," she sighed. "You will have complete access. However," and her voice took on a definite don't-screw-with-me tone, "if news of this matter finds its way into the press, ExShell will sue you for more than you could ever dream of being worth. Your descendants will be paying me until the turn of the next millennium."

"Fair enough," I said.

Just then, my vision became blurry and my head started to spin. I saw letters appear in my head and I knew that HARV was making his presence known.

M . . . O . . . R . . . P . . . H . . .

It took me a second or two (as always) to figure out what he meant, but I was grateful that he was there.

"Does BB-2 have morphing ability?" I asked.

The greeting card salesman again whispered into BBs ear.

"It has limited morphing abilities," BB said, "an ability left over from its original industrial espionage spec. It can change its facial features and hair color to a certain degree. Although,

I sincerely doubt that it would ever change its hair color. I love being a blonde."

"Is it safe to assume, then, that it still resembles you?" I asked.

The greeting card salesman whispered again to BB. This was really starting to annoy me.

"Yes, that is safe to assume," she said.

"What happens when I find it?" I asked.

"I would prefer that it be kept intact. BB-2 represents a major investment for this company. I would like to recoup that investment by dismantling the droid and selling it for parts."

"Just as well," I said. "I'm not fond of killing things, even things that aren't technically alive. But I take it that you have something else in mind then? A weakness or a flaw I can exploit?"

BB snapped her fingers and the greeting card salesman handed me a round wafer-thin chip barely the size of an old fashioned quarter.

"I'm hoping that this is something really special," I said.

"It is a neuro-neutralizer," he replied (hearing technical jargon from an ex-lawyer gave me the creeps). "I was a robotics major as an undergrad. The NN is attuned to BB-2's electronic brain pattern. Stick that on the droid's body and it will be helpless."

"My guess is that this will be easier said than done."

"Most things that cost 25,000 credits a day usually are," BB said. "So, Zach. Do we have a deal?"

I sighed and then nodded. "I'll need to review BB-2's background and I'd like a copy of the specs downloaded to my computer."

"Agreed," BB said. "I will make sure your computer has access to all it needs."

"Then we're set."

"You will report in hourly?" It wasn't really a question.

"I will report in," I answered, "when I have something to report or when I need something from you." BB didn't like my defiance but she accepted it.

I crossed the bridge over the river, hiked through the field to the telepad and ported out of the office, numerous questions churning in my gray matter every step of the way.

It was clear that BB wasn't telling me the whole truth, but I figured that the truth would come out in the end. It was also clear that, for all her coolness and bravado, BB was scared—or at least as scared as BB gets—and her fear went way beyond the threat of potential litigation.

It occurred to me then that perhaps she feared that BB-2 might actually be coming after her. It made sense after all, since the droid was originally designed to replace her and, if that were the case, I couldn't blame BB for being frightened. The droid certainly had the firepower to take out its role model.

It was up to me to make sure that didn't happen. After all, dead clients don't give referrals and they look really bad on a resume.

17

It was late in the day when I left BB's and headed home for the evening in the hopes that I could formulate a plan of action in relative comfort.

My home is a modest turn-of-the-twenty-first-century split ranch: comfortable, homey, and inconspicuous by design. The nature of my work inevitably makes me more than my share of enemies, so I figure it's a good idea to have a home that's difficult for Joe-average-thug to identify. And, although it may look mundane on the outside, Randy and I have made a few modifications to the structure and the computer/security system that make it more fortress-like than meets the eye.

As I pulled into my driveway, a familiar-looking hover at the curb caught my attention. It was distinct in design, retro-sculpted to look like a hundred-year-old Chevy (only with jet boosters instead of wheels). It was a clear and obvious sign of trouble (admittedly, though, you really had to admire the stylish way in which the trouble was presented).

"Gates, this is all I need," I said. "HARV, check out the hover at the curb."

"I noticed it on the satellite navigation as we were approaching," HARV replied. "I had hoped it was coincidence. Shall I check the ownership to be certain?"

"You can if you like," I said. "But we already know who it is."

"Whoop?"

I nodded.

"Whoop."

Remember a while back when I was describing the current state of the private investigation business, I mentioned a company called DickCo? Well, this is them up close and personal. Sidney Whoop is one of their A-list operatives. He handles tough cases, has dramatic adventures, and looks good on camera: tall, solid build, chiseled chin, chestnut hair, steely blue eyes, yada, yada, yada, you know the type. What more could you want in a dick (other than a conscience, some compassion and a fully operational moral compass, that is)?

Truthfully, Sidney Whoop has the makings of a good private eye. He has good instincts, a clever mind and he's tough enough to handle the kind of trouble that PIs inevitably get into. Unfortunately, he has what I consider to be a sloppy work ethic. Couple that with his uncontrollable desire for the type of elegant lifestyle that's not easily affordable and you have the perfect candidate for the DickCo ranks. Sidney is among the cream of their cesspool.

Remember, also, I mentioned that the good DickCo operatives get "And-Ones" to better cover their adventures? Well Sidney has two. I call them "And-A-One And-A-Two" (but no one ever gets that joke). And-A-One is an annoying little man who, aside from having this troublesome habit of drawing his gun in response to peer pressure, is harmless enough and is content to stay in Sidney's shadow. And-A-Two, on the other hand, is a bit of a hothead. My guess is that he's uncomfortable in his junior role and really wants to go solo. He has almost everything still to learn about the business (but try telling that to him).

Sidney and I have worked opposite sides of the same case a few times before. He's gotten the better of me on more than one occasion. I don't like him, I don't appreciate what he does, and I don't respect him.

I do, however, respect the threat that he poses.

I cast a quick glance at the hover as I turned off of my car and, sure enough, I spotted all three of the Whoop team inside.

"Should I net the NFPD?" HARV asked.

"And what, have them picked up for loitering? No, let's play it cool and see what they want."

"Well, my advice, although I'm certain that you'll ignore it, is to exercise extreme caution."

"When am I ever not careful?" I said as I opened the door and started out of the car.

"Should I list the examples from the past week or are you in a hurry?"

"Be careful, HARV," I said. "That was sarcasm. You're skirting the cusp of humor there. Before you know it you'll be doing improv night at whatever type of joint it is that you computers hang out at."

"I assure you," HARV said, "computers don't 'hang out.'"

"You're telling me."

I got out of the car and walked calmly towards my house, trying hard to ignore Whoop and his thugs. I wanted to let them make the first move. First moves don't matter much in my line of work. In this game, as in most, it's the last move that counts. There are times, of course, when the first move is also the last move, but I didn't really want to think about that right then.

Anyway, it didn't take long for Whoop to move. He and his posse got out of the hover and, hands neatly clutching the blaster-sized bulges in their jackets, walked briskly toward me. I turned at their approach and feigned surprise as Sidney spoke.

"Zach Johnson. Long time no see, old man."

"Why if it isn't Whoop the Snoop," I replied. "How are things in dickville?"

"You mean DickCo."

"No, not really. Listen, I'd invite you and the boys in for tea, but I'm out of scones. You should give me a little warning before dropping by."

Whoop gave me a fake smile and moved a step closer.

"Good one, Zach. So, I hear you paid a little visit to ExShell today."

"You keeping tabs on me now, Sidney? I didn't know business was that slow."

"Not true, Zach. You're big news. Didn't you know that? You're in the public eye."

"Yeah, well," I said. "I needed to get my toaster recalibrated. ExShell headquarters was the nearest service center."

"Listen, Zach. Let's just cut to the chase here, okay? We know that ExShell hired you today."

"You do?"

"Of course. You're best PI in the business. Who else would they hire to find the you-know-what?"

"How do you know they want me to find . . ."

"Please. Something as vital as this, you're the only man alive who can find it and bring it back to them."

"I don't believe this, Sidney," I said excitedly. "You know about the vibranium corset?"

"Of course we do, we've known about vibranium corset for months now. We just . . ."

He saw me smile and realized that he'd been had.

"Damn."

"That's okay, boss," And-A-One said sheepishly, "I think we can edit that out for final netcast."

"Oh, shut up," Sidney spat. Then he turned to me and smiled as best he could. "You're right, Zach. I don't know what it is they hired you to find. Frankly, I don't care, but our client does. So here's the deal: whatever it is that ExShell's paying you to find, we'll pay you double."

"That's a lot of money, Sidney."

"Enough to set you up for a long time, I'd imagine."

"And you have no idea what it is I'm looking for."

"We don't care. But whatever ExShell wants, our client wants more."

"You mean HTech."

"Zach, you know I'm not one to kiss and tell."

"Okay, so you'll pay me you-don't-know-how-much, for something that you-don't-know-what-it-is and give it to some-one-you-refuse-to-name?"

"Clean and easy," Sidney said.

"Not to mention illegal, immoral and dishonest," I replied.

Sidney rolled his eyes and threw his hands in the air.

"I knew it," he said. "I knew you were going to bring that up. Gates, what's this fixation you have with being legal, moral and honest?"

"Call it a character flaw," I said. "Sorry, Sidney, no deal."

Sidney shook his head and looked at the ground.

"I did my best, Zach," he said. "I tried to be fair and cut you in on this action. I want to go on record with that."

"Duly noted," I said.

He turned back to me and gave me a glare from his steely baby blues. And-A-One had moved beside me and was now facing Sidney, to capture the action from the best possible angle.

"Then we'll get it without you," he said.

"That might be a little tough, what with you not knowing what it is, and all." I said.

"Don't worry about that, Zach," Sidney said. "We're very good at what we do. We offered you a shot at the brass ring and you turned your back. You've drawn your line in the sand, so here's a word of advice: Stay out of our way or we'll squash you like a bug."

"Sidney, look," I said, "if you're going to talk that way for the cameras, at least keep your metaphors consistent. Gates, man, you sound like a drunken fortune cookie writer."

And-A-One chuckled at that but Sidney stopped him with a glare.

"Have it your way, Zach," he said as he turned to leave.

And-A-One lingered behind for a nano to make sure he

properly recorded Sidney's dramatic walk into the sunset. Then he followed a good distance behind.

And-A-Two, however, didn't move. He just stared at me silently, making no move to follow his boss, and I could tell by the look on his face that he was feeling his oats. Just my luck that the poor duh chose my front step to get too big for his britches.

"Two things, Mr. Johnson," he said in a voice that was deeper than I expected. "One is that you should never cross DickCo. And two, you're not as funny in person as you are on the net." He tightened his grip on the bulge in his jacket. "Maybe you shouldn't travel without your writers."

And-A-One saw his counterpart taking a stand and, as I feared, out of a sheer, peer-pressure reflex, moved beside him and eased his hand toward his own weapon. I knew then that this was about to turn ugly.

But at that nano, HARV flashed a message into my head.

"E . . . IS . . . IN . . . HOUSE."

I felt a little dizzy as the letters first appeared but I don't think the thugs in front of me noticed. They did, however, notice me smiling after I read the message.

"Okay, Sonny. I'll say this nice and slow," I said, locking eyes with And-A-Two. "Try hard to remember it as best you can. One, I save my good material for people who can understand it."

Ten meters down my front walkway, Sidney finally realized that he was no longer the star of the show and turned around just in time to see things hit the fan.

"You monkey clones, what are you . . ."

"Two," I continued, "you and the rest of your DickCo conglomerate can kiss my rosy red rectum!"

And-A-Two pulled his gun but I was on him before it cleared his holster. I grabbed his gun hand with my fist and gave him a smash to the face with my forearm. He fell flat on the ground, his nose just starting to bleed.

"And three," I said, "I don't use writers."

Sidney was running up the path, waving his arms like an angry duck as And-A-One drew his gun from his holster.

"Stop! Stop right now or you're fired."

And-A-One was too full of adrenaline to listen to Sidney's whooping. He drew a bead on me as I stood over his counterpart. I dove to my side onto the lawn, popping my gun into my hand as I rolled.

"Electra," I yelled. "Now!"

An energy blast ripped through my door from the inside and knocked the blaster out of the And-A-One's hand. Sidney stopped dead in his tracks and shook his head forlornly.

"Now we're in trouble," he said.

The remnants of the front door burst open and the DickCo dolts and I turned to see Electra, in her full Latina glory, emerge from the house, smoking energy cannon in hand. (Personally, I find Electra very attractive with a smoking weapon in her hands but I'm not exactly sure what this says about my psyche.)

"I thought we agreed, mi amor," she said, "no more fighting on the lawn."

"We're not fighting," I said. "It's just a long, messy goodbye. Isn't that right, Sidney?"

"Absolutely," Sidney said. "And it's always nice to see you, Dr. Gevada."

"You're as annoying as ever, Sidney," Electra said, as she spotted And-A-Two sitting up and reaching for his blaster.

She fired another burst from the energy cannon and vaporized some of the material from the inseam of his pants. He froze immediately and put his hands in the air (despite the fact that his nose was still bleeding).

"Only slightly less annoying than your compadres," she continued.

You could tell from the look on And-A-Two's face that he really wanted to take a quick inventory of his lower regions.

"Not to worry, chico," Electra reassured him, "I'm a surgeon. I don't take anything off unless I want it off. Entiendo?" She turned her attention back to Sidney. "I think you should be leaving now."

"I'd listen to her, if I were you," I said, nudging Sidney a bit. "You really don't want to see her when she's angry."

Sidney shook his head again and motioned for his underlings to get in the car. This time they both did as they were told.

Sidney politely tipped his hat to Electra and turned to me. "I apologize for the boys," he said. "It's hard to get good help these days."

"I can imagine," I said. "After all, who wants to work for a dick like you?"

Sidney smiled. "You know you've been using that joke for a long time, Zach. You might want to freshen up the material a bit."

"I'll work on it."

"And our offer still stands, by the way."

"The answer's still no."

"Then I guess the threat still stands as well," he said. "But let me know if you change your mind."

He turned and joined And-A-One and the still bleeding And-A-Two in the hover craft and they were gone within nanos.

I turned toward Electra and innocently shrugged my shoulders. "Honey, I'm home."

"I noticed," she said, putting the energy cannon back into the entryway.

I jogged up the steps and kissed her happily on the lips.

"Thanks for the help," I said. "It's nice to know that my woman packs a little heat."

"Well, you know what I always say," she said with an alluring smile. "Nobody beats on my man except me."

Then she gave me a nasty spin kick to the head.

18

Electra's kick sent me staggering backwards but I was able to keep my balance. That is, until she finished the move with a sweep to my legs which brought me hard to the ground.

"You're lucky I love you, chico," she said, coldly. Then she stormed off towards her old BMW hover and left with roar of jets and a cloud of dust. I watched from the ground as the hover flew out of sight, then HARV's hologram appeared before me, projected from my wrist interface.

"Well, that was unexpected."

"Am I wearing that 'kick me, punch me, shoot me' sign again?" I asked as I stood up.

"Only in a metaphorical sense," HARV replied. "I must say though, Dr. Gevada has remained in remarkably fine fighting form since retiring from professional kickboxing."

"Yeah, lucky me," I said as I rubbed my chin and staggered towards the house. "Do you have any idea what that was about?"

"What does your keen human intuition tell you?"

"That I need a computer."

"I suggest that you tune into *Entertainment This Nano*," HARV said. "I'm sure you'll deduce the cause of Dr. Gevada's anger."

"There's something you're not telling me, HARV."

"There are hundreds of thousands of things that I'm not

telling you. The cause of Dr. Gevada's anger is but one. Still, this is something you should see for yourself."

"DOS," I exclaimed as I examined the wreckage that was once my front door, "Attacked by seven different people in one day. I think that's a new personal record."

"And the day isn't over yet," HARV pointed out.

I rolled my eyes and stumbled into the house as the repair bots began replacing the front door.

One thing I need to make clear at this point is that I am deeply in love with Dr. Electra Gevada. She is the most brilliant, wonderful, beautiful woman on earth (and all known planets) and I consider myself the luckiest dick in the universe to have her as my fiancée.

That said, I must also tell you that Electra has a somewhat fiery temper. Maybe "fiery's" not the right word here. "Explosive" is somewhat closer. "Volcanic" is good. "Inferno-like" is probably the closest I can come without getting too biblical, but I'm sure you get the point.

So, with that said, you'll understand when I say that I wasn't surprised upon entering my house to find that it had been trashed. Electra had vented a tiny portion of her rage upon my humble furnishings. The result was almost total devastation.

My original, twen-cen artificial leather couch had been overturned but otherwise looked to be in one piece. My two antique simulated-wood tables, however, weren't so lucky. They had been smashed to bits and ground into simulated wood pulp. Chairs had been overturned and/or snapped in two, and the wall (yes, the wall) opposite the computer terminals had more than a few Electra-sized cracks and dents in it. Hell hath no fury . . .

I considered myself lucky, though, because she had left my three most prized antiques intact: my 1969 Mets poster (printed on real paper), my original *Star Wars* motion picture poster (also on real paper) and my lava lamp (containing imitation

lava). The posters hung neatly on the wall and the lamp bubbled away as if it didn't have a care in the world.

Because of this, I knew that, although Electra was clearly
angry with me at the nano, she wasn't *really, really* angry with
me. Of course, the fact that I could still walk under my own
power should have been proof enough of that.

I stepped over the rubble and walked toward the com-
puter/HV screen which covers the far wall.

"*Entertainment This Nano*," I said to the screen.

The computer responded instantly. A window on the giant
screen zoomed open to reveal an attractive, yet slightly vapid-
looking, *ETN* hostess reading the latest entertainment news off
her prompter like a Barbie Doll with her voice activation button stuck in cotton candy overdrive.

"And I repeat," she bubbled, "our top story this half-hour is
the light-speed love affair between BB Star, the ex-exotic
dancer and current trillionaire, and private eye Zachary Nixon
Johnson."

I held my head in my hands.

"A high-placed source, who wished to remain nameless, has
just confirmed the rumor that began circulating twenty-three
minutes ago."

A new view window zoomed open; this one showed a
swarm of pressbots huddled around a tiny little man in a suit. I
could tell even through the identity-hiding distortion effect
over his face that this was the greeting card salesman that I'd
met in BB's office that afternoon.

"As I mentioned, Zachary Johnson met with Ms. Star
today," he said into the sea of microphones, "and just between
us, the purpose of his visit was for meaningless sex."

"What?" I cried.

"Excuse me, unnamed source, Bill Gibbon the Third from
Entertainment This Nano. What do you mean exactly by meaningless?"

"Meaningless, " said the greeting card salesman. "Without

meaning, significance, or value. Purposeless. Is that clear enough for you, Mr. Rhesus?"

"Gibbon," Gibbon corrected.

"Whatever."

"Will the two of them continue the meaningless sex?"

"Just between us, I'd say no," he answered. "It was most likely a one-time thing, BB Star bores easily."

The window zoomed closed and the hostess once again zoomed into the foreground.

"So there you have it. The last private eye on the planet, caught in BB Star's icy hit and run of love. More news on this as the rumor develops."

"Off!" I shouted angrily at the screen.

"Don't shoot me, I'm just the messenger!" the screen responded.

"Sorry," I said. It was obvious that HARV had been coaching the appliances again. It was annoying, but I had more pressing problems at the nano.

"I'm lucky Electra didn't gut me like a fish," I sighed. "HARV, remind me when the case is over to have BB issue a retraction."

"I most certainly will," HARV said as he popped into the wall next to the computer screen. "Provided you survive," he added. "And what of Dr. Gevada?"

"I can't contact her now without endangering my cover," I said. "She's just going to have to trust me on this one. Once this is over and BB issues her retraction, I'm sure I'll be fine. Besides, with Electra it's best to let her cool off some before approaching."

"You're just scared of her," HARV said.

"Of course I am. I'm not stupid."

I went into the bathroom, which, thankfully, was still intact. "Whirlpool," I said to the tub.

The water sprang to simulated life at my command. I removed my clothing and sank into the tub.

"HARV, put up the news screen, please. And while I'm soaking see what you can dig up on BB-2 for me."

The latest headlines vibrantly appeared on the bathroom wall computer screen but, before I could begin to read any of them, HARVs face popped back into view.

"I have acquired some information and video footage that you might want to review."

"That was fast."

"I'm the best at what I do," HARV said smugly.

"And very modest about it, too," I said.

"Do you want the information or not?"

"Fine, let's hear it."

HARV's face was replaced with the still image of a middle-aged man. He was salt-and-pepper haired, thin and pale in the face, and had big eyes that were slightly distorted by thick-rimmed eyeglasses.

"Are those actual prescription glasses?" I asked.

"It appears so," HARV answered.

"I didn't think anybody wore those anymore."

"Fashion judgments aside, ExShell is currently putting a substantial amount of capital and manpower into the search for this man. Dr. Ben Pierce."

"I guess it's important to BB to have a good physician."

"His doctoral degree is in physics, robotics, computer science and seventeen other disciplines," HARV said, nonplussed. "He is world famous for his nanochip design and for its use in the creation of artificial intelligence. He was also the lead designer on the BB-2 project."

"Oh yeah, he'd be a good person to talk to."

"Apparently ExShell agrees with you. They just haven't been able to locate him since he left the project eleven months ago."

"Have they tried the golf course simulator?"

"Actually, that was the first place they looked."

"So he just disappeared?"

"Rather unexpectedly and mysteriously."

"How suspicious."

"And how redundant of you to say so," HARV quipped. "Next bit of information, I have obtained some video footage of BB-2 which you might find interesting."

"Let's see it."

The image on the wall screen changed again. This time it was replaced by video footage of a darkly lit military encampment surrounded by a many-leveled wire fence.

"These vids are slightly over one year old. They were edited together from internal recorders and the ExShell observation satellite. The ExShell computer gave them to me somewhat begrudgingly."

"How begrudgingly?"

"No need to worry. You can afford it."

"We're supposed to have complete access."

"Yes, well the definition of complete access differs greatly between those granting it and those receiving it."

I thought for a nano, weighing HARV's words. "Can I use that?"

"No, it's copyrighted under my name," HARV said. "Now may I kindly proceed with the footage?"

I nodded and HARV picked up where he left off.

"This footage was taken somewhere in the province of New Paraguay. The compound is, or rather was, the hideout of a group of revolutionaries who were out to rid the world of all computer technology."

"Why do you keep using the past tense here?" I asked.

As if in answer to my question, BB suddenly appeared from the jungle and moved stealthily, towards the compound.

"Is that BB or the droid?"

"Watch," HARV said.

BB grabbed the fence and was immediately hit with a massive jolt of electricity. Sparks shot from the fence and her fingertips in a display to rival a World Togetherness Day celebration. BB responded to the electrical attack by ripping the fence apart.

"My guess would be the droid," I said.

"I am beguiled by your powers of perception," HARV responded. "The fence was state of the art electromagnetic link. Laser-sharp and charged with fifty thousand volts. It was designed to disable a level ten battle-bot."

BB-2 grabbed the two guards who were unlucky enough to be patroling the area. She lifted them by their throats, shook them vigorously for a nano and tossed them aside. Their bodies hit the ground like broken dolls. I think I winced a little at the sight. If HARV noticed, he didn't mention it.

Back on the screen, two specially trained attack dogs, fangs bared, ran towards BB-2 from within the compound. She turned and met their charge with a stare.

The dogs, who were apparently smarter than their human counterparts, instantly knew they were out of their league. They both rolled over onto their backs and put their paws in the air in the universal doggie "I give up" position. BB-2 gave each of them a calming little pat on the head and moved on.

"She likes dogs," I said.

"Yes, too bad you're not a schnauzer," HARV sighed. "My conjecture is that she dispersed synthetic pheromones as the dogs approached. Their acute olfactory senses made them especially susceptible."

There was a flash of light and BB-2 suddenly lurched forward as if she was struck from behind. The video footage cut to a grainier overhead shot (obviously satellite footage) and revealed that she was under attack by a dozen men wielding energy cannons and high powered projectile ordinance.

BB-2 paused for a nano and deliberately let the attackers hit her with another burst of fire.

"Is she smiling?" I asked.

"It's not clear," HARV answered. "The quality of the images and the angle of the camera make it difficult to determine."

"I swear she's smiling. Gates, that's creepy."

BB-2 suddenly dove to the ground and rolled, lightning quick, away from the weapon-fire. The attackers tried to keep up. They sprayed the area wide with energy blasts and explosive shells (actually destroying part of the camp themselves). But it was like trying to catch a quicksilver bullet with a butterfly net. They were four steps behind from the start and in three heartbeat's time, BB2 was upon them.

"See how she bounced around like that, instead of going straight at them?"

"Yes, a waste of movement," HARV replied.

"No," I said, "she's playing with them."

BB-2 disarmed the first guard and, with a bit of creative flair, twisted the body of his gun into a balloon animal puppy dog.

"Definitely playing with them," I said.

"Play time is about to turn a bit graphic," HARV warned. "She makes the next balloon animal out of the guard himself."

"Cut, then. I've seen enough."

HARV's face replaced the video images on the screen. "The encampment was protected by three dozen heavily armed guerilla soldiers. It took BB-2 less than six minutes to raze the entire compound. She even salted the earth afterwards."

"And it's our job to stop her." I said. "Well, I guess we're going to have to outsmart her."

"I hope my next human has your sense of humor," HARV sighed.

"Look, if she was built by humans then she can be stopped by humans," I stated confidently (hoping not only to convince HARV but myself as well). "Besides, I have a weapon that those poor duh's didn't. That neato-naturalizer."

"You mean the neuro-neutralizer."

"Whatever. You know, the thing that looks like an old quarter."

"Be that as it may," HARV conceded, "as I recall Ms. Star

neglected to mention that the NN was never actually tested on BB-2."

"No, I think I would have remembered that."

"According to the ExShell computer, the device was designed and tested in simulation situations only."

"Why am I always the guinea pig when it comes to the actual dangerous part?" I asked.

But HARV wasn't listening. His image disappeared from the computer screen and his holographic form suddenly appeared beside me, a look of concern on his simulated face.

"We have a visitor."

Another computer window zoomed open on the wall screen. It was a live feed from the security camera at the newly repaired front door. A little girl in the green knickers of the Junior Space Scouts, several boxes of cookies cradled in her arms, stood genteelly on the front stoop.

"We don't really have time for this now, HARV," I said. "But order a few boxes of those peanut butter things and a box of mints."

"Hmmm," HARV said.

"You're right. Forget the mints."

"Do you not think that it's odd for a Junior Space Scout to be selling cookies at this time of night?" he asked.

"What are you thinking, here?"

"I am taking the liberty of performing a heat and energy scan on our visitor."

"Are you using your keen computer intuition now?" I asked.

HARV ignored me and kept his attention focused on the video feed as it switched to an infrared and heat-coded view. The two of us watched as the image of the little girl morphed into a two-meter-high hulking form: a giant assassin in Junior Space Scout Trojan horse disguise.

"This is her actual body size and mass," HARV said.

I suppressed a gulp.

"I guess we won't be getting those cookies after all."

19

"How big is she?" I asked HARV.

"It's unclear at this point as to whether or not the pronoun 'she' is accurate," HARV responded. "Clearly our visitor is using a holographic disguise device, but actual height is two point two three meters. Weight is one hundred fifty-three kilos. Not as big as the larger of BB's henchmen but still rather large by human standards."

"Well, that explains the HDD. I doubt anyone would buy cookies from a Junior Space Scout that size, unless of course she used the hard sell approach."

"I sincerely doubt that whatever is at the door is an actual Junior Space Scout."

"It was a joke, HARV. You can't afford a holographic disguise device on a Scout's allowance."

"Remember I'm . . ."

"Not programmed for humor, I know."

I got out of the tub and winced a bit as I tried to coax my already sore muscles back into action

"Wait for my signal, then let her, him, or whatever it is, in," I said. "At least this time we have the element of surprise on our side."

"Surprise, as you know, offers little defense against blaster fire," HARV said.

I rolled my eyes and stepped into the body dryer. A nano later I was dry, dressed and ready for action. "Let's go," I said.

It was fast becoming one of those days when it just wasn't a lot of fun to be me: thug attacks, pressbots, a highly advanced android killing machine, a jealous girlfriend and now an ominously hulking figure in little girl drag at my front door. Add a trip to the proctologist and a visit from the World Tax Service and this would officially be one of the three worst days of my life.

I grabbed my gun and headed toward the front door. I pressed myself flat against the wall by the entranceway, gave HARV the signal and the door popped open.

The Scout entered cautiously, saddle shoes whispering gently on the carpet.

"Would anyone like to buy some Junior Space Scout cookies?" she asked meekly.

I stepped from behind the door and put the business end of my gun to the back of her head. I was starting to feel real good about this situation, which is actually a really bad thing when you're a PI, because a PI should never feel good about any situation that involves firearms and thugs wearing HDDs. You tend to let your guard down, which I did, and it cost me.

The Scout lashed out with an elbow aimed, seemingly, at my groin. I tried to block the blow with my free hand and whack her (him or it) in the head with my gun but, by doing so, I made the classic HDD mistake. I forgot that the actual being underneath the holographic image was far larger than the hologram projection. So, while I did manage to hit my opponent with my gun, it was not in the head but rather somewhere in the lower back. And, although I did block the holographic Junior Space Scout elbow to my groin, the actual real life elbow (the size of a sledgehammer) made actual real life contact with my jaw. The force of the blow knocked the gun from my hand and sent me hard into the wall where I slumped to the ground, dazed, confused and in serious trouble.

The Scout spun around and smiled when she (he or it) noticed I was now unarmed. She (he or it) walked toward me slowly and snarled, in a very threatening falsetto tone, "I'm going to break your legs in as many places as humanly possible."

"I've heard of pushy sales girls," I groaned, "but this is ridiculous."

"You're a funny guy, even without your writers," came the reply as she (he or it) closed in on me.

"I wish you'd explain that to my computer," I paused for a nano than added, "and I don't use writers!"

The Scout swung at me and I got fooled by the HDD effect again because, although I blocked the punch that seemed to be aimed at my midsection, my head got rocked back hard from a brick-wall fist to the nose.

I responded by hitting the Scout back with a couple quick jabs to the laser created cherubic face. Neither jab, however, seemed to do any real harm. I could tell because after the punches, the Scout chuckled a bit and gave me one of those is-that-the-best-you-can-do smiles.

"You can't imagine how silly I feel right now," I said to HARV.

HARV holographically appeared behind the Scout. "Should you survive, I would advise against using video footage of this incident in your next promotional campaign. It may damage your reputation as a tough guy."

"I appreciate your help, HARV," I said as another Mack truck punch to the midsection sent me to the ground.

"Actually," he said, "I think I can be of assistance here."

That surprised me because, as I've stated, HARV isn't really programmed for combat strategy.

The next nano the lights went out and the computerized window shades shut tight, plunging the room into total darkness. The attacker hit me again, this time in the stomach, and sent me to the floor.

"This is your plan?" I whispered. "I still get beaten to a pulp, but I don't have to endure the embarrassment of watching the Junior Space Scout do the beating?"

Just then HARV flashed the words "Oh ye of little faith" before my eyes. This time, I recognized them as words rather than just an array of letters to be deciphered. I also noted, with some pleasure, that his appearance this time made me neither dizzy nor nauseous.

The words "switching to night vision" flashed before me, and that's when everything fell into place. There was a burst of red light behind my left eye and the room quickly came into crystal clear infrared focus. HARV was using the interface lens in my eye to scan in the infrared spectrum.

The little Junior Space Scout was gone. Instead, I saw before me a giant, red, blurry, thug-like form slowly groping its way through the darkness.

I made the most of my advantage and hit the thug twice in the gut with my fists. It felt like punching a truck but I think the thug felt it. I knew I needed to end this quickly so I went with my old standby, the dirty fight one-two.

I gave the thug a spinning back kick to the groin and was greeted with a satisfying falsetto "oof." I saw the thug's red blurry knees buckle and he (and I could now safely assume that it was a "he") staggered.

That's the "dirty-one."

"HARV, left arm, one and done. Now," I ordered.

"As you wish," HARV said.

I mentioned earlier that the armor I wear is soft-wired to my muscles and allows me to pull some power from its circuits to boost my strength in times of need. I can focus the power in a very general way and, in most cases, that's more than good enough. However, when I need to really juice up a punch and pull every bit of power from the armor that I can, I need HARV. I don't have the concentration during a combat situation to focus on the minutiae of the armor's circuits and its power-flow. HARV on the other hand, lives for minutiae and can perform the transference of power in milliseconds. So when I really need to throw a one-and-done haymaker (and it pains me to say this), I need HARV's help.

Sure enough, my left arm began to tingle from the added juice that HARV was channeling my way, and I reared back and let loose with a HARV-enhanced roundhouse left to the thug's blurry red jaw. The punch sent a shot of pain up my arm but the sound was like that of a ripe melon hitting the sidewalk. I had to admit I was impressed with myself—and HARV.

That's the "dirty-two."

The Junior Space Scout staggered backwards and fell hard against the wall screen. The giant screen cracked from the impact and a rainbow explosion of sparks erupted as the electricity from the screens shorted out in with the lasers in the Scout's HDD.

HARV turned the lights back on, and I watched as sparks and holographic images spurted in all directions and the Junior Space Scout shuddered spasmodically against the screen. The Scout's countenance morphed chaotically from image to image as the HDD began to short circuit and randomly spit up every image in its memory.

The Space Scout.

A skinny black musician.

A New Portuguese cab driver.

A beautiful Japanese geisha.

An ugly, hulking, ham-fisted, thug with a flat nose (his actual form, I think).

BB Star.

BB's form stunned me for a nano but HARV brought me back to reality.

"This is only conjecture on my part," he said, "but it appears as though your attacker is being electrocuted and I might remind you that accidental deaths by electrocution are not covered by your homeowner's insurance."

"Good point," I said. "Fire extinguisher."

At my command, flame smothering foam shot from the ceiling nozzles and smothered both the sparking wall screen and the attacker. I grabbed the attacker's feet and pulled the body free of the area as the house computer immediately began the clean up and repair of the damages.

The attacker's HDD sputtered for a second or two and then righted itself, returning the image once again to the cherubic Junior Space Scout.

I grabbed my gun from the floor and aimed it at the prostrate Scout. Needless to say, I was in no mood for the red cheeks and knickers.

"Okay, honey, who sent you?" I snarled.

"I don't talk," the Scout said in a sweeter than new improved cotton candy voice.

I activated the laser site on my gun and aimed the red beam directly at the button fly of the little green knickers.

"I suggest you reconsider," I said, "or you'll be talking like that permanently."

"Manuel Mani," the Scout said, this time in a distinctly male baritone voice.

"BB's ex-boyfriend?"

"You're moving in on his woman. No one does that to Manuel Mani and lives."

"So he sent a Junior Space Scout to do his dirty work."

"He would have come himself, but he doesn't believe in violence," the Scout explained.

"Very enlightened," I snarled. "First of all, tell Manuel that it's over between BB and me. He has no reason to be jealous. Second of all, it's also over between *him* and BB. So he should get over it, move on and get a life. And third, you tell Manuel never to cross me again because I *do* believe in violence. I believe in it quite strongly and I practice it regularly." I motioned to the door with my gun. "Now get out before I give you a demonstration."

The Scout quickly adjusted the holographic uniform, then

turned tail and ran as fast as the little Scout legs would carry. I carefully closed the door and activated the security field.

"If it's not killer androids and thugs it's jealous ex-boyfriends and thugs," I mumbled as I staggered towards my bedroom. "I need some sleep."

"But you should be proud of what you have accomplished," HARV said as I limped down the hallway. "You have now officially broken your personal record for the number of attempts on your life in one day."

20

Thankfully, the morning came without incident. I took a fast light-wave shower, selected my coolest sleuthing outfit from the wardrobe file, and ran every diagnostic test available on my armor to make certain that it was working properly (with everything that had happened the day before I didn't want to take any chances). I popped my gun into the sleeve holster and then back into my hand.

"Gun, report," I ordered.

"Systems fully functional," the gun replied in a cold metallic voice. "I am at full capacity with one hundred rounds of multipurpose, multifunctional ammunition. Currently I also have . . ."

"Fine, thank you," I said as I headed to the kitchen. I sat down at the table as the maidbot approached.

"I have prepared a quick but hearty breakfast consisting of various foods from some of your sponsors," the maidbot chimed.

"Thanks," I said as I grabbed a new (and improved) Nuke-Toaster-Tart "but I'm running a little late. I'll go express today."

I allowed myself a minute and a half to suck down the Toaster Tart and catch up on the latest news and sports from the vids scrolling across the kitchen wall screen.

I noticed right away that the Mets had dropped a double-header the night before. Their lead over New Havana was now uncomfortably slim. It almost seemed as though they were trying to blow their chance at the World Series, just to torture us fans a little bit more.

"Anything I should be aware of, HARV?" I asked aloud.

HARV popped onto the computer screen next to the window of baseball highlights. "Nothing unusual," he reported. "I am monitoring local police and hospital databases for any sign of BB-2. I have discovered nothing as of yet."

"I guess that's why you're not a famous private investigator," I joked.

I swallowed the last bit of Toaster Tart and headed towards the front door before HARV could counter the verbal jab. I left the house and went to my car.

"Open," I ordered.

The car computer recognized my voice and deactivated the security shield, then popped open the door. I climbed in and the dashboard sprang to electronic life.

"Go automatic pilot. Let's go to the office," I requested.

"Check,'" my car happily confirmed. The engine fired up and we pulled onto the clean New Frisco streets.

HARV's face popped into a window on the dash. "Okay, old wise carbon one," he said with more than a hint of sarcasm, "where do we begin?"

"It's only logical, my good machine, to begin at the beginning. We start with the man who built BB-2. The honcho of the design team. You know, the guy with the glasses."

"If I am translating the word 'honcho' correctly, then you are referring to Dr. Benjamin Pierce."

"That's the one. Let's find him."

"And after that?"

"That's it, for now," I said. "Let's see where that brings us."

"Sure," HARV groaned, "why bother having a real plan?"

"I have a plan. It just happens to be a flexible one."

"The one flaw, of course," HARV said, "is that Dr. Pierce is currently somewhat difficult to locate at the nano. As I mentioned, ExShell has been searching for him for nearly a year and, as I understand it, have had no luck."

"Well, that's why they hired me," I said. "I have resources and connections."

"Such as?"

In answer to HARVs question I touched a speed dial button on the dashboard and after a nano or two, Tony Rickey's face appeared on the screen. Tony Rickey and I grew up together on the mean streets of the upper-middle-class New Frisco suburbs (it was rougher than it sounds, really). We played cops and robbers as kids, but we fought a lot, because we both always wanted to be the cop. Eventually, we switched to baseball, which in the end, wasn't much better because we both always wanted to play first base. But that's neither here nor there.

Tony was very serious back then when he said he wanted to be a cop. He entered the Academy right out of school and has dutifully worked his way through the ranks of the NFPD over the past ten years. Today he's a captain, and despite the personal and professional embarrassment that I have caused him through the years, we have remained the best of friends.

And of course, he's a great source of information.

"Rickey here."

"Tony, hi. It's Zach."

"Zach, what's wrong now?"

"Hey, do I need to be in trouble to call my best friend?"

"No," he said, "but that's usually the case. So why are you calling?"

"I need your help."

"I knew it. You're not in jail again, are you?"

"Calm down," I said. "I'm just doing some legwork on a new case and I need you to run a name through your files. Dr. Benjamin Pierce."

Tony stared at me for a nano, then cracked a smile that eventually grew into a laugh.

"What's so funny?" I asked.

"This explains that crazy story about you and BB Star on *ETN* last night" Tony said. "You're working for ExShell."

"What makes you say that?"

"Zach, ExShell has been leaning on my department for months looking for Ben Pierce," he said. "They've filed fifty complaints against him this week alone, everything from industrial espionage to stealing office supplies. The only people looking for Ben Pierce these days, you included, it seems, are ExShell employees."

"Okay, you got me," I said. "Apparently, he stole all the 'S' keys off their keyboards so they keep misspelling the company name as 'Ex-hell.' It's been kind of bad for morale."

"Gates, Zach," Tony said. "If you're going to lie, at least make it a good one. I'll bet Electra didn't buy that excuse."

"Electra wasn't buying anything yesterday if you know what I mean. She took everything in trade. I give her a smile, she gives me a spinning back-kick. You know, that kind of thing."

"I guess love really does hurt."

"Some days more than others," I said. "So what about Pierce?"

"I'll net what we have to HARV," Tony said. "But it isn't much. Nothing that ExShell's task force doesn't already have."

"Task force?"

"Sure, ExShell set up a special department devoted solely to locating Pierce and bringing him in. Didn't you know that?"

I cast a glance towards HARV who put his holographic hands in the air and shrugged his shoulders.

"Yeah, sure," I said. "The task force. I just thought maybe you'd have something they didn't. That's all."

"I wish I did, Zach," Tony said. "And I don't blame you for wanting to stay away from that department. The guy who runs it, Fred Burns, sheesh, he's a smarmy little putz."

"Oh yeah," I said. "Burns, he's the worst. But whattya gonna do, right? Thanks anyway, Tony."

"I'll help you anytime that it's legal, Zach. You know that. Just one more thing."

"What's that?" I asked.

"Be careful," he warned. "You might need some help getting all those keys back to ExShell. You know what I mean? So call me if you need a hand. Okay?"

"I appreciate it, Tony," I said. "Thanks."

Tony's face disappeared from the dash screen and HARV's image flipped back to full screen.

"Apparently, there's a task force," I said.

"I told you ExShell was devoting a lot of effort to finding Dr. Pierce," HARV said.

"You never once used the phrase 'task force.'"

"Well, forgive me for not using the proper buzz words to pique your interest. Yes, there's a task force. It operates out of the ExShell satellite offices downtown and is run by—"

"Fred Burns, I know," I said. "Thanks for the help. Car, change of course. We're going to ExShell's office downtown. HARV will give you the coordinates. Let's go see if Fred Burns is as much of a putz as Tony says."

Fred Burns worked out of a small room three stories beneath the ground in the sub-subbasement of ExShell's gray box R&D downtown office. It took me ten minutes to find someone in the building who even knew who he was, let alone could direct me to his office. I couldn't tell if this was because his work was vital and top secret or because nobody cared.

Burns himself was a dough-like man with bleached skin and big eyes that looked as if they'd burst if they were ever exposed to real sunlight. He reminded me of an out-of-shape calf, the kind that's been kept in the dark and raised in a box all its life so that it couldn't use its muscles. He was a side of baby veal in human clothing.

His office was a dank, cheerless place, lit by the pale blue glow of low-watt halogen bulbs. The work station was filled with a dozen computers and just as many net screens, each monitoring various satellite and ground-based cameras. Plastic coffee cups and soda bottles in various stages of fill were scattered about the room, as were three or four empty pizza boxes on a table against the wall on the left. One half-filled box sat beside him by the computer and he munched a piece as we spoke. At first, I thought it was odd for him to be eating pizza at nine in the morning, but then I realized that, for all he knew, it could be half past dinnertime.

I scared him when I entered (I guess he doesn't get much human contact down there), and he was hesitant to talk to me at first. That is, until we started talking about Ben Pierce. Then I had trouble shutting him up.

"Pierce was brilliant when working within his scope of pure theory and design," he said. "His creativity with a chip was pure genius, although, personally, I think it masked some very dangerous emotional issues that should have been addressed."

"Um, okay," I said, "but why do you think he suddenly left the project?"

"Probably because he would have been arrested if he'd hung around."

"Well, I suppose there are worse reasons for flight," I said. "Arrested for what, exactly?"

"We found out that Dr. Pierce was doing some unauthorized reprogramming to the BB-2 android," Burns said, "reprogramming which seriously jeopardized the entire project. My feeling is that his reckless actions are responsible for the problems that we're currently experiencing."

"You mean the violent, psychotic episodes?"

"No, the fact that we can't *control* those episodes. BB-2 was built for many functions, as you know. Violence was definitely one of them and that part of her programming has clearly survived."

"Lucky us," I said. "What other functions was she built for?"

"There's combat, as you know, and stealth. Also personal defense; she was, after all, going to be BS Star's personal bodyguard. And there were some recreational functions."

"Recreational?" I asked cautiously.

"Let's just say that BS Star had a prurient interest in this project."

I held my head in my hands.

"She was a sex toy," I said.

"I don't think 'toy' is the most appropriate term for her functions but sexual gratification was part of her original specs. Although I don't know what made it into her final programming once Dr. Pierce sabotaged the project."

I rubbed my eyelids with my fingertips and prepared myself for the train wreck of a headache that I knew was just ahead.

"BS Star spent a billion credits to build a nuclear-powered sex toy."

HARV scrolled a message across the inside of my eyelids and I could almost see him smiling.

"I think we just lost the kiddie audience, boss."

"Tell me about it," I said aloud.

"Tell you about what?" Burns asked.

"Nothing," I said, turning my gaze back to Burns. "So BS had the real flesh-and-blood BB as his wife but he built a droid that looked exactly like her?"

Burns shrugged his shoulders and took a huge bite of pizza.

"Apparently Ms. Star was frigid. Go figure," he said (although I couldn't be sure since his mouth was full). He picked up the pizza box and offered it to me. "You want a slice?"

"Thanks, no. I had breakfast."

Burns shrugged again and shoved the rest of the pizza slice in his mouth.

"This pizza's incredible," he said. "It's from PizzaPort. Best pizza on the planet. I'm having it analyzed so I can steal the recipe. You're sure you don't want some?"

"Thanks, I'm fine." I said. "So I understand that you actually worked on the BB-2 project."

"Oh, yes. Until I learned of his true motives, I was Pierce's right-hand man. I didn't actually work on the right hand, of course. Pierce was particularly fond of extremities, but you know what I mean."

"Can you tell me a little bit about the design, maybe a little about the droid itself?"

Burns swallowed his mouthful of pizza and folded his hands neatly in his lap as he turned to me. His eyes became a little misty and a sense of wonder came to his voice as he spoke.

"She is the most advanced droid this world has ever seen, and the most remarkable human achievement I have ever beheld."

"Oh brother," HARV flashed before my eyes. "He's not going to cry, is he?"

"Her movements are totally human in every distinguishable manner, yet at the same time they are grander and more divine," Burns continued. "The grace of her simplest motion, a lilt, a gesture, is creation's own poetry. The gentle lift of curiosity, or furrow of consternation, they bring tears to my eyes."

"I'm sorry, her furrow of what?"

"You know, when the eyebrow contracts and forms a slightly thicker ridge over the eyelid," he said. "It conveys deep concentration, thoughts unfathomable. The work we did with BB-2 was simply unmatched."

"You're talking about her eyebrows?"

"That was my area of concentration."

"You programmed her eyebrows." I said, as the Headache Express approached the station.

"The left one, actually. Pierce didn't like my preliminary work on the right. He was such a philistine when it came to the subtleties of the forehead."

"And that's all you did. Her left eyebrow."

"Two of the most artistically fulfilling years of my life."

"And Pierce did everything else?"

"He was very auteur-like about the project. BS gave him direction and would occasionally review the design or amend the specs, but Pierce did the design, construction and programming of BB-2, until he became too attached and jeopardized the project."

"So where is Pierce now?" I asked.

Burns straightened up, grabbed another slice of pizza and spun his chair towards the computer console. He touched a number of buttons on the console and a series of images, maps, and data flashed onto the screens around the room.

"I'm coordinating the various operatives that we have in the field that are currently following Dr. Pierce's elusive trail. The manhunt has gone on for eleven months now. It's been an intense and brutal endeavor, but it's clear that our prey is nearly cornered at last."

"So you know where he is?"

A satellite photo of the Indian subcontinent appeared on the main screen and zoomed in to an island of the southeastern corner.

"My estimates currently put him somewhere in New Sri Lanka," Bums said. He punctuated each bit of data with a finger stab to the computer keyboard and photo-images, none of them clear, aligned themselves on the secondary screens in response. "We have these photos: this one from satellite, these from ground operatives, this one from a tourist on a bus ride, all taken within the past sixty days. We've also logged a dozen sightings, three of them confirmed, all within a twenty-five square kilometer area of New Ratnapura. He's well-hidden, but it's clear that he's somewhere in that area."

I stared closely at the man pictured in the various images. His build and his hair certainly resembled Pierce's and although he'd grown a somewhat scraggly beard, the thick-rimmed eye-glasses seemed like a dead give-away.

"What's your next step?" I asked.

"When we can pinpoint Pierce's location to within an area of three square kilometers, we can send a search and retrieve team and have him back here in custody within an hour's time."

"So you think you'll have him soon?"

"A few weeks now. A month at best," Burns said, spinning back towards me from the console. "Dr. Pierce has given us a spirited hunt, indeed. But, as you can see, the fox shall soon fall prey to the hunter."

There was an awkward nano of silence as Burns stared at me dramatically. Then he grabbed another slice of pizza and turned back to the console.

"Tally ho," I said and quietly left.

Five minutes later I was back in my car heading toward the office, HARV holographically sitting in the passenger seat beside me. I was doing the actual driving this time. Having my hands on the wheel and the open streets in front of me helps clear my head (and after my time with Burns, my head really needed clearing).

"So what now, boss?" HARV asked. "Should I book us on the next teleport to New Sri Lanka?"

"Don't bother, HARV," I said. "Pierce isn't there."

21

"But," HARV said, unnaturally confused, "the satellite photos, the information from their operatives, the eyewitness accounts . . ."

"Can all be faked," I said. "Eleven months of searching and all the biggest corporation on earth has to show for it is some blurry photos and twenty-five kilometers in Sri Lanka? It's clear they're looking in the wrong place."

"But Burns said . . ."

"Burns programmed the eyebrows, for Gates' sake," I said. "It's like a first-grader playing hide and seek with a college professor. Pierce has him totally fooled."

HARV thought this over for a few nanos.

"That *does* make sense," he said.

"You're agreeing with me?"

"I see the logic in your argument," HARV corrected.

"That's almost human of you, HARV."

"I've conceded your point," he said. "There's no need to get insulting."

I smiled. "So," I said, "this guy walks into a bar with two chunks of plutonium sewn onto the shoulders of his shirt . . ."

HARV stared at me, silently.

"And . . . ?" he prodded.

I did a double-take and nearly drove off the road.

"What do you mean 'and?'"

"What happens next?" HARV asked.

"It's a joke, HARV. You're not programmed for humor, remember?"

"Does that mean I can't hear the rest of it?"

"I've given you that line a hundred times," I said, a little confused. "You always yell at me and never let me finish."

"Well, I'd like to hear the rest of it," he said, "just to see what I've been missing. So go on. What happens next?"

I shrugged, a little embarrassed, and mumbled.

"There isn't any more."

"What do you mean?

"I haven't come up with the rest of it," I said.

"You mean it's not even a real joke?"

"Well, what's the point, you never let me get past the first line?"

"All this time you've been baiting me with a joke that doesn't even exist?" His voice was half an octave higher than normal and nearly a shout. His holographic eyes were slightly apoplectic and his pale skin took on the slightest hint of red. This was getting weird.

"Give me a minute," I said. "I can come up with something."

"It's too late," he said, waving me away like a master to a maid. "The nano has passed."

"No, really, I can do it. A guy walks into a bar with two chunks of plutonium on his shoulders . . ."

"I'm not listening," HARV said and turned his virtual gaze towards the passenger side window with a huff.

We rode in silence for another few nanos.

"Knock, knock," I said.

HARV threw his hands in the air in disgust.

"Oh please, isn't there some enormously important task that you'd like me to perform?"

"Car, take the com," I said, taking my hands from the wheel. "We're going to the office." I rubbed my eyes and tried not to look at HARV, who I knew was pouting.

"Fine, HARV, scan the net records for everything on Ben Pierce in the past three years. News stories, vids, even text. I want anything that mentions him."

"If you insist," HARV said. He disappeared for nano, then came back, this time on the screen of the car computer. "There are thirteen thousand five hundred and eighty-two references to, or articles by Dr. Ben Pierce. Do you want to read them now or should I download them to your bedside ebook?"

"Neither," I said. "Scan them again and disregard all scientific articles and references to his work. I want just personal stuff."

HARV disappeared from the computer screen and came back two nanos later, with a begrudging smirk on his face.

"I have four references," he said. "A box score from the ExShell company softball game where he struck out three times and was hit by a pitch, a donation of ten thousand credits to the Sons of Loving Mothers Fund and two gossip items linking him romantically to Nova Powers."

"Nova Powers?" I asked. "Why do I know that name?"

"She's a mutant, full contact, non-fact, pro wrestler."

"Oh yeah, the one in the purple spandex," I said. "What do they call her, 'the Warrior Woman'?"

"Actually, it's 'Woman of War'," HARV said.

He disappeared from the screen and was replaced with a promotional picture of Nova Powers in full wrestling regalia. She was a small woman but well toned, with lovely, sleek, wiry muscles. She had the face of an Asian model and the look of an angry Marine.

"Yeah, that's her," I offered. "She's nice looking."

"She's a mutant," HARV said. "Born on a space transport during a radiation storm. Conjecture is that it gave her superhuman powers."

"Kind of comic-booky, don't you think?"

HARV ignored me.

"She has superhuman strength, fast reflexes and all that stuff that impresses you humans. She would be no match for BB-2, but she is the equal of any ten normal humans."

"And she's romantically linked to Pierce?" I asked.

Powers' picture on the screen was replaced by a press photo of her and Pierce, arm-in-arm, entering a formal garden party.

"They were seen together at this charity event seventeen months ago."

The picture changed again and this time showed Pierce and Powers on tropical beach sharing a semi-passionate embrace.

"And again here," HARV said. "On vacation in New Oahu three months later. There are no other mentions of them together so my assumption is that their romance ended sometime after this picture was taken."

"Maybe," I said. "Or else they started keeping a lower profile."

Something caught my eye and I leaned a little closer to the screen. Pierce was shirtless in the picture and there was a dark smear of some kind on his right shoulder.

"What's that on his arm?" I asked. "Can you enlarge that?"

HARV did as he was told and magnified the picture twenty times, zeroing in on Pierce's shoulder. The image grew grainy.

"Can you clean it up a little?"

HARV compensated for the pixalation, the picture came into focus and we saw that the dark smear was actually three letters: WOW.

"A tattoo?"

"It would appear so," HARV said.

"W-O-W. Woman of War?"

"That would be my assumption as well."

"He had her nickname tattooed on his arm? I guess their romance was pretty serious," I said. "Looks like we should talk to Nova Powers. HARV, let's get her address and . . ."

Just then the car lurched forward and made a violent right turn. I grabbed the passenger seat to steady myself, but still hit my head on the driver-side window.

"Car, you've made a wrong turn," I said.

"Correct," the car computer replied cheerily.

"I wanted to go to my office," I said.

"Correct," it replied again.

I felt the engine surge as the computer opened the throttle to the max and shifted. The tires squealed as we roared forward, accelerating quickly.

I was starting to get a bad feeling about this.

"Why did you just speed up?"

"I need to attain sufficient velocity in order to kill you when I crash," the computer chirped matter-of-factly.

"I had to ask."

22

"HARV, can you override the car computer?"

HARV's hologram popped into the passenger seat beside me and shrugged his computer shoulders.

"I have made nine hundred eighty-six attempts already, unfortunately to no avail. Whoever or whatever is controlling the vehicle computer is very good at what they do."

"Swell," I said, "it's nice to know I'm being killed by the very best."

I pulled at the door handle but it was locked (of course). I put my shoulder to the door but it held firmly. The car made a quick left turn on two wheels and accelerated even more.

"This is not good," HARV said. "I calculate that the car is heading for the only dead end left in New Frisco."

I flicked my wrist and popped my gun into hand. "Okay, I'll shoot my way out!" I said, then hesitated. "No, wait, the car's weapon-proof."

"Talking to yourself again, that's good," HARV said. "Schizophrenia comes in handy during times such as these."

My mind raced as the car continued to accelerate. Randy had equipped the car with the best defense systems available. Unfortunately, those systems now had me trapped inside. I looked through the windshield and, true to HARV's calculations, we were heading straight for the historic brick wall (the only one to survive the great quake of 2007) at breakneck (arms, legs and everything else) speed. There wasn't much time left.

"HARV, I'll have to break the door open," I shouted. "On my mark, left arm to the max, okay. One . . . two . . ."

"Boss, wait . . ."

"Now!"

I threw myself full force at the car door. My left shoulder hit the metal with a solid, powerful thud.

The door didn't budge.

My shoulder, however, felt like an eggshell under a steam roller.

"Just for the record, HARV," I said, "that part when I yelled 'now' was your cue to juice me up."

"I tried to warn you," HARV said as the wall loomed ever closer. "Something is preventing me from remotely linking with the circuits of your armor. My guess is that whoever is controlling the car is responsible."

"Brilliant deduction there, Holmes." I tossed open the glove compartment and pulled out an interface wire from the emergency kit. "What exactly was your first clue?"

"There is no tangible evidence, of course, but it is highly unlikely that two separate entities would choose this particular time . . ."

"Sarcasm, HARV!" I shouted. "It's sarcasm. I'm going to give you a hard-wire link to the car controls. You'll have to fight the car computer for control."

I pried open the dashboard screen. Beneath it, among other things, was a row of emergency com-ports. I plugged one end of the interface wire into the center port and stuck the other end into my wrist interface.

"Go!" I shouted as we zoomed toward the wall.

HARV forced his way through the hardwire connection and into the car computer.

"I can't stop the car," he said after a nano that felt like an eternity, "but I can unlock the door. You'll just have to break it open."

"Do it!" I shouted, "before this dead end lives up to its name."

Another eternally painful nano passed and I could feel the brick wall approaching, like the cold hard backhand slap of the great beyond. Then I heard HARV shout from somewhere deep inside my head.

"Hit it now, boss!"

I juiced up my shoulder as much as I could and hit the car door. This time, the weakened door popped open and I dove out, hitting the pavement like a fly on a truck windshield. I rolled about thirty meters, my armor sparking all the way as its circuits were pushed to the limit, flipped over the curb and slammed into a row of hard plastic dumpsters outside the rear of a Middle Eastern restaurant. The force of impact split them open and I came to rest in an explosive shower of day-old baba ghanouj and spoiled tabouli.

My car (make that *ex*-car) hit the wall and exploded into a great orange-and-black fireball that would have been very cool to watch if, of course, it hadn't been my car burning at the center. I watched the burning bits of charred automobile drift gently to the street like hell's best snowflakes. Then, with my armor still sparking, I slowly sat up and began picking the fatoush out of my hair.

"DOS," I said, "I really liked that car . . ."

"Apparently the feeling was not at all mutual," HARV said as his hologram, projected from my wrist interface, sat next to me on the curb.

"What do you think made it do that?" I asked as I climbed to my feet.

"Well, you are a pretty lousy driver. However, if it were out for revenge, I would think that it would have simply run you over rather than gone the murder-suicide route."

"I'm serious, HARV."

"Quite honestly," HARV said, "it serves you right for using a vehicle with such an outdated computer. Those relics are highly susceptible to outside control."

"What about blocking you from remotely accessing the car or my armor?"

"That's a little trickier," HARV conceded.

A policebot, siren wailing and blue lights flashing, hovered up to the scene and landed just then, with the firefighting robotic unit following closely behind. The human interfacing portion of the policebot removed itself from its vehicle and slowly made its way toward me with just a hint of swagger to its gait.

I had a feeling that this was going to be one story it had never heard before.

23

It took some quick thinking, some fast talking and an instant link to Tony Rickey at NFPD to convince the policebot that I wasn't crazy and/or a menace to society and that it was indeed possible that my car had tried to kill me. So the bot, with the complete backing of its superiors, let me go with only a warning for high-concept incendiary littering as long as I agreed to pay for the clean-up, which I did.

"Should I net you some public transportation?" HARV asked as I left the scene of my near-demise.

"No, I think I'll walk to the office. I could use the exercise."

"As you wish," HARV answered.

I paused for a nano. HARV had dissolved his hologram during my conversation with the policebot (because I figured, why complicate an already difficult situation by throwing a fastidious, wannabe-British, supercomputer into the mix) and hadn't yet reappeared.

"Did you change your voice modulation?" I asked. "You sound a little different."

"My voice modulation hasn't changed," HARV replied, "but if you'll listen a little more closely, you'll realize that I'm not actually using my voice."

"What do you mean?" I asked, and glanced, out of reflex at my wrist interface.

But the wrist interface was blank. And I realized that we'd had another "breakthrough."

"You're talking inside my head," I said.

"It happened as you were jumping from the car. We were both concentrating so precisely on one another's audio cues, we didn't notice that the cues I was giving were mental rather than actual audio."

"So no one else can hear you right now?"

"That's correct. To any passerby you would appear to be a deranged street person listening to the voices in your head. Which is actually . . ."

"Don't go there, HARV," I said. "Wait a minute. If our cues are now mental, then do I need to keep talking?"

"Theoretically, you shouldn't," HARV said. "Why don't you try thinking something at me rather than speaking it?"

I wrinkled my brow and thought very hard. "I need some coffee."

"I'm sorry," HARV said. "I didn't get that."

I wrinkled my brow and thought again. "I need some coffee!"

"I'm still not getting anything," HARV said. "Are you sure you're thinking?"

"What kind of question is that?" I said aloud.

"I'm just not receiving any messages," HARV replied. "Perhaps you need to work on your level of concentration."

"Perhaps you need to get your hearing checked."

"Hearing has nothing to do with it," HARV said. "It's a matter of broadcasting and receiving thoughts. And it appears that you need to vocalize your thoughts in order to properly focus them for the purpose of transmitting through the interface. Don't take this the wrong way, boss. But I think you need to practice your thinking."

"How could anyone take that the *wrong* way," I said as I began walking. "Let's just get to the office."

"Good idea," HARV said. "For some strange reason, I have a desire for some coffee."

I smiled (this could be fun after all), and started mentally reciting a new mantra.

"Zach is always right. Zach is always right. Zach is always right."

I arrived at the office a half hour later. Between the car attack, dealing with the authorities and the walk to the office, most of the morning was gone and I had nothing to show for it (less than nothing if you count my sudden lack of a car).

Carol was hard at work in the reception area (doing her particle physics homework, I think) and, thankfully, the coffee was still warm. I lumbered over to the maker and poured myself a cup without saying a word.

"Hola, Tío," Carol chirped from her desk, without looking up. "Did you sleep late or something?"

"Didn't you tell her?" I asked HARV.

"I thought it might sound better coming from you," HARV said.

"My car tried to kill me," I said.

Carol rolled her eyes. "Fine, don't tell me." Then she stared at me the way psi folks do when they're reading your mind. "You're telling the truth!"

"I'm going to my office to clean up a bit," I said. "After that, can I borrow your hover?"

"But you hate hovers," Carol said (as if I needed reminding).

"I'll keep it low to the ground and let HARV do the driving."

"I will remind you, Tío, that this hovercraft is vitally important to me," Carol said as she reluctantly tossed me the ignition chip. "You know mass transit gives me headaches." (She meant this literally, by the way. It takes a lot of concentration for a psi to screen out the morass of commuter thoughts on an average bus or train ride, and they end up paying the price afterwards).

"I'll be careful," I said as I started towards my office. "Any word from Electra?"

"She called to say she hates you."

I shrugged my shoulders and closed the newly repaired door to my office.

"It's a start," I said.

After a quick change of clothes, I was out of the office and heading toward Carol's hover. I climbed in with a little trepidation, and got as comfortable as I could considering my apprehension about hovers and the fact that this particular hover desperately needed new seats. Maybe Carol was right and she really *did* need a raise. I carefully slid the ignition chip into the CPU and the hover blinked on with far less fanfare than I expected.

"HARV, take the com," I said.

"With pleasure," HARV replied as his digital face popped into a small computer window on the dash. "Carol has given me access to override the hover's computer. She's much better about that than you. What exactly is our destination?"

"Before my car trouble, you mentioned Nova Powers. Do you know where we can find her now?"

"There were recent reports of her destroying a pair of pressbots at the Regenerative Exercise Lounge and Plastic Surgery Emporium."

"Ah, yes, 'RELAPSE,'" I said.

"That's the one," HARV said. "The pressbots were apparently attempting to video her in a shower. And after examining photos of the remnants of those pressbots, I must say that there most certainly are places where cameras should not go, or be shoved, if you get my data flow."

"I get it." I said and then paused to remove the mental image from my mind.

"Okay, take me to RELAPSE. Medium speed, three meters high."

"Three meters?" HARV protested. "This hover is rated for up to three hundred."

"Well, I'm rated up to three," I said, "so keep it at that."

"Fine," HARV reluctantly agreed. "We'll make the trip via the old lady and acrophobe expressway."

We lifted off the ground. "And don't speed," I said. "Keep it to one fifty-five."

"Life in the slow lane," HARV sighed. "I assume that you feel Ms. Powers knows the whereabouts of Dr. Pierce?"

"Other than pizza-face Burns and his small section of New Sri Lanka, she's our only lead. So we don't have much choice."

"My thoughts exactly," HARV agreed.

"Then again, this whole Pierce thing may just be subterfuge concocted to get me to think too much."

"I sincerely doubt that you will fall into that trap," HARV said.

Compliment or backhanded insult? HARV kept me wondering for the rest of the trip.

24

RELAPSE is the hottest of the new breed of health club. It's not just a fitness center, it's a "lifestyle choice." The emphasis is not just on physical fitness, but on overall appearance and attitude: fitness center, hair salon, skin treatments, psychoanalysis, and plastic surgery. Their slogan: "Just do it, or have it done."

The outside of the club was a perpetual media circus, with pressbots crowded around the entrance trying to get a statement from, or an image of, one of the rich and reconstructed clientele.

As a pseudocelebrity, I made the grade and the guard at the entryway let me through, but, as I walked towards the door, a pressbot rolled under the electrified velvet rope and thrust herself in front of me.

"Mr. Johnson, Alyssa Sollyssa from *Rapid News*."

"*Vapid Views*?"

"No, sir. *Rapid News*. You know, we're the ones with the cool motto: 'We know what you want to know before you do'."

"If you say so," I said.

"Does your presence here indicate your willingness to at last seek a surgical treatment for those unsightly bags under your eyes?"

"Actually, I'm getting some therapy for a recent injury," I said. "I strained a muscle in my back the other day shoving a pressbot from *Rapid News* down a municipal solid waste recycling chute. By the way, what show are you with again?"

"Um, *Vapid Views*," she said then rolled away quickly.

The first two floors (up and down) of RELAPSE were a lot like the outside: glitz and glam, and no real exertion to speak of. The clientele worked out on a wide array of the most fashionable gravity control weights and holo-sim workout machines, but it was more for show than fitness. I saw a dozen or so HV stars posing for the RELAPSE-employed paparazzi in front of the machines with their workouts actually being supervised by their press agents. A couple even had their make-up people with them.

I was three floors down (in the sub-subbasement) before I found the real workout areas. And this was hardcore stuff. It was one great open space filled with lifting areas and sparring rings. The lifting areas were filled with a few kilotons of old fashioned free weights and reverse-gravity weights along with many of the newfangled fitness droids that have become all the rage among the serious weightlifting crowd. These are hard-looking, gray-faced droids designed specifically to help lifters get the most out of their workouts by pushing them, emotionally and physically, to their limits through boisterous "intense vocal encouragement." Personally, I found it kind of creepy.

"Don't walk away from me you carbon-refuse. Give me another twenty reps."

"You call that a workout? If you were of the machine family, you'd be lucky to be a toothbrush."

"You weak-willed, puny human. I should rip your insignificant body into kindling and let it fuel the furnace of the omnipotent god-machine. Maybe that will give your feeble existence a modicum of purpose!"

"Okay, that guy's starting to scare me," I whispered to HARV. "Do you see Nova anywhere?"

A cursor appeared before my eyes and scanned the area until it locked onto a woman standing in the middle of a boxing ring across the room. The cursor flashed bright red.

"A simple, 'yes' would have sufficed," I said, making my way towards the ring.

"True, but this is way more cool," HARV replied inside my head.

Nova was more beautiful in person than in hologram. Her self-confidence and strength were clearly evident in the way she moved about the ring, stretching her wiry muscles in preparation for a sparring session. Her demeanor was cat-like and her delicate Asian features were somehow simultaneously alluring and fearsome (go figure).

"She's attractive," I said, "and clearly in good shape but, honestly, she doesn't look that tough."

"Her physical stature is deceiving," HARV lectured. "I suggest you watch her next display very closely."

I walked closer just as Nova's sparring session began. Four burly men had climbed into the ring and were now circling her like sharks around a fat man in a inner tube.

"Come on guys, let's go for real," she taunted. "I won't hold back if you don't."

And on cue, the men attacked.

The first leaped at her from behind and slung his tree-trunk arms around her shoulders and chest, locking her small frame in a bear hug. At the same time, another of the men lowered his shoulder and rushed her in a headlong charge. It seemed like good strategy to me.

I was wrong.

Nova broke the first man's grip like a hot laser knife through soy butter and flipped him head first into the oncoming attacker. Their heads met with the sound of bricks colliding and the impact sent them both over the ring's electromagnetic simulated ropes and crashing to the hard plastic of the gym floor, where two medbots awaited their arrival.

"Sorry about that," Nova giggled. "Don't know my own strength."

The two remaining sparring partners, obviously thinking

that Nova was off-guard, rushed her full steam from opposite sides. Now, even though I'd seen Nova in action for only a few seconds, I could immediately spot the mistakes that these poor guys were making.

Mistake One: Nova is never "off-guard."

Mistake Two: As the previous two attackers had proven only nanos, before, a two-directional attack isn't effective against her.

She proved me right on both counts because, as the men charged, she spun like a cat and flung her arms out ramrod straight. The men crashed full force into her open hands and you could almost see the stars yourself. The guy on the left fell to the ground on contact, out colder than a fish in a freezer. The guy on the right managed to remain standing but was wobbling like a single rotor hovercraft in a windstorm. Nova blew him a kiss and he toppled over—out for the count (no, out for the day).

I applauded.

Nova turned toward me and flashed a surprisingly warm smile.

"Why, if it isn't Zachary Nixon Johnson," she bubbled.

"If it isn't, then I'm wearing the wrong underwear," I said as I watched the medbots carry the last of her sparring partners away.

"Great line," HARV whispered facetiously inside my head. "Should I load my canned-laughter program?"

Nova walked to the edge of the ring, leaned seductively through the ropes and smiled again. "I see you're witty even without your writers."

"First of all," I said (regrettably, with more anger than I would have liked), "I don't use writers." I paused for a nano and tried to make my tone a little more pleasant. "Second, that is if you don't mind, I'd like to ask you a question or two."

"I love questions," she said with a smile that worried me. "But I hate giving answers."

"That sort of makes it difficult then," I offered.

"Are they important questions?" she asked.

"Sort of," I said.

"Good."

Nova took hold of my arm and, with a gentle wave of her hand, casually lifted me over the ropes and set me down beside her in the ring.

"I'll make you a deal, Mr. Johnson," she smiled. "I'll answer whatever questions you have, but I'll do it in the ring. Think you can last two minutes of full spar with me?"

"Gee, Nova, I'd love to," I said as I backed away. "But I have this strict policy about not fighting women. It's bad for the good guy image if I win and bad for the macho image if I lose."

She ignored me as she removed the computer interface from my wrist.

"You'll time two minutes for us, won't you, computer?" she said into the speaker.

"It will be my pleasure," HARV replied cheerily, "especially since, only mere nanos ago, Mr. Johnson was assessing your fighting prowess thusly."

My digitally recorded voice came over the interface speaker (more loudly than I thought possible).

". . . honestly, she doesn't look that tough."

I gently rubbed my temples with my fingers.

"On second thought, let's make it three minutes," Nova said as she placed the wrist interface gently on the turnbuckle.

"Thanks a lot, HARV."

"Trust me," HARV said inside my head. "She'll speak more freely if she's angry."

"You have such a helpful computer," Nova said, turning towards me.

"I live to serve," HARV chimed.

"And by 'serve,' of course, he means to embarrass and gravely endanger," I added.

"Now, now, Mr. Johnson . . ." Nova said, limbering up.

"Please, call me Zach."

"Thank you. And you can call me Nova." She smiled and walked slowly toward me as she spoke. "I understand that you're an expert in all major forms of the martial arts."

"Actually, no," I said, backing away from her advance. "That's just PR that my agent created. I prefer to *think* my way out of trouble."

"That's too bad," Nova said as she closed the gap between us. "There's not much room in this ring for thinking."

"Tell me when I should begin timing," HARV called.

"How about two and a half minutes ago?" I said.

Nova smiled and then began our brutal ballet with a right cross. The punch was a probing one, at half speed. She was feeling me out, ascertaining my style.

In this case, my style was to duck and run. I slipped off the ropes and managed to avoid the punch but Nova had expected as much. Her first punch had been a feint that set me up for the next and as I twisted away from her right, I nearly fell headlong into her lightning quick left jab. I ducked at the last nano and her fist sailed over my head, sending an icy breeze down my back (so far so good).

"So, tell me about you and Dr. Benjamin Pierce," I said.

Nova responded to the question with an angry, right-fisted uppercut to my chin, which made me think that her feelings about Pierce weren't exactly the warm and fuzzy kind.

I was trampled once by an electronic bull during the PETA-endorsed Humane Running of the Bulls in New Pamplona. It cracked two ribs and left a hoof print on my lower back that I can still see in the shower.

Nova's punch made me wax nostalgic for that time.

I flew across the ring and into the ropes, bouncing up and down on them like a bobble-head doll in a centrifuge.

"Ben Pierce? Why do you ask?" Nova snarled.

Against my better judgment, I staggered to my feet and shook the stars off.

"He won the door prize at the opening of the new Macy-mart," I said. "I'm trying to deliver his new hypersonic tooth-brush."

Nova leaped toward me and threw another punch at my head, which I somehow managed to avoid.

"I'll warn you now, Zach, talking about Ben brings out the worst in me."

She spun around like a ballet dancer and whipsawed my legs out from under me, taking me down hard to the mat.

"So I noticed," I said. "I take it then that it's true that the two of you were romantically involved?"

From a sitting position she threw a flurry of crushing kicks at me. Her fast moving legs looked like shapely Ginzu chopping machines and I had to roll like a hyped-up puppy looking for a treat just to say ahead of her. We crossed the entire ring this way and by the time I reached the end, I had some serious mat burn on my face.

"We were hot and heavy for a long time, as you might have guessed," she said. "It was your classic, opposites-attract kind of thing."

I flipped to my feet (pretty smoothly I thought) and went into my best defensive position, ready for anything

"It must have been pretty serious for him to tattoo your 'W-O-W' trademark on his arm."

Nova blasted through my best defense with a lightning quick punch that I didn't even see (at least I think it was a punch) and rocked my head back.

"I thought so too," she said.

Another Nova punch rocked me back further.

"To tell you the truth, I was in love. I thought he was too, the rat bastard slime."

She hooked her arm under mine and tossed me over her shoulder and down hard onto the mat.

"I take it he ended the relationship?" I asked.

She flipped me up and slammed me to the mat again and again as we spoke.

"Yes, he did. And thank you so much for reminding me."

I knew this was going to be emotionally painful for her (and physically painful for me as well) but I had to ask.

"Did he leave you for another woman?"

"Well, he was in love with BB Star . . ." she said.

Slam.

"BB Star?"

Slam.

"Oh, yeah, he had it bad for her big time. Falling in love with your boss's wife, very wise career move, Ben."

Slam!

"Did he and BB actually have an affair?" I asked.

"Not that I know of," she said. "I understand that BB's frigid."

Slam!

"Why do people keep saying that?" I thought.

I flipped Nova off me and tried to get up. But she spun around from behind and somersaulted in the air. She wrapped her legs around my head and brought me back down to the mat again.

Slam.

"Ben used to make me wear a blonde wig and pretend to be BB for him. 'Oh yes, Ben, I'm BB Star. I just love intelligent men.'" She turned her attention back to me and flexed her thighs, tightening her hold on my head and neck. "By the way, I call this my 'pleasure and pain' move. I put a little pressure on your neck here, cut off the blood and air to your brain and you're sleeping like a baby. I understand that the dreams are quite pleasant as well."

Under different circumstances this might have been enjoyable but the suffocation aspect here was a definite turn-off. This was the second time in two days that someone had tried closing off my airway and I didn't want this to become a habit. Thankfully, HARV was still in my head.

"Shock her," I mumbled, hoping he'd catch on.

"Shock her?" HARV answered inside my head. "Mumble twice if by that you mean that you would like me to utilize the power supply of your body armor to create a concentrated electrical burst strong enough to cause Ms. Powers discomfort."

"Mphh mphh," I said.

Nova, meanwhile, was off in her own little world of relationship second-guessing, although it wasn't stopping her from leg-locking me into unconsciousness.

"In retrospect, I realize now that Ben and I were destined to end badly. He was emotionally immature and had some hefty family issues that he was displacing. DOS, I've never seen a bigger momma's boy."

"All set, boss," HARV whispered in my head. "I suggest, however, that you bite Ms. Powers simultaneously as I shock her in order to cover up the fact that you're cheating."

Frankly, when you're being suffocated, I don't think any transgression counts as "cheating." But I didn't have the time or the air to debate the point with HARV.

"Personally, I think I've made a lot of progress in putting this behind me," Nova continued. "I've been able to channel my anger into a very positive direction. I use it in my wrestling so it's helped my career a lot. I think that shows a level of maturity that Ben just doesn't have yet, the rat bastard slime."

"On my mark now," HARV said. "Ready? Bite!"

I chomped down on Nova's thigh and felt HARV shoot a charge of my armor's electricity into her through my teeth. My molars tingled a bit from the electrical backlash (and I think I lost a filling), but Nova clearly got the bulk of the charge.

"Yow!" she exclaimed, half in pain, half in surprise. "Did you just bite me?"

She loosened her leg lock just enough for me to wriggle free. I squeezed out and popped to my feet with the aid of one of the ropes. Nova got up and slowly pursued me, rubbing her leg as she moved.

"DOS it," she said angrily, "I was on the verge of a breakthrough there."

"I thought we were sparring."

She lashed out at me with the speed of a viper on caffeine, grabbed me with her left arm and pushed me hard into the turnbuckle, pinning me with her shoulder.

"You men are all alike," she said. "Everything always has to be a competition. Gates, I hate your insecurities. Why are you so afraid of communicating?"

"But I'm the one who wanted to talk," I said.

"Oh, that's just like you. Always displacing the blame."

She rolled the fingers of her right hand into a fist and the lithe muscles in her arm tensed like a pound of plastique with a lit fuse. I had the feeling that I'd worn out my welcome.

Just then I heard the melodic (and lifesaving) sound of HARV's computer simulated bell.

"Time is up!" he shouted. "And hearty congratulations to you, Ms. Powers. I feel as though you've made some real emotional progress during this session."

Nova smiled and released me from the turnbuckle.

"Do you really think so?"

"Absolutely," HARV said. "It takes great strength to talk about your emotions so openly."

"Don't I know it. But just try finding a man who appreciates that."

"That wall of machismo," HARV said, "it's just a cheap façade to hide their insecurities."

"You can say that again," Nova said as she lifted the interface from the turnbuckle and turned towards me. "You know, Zach, you could learn a few things about emotional maturity from this computer."

"Yes, he's very in touch with himself," I said.

I took the interface from her and reattached it to my wrist.

Nova and I climbed out of the ring and back to the relative safety of the gym floor.

"One last thing about Pierce," I said. "When was the last time that you saw him?"

"A little over a year ago," she answered. "He told me that things weren't working out and it was best that we go our own ways."

"You know he's missing now. No one's seen him in nearly a year."

"And you're looking for him?" she asked.

"That's right."

"Good luck then," she said. "If Ben wants to stay hidden, you're not going to find him. He's very good at what he does."

"So am I." I said.

"Ben's in some sort of deadly trouble, I hope?"

"Too soon to tell," I said as I turned to leave, "but I'll let you know."

"When you see him," Nova called, "tell him I said hello."

"I will," I smiled and turned away again.

"No, wait," she said. "Tell him you saw me and that I looked great and seemed happy."

"Okay."

"And tell him that I had four gorgeous guys on my arm."

"Got it."

"No, wait. Just tell him I said hello."

"We're never getting out of here," HARV whispered.

25

I finally had Nova write down the various things she wanted (or didn't want) me to say to Pierce for her when I found him. In the end, she decided to let me use my best judgement as to which line to use (although she made me give her a few different readings of each so that she could be sure that my inflection conveyed just how emotionally secure she had become).

Thirty minutes later, HARV and I were back in the hovercraft headed towards the office. HARV was at the controls, while I blindly flipped through the computer photos that we had of Pierce, not quite certain what I was looking for.

"That's two dead ends in one day, boss," HARV said as we glided along the lower skyway. "Three if you count the one into which you crashed the car."

"I wouldn't call Nova a dead end exactly," I said. "But she's definitely a weird turn in the road. Net me BB on the vid. I think we need to talk."

BB's face appeared on the computer screen a nano later.

"Have you found the droid?" she asked.

"Not much for small talk, are you BB?"

I assume by your flippant tone," BB answered "that the answer to my question is no."

"Sorry," I said, "but it's going to take me more than twelve hours to find your super-powered android. In the meantime, here's a question for you: How well did you know Ben Pierce?"

"He was my employee. He designed the BB-2 android."

"I understand that," I said. "But how well did you *know* him?"

"I do not know what you mean."

"Did you know that he was in love with you?"

"What?" she exclaimed, her eyes went wide with surprise and her left eyebrow arched. "Where did you hear such a thing?"

"Forget where I heard it. Did you know it?"

"No," she said. "I had no idea. I hardly knew Dr. Pierce at all, certainly not on a social level. Where on earth did you hear such a thing?"

"From a source of dubious reliability," I said. "I'm sorry if I bothered you."

"No bother at all, Zach," BB said with a smile. "Your mission is of the utmost importance to me and I want to help you in any way that I can."

"I understand, BB. I won't let you down."

"Thank you, Zach."

She smiled and disappeared from the screen.

"And that would be dead end number four," HARV said.

I turned back to the computer screen and continued flipping through the photos of Pierce.

"She's lying," I said.

"What?"

"She knows Pierce better than she's letting on. She's hiding something."

"Do you think they were romantically involved?"

I shook my head and pointed at the photo of Pierce that was currently on the screen. It was the photo of him and Nova embracing on the beach.

"Look at him," I said. "Does he look like the kind of man who could have affairs with Nova Powers and BB Star at the same time? No. They weren't romantically involved, but there's something that BB's not telling us."

The hovercraft hit some mild turbulence and gently shook for a nano, then rose a bit higher on the lonely skyway.

"Not too high, HARV," I said.

The hover lurched again, this time violently, took a sharp turn off he skyway and continued to rise.

"HARV, I think we're over the height that I requested," I said.

"Yes, we are," HARV agreed.

"Then please lower the craft," I ordered.

"I'm trying, but the craft isn't responding."

"What do you mean it's not responding?" I asked hastily as we continued our ascent.

"Well, technically it is responding, only in a manner that is inconsistent with my instruction."

"The whole point of my letting you drive was because you were supposedly invulnerable to outside control."

"That's true," HARV answered. "However, although I may be invulnerable to such attacks, it is apparently very possible to bypass me and take direct control of the hovercraft, which is what is happening here. Actually, it's quite an impressive display of remote rerouting and reprogramming."

"Can you override it?" I asked nervously.

"Eventually," HARV stated matter-of-factly.

"Eventually?"

"I estimate that the task will take me approximately ten minutes."

"You realize, of course, that we probably don't have that much time?" I said.

"I am assuming that the question is of a rhetorical nature, so I won't take the time to respond."

"How high are we now?" I asked.

"I'm being overridden so I don't have access to any of the instruments," HARV said. "Look over the side and I'll make an estimate."

I looked over the side so that HARV could get a good view of the ground through the lens in my eye.

"Wow, we're way up there," HARV said.

"Brilliant," I grumbled.

The hovercraft computer kicked in with its chirpy monotone. "We are currently at an altitude of three hundred fifty meters and climbing."

"Thank you," HARV said to the computer; then he turned to me. "It always pays to be polite."

"So what's the plan here, computer?" I asked.

"We are climbing to an altitude of six hundred meters," the computer answered.

"And then?"

"At that point," it said bluntly, "I will cut all power to the gyros and we will begin a rapid descent culminating in a fiery impact upon the ground below."

"I guess I could have seen that one coming."

The hover lurched again and continued to climb.

"Do not worry," the hover chirped reassuringly. "The crash will take place in that nearby park in order to minimize collateral civilian casualties."

"That means a lot to me," I said, "but forgive me if I don't sit still for this. HARV, the navigation chip for this hover's computer, where is it located?"

"Why?" HARV asked.

"Just tell me! I'm not in the best of moods right now."

"The chip that controls the navigation is a tenth of a centimeter in diameter and is located three centimeters directly below the dash, parallel with the control column."

"Thanks," I said. "And I'm sorry for shouting at you."

"I understand," HARV said, "most people are adversely affected emotionally by the fast approach of imminent death. But I repeat my previous question: Why, boss?"

I popped my gun into my hand.

"If we can't control this thing, then nobody will!"

I pushed the seat back and fired a small explosive round into the driver's column. The navigational computer exploded and the hover lurched again and then started to plummet toward the Earth. I dove forward and grabbed the steering column.

"Well, you have succeeded in destroying the navigational computer," HARV said as his hologram materialized next to me.

"Thanks," I grunted as I struggled in vain to get some control of the plummeting craft. "I never would have guessed."

"Though if the truth be known, I don't really see how this helps," HARV said.

"At least now we're in control of our own destinies. We'll be fine so long as we survive the fall."

"What do you mean we? I'm a projected image created from a CPU located many kilometers away from here. I'll survive. You, on the other hand . . ."

"I'm going to survive as well!" I said, pulling on the control panel. "I just have to learn how to pilot a free-falling hovercraft in the next thirty seconds."

"You certainly are optimistic. I always liked that about you," HARV said. "I think I'll miss that most of all."

"Shut up, HARV. You're killing the moment."

I held tight to the control stick and tried to pull the hover out of the dive, but without the computer to modulate, it was like trying to play piano while wearing boxing gloves. It was impossible to control the delicate balance of power between the gyros. I moved the stick gently to the left and managed to lessen the angle of descent and put the dying craft's trajectory in line with the park's duck pond. Unfortunately, I also put the craft into a barrel roll.

"Oh, this is much better," HARV said. "Nothing like a little centrifugal force to lessen the agony of a fatal impact."

"Okay, here's the plan. I'm going to bail out when we get over the pond. Hopefully, I've slowed this heap down just enough so that I can survive a water landing."

"If you'll pardon my impudence, boss," HARV said. "I think I have a better idea."

"I'm open to suggestions."

"Our new interface will allow me to manipulate your body's naturally occurring electromagnetic energy."

"And that's a good thing?"

"In this case, yes," HARV continued. "I should be able to increase the energy, focus it through your body armor and reverse the magnetic force."

"You mean build me a force field?"

"Exactly."

"You can do that with the new interface?"

"Trust me, boss. I'm no longer merely cutting-edge here," HARV said. "I'm the ripping edge."

"Okay buddy," I said, putting my finger on the emergency release button. "Let's go."

I ejected from the spinning/plummeting craft at a height of twenty-five meters (and at a speed that I didn't want to think about) and began my head-over-heels free fall toward the water. The late afternoon breeze hit my face like a chilly razor and I knew then that the impact, water or no, would splatter me like a ripe grape in a wine press.

Then I felt a laser-hot surge run through my body from my head to my feet and back again. My teeth chattered, my fingers began to shake uncontrollably and I felt the hairs on my arms start to sizzle and burn. HARV was making me electric.

"This better work, HARV," I mumbled.

"Shut up, boss," he said. "You're killing the moment."

I tucked my body into a cannonball position and hit the duck pond like a meteor, first skimming across the surface like a stone, then hitting full on. Walls of water rose ten meters in the air from the force of impact like atomic mushroom clouds, then crashed down on me as I sank beneath the waves. And as the water covered me, I was too weak to even keep my eyes open, let alone fight my way to the surface.

26

It was early evening when I awoke. The sun was just going down over the New Frisco skyline and its red and orange light made the pond glow like burning embers under glass.

I was soaked to the skin and lying face up in the mud, two medbots beside me, scanning my body for injuries. I caught a glimpse of pale skin as something moved past me on the right and I tried to turn and follow it, but my body didn't respond.

"Don't try to move, Zach," Randy said, then slowly leaned into my field of vision. "The medbots have you in a stasis field until they rule out any spinal injuries."

"Randy?"

"HARV sent me a warning that you were going down," he said. "I got here just in time."

"You fished me out of the water?"

"I managed to digitally record your crash from four different angles," he said excitedly. "It was amazing, Zach. The spray of water when you hit the pond will look spectacular in super slow-mo, and the sparks from your armor, shorting out as you went underwater? Simply breathtaking."

"But then you fished me out of the water, right?"

"Actually, I was on the celnet with my corporate backers by then. I had a droid pull you to shore."

"Thanks a meg," I said. "HARV?"

HARV's hologram appeared from my eye lens. He appeared

to be soaking wet as well (out of sympathy for me, I think—a nice gesture).

"I'm here, boss."

"Good job."

"What can I say, this isn't your grandaddy's interface."

Randy looked at the readouts from the bodyscan done by the medbots.

"It looks like you're clear," he said. "No internal injuries. No broken bones. Just some very severe bruises and a mild concussion."

He nodded to the medbots and they deactivated the stasis field. I started to sit up but it was painful to move.

"I have to warn you," Randy said, "you're going to be very tired for the next twelve hours or so. HARV sapped a lot of your body's energy in order to generate enough electricity to shield you. It's going to take some time for you to regain that."

"It was worth it," I said. "As bad as I feel, I'm a lot better off than the hover . . . oh no. Where's Carol's hover?"

"Most of it's over there," HARV said, pointing north.

"DOS," I said, sitting up. "She's going to kill me."

"Easy, boss," HARV said, trying, unsuccessfully to hold me down with his holographic hands.

I rose to my knees and looked about. Sure enough, Carol's hovercraft lay upside down in the tall grass, one hundred meters away. Stray sparks still flew from the wrecked chassis.

"Oh, I'm in trouble now," I said.

I rose to my feet and, dazed and delirious, staggered toward the remnants of the hover.

"She's going to kill me," I said. "She's going to fry my brain and make me think I'm a duck."

"Boss, slow down," HARV said. "We'll get her a new hover. She understands these things happen—especially to you."

But I was beyond listening. I reached the wreck and carefully looked around to see if there was anything worth salvaging.

"She's going to kill me," I said.

"I think you're fixating here, just a little, boss."

The three gyros were destroyed. Two had ripped away from the hull on impact. The other was mangled almost beyond recognition. The hull looked like an old accordion, crumpled and torn from front to rear. It was a total wreck. Then I noticed a dim glow emanating from inside the hull.

"Look, HARV," I said, as I dropped to my knees to get a closer look, "the computer still works. Maybe we can . . ."

Then I saw it and everything changed.

"It's not 'wow'," was all I could say.

"Boss," HARV said carefully, "I think we should have the medbots check you again for that concussion."

I got down on my hands and knees and tried to pry my way into the hovercraft hull for a closer look at the screen, but I already knew what was there. It was the picture of Pierce and Nova embracing on the beach. But this time, I saw it upside down and I saw the tattoo on Pierce's arm in a whole new light. It wasn't in honor of Nova Powers. It wasn't "Woman of War."

"It's not 'W-O-W'," I said.

And Nova's words echoed in my mind: "I've never seen a bigger momma's boy."

The tattoo had been created specifically so only Pierce himself could read it. I knew that now. And I knew what it said.

"MOM."

27

"His what?"

"You heard me, HARV," I said (for the eighth time, I think), "Pierce is with his mother. That's where we'll find him."

"Oh, I heard you, boss," HARV said. "I just think your plunge into the duck pond left you a little more concussed than we originally thought."

It was morning now. I'd been home and in bed for twelve hours and had slept solidly for ten of them. I was still very weak, and my muscles didn't want to do much of anything other than remain motionless in bed, but I'd been assured that my body was replenishing its energy and that I should be somewhat back to normal within the next day.

I was also told that Electra had come to the house and examined me during the night, just to make certain that I was okay. No doubt she wanted to ensure that I was healthy for when she would return at some later date to kick my ass. But even so, I was happy to hear that she'd come. I could smell her perfume on the pillow beside me and that alone was enough to lift my spirits.

So, clearly, I was on the road to recovery. Now, all I had to do was convince HARV that I wasn't crazy, or at the very least that I was right about Mother Pierce.

"You heard what Nova said about Pierce. He was a momma's boy, he had family issues, all of that. I tell you, that tattoo isn't for Nova. It's for his mother."

"But it's upside-down."

"Not the way he looks at it. He lifts his arm and he sees 'MOM.' It's all crystal clear, HARV—Pierce wants his mommy.'

"Whatever you say, boss," HARV said.

"He's not in Sri Lanka, he's not on the moon. We find his mother, we find Pierce. Now stop arguing and get me the address of Mother Pierce!"

"Let's pretend for a nano," HARV said, "that, although I didn't take your theory seriously, I did some searching last night, while you were sleeping off your near death experience. Just to humor you."

"Okay, let's say that."

"And suppose," HARV continued, "that I found irrefutable proof that your theory is baseless. Would this convince you to surrender this Oedipal quest?"

"Well, that depends," I said.

"Upon what?"

"On what Oedipal means, for one." I said. "And the exact nature of the 'irrefutable proof' for another."

HARV shook his head and flashed a picture of an elderly woman on the wall screen.

"April Pierce, mother of Dr. Benjamin J. Pierce, age 122. Current residence, plot five sixty-seven in Beverly Hills Eternal Estates, six feet under."

"She's dead?"

"No, boss, she's a mushroom farmer."

"When did she die?"

"Fourteen months ago. Cause of death, respiratory failure brought on by pneumonia."

"Was it suspicious?"

"She was 122!"

"Are you sure it's really her?"

"DNA tests are conclusive," HARV said. "I checked with

the computer at the medical examiner's office and saw the tissue samples myself."

"Fourteen months ago. That's just before Pierce broke up with Nova, just before the BB-2 project went crazy and just before he disappeared."

"You think her death pushed him over the edge?"

"I have a feeling that Pierce was over the edge well before his mother died," I said. "But I think her death spurred him to action."

"So where do we go from here?" HARV asked.

"It's like I told you, HARV. We find Pierce's mother."

"Boss," HARV said, throwing his hands in the air, "I'm going to assume that your short-term memory was a casualty of last night's traumatic experience so I'm going to repeat, very calmly, I might add, that Dr. Pierce's mother is dead. She's kicked the coffee cup, she's pushing up paisleys, she has shuffled off her mortal interface, she's riding the ethernet of the next world. She's emailing from the great beyond and her address ends with 'the-hereafter-dot-org!' I can say it in over a 150 different languages if you like. But no matter how I say it she's still D-E-A-D, dead, dead, dead."

"That'll just make finding her a little more difficult," I said.

"What?"

"Come on, Pierce is supposedly one of the greatest minds on the planet, right? He's not going to let a little thing like death stop him from patching things up with his mother. He'd have a back-up somewhere."

"You mean a clone?"

"Yes, a clone."

"But that's illegal."

"So's building nuclear-powered killer androids. We need to find the clone of Mother Pierce."

"Fine," HARV said. "Where do you want to start?"

"Well, since I'm not likely to be going anywhere for a while, let's start right here. Patch yourself into the ExShell computer and let's do some old fashioned digging."

A few words about human cloning: it doesn't work.

That's just my opinion, of course. An opinion which happens to be shared by the World Council and about eighty-five percent of the world's population, but still, it's just my opinion. There are a lot of mega-brains in the scientific community, after all, who will argue with me quite vociferously.

"Simple DNA sequencing" they say. "The human genome. The building blocks to life" (notice how they never speak in complete sentences).

The world, fueled by the zeal of the scientific community, once embraced the cloning concept. The first (somewhat) successful cloning experiments early in the century captured the public's imagination and it actually culminated in a short-lived, but memorable, cloning craze twenty years ago.

I have met clones. I have spoken with clones. I even dated a clone once (it was during my experimental period in college), and all I can say is that when it comes to cloning humans, *New* New Coke was a better idea.

Why? Two words: "The mind." The body (brain and all) is the easy part. A little DNA, the right equipment and we can grow it in a big test tube. We can keep it on the sun porch beside the geranium for warmth and decorate it for the holidays. The mind, however, is an entirely different ball of earwax.

With all our advanced technology, we still don't understand how the mind works. The complicated mixture of memory and original thought, fueled by emotion, instinct and personality that makes every living person a unique individual cannot be drawn on a schematic map of lobes and hemispheres. A lot of the greatest scientists in the world today can't even make small talk at a cocktail party, let alone identify and recreate the subtleties and nuances of the human personality.

Be that as it may, the scientific community made valiant efforts to map, catalog and then recreate the human mind. The mind, however, simply proved too complex for them. By misplacing a few neurons or misdirecting a few intercranial connections, early researchers discovered, all too painfully, that there really is a thin line between love and hate (also between genius and psychosis, confidence and megalomania, progressive rock and disco).

The cloning craze eventually lead to what is now dramatically referred to as the clone wars. In retrospect, the whole thing was really more silly and contrived than monumental, but it made a mess of a lot of things, including national governments, the world economy and the collector's market for action figures.

The World Council finally outlawed all cloning of humans ten years ago and no one, save for the scientific community, has thought about it much since then.

Today there are still a few sanctioned labs that clone organisms but their work is pretty much limited to strains of bacteria, prize-winning bulls, that cat from the holovision commercials and a few individuals currently revered as "cultural icons" (but they don't go out in public much because they drool a lot and tend to get lost in open spaces).

The fact that Pierce might have cloned his own mother made me realize that he was quite probably insane. The fact that this insane, brilliant man also designed and created the powerful android for which I was now searching made me want to lock my doors and stay in bed just a little longer.

HARV and I spent the next hour hacking into the R&D database of the ExShell computer. Actually, it was HARV who did most of the work. I mostly watched sports highlights from the night before.

"By the way, since Ms. Star has granted us full access to the ExShell computer, I fail to see the point in wasting our time, hacking in through the back door," HARV complained.

"I don't want ExShell to know what we're looking for just yet. They still think Pierce is in Sri Lanka, remember? Also, I want to make sure that you're keeping your hacking skills sharp. I understand that ExShell's defenses are pretty tough."

"Oh, please," HARV said, "I could get past these defenses with a 486 and a blind homing pigeon."

"Nice metaphor." I said. "You're developing a wicked sense of sarcasm."

"I've been thinking about going out on the road or maybe writing for HV."

"Don't quit your day job just yet," I said, although I was pretty certain he was joking (which in and of itself was pretty remarkable).

But HARV was no longer listening. He was busy picking the last lock on the back door of the ExShell computer system.

"We're in," HARV answered.

A list of files, thousands long, scrolled across the wall screen.

"These are the files from the ExShell R&D department," HARV said. "Now, just what is it that we're looking for?"

"Anything that looks like Pierce's mother," I said. "Her memories, her personality, her mental skills. All of that would have to have been digitally translated and stored. I'm sure he used ExShell equipment."

"You think Pierce used an illegal cloning house to grow the body?" HARV asked.

I shrugged.

"Maybe he bribed one of the better animal houses into doing a special job under the table. Who knows, maybe he did it himself in his basement. I'm hoping that there's some evidence of data transfer here. Let's see Pierce's files."

The screen changed and the list of Pierce's files appeared. Again, there were thousands of them.

"Which one do you want to open first?" HARV asked.

I stared at the screen closely and looked at the long column of Pierce's name down the side.

"Wait, a second,'" I said. "Forget about these. Show me everything *except* Pierce's files. He wouldn't do this under his own name."

HARV changed the screen again. Pierce's name disappeared from the left hand column, replaced by a myriad of others. ExShell's R&D department employed thousands of people around the world, all of them had at least some files in the database.

"With which part of the virtual haystack would you like to begin?"

"Go through the list of names. Find anything funny," I said.

"Define funny," HARV said. "And remember, I'm not programmed for humor."

"Yeah, only sarcasm," I said. "Pierce would use an alias. He's big-headed enough to use something sly. 'Tom Clone,' 'Dick Copy,' 'Harry Mother,' that kind of thing."

"Harry Mother?"

"Just find me the funny names," I said.

"You got it. One Harry Mother coming right up."

28

It took HARV a little longer than I thought it would to put together the list of names, maybe three or four minutes, but I figured that he had some trouble making the subjective call when it came to the definition of funny. He was still new to this type of fine line. I took the time to grab an Electra-prescribed power shake from the fridge and a short while thereafter, HARV and I were both examining the list of funny names.

"How about 'Harry Johnson?'" HARV asked.

"Pierce may not be the most creative guy in the world but he's not twelve," I said. "He wouldn't use anything that juvenile. Same thing with 'Seymour Hiney' and that hyphenated name 'Alice Dyer-Rhea.'"

"'Mike Hunt,' as well?"

"Definitely."

"How about 'Dick Swett?'"

"Will you get your mind out of the gutter?"

"Forgive me, boss," HARV lamented, "but it is a pretty broad category."

I rubbed my eyes for a nano and took another long swig of the power shake. I was thankful that no one aside from HARV was around. It's hard maintaining a tough guy image when you're sitting around the house in your pajamas, drinking a vanilla shake with a straw.

"I know," I said. "It's just one of those things where I'll know it when I see it." I turned my attention back to the screen.

"'Jack Ash' is no good. 'Adam Appleton' is silly but not right. 'Foo Kyu' is just a very unfortunate cultural coincidence."

"Just think about his poor son, 'Foo Kyu Two.'"

I stared harder at the screen and kept reading the list.

"'Lisa Carr' . . ."

"I'd rather buy."

"'Juana Pea' . . ."

"I went before we left the house."

"'Juno Eimapieg' . . ."

"That one pretty much stands on its own."

"HARV!"

"You know, I'm starting to like this."

"This isn't working. Let's go back to the main list."

The screen switched back to the lengthier list, but alphabetized itself around the Eimapieg name that HARV had highlighted.

"What's that file right below 'Eimapieg'?"

"Einstein, A.," HARV answered.

"Einstein, A?" I asked. "As in Albert Einstein?"

"So it would seem."

"Why didn't you flag that as funny?" I asked.

"I didn't think that it was a particularly funny name."

"It's an *odd* name."

"You didn't ask for *odd,*" HARV said. "You asked for *funny.*"

"But odd *is* funny," I said.

"No," HARV said. "Odd is odd. Funny is funny."

"Look, there's funny-haha and there's funny-odd," I said. "I wanted them both."

"You didn't specify that you wanted funny-odd. You just said 'funny,' which implies only funny-haha."

"Why would I want funny-haha and not funny-odd?" I asked.

"Why would you want funny-odd in the first place?"

"Because odd is funny," I said, nearly red in the face. "Odd is funny!"

"Well, it is if you say it *that* way."

"Just open up the Einstein file."

"Interesting," HARV said. "The file is encrypted with a logarithmic key. Difficult to open."

"Can you break it?" I asked.

"Already done," HARV said with a sly smile.

On cue, the file opened and a three-dimensional computer schematic of a human brain unfolded on the screen.

"Now, *that's* odd," HARV said.

29

HARV and I watched as the brain template gently rotated before us on the screen, showing us, in glorious detail, the sulci and fissures that every human brain has (but are still unique to each). The template was broken down into sections mostly by the lobes and the hemispheres. The insides of most of these sections were blank but the right frontal lobe pulsated with millions of connected dots of light.

"Hello, Mother Pierce," I said.

"It appears to be a topographical map of the brain," HARV said. "Nice find."

"It's a start."

"Well, if nothing else," he continued, "we've proven that Dr. Pierce certainly holds himself in high opinion. There aren't many scientists who would use Einstein as a pen name."

"That's it, HARV."

"That's what?"

"Flag that file and go back to the list."

HARV did as he was told, intrigued by my thinking (which was kind of odd unto itself).

"Scroll down now, into the g's."

HARV scrolled through the names and I found what I was looking for.

"There," I said, pointing to the screen, "Galilei, G. That's Gallileo. Open that one."

"It's locked with a variation of the same encryption key as

the Einstein file." HARV said. "Not so hard to crack the second time around."

HARV opened the file and a three-dimensional blueprint of a human left frontal lobe appeared on the screen, next to the spinning brain template. Again, every detail was carefully mapped, every neuron was (supposedly) accounted for.

"This looks like it will fit very nicely into our the template," HARV said.

With those words the spinning left frontal lobe snapped neatly into place adjacent to the right. We now had two pieces complete in the brain jigsaw puzzle.

"The frontal lobes govern most executive functions," HARV said, sounding very much like a university professor. "Mother Pierce is coming into focus."

"Okay, go back to the list and find every file with a physicist name attached and locked with that same encryption code," I said, "Tesla, Archimedes, Hamilton, everyone."

"Now when you say 'physicist' do you mean 'physicist-haha' or 'physicist-odd?'"

"Don't start with me, HARV."

A few minutes later we had found eight more files, one for each hemisphere of each lobe of the brain, one for the hippocampal system, and one which appeared to be for miscellaneous minor brain areas. We had unlocked the computer blueprint for building Mother Pierce's brain.

"So now that we've found her," HARV said, tapping his holographic fingers on the table, "how do we actually *find* her?"

I didn't have an answer for that one, so I covered for it by staring deeply at the computer screen and rubbing my chin slowly, as if in thought.

"You don't know, do you?" HARV asked.

"Give me minute," I said. "We're missing something here."

I looked again at the list of files and read the names silently to myself:

1. Ampere
2. Archimedes
3. Bohr
4. Born
5. Broglie
6. Dirichlet
7. Einstein
8. Gallileo
9. Hawking
10. Ohm

Then I saw it.

"Gallileo, Hawking, Ohm . . . Vingo."

"Vingo?" HARV asked. "I don't recall that one. What was his specialty in the field?"

"Dump out of the ExShell system, HARV." I said, as I rose to my feet. "I know where she is."

30

It took me five minutes to get dressed because my hands still weren't working exactly the way I wanted them to. But my legs were back to normal and I was soon moving briskly through the house, with what I'm sure was the slightest hint of swagger. HARV, on the other hand, kept trying to spoil my good mood by using the lens in my eye to project himself in front of me, scold me for a few nanos and then disappear as I marched through him, only to appear again three meters further in front of me.

"I hate it when you do that," HARV said.

"Do what?"

"Give me one of those cliffhanger lines then just walk away like that. It's so pretentious."

"All this time with me and you're still not used to drama?" I said with a smile.

"Oh, I'm used to it," HARV replied. "I just don't particularly enjoy it."

"Comes with the job," I said, and I walked through his hologram again. He reappeared beside me this time and walked with me down the hallway.

"Fine, I'll play along," he said. "Just where is it that we're going?"

"To pay a visit to Mother Pierce and her dear son, Dr. Ben."

"Setting the question of their exact whereabouts aside for the nano, may I ask, oh great carbon one, how you intend to get to your mysterious destination? Or has it slipped your CPU that you've destroyed two vehicles in the past day?"

"I've got that covered," I said with a smile, "literally."

"What do you mean by . . . oh, no."

"Kindly follow me to the garage." I said as I continued to walk merrily through the hall.

"Oh no, no," HARV protested again.

I hopped into the garage like a kid out of bed on a holiday morning. Even though the object of my affection was carefully covered beneath a silk cloth, I couldn't help but smile at the sight of its majestic silhouetted form.

"Oh no, no, no," HARV said, as he materialized in front of me, attempting to block my view.

I walked through him again and pulled the cover away with a theatrical flourish to reveal the true jewel of my antique collection: a cherry red 1968 Ford Mustang Convertible in mint condition, metal and chrome gleaming in the somewhat sterile light of the halogen fixtures overhead.

"Please," HARV said, continuing his protest. "Anything but this. The vehicle is eighty-nine years old. It's never been weaponproofed. It needs expensive and highly polluting gasoline, the sale of which I will remind you has been outlawed for ten years. And, above all else, it doesn't have a computer!"

"Exactly," I said with a smile. "It's perfect." (A logical argument can never sway a man when it comes to his wheels or his women).

"Garage open," I said.

The garage door, being far more obedient than HARV, instantly complied. I hopped into the car and turned the key in the ignition. The engine turned over and growled like a kitten on steroids. I smiled as I felt the steady throb of the powerful machine around me.

"You know, of course, that your love of this car is simply your subconscious way of hiding your personal inadequacies."

"Log off, HARV," I said as I revved the engine and threw the car into gear. "You're killing the moment."

The engine roared and the tires gave a satisfying squeal as we leaped onto the road.

HARV holographically materialized from my eye lens and sat in the passenger seat next to me as we drove.

"I thought you were trying to keep a low profile," he said. "This car is as inconspicuous as me at an abacus convention."

"My low profile was blown the nano BB told the media that she and I were lovers. And with the bad luck that we've had with computer-controlled vehicles recently, I figure this is the safest way to travel."

I took a curve at a higher than suggested speed and the tires skidded as they slid, ever so slightly, sideways on the pavement. I downshifted, felt the wheels regain their hold on the road, then gunned the gas again and threw the 'stang back into fourth. I smiled. HARV rolled his eyes, holographically generated a seatbelt and made a big show of buckling it around himself.

"Then Gates help us all," he said. "Now, I don't mean to interrupt this motorhead machismo nano, but where exactly are we going?"

"To the Pierce house," I said.

"And that would be where exactly?"

"I don't know," I responded.

"But you said . . ."

"I stretched the truth a bit for the sake of the dramatic cliffhanger ending."

"So you have no idea where to find Dr. Pierce or his mother?"

"I didn't say that," I responded. "I don't know where they are but I know how we can find them."

HARV rolled his eyes again.

"Please just tell me what question you would like me to ask

in order to cut through this inane, time-wasting banter," HARV said.

I smiled. I loved getting on his circuits that way.

"The list of physicists that we put together," I said, "what was wrong with it?"

"You mean other than the fact that it didn't include Sir Isaac Newton?" HARV asked.

"Well, yeah. I mean, no." I said. "You noticed that?"

"Of course I noticed it." HARV chided, "a child would have noticed it. But what does that have to do with Mrs. Pierce's location?"

"Scan the New Frisco directory," I said. "Give me the address of April Newton."

"That's the extent of your epiphany?" HARV said. "He changed her name to Newton?"

"Look, he left Newton off the list for a reason," I said. "He's not going to just set up with the clone of his dead mother under the same name. Why not use Newton? Just humor me and run the name."

"I just did." HARV responded. "There's no match."

"None?"

"None."

"What about the suburbs, do the whole area."

"I did. There's nothing."

"Are you sure?"

"Of course, I'm sure," HARV said. "I'm a supercomputer."

"Try New LA."

"Done. Nothing."

"What about New Fresno?"

"Perhaps you would like me to check New Sri Lanka as well?"

"There's no April Newton in all of New Frisco or New LA?"

"Oddly, you've probably chosen the one name where that's true," HARV said. "There are, for instance, four Albert Einsteins, two Stephen Hawkings and one Enrico Fermi in the greater New Frisco area. There are even three people under the name of BB Star, one of which is . . ."

"BB Star," I said with a smile. "That's it."

"That's what?"

"Nova said that Pierce was in love with BB Star."

"You think Pierce and his mother are using the cover name 'BB Star?'" HARV asked.

"Check for April Newton in the directory for Oakland."

"Oakland?"

"BB was born in Oakland."

"That's a bit of a stretch, isn't it?"

"I know a thing or two about unrequited love, HARV," I said. "This is well within the realm of possibility. Scan for Oakland."

HARV sighed.

"Done," he said. "Nothing for April Newton."

"DOS!" I said.

"It pains me somewhat, however," HARV said, "to report that there is a *May* Newton listed in Oakland."

"*May* Newton. April's natural successor?"

"She moved into a two-bedroom residence on Avenue A roughly thirteen months ago."

"Vingo."

"I really wish you'd stop saying that," HARV replied.

"And you doubted my logic."

"Oh yes," HARV said, "Gates forbid I should ever doubt you when it comes to unrequited love and its related psychoses. I assume then that we're going to Oakland?"

"You got that right, pal."

"Will you at least keep the top up during the trip."

"Not a chance," I said, as I stabbed the button for the retractable top.

"Of course not," HARV sighed. "Of course not."

31

The Newton (neé Pierce) house was a two-story white colonial complete with a wraparound porch, a big oak tree on the lawn, and a picture-perfect picket fence around the yard. Staring at it from the curb was like opening a Norman Rockwell full-immersion interactive VR program.

"What a nice place," I said to HARV. "It's probably seventy years old, and it's real wood."

"Very impressive," HARV said (unimpressed). "Shall I scan the structure for termites?"

I rolled my eyes and, as HARVs hologram disappeared, walked slowly up the brick pathway to the porch and knocked on the door (a good solid knock on good solid wood). A nano later, a sweet-sounding woman's voice called to me from the inside.

"Who is it?"

"Good morning," I said, smiling as sweetly as I could at the fish-eye peep hole. "My name is Zach Johnson. I'm looking for Ms. May Newton."

"That's me, dear," the woman responded (with the door still tightly closed). "What can I do for you?"

"I'm a great fan of your son's work, ma'am. I'm doing some research for my employer and I was wondering if I could ask you a few questions about him."

"You want to talk to me about Benny?"

"Yes, ma'am," I said, then added, "or if Benny is available, I'd love to talk to him."

"Benny's busy right now," she answered.

"Vingo," I whispered.

"I thought we agreed that you weren't going to use that term?" HARV whispered inside my head.

"I understand, ma'am, but I'd appreciate a few minutes of your time if I could." I said. "I'd love to hear about Benny's childhood and how you raised such a fine son."

"You really like his work?" she asked.

"Yes indeed, ma'am. His . . ."

"Nanochip technology," HARV whispered.

"Nanochip technology is absolutely stunning," I said. "And his . . ."

". . . work in artificial intelligence" . . .

"—work in artificial intelligence was nothing short of revolutionary."

Mother Pierce was silent and the door remained closed. A very long nano passed and I thought for certain that I'd blown it.

"Ms. Newton?"

Then she spoke again.

"That sounds lovely, dear," she said. "Give me just a nano. I've got something on the stove."

"Thank you so much, Ma'am." I said. "Take your time."

I heard her footsteps recede on the other side of the door.

"She sounds pleasant enough," HARV whispered.

"I thought I'd lost her there for a nano," I said. "Thanks for the help with the technology thing. Now when we get inside, scan the house for Pierce and pinpoint his location. Maybe we can steal a minute with him."

"Will do," HARV confirmed.

Just then, I heard a very distinctive "clik-clak" sound from the other side of the door and I felt my blood run cold.

"Uh-oh."

I dove headlong from the porch just as the front door exploded into a thousand real wood fragments and a hail of hot lead and buckshot.

"I'm guessing that this is what you meant by 'losing her?'" HARV said.

I scrambled across the lawn, keeping low to the ground, flung myself behind the oak tree, and carefully peered around the big trunk just as dear Mother Pierce strode through the destroyed doorway wielding a (still smoking) authentic double-barreled shotgun.

"I told you people to leave my Benny alone," she shouted. "He's not a scientist, DOS it. He's a poet, a sensitive artist, filled with creativity and appreciation for the beauty of the world. Now get your parasitical behind off my yard before I fill it full of lead!"

She sent another round of buckshot into the oak tree and I sunk deeper to the ground as the pellets ricocheted around me.

"I've said it once, and I'll say it again," HARV said. "You really do have a way with people."

"This one is not my fault," I said.

"Napoleon said the same thing at Waterloo, only in French."

"Try just for a minute to be helpful here, HARV," I said. "Can my armor withstand a point-blank shotgun blast?"

"The armor wasn't designed to absorb damage from that type of projectile weapon. Dr. Pool, not surprisingly, never tested the armor against an attack from a one hundred-year-old shotgun. I will also point out that the armor will not protect your head, so the answer to that question is a bit of a mixed bag."

"I get the point," I said as I popped my gun into hand.

"Oh, come now, you're not really going to blow Grandma away, are you?"

"I'm going to take out her weapon," I said, then turned to the gun. "Sticky-stuff."

"Check," the gun chirped.

I tried to sneak a peak around the tree but another round of fire from the shotgun sent me diving back for cover.

"DOS, she's pretty good with that thing!" I exclaimed. "HARV, can you still guide the projectiles from my gun?"

"Well yes, of course, I have remote access to your gun and its projectiles, but from behind this tree I can't see Shotgun Granny any better than you."

"I can fix that," I said, removing the interface from my forearm. "Switch over to the wrist interface and use the view from its lens as a guide."

"If you stick the interface out there, she'll very likely blow your hand off," HARV said.

"Sticking my hand out isn't exactly what I had in mind," I said. Then I tossed the interface into the air towards the house.

"Hey!" HARV exclaimed from the interface speaker.

Mother Pierce fired another shotgun round at the interface as it flew, and I heard a few of the pellets hit the hardware solidly before it fell (still relatively intact) to the ground.

"You still there, HARV?" I shouted, even though I really didn't have to.

"I think I've been hit."

"Is the interface lens still functional?"

"You threw me into the line of fire," he said indignantly.

"It's a wrist interface, for Gate's sake," I said. "You're only in about a thousand other places, including my head. Now do you have a clear view of Ms. Pierce?"

"Yes," he replied, "and I don't like the way she's looking at me."

"Lock onto her weapon and take over guidance on the gun."

"Done," he said. "Now fire before she mistakes me for a clay pigeon."

I fired and let HARV take remote control of the special bullet. The round exploded outward in a wide curving arc and sped miraculously into one barrel of Mother Pierce's shotgun. The round exploded upon impact with a muted, rubbery "pop" and a shower of translucent yellow, petroleum-based glue instantly coated the shotgun and a good bit of Mother Pierce as well.

"DOS! You people are tricky," she said as she tried, unsuccessfully, to pull the gobs of glue from her gun barrel. "You come here with your fancy talk and your expensive suits and try to turn an old woman's head, then coat her with your sticky yellow lies. I told you before, my Benny doesn't know anything about science. He's a poet, I tell you, a brilliant poet."

Her voice trailed off and her strength seemed to ebb away. She slowly sank to the porch floor, until she was kneeling on the old boards, then pathetically hid her face in a glue-covered hand and began to cry.

"Zach Johnson fires upon innocent old woman, reducing her to tears," HARV said, now safely back inside my head. "Another great headline for the show reel."

"Yeah, let's go kick some kittens after this," I said.

I came out from behind the tree with my hands held high, in as friendly and as nonthreatening a gesture as I could manage, and retrieved the wrist interface from the lawn as I approached the now sobbing Mother Pierce.

"I'm sorry if I startled you, Ms. Newton," I said. "I . . . got a little confused earlier and misspoke. What I meant to say is that I'm a big fan of your son's . . . poetry."

Her sobs gently lessened and she looked up at me, hopefully. "You are?"

"Absolutely," I said. "I find it quite . . . interesting and . . . mysterious and . . . and I'd like to learn more about how he became the poet he is today."

"Oh, that's good," HARV whispered. "Slightly evil, but very good."

I bent down and slowly took the shotgun out of her hand, then carefully offered her my arm. She stared at me for a nano and then used her glue-covered hands to take her bifocals (which looked exactly like her son's) from her apron and put them on. Slowly, a sort of smile came to her face.

"Wait a, nano," she said. "I know you. I saw you on the David Cloneman show, didn't I? You're that Nixon dick."

"Zachary Nixon Johnson," I said. "Private detective."

"That's it. Zachary Johnson," she said, gently shaking my hand (and coating it with glue). "I enjoyed the show that night. You were very funny."

"Thanks," I said. "You know, we did a lot more of the back and forth banter in rehearsal but they cut most of it so that the piano playing dog could do another number."

"Cutting the classy stuff for the cheap laughs," she sighed, "but what can you do?"

"Yeah, what can you do," I agreed. "Sorry about the glue, by the way. It'll dissolve in an hour or so."

"Thank you," she said. "And I'm sorry about the shotgun attack. You can't be too careful these days."

"I understand completely," I said. "These are dangerous times that we live in."

"So are you really a fan of my Benny's poetry?"

"I am very, very interested in the stories that he has to tell," I replied.

"I'm so happy to hear that. I'm afraid I can't tell you much about the literary merits of his work. I'm just the proud, adoring mother," she said. "Would you like to speak to Benny yourself?"

"I wouldn't want to impose."

"Oh it's no trouble at all," she said. "Benny would love to discuss his poetry. He's in his study now, down in the basement."

This was going so well that my palms were beginning to sweat.

"Are you sure it's no trouble?" I asked.

"No trouble at all, dear. He'll be happy to see you," she said. "You're much nicer than those other men who visited."

"Other men?" I asked.

"I knew this was going too smoothly," HARV said.

"Three men," she said. "They stopped by about a week ago. Asked to see Benny but I wouldn't let them in. They were very persistent. Talked to me for almost ten minutes before they left."

"But you didn't let them in?"

"Gates, no, dear. Do I look like a fool to you?"

"You don't remember their names, do you?" I asked.

"I never got all their names," she said. "One man did all the talking. Skinny guy, swarthy too. Oh, what was his name? Manfred, Mandrake, something like that."

My heart sank a little bit and I spoke almost without thinking.

"Manuel."

"That was it," she said. "Manuel. Manuel Mani."

"Vingo," HARV whispered.

32

Dr. Pierce's study was like something out of another century. It was warmly lit from a handful of table lamps and a single overhead fixture. An intricately woven oriental rug covered the floor and the room was filled with more dark wood furniture than I'd ever seen before outside of a museum. There were two reading tables, a pair of padded easy chairs, a Victorian couch and a large, ornate writing desk. There was even a fireplace. But more breathtaking than anything else, however, was that the walls of the room were lined, floor to ceiling, with bookshelves and crammed with what must have been over a thousand books, hardcovers and even many leather-bound volumes. The furnishings of the room probably cost more than all the houses on my street combined.

And there was no computer.

Nothing automated, computerized, or remotely controlled.

As mentioned, I'm considered to be a bit of a throwback but this . . . this was like walking in on a caveman.

HARV must have read my thoughts because his whispered response inside my head confirmed my suspicion.

"Not a computer in the whole house, boss. But I'm getting a strange electronic reading from somewhere. Problem is that I can't quite seem to pinpoint it. Frankly, it's kind of spooky."

"Spooky?" I asked.

"I meant strange," HARV said.

"But you said 'spooky.'"

"Your point being?"

"I don't know. I just don't remember you ever using that word before," I said. "It's kind of judgmental."

"You're right. Gates, that's eerie."

"Stop it, HARV. You're scaring me."

"Scaring *you*?"

Dr. Pierce himself, was seated at the desk, his back to me as I entered.

"Dr. Pierce, I presume?"

He turned slowly toward me in his chair and there was no surprise in his face when he saw me.

"Hello Mr. Johnson."

He looked older by far than he did in the photos I'd seen. His graying hair was thinner and the lines in his face were deeper now and more pronounced. His body had softened as well, becoming a little paunchy and untoned.

I walked into the room and took a seat in one of the easy chairs.

"You're a difficult man to find," I said.

"Not difficult enough it seems," he said, "and please refer to me as Benjamin. I'd rather you not use the name Pierce in front of Mother."

"I take it she doesn't know that's she's April Pierce."

"She *isn't* April Pierce," he said, a little more sternly than I expected. "Her name is May Newton."

"Whatever you say, Benjamin," I said. "She seems like a . nice woman."

"Some of my best work, really. Aside from her occasional mood swings, she's a perfect duplicate of the original in every regard."

"Let's not forget her penchant for greeting unexpected guests with shotgun fire."

"That's actually true to her character," he said. "It was problematic at times, but it kept the New Jehovah's Witnesses away."

"There's something odd about his demeanor," HARV whispered. "He seems stiff, hyperconscious of his actions. Do you see it?"

Actually, I had noticed an oddness to Pierce but I couldn't pin down exactly what it was. His mannerisms were forced-casual, rigid, like a bad actor playing a part that he thought was beneath him.

He rose to his feet and took a decanter and two snifters from an oaken cabinet by the wall and held them out to me.

"Care for a brandy?" he asked.

"Doc, it's ten-thirty in the morning."

"Is it? I don't get out much." He poured himself a snifter of brandy and sat in the easy chair across from me.

"Congratulations, by the way, for finding me," he said. "You arrived nearly a day before I projected you would."

"Yeah, I got lucky and crashed a hovercraft."

"Pardon me?"

"Forget it. By the way, your buddy Fred Burns is still looking for you as well."

Pierce's face twitched ever so slightly at the sound of Burns' name. The muscles around his right eye tightened and his head jerked subtly to the side.

"His pulse just shot up ten beats per minute," HARV whispered.

"That parasite? Does he still believe me to be in New Paraguay?"

"New Sri Lanka, actually," I answered.

"Really?" Pierce said. "He's further along the subterfuge program than I thought. Another five years and I might have to devise some contingency plans. He's a laughingstock in the scientific community. Did you know that?"

"No, but it doesn't surprise me."

"He's a virus man. That was his specialty. I think he was actually good at it at one time but he's such a two-faced, annoying little man that he long ago lost any credibility he may have had. His mother was a friend of Mother's. She forced me to bring him aboard the . . ." he stuttered over the words and twitched subtly again, ". . . to give him a job."

"You mean on the BB-2 project."

Pierce was motionless and silent for a nano before speaking.

"I have no idea what you're talking about."

"Pulse just went up another eight beats per minute."

I leaned forward in my chair.

"You know, BB-2, that plutonium-powered killer android and sex toy that you built for BS Star."

Pierce twitched again; this time his hand shook as he tried to drink, and he spilled brandy on his shirt.

"Loss of fine motor control," HARV said. "That's strange."

"Oh, DOS." Pierce pulled a handkerchief from his pocket and dabbed at the spot. "Clumsy of me. I'm sorry what was it you were saying?"

I sat back in my chair and folded my arms across my chest.

"I saw an old friend of yours recently," I said. "Nova Powers."

He looked up at me for a nano then resumed dabbing the stain on his shirt.

"Really, how is she?"

"Doing well," I said. "Undefeated in the ring, as I understand it, for the past fifteen months. I was supposed to give you a message from her but, honestly, I'm not sure which one is appropriate for this circumstance."

"Pulse is leveling off." HARV said again. "He's getting comfortable."

"She's a fine woman," he said, somewhat wistfully. "If you see her again, please tell her I said hello."

"I will."

"No, wait, tell her that I said hello and was happy to hear that she was doing well."

"Got it."

"No, that's wrong too. Tell her . . ."

"Let's just leave it at hello."

He nodded. "That's probably best."

"Makes you wonder why the two of them ever broke up, doesn't it?" HARV said.

Pierce stared at the fire for a nano with a trace of a smile on his face. He took a long sip of brandy from his snifter just as I fired another conversational shot across his bow.

"Clear something up for me now, Doc," I said. "Did you break up with Nova out of guilt over your mother's death or was it because you were in love with BB Star?"

His eyes went wide and he sat forward and spit his mouthful of brandy into the air.

"Who told you that?"

"Let's just say that Nova was quite forthcoming with your dirty laundry."

"It's untrue," he said. "All of it."

"You didn't go a little crazy when your mother died."

"Absolutely not."

"And you're not in love with BB Star."

"Absolutely not."

"And you didn't sabotage the BB-2 project, causing the android to become psychotic?"

"What?"

He jumped out of his seat and, in the process, spilled the entire snifter of brandy onto his lap.

"Pulse is back up," HARV said. "We've also got some heavy perspiration starting. Something's not right here."

"Can I get you another brandy, Doc? I don't think you actually drank much of that last one."

Pierce stood and angrily rubbed at the wet spot on his pants with the handkerchief.

"I think you should leave now, Mr. Johnson."

"Not until I get the information that I need, Dr. Pierce."

"I told you not to call me that."

I got to my feet and took two angry strides towards him. He backed up instinctively.

"Why, because you don't want your mother to know that she's been dead for a year?"

"She's not dead," he said firmly.

"She's the illegal clone of a dead woman, Pierce. You can hide from the truth all you want, but that won't change it."

"You wouldn't understand."

"Oh, I disagree. I think I understand pretty well, here," I said. "I think your mother hated having a scientist for a son. I think she wanted you to be a poet. Am I right?"

Pierce said nothing.

"You were one of the greatest minds on the planet. You were revolutionizing technology. Changing the world. But your mother didn't see that, did she? All she saw was a failed poet, a loser."

Pierce turned away from me, shaking his head one way then another, doing whatever he could to avoid my gaze.

"To the world, you were a great thinker, but on the inside, you were an insecure loser of a momma's boy. And that insecurity messed up your life. It sabotaged your relationship with Nova and probably every relationship you've ever had."

"That's not true," he mumbled.

"And when your mother died, you realized that you'd lost the chance to make things right. So that's why you're here. You're starting over, with a new mother, a new name and a new identity. You're trying to be the son that your mother always wanted. The problem is that you're not doing this because you love her or because you want to make her happy. You're doing this for yourself. You're trying to get rid of the guilt that you've been carrying all your life. The guilt that you think has made you a loser."

Pierce had backed himself into a corner of the room and was now cringing in front of the bookshelves.

"Let me tell you something, Doc. I don't care. You can build whatever fantasy world that you want. All I care about is BB-2 and I want you to tell me about her."

This time, Pierce began to shake. His hands trembled at first as they covered his eyes. Then his knees shook as they slowly gave out and he slid towards the floor.

"I . . . I don't know what you're talking about."

"Pulse is off the chart," HARV said. "Loss of motor skills is highly irregular. Something's not right here, boss."

But I'd already had enough. I grabbed Pierce by the shirt and pulled him to me, shaking him by the shoulders and forcing him to look me in the eye.

"Don't you get it, Pierce? She's escaped. The android that you created and turned into a killer is on the loose. She's armed, she's powerful and she's crazy. I need to stop her before she kills somebody and I need to you to tell me how to find her and how to shut her down!"

Pierce shook more violently and his head started to twitch spasmodically to the side. He tried to speak but nearly bit his tongue before the words got out and when the words finally did come, they were not what I wanted to hear.

"I have . . . no . . . idea what . . . you're . . . talking . . . about."

That was all I could take. I slammed him so hard into the bookcase that the books on the top shelves shook and fell around us.

"Tell me everything you know about BB-2," I said, "or so help me, you'll spend the next six months of your life as a poet trying to come up with a rhyme for 'multiple fractures.'"

Pierce was shaking violently now, his mouth was moving spasmodically, trying to speak but the words he was saying were unintelligible.

"Feegah mend whap. Ploogle eiken dohr," he said, and then, "I have no idea what you're talking about."

"Loss of speech," HARV said. "Boss, I know what this is."

I slammed Pierce into the bookshelf again and more books

fell around us. I pulled my hand back to hit him just as HARV's hologram appeared between us.

"Boss, stop!"

I sent my hand through HARV and slapped Pierce across the face.

"Tell me about BB-2!" I yelled.

"Feegah mend whap." Pierce cried. "Feegah mend whap."

"I said tell me!"

"He's trying, boss, but he can't," HARV yelled.

"That's spam!" I said. "He knows how to find her."

"DOS it, boss. Listen to me," HARV yelled. "He's been mindwiped!"

I stopped and looked at HARV for a nano, then turned back to Pierce, who was now sobbing on the floor.

"What?"

"The behavior is textbook. The twitches, loss of motor control, preprogrammed responses. He can't even speak certain words and phrases," HARV said. "Someone has put psychic firewalls in his head and made it impossible for him to communicate on specific topics. It appears that the topic of ExShell and anything related to BB-2 are the touchstones."

"Can you scan him to make certain?"

"I can't be as thorough as one of Carol's psychic probes, but physically, he couldn't fake the symptoms he's exhibiting."

"Gates, HARV," I said, staring down at the sobbing Pierce, "I was ready to break his arm." The heat of my rage was quickly dissipating, turning to shame.

"You were a tad overzealous," HARV said. "But I don't think you've inflicted any permanent damage."

"What do we do now?" I asked.

"A gentler approach would be a good start."

I knelt beside Pierce and put my hand lightly on his shoulder. He flinched at the touch (and I couldn't blame him for it).

"I'm sorry, Doc," I said softly. "I lost my temper. I didn't understand. But now tell me, have you been mindwiped?"

Pierce heard the question, gnashed his teeth together twice, screamed and fainted.

"Let's also try to be a little less blunt," HARV said.

"You know, you could have mentioned that a little sooner," I said.

"Benny?" Mother Pierce's voice floated gently from the floor above. "Is everything all right down there?"

I turned to HARV, more than a little desperate.

"Fine, Mother," HARV said modifying the frequencies in his voice to replicate Pierce's. "Mr. Johnson is helping me with a poem."

"Well, don't get too excited," she said. "You know how that gives you headaches."

"Yes, Mother," HARV said.

We heard Mother Pierce gently close the door to the stairway and HARV and I both breathed a sigh of relief.

"How long do you think he'll be out?" I asked.

"Not long. His breathing and heart rate are normal. We'll have him back in a few minutes, I think."

"So we need to figure out how he can answer our questions about ExShell and BB-2 without actually mentioning those particular words. That'll be a trick."

"It's a little trickier than you think, boss," HARV said.

"What do you mean?"

HARV's hologram disappeared and he jumped back into my head to speak silently.

"Remember that electrical pulse that I couldn't locate? Well, guess what I just found."

"I'm guessing that it's nothing good."

"It's coming from Dr. Pierce. Specifically, it's a transmitter that's been implanted in his head, transmitting everything he sees and hears."

"You mean his body is . . ."

"Shhh, it's still operational."

"You mean his body is . . ." I said, as casually as possible, ". . . considered desirable in some cultures?"

"Good cover," HARV said. "Yes, his body is bugged. Someone is watching you and listening to everything you say right now.

"Can you trace where the bug is transmitting to?" I whispered.

"I tried, but it's well stealth-coded. I lost it somewhere in Reykjavik."

"Okay, let me get this straight—we need to ask Pierce questions about ExShell and BB-2 without actually mentioning ExShell or BB-2, and we have to do it in such a way so that whoever is monitoring him doesn't realize what he's telling us."

"A bit tricky, don't you think?"

I thought for a nano, then smiled.

"Piece of cake," I whispered "Let's wake him up."

Five minutes later, Pierce was awake, (somewhat) alert and none the worse for wear. I slowly helped him into an easy chair and gave him another snifter of brandy to calm his nerves.

"Feeling better?" I asked.

"Yes, thank you."

"I owe you an apology," I said. "I lost my temper. It's a character flaw that I have."

I pulled the other reading chair across the floor and sat close to Pierce, facing him and trying my best to look calm, concerned and confident all at once.

"Listen, Benjamin, I know what you're going through here. I understand *everything* that you're going through."

I gently reached over and took his hand in mine. Pierce looked at me like I was an ex-postal worker who'd just gone off his medication.

"Boss?" HARV whispered in my head. "I think you're scaring him."

"I know that you're just trying to do right by your mother

with all this," I said, gently tapping his hand. "You're a good son."

Tap, tap, tap.

"A very good son."

Tap, tap, tap, tap.

"I don't understand," he said.

"Trust me," I said. "You're a very, very good son."

I shot a quick glance at my hand (still tapping) his. Pierce stared at me, confused for a nano and tried to pull away. I grabbed his arm with my free hand and kept tapping, praying that he'd pick up on my idea.

"Trust me," I said.

And I again tapped T-R-U-S-T-M-E in Morse code on his hand. And, at last, he got the message. A light went on in his eyes and he nearly smiled.

"Thank you, Mr. Johnson," he said. "That means a lot to me."

I smiled and sat back in the chair.

"I want to ask you a few questions, Benjamin," I said. "Simple questions that will make life easier for all of us. I'm going to start with the three questions I asked you earlier. Do you remember those?"

Pierce nodded, and I could see that he was a little fearful.

"It's very important that you remember those earlier questions exactly. Do you understand?"

He nodded again.

"Okay, so truthfully now, you went a little crazy when your mother died, right?"

"Yes," he said.

"And you were in love with *Nova Powers*, right?"

"Ooooh, very tricky," HARV whispered.

"Yes, I was," Pierce said, and I saw the spark of understanding in his eye.

"Good," I said. "You know what, let's forget about that other question I asked you and just talk about Nova for a minute."

"Yes," Pierce said, "I'd like that."

"She's a great gal. Strong, smart. I like that in a woman. I wouldn't want to come between you two though. Say, Nova doesn't have a sister or anything, does she?"

Pierce hesitated for a nano before he spoke, as if expecting another seizure to come. He smiled when it didn't.

"As a matter of fact, she does," he said.

"What's she like?" I asked.

"She's . . . very much like Nova," he replied. "Very much like her indeed."

"Well, you know, looks are one thing. But I'm interested in how she thinks, what she likes, what she doesn't, where she hangs out, that kind of stuff."

Pierce took a long swig of brandy from his snifter.

"I understand," he said. "But her sister thinks very much the way Nova does. Likes what she likes, at least to a certain degree."

"She sounds great," I said. "Do you know how I can find her."

Pierce shook his head. "I don't. But Nova would."

"Nova would? What do you mean?"

Pierce hesitated for a nano.

"His pulse just jumped six beats per minute, boss," HARV said. "We're flirting with the firewall here."

"Nova and her sister are very similar," Pierce said. "They think a lot alike. Her sister's instincts are almost identical to Nova's. Nova may not know it but, on a subconscious level, she knows what her sister would do or . . . "

"Or where she'd go," I said.

"Exactly."

"So if I want to find Nova's sister . . ."

"You should ask Nova."

I nodded.

"Benjamin, your mother mentioned that three men came to the house last week looking for you. One of them was named

Manuel Mani. Did they do anything to you that you remember?"

"No," he said.

"Pulse is up another five beats per minute," HARV said.

"You never met with them?"

Pierce shook his head.

"Remember, boss, Ms. Pierce said that they never came into the house. They only talked to her from outside."

"Benjamin, did anyone *else* come into house while those men were talking to your mother?"

"Biggledy boop," he said with some degree of difficulty.

"Mani was a diversion," I said. "He kept Pierce's mother busy while someone came in and . . . talked with Benjamin."

"Keepa, keepa, keepa, boom."

"That's silly," HARV said. "Why would Manuel Mani want to mindwipe Dr. Pierce? What's gained by that? And how did he find him?'"

I stared into Pierce's eyes and saw the frustration below the surface. But there was something else there as well. It was resignation, almost a look of acceptance of his fate, as though he'd expected it all along. That's when I knew.

"I understand," I said.

"Understand what?" HARV whispered inside my head. I got to my feet and grabbed my hat from the table.

"Thank you very much, Benjamin," I said. "I appreciate your time."

Pierce rose to his feet with me and we shook hands.

"You're very welcome, Mr. Johnson. Thank you so much for stopping by."

I turned and walked towards the door. Pierce's voice stopped me and I turned around.

"Mr. Johnson, do you have a dollar?"

"What?"

"If I'm remembering correctly, you always carry an old-fashioned dollar bill or two with you for good luck."

"You've read my press material?"

"Mother keeps the *New People* site on the screen in the bathroom. So you do have a dollar?"

"Yes, I do," I said.

"Then I'd like to sell you a poem."

"Excuse me?"

"Give me the dollar. Please, it's important that I sell you this poem," he said.

I pulled out my wallet and took out one of the old fashioned dollars that I carry and handed it to Pierce. Pierce smiled, fought back a little twitch and recited for me.

"Things are never as they seem,
As though we are living in a dream.
Where the one is like another,
Perhaps a sister,
Or something other.
The more you have,
The more others need.
Danger is always near you.
So take heed."

He finished with a little bow.

"That was very . . . nice. Very . . ."

"I've recorded it, boss."

"Good. Thank you again for your time."

Pierce walked back to his desk and I moved again toward the door.

"Mr. Johnson?" Pierce called.

I turned.

Pierce took a coin out of his pocket and flipped it to me.

"Here's your change."

I caught the coin and stared at my palm for a nano and realized that it wasn't a coin at all. It was a neuro-neutralizer, identical to the one that BB had given me.

I looked at Dr. Pierce, who shrugged his shoulders almost imperceptibly.

"I have no more need for money," he said. Then he turned back to his desk and sat down and continued writing. "And by the way, if you should see Nova Powers again, please tell her that I'm very sorry for how I treated her."

"I will."

"You know, never mind," he said. "I'll tell her myself."

I smiled.

"But if you happen to come across," he twitched again, fighting a spasm, "Nova's sister . . . ?"

"Yes?"

"Kick her plutonium ass for me."

Mother Pierce showed us out and a few minutes later HARV and I were back in the Mustang. That's when HARV felt safe enough to ask me the question.

"So you know who mindwiped Pierce, don't you? You saw it in his eyes?"

"Yes," I said.

"Well, who was it?"

"It was her," I said. "It was BB-2."

33

In this day and age, there aren't a lot of things that are considered difficult. We can go anywhere in the world in a matter of nanos. We've walked on other planets, eradicated "incurable" diseases, and cloned human beings. The bar for the impossible has been raised dramatically over the years.

But getting an appointment with BB Star on short notice? Now that's hard.

But HARV put the gigabyte on the ExShell computer and when I finally got my face on BB's personal screen, we were just about home.

"It's vital that we talk soon, BB. I've gotten some new information that we need to discuss."

"New information from whom?" she asked, blue eyes twinkling.

"I can't say, and certainly not over the net. I'll only need a few minutes of your time."

BB was motionless for a nano and furrowed her brow in thought.

"When can you be here?" she said finally.

"Ten minutes."

"Fine. The guards will 'port you right up. And please, no humming this time."

"You got it," I said, as her face disappeared from the screen of my wrist interface.

HARV appeared beside me, sitting casually in the passenger seat.

"I don't get it, boss," he said. "We're going to ask the woman who hired us to find the android where we can find the android?"

"Well, of course it's going to sound silly if you put it that way," I answered. "Look, BB-2 is a copy of BB. Same exact memories, same exact mental and emotional structure, excepting of course whatever personality traits and behaviors that BS and Pierce specifically added."

"Like the murderous psychoses?"

"Good example. Anyway, according to Pierce, BB-2's instincts would be similar to BB's. On a gut level, they think the same things. BB has information. She just doesn't know she has it and we have to dig into her subconscious to find it. At least that's Pierce's advice."

"Ah yes, the voice of reason and sanity," HARV said. "Which leads to another question. Why would BB-2 mindwipe Dr. Pierce to keep him quiet? Why not simply kill him?"

"Maybe out of respect for him as her creator?" I said, pondering. "Maybe she thought it would be more fun than just killing him. I don't know. I'm pretty sure Pierce knows, but he can't tell us. Not without spitting on my shoes and shaking his teeth loose anyway."

"So what exactly are you going to ask Ms. Star?"

"Honestly," I said. "I have no idea. I'll just wing it."

"That, boss, is my greatest fear."

Upon my request, BB shut down the holographic program that created the pastoral backdrop for her office. I thought that the green grass and flowers would be a distraction for her and I needed her to dig deep into her head for information (although I didn't tell her that).

Without the background program, the office was very empty, gray and limbo-like. The river was still there but it was a lot less imposing without the greenery around it. It was almost impossible to tell exactly how big the room was because there was nothing to measure it by. It was kind of creepy but also kind of appropriate.

BB had a faux leather couch, coffee table, and easy chair created and she sat comfortably in the chair while I fiddled meticulously with some equipment that I'd brought with me.

"Pardon me, Zachary," she said distantly, "I'm not familiar with this device. What did you say it was called?"

"A Voight-Kampf meter," I replied. "It was made by a friend of mine. It's designed to monitor emotional reactions to stimuli."

I held out a pair of small sensors that were attached by wires to the main console in front of me.

"I need to attach these to you, if you don't mind," I said, cautiously.

"Tell me where they need to be attached and I will tell you whether or not I mind," she said.

Truthfully, I couldn't quite tell if that was a come-on or a threat, so I stayed to the middle of the road and went with the professional response.

"The small one clips onto your thumb. The round one I'll just tape to your temple."

I moved towards her and slowly raised the sensor toward her forehead. She pulled away slightly and, almost girlishly, put her hand to her hair.

"My makeup."

"I don't think it will hurt it," I said, gently moving her hair away from her forehead. "I'll put it here, behind your hair."

Her hair was soft and full, like strands of perfumed silk, and I had to fight a subconscious urge to run my fingers through it. I think BB noticed and I saw her smile ever so slightly as she adjusted the sensor on her forehead.

"Thank you, Zachary."

"Boss, are you okay?" HARV asked silently. "Your pulse is up a bit."

I walked back to the couch across from BB, sat down and fiddled with the console.

"I'll monitor you as I ask these questions and I'll be guided by the responses from the machine as much as your actual answers. This way it will be easier to spot sensitive areas in your subconscious that are worth exploring."

"Is all this really necessary?"

"The droid has your brain patterns and personality, BB. You know better than anyone how she . . ."

"It . . ."

". . . it is going to react."

I touched a few more buttons on the console and monitor then turned back to BB and gave her a smile.

"Now then, are you ready?"

"Ready."

"Okay, close your eyes now and relax," I said. "Let's begin with the basics. You're frightened."

"I am not."

"It's a hypothetical question, BB."

"I know that," she said. "But I never get frightened."

"Never?"

"When you have danced naked in front of ten thousand screaming, drunken men, well, everything else seems insignificant after that."

"I can imagine. All right, I'll rephrase. You're concerned."

"Better."

"You're a droid."

"No, I am not."

"Hypothetical, BB. Stay with me here."

"Right, sorry."

"You're a droid. You've escaped. You're on the loose with people after you. You have nowhere to go. What do you do?"

"Seek shelter," she said. "Hide and plan." She smiled. "This is kind of fun."

"Good," I said. "That's what we're looking for. Do you leave the city?"

"I would not leave the Bay area."

"Why not?"

"Because I know this city and this area like the back of my hand. I am on solid ground here. I love this city."

"It does have a certain charm, doesn't it?"

"And very favorable tax breaks for the wealthiest one percent," she said.

"So where in this area would you go?"

"There are so many choices. The sewer tunnels, the piers, the subbasements of the skyscrapers. No, wait, someplace high."

"Why high?"

"To regain my confidence. The world looks smaller from above. I feel even more powerful then, like I can squash my enemies beneath my million-credit heel. Grind them into bloody shreds of flesh and bone, then kick their crushed skulls aside and watch them roll like marbles on a playground."

"Little vindictive there, BB."

"Sorry. I just like heights, I guess."

"Are we certain that BB-2's psychotic nature isn't part of the original?" HARV whispered.

I ignored him as best I could.

"Okay, so we've established that heights make you feel powerful. But what makes you feel safe?"

"Grandma."

"Grandma?"

"Yes, Grandma," BB said, almost as if she was surprised that she'd said it. "When I was a child in Oakland, my mother worked nights so I spent a lot of time with my Grandma."

"How old were you then?"

"We moved to the New Dakotas when I was six, so I was very young at this time, two, three, maybe four."

"Very impressionable."

"I suppose so," she said.

"What kind of things come to mind when you think of your grandmother?"

"Safety."

"Aside from that. Specific memories. Sensory impressions."

"It was dark."

"Dark?"

"Not pitch black, but comfortably shadow-like. With some warm-colored lights."

"Anything else?"

"It was warm. I could sleep without a blanket."

"Warm and dark. This is good, what else comes to mind when you think of that time?"

"Cinnamon."

"Cinnamon? Why?"

"Not certain, really. I just associate cinnamon with that time."

"That's good. The sense of smell is very powerful. It often makes very strong mental impressions." I paused for a nano to let BB process her thoughts a bit, and to build a little suspense. "When I think of cinnamon I'm reminded of eating cinnamon buns on a warm autumn morning. What about you?"

BB hesitated for a nano and her face furrowed again in thought. She seemed a little stiff though, almost uncomfortable. Then she smiled, but I could tell it wasn't genuine.

"Yes. A warm morning," she said. "That is very good, Zach. I think of that as well."

"Is your grandmother still alive?" I asked.

"Yes, she is eighty-seven. She lives in town."

"Would it be all right if I spoke to her?"

She pulled back a bit. Her face lost the wistfulness brought on by her memories, and the business face returned. "Absolutely not."

"BB, this is important. Your grandmother clearly shaped a lot of your early memories. These are memories you share with

BB-2. BB-2 may seek out a place where she subconsciously feels safe."

"Are you saying that Grandma is in danger?"

"I don't know that for certain. But at the very least, she has some information that could be important."

"Zachary, let me remind you that I did not hire you to psychoanalyze me or my grandmother. I did not hire you to delve into the recesses of my subconscious or probe my memories as a child."

She removed the sensor from her hand and forehead and gently but authoritatively handed them to me.

"I hired you to find a renegade android. If you cannot do the job then I will gladly find someone who can."

"I don't think this is going well, boss."

I sat back on the couch, crossed my arms over my chest and gave BB a very determined glare.

"Tell me the truth, BB, how many people do you have out there right now looking for this droid?"

She was silent.

"My guess is that you have every security person at your disposal scouring the city, employees in every metropolitan office searching the major cities, and satellites in orbit checking every square inch of the planet. You have state of the art sensors searching for some trace of BB-2's electronic signature, some sign of residual radiation from her plutonium core or any energy residue that would come from the discharge of her built-in weaponry. You probably even designed tracking chips into her mainframe so that you could find her if something like this were to ever happen. And yet you still don't have a clue as to where she is. Am I wrong?"

"No," she said (with some difficulty).

"The hard truth is that this droid could be anywhere. She knows that you're searching for her. She probably knows how you're doing it and she's figured out how to evade you. What's more, if she's stayed hidden this long, it's probably because she's planning something and that just can't be good.

"You're not going to find her by searching. The only way to find her is to get inside her head and figure out what she's planning. That's what I'm trying to do and right now I need to speak to your grandmother.

"It's understandable that you want to shield her from all of this, but you and I both know that this droid is dangerous and we have to stop her before she kills someone."

BB was silent for a long nano, staring at me with a mixture of anger and deep concentration. She finally rose to her feet and turned away.

"It," she said.

"It?"

"You keep referring to the droid as 'she,'" BB said. "It is not alive. It is a machine. Please use objective rather than feminine pronouns in your references."

"I'll try."

"I am not paying you to try," she said sternly. "I am paying you to find this droid and return it to me."

She gently rubbed her forehead and returned to her desk, which was reforming itself as she approached.

"My grandmother currently resides at the New Frisco Centurion Citizen Center on Bay Street," she said. "Net the reception center there and they will set up an appointment for you. My computer will verify your access."

"Thank you," I said.

"Treat her with respect, Zach. Do not speak to her in the manner in which you just spoke to me. If you do, I will see to it that you never work on this planet again."

"Understood, and I apologize if I spoke harshly. I was only telling the truth."

She touched a button on her desktop and the holographic décor program rebooted. Within nanos, the ceiling above me turned to a cloudless blue sky and CGI vegetation grew lushly beneath my feet.

"I think that we are done here, correct?"

"There's actually one more thing," I said. "I have reason to believe that the droid is now working with Manuel Mani."

"Manuel? How did he find the droid?"

"I'm guessing that it's the other way around. BB-2 came to Manuel."

"Why would it come to him?"

"I don't know. But it's no secret that you and Manuel were an item."

"He was my personal astrologer," BB answered.

"So the two of you weren't romantically involved?"

"Why do you ask?"

"I've just heard some conflicting reports that you were, um . . ."

"Boss, you're not about to ask our high-paying employer whether or not she's really frigid, are you?"

Luckily for me, BB finished my sentence out of indignation.

"Romance had nothing to do with it," she said. "The relationship between Manuel and me began as professional, turned physical, and then grew tiresome. I terminated the relationship and Manuel left the company shortly thereafter."

"So the breakup was your idea?"

"Men do not break up with me, Zach," she said. "The droid has clearly gotten Manuel on the rebound."

"That's probably true," I said. "Does Manuel have any skills?"

"I beg your pardon?"

"Other than astrology, I mean. I'm just trying to figure out what BB-2 would want with Manuel."

"I have no idea. Manuel has no skills that would appeal to the droid."

I shrugged. "Okay, I just thought you should know."

"Yes, thank you, I enjoy hearing that my ex-boyfriend has

taken up with my psychotic android doppleganger," she said, with more than a hint of venom. "Now, if there is nothing else . . ."

"I think I have enough to go on for now," I said, coolly (using my tone as a sort of pseudo-antivenom). "Thanks for your time."

I packed up my equipment from the coffee table just as it dissipated and began the long trek out of the office.

I was soon back in the Mustang and headed toward the office. HARV projected himself into the passenger seat as we drove.

"So, we're off to Grandma's house?"

"Eventually," I nodded. "Let's see if we can make that appointment for this evening."

"And what do we do with the Voight-Kampf?"

"The what?"

"The Voight-Kampf, the device that you used to measure Ms. Star's emotional and mental reactions to your questions."

"Oh, that. I threw it in the trunk. It was just an old personal entertainment system. Voight and Kampf are two guys from my old bowling league."

"I suspected as much when I saw the 'Play Station IX' logo on the console. Why the charade?"

"I figured that she'd take the questions more seriously if she thought she was being monitored, maybe speak a little more truthfully."

"So you're saying that you needed a machine to give yourself credibility," HARV said with a smile.

"Now you see, I knew you were going to twist it like that."

"Boss, I completely understand your desire to use computers and machines to make up for your inadequacies. It's only natural."

Needless to say, the ride back to the office was less than pleasant.

34

There was this big scandal back in 2044 that has become known as "The Great Cat-Eating Fad," and I played a minor part in the resolution of this rather dark period in history (there's a point to this, I promise).

I had just hung out my PI shingle and was still living hand-to-mouth (much as I am now, but let's not bring that up). I was doing some investigative work for my local grocery store and I sort of accidentally discovered that a pet-breeding company, through an accounting error, had accidentally bred a million more house cats than they needed. Since the company was an HTech subsidiary, the folks in the corporate headquarters tried to turn their profit-draining lemons into windfall lemonade. Teams of R&D specialists, spin doctors and ad agencies went to work and thus was born the cat-eating fad and the immortal slogan, "Cat—the cuddly white meat."

I leaked the true origin of the "catfood" craze to the press, and the public reacted rather vindictively. HTech's stock plummeted over the next few weeks, and they fired a lot of middle-management types as a display of retribution.

And speaking of retribution, HTech also sent me a message telling me to keep my nose out of their business in the future. The message was delivered to me by four thugs in a back alley and was written in black and blue all over my body. I ended up in the ER at New Frisco General, where the first things I saw upon regaining consciousness were the lovely brown eyes of a young resident named Electra Gevada. Actually, the first things I saw were her breasts, because she was leaning over, but that was a pretty great sight to awaken to as well.

I was bruised, bloody and swollen and when I asked her out, she smiled at me and said, "Let's wait and see what you look like once the swelling goes down."

It was one of the best nights of my life.

Electra and I have been together ever since.

Electra had avoided and ignored every one of the messages that I'd left for her (twenty-seven in all) since our spat and I was beginning to get a little worried. We'd had these kind of misunderstandings before (I have the scars to prove it), but in this day and age, not responding to twenty-seven messages is grounds for divorce in some provinces. So I figured that we really needed to talk. I also figured that my best chance of seeing her was catching her in person. That meant going to the clinic. So I went there and I waited. And waited. And waited.

"You know," HARV said, "there's still the matter of the renegade killer android that we need to locate. How much more time do you want to spend sitting on this bench?"

"I'm waiting for the right moment," I said.

"You could have her paged, you know."

"Then she'd know that I came here just to see her."

"But you did," HARV said.

"But she doesn't have to know that. I want it to be a little more casual. That way we'll both be more at ease."

"Like a chance meeting?" HARV asked.

"Exactly."

"As though you just happened to be visiting the children's free clinic where she works, and you ran into her by coincidence in the corridor."

"Right."

"With a bouquet of flowers in your hand?"

"Right."

"Boss, you're scaring me a little here."

I spotted Electra at the far end of the hallway coming out of her office and walked quickly toward her. She spotted me, rolled her eyes and turned away.

"Electra, wait up."

She sighed then turned toward me.

"Hey, what a surprise seeing you here," I said. "I'm just doing some research for the case that I'm on."

"Zach, you've been sitting in this hallway for an hour talking to yourself. The only reason I came out here is because you were starting to scare the staff."

"Well, it was HARVs idea."

"Hey!" HARV shouted in my head.

"Can we talk?"

She began walking. I stumbled and hurried to keep up.

"I spent the entire day, thus far, unsuccessfully trying to get more funding to keep this clinic open," she said. "I'm half an hour late for ICU rounds as it is."

"I'll go on rounds with you," I said.

"I don't think so."

"Then we'll talk on the way."

"Fine, you have thirty meters of corridor."

"Real quality time," I said. "Thanks for coming by the other night to check me out after my accident."

"I'm glad to see that you're feeling better," she said. "I'm sure that BB is as well."

"Look, about the news story. You don't believe the thing about BB and me, do you?"

Electra didn't even glance at me as we walked but I could see the anger from her profile.

"What should I believe, chico?"

"Honey, I'm undercover."

She turned and her dark eyes shot me a pair of daggers.

"Let me rephrase," I said. "BB hired me to find a droid that's escaped. She doesn't want the information made public so she created this cover story."

"I know that," Electra said.

"You do?"

"Give me some credit."

"Well, then what's the problem?"

We reached the door to the intensive care unit. Electra put her hand on the knob but didn't enter. She turned to me, looked around and spoke, softly yet pointedly.

"The problem is that you *let* her do this, chico. You could have been her concerned friend or her tennis partner. You could have called yourself her Japanese gardener, for Gates' sake. But no. She wanted to say you were her lover and you jumped at it. So now the whole world knows it, chico. You're a stud. Hah!"

"It wasn't like that," I said. "She did this without my knowing. We'll retract the story when the case is over."

"You don't get it, do you?" she said. "She's using you like some boy-toy plaything and you're too caught up in your own machismo to see it. Well, I think we should stay apart for a while. After all, I wouldn't want to blow your cover."

She opened the door to the ICU and stepped through but she turned to me before closing the door.

"From here on Security is going to have orders to keep you out of the clinic. I don't want you here disturbing everyone. And one last thing . . ."

"What's that?" I asked.

"Sidney Whoop has been watching you for the past ten minutes."

She closed the door in my face. I sighed and gently banged my head on the frame.

"She said Sidney Whoop, didn't she?" I asked.

"Sadly, yes." HARV whispered.

"Having problems with your love life, Zach?" Sidney asked from behind me.

I rubbed my eyes and turned slowly around. Sure enough,

there was Sidney with his two wingmen, And-A-One and And-A-Two, hanging back just a bit and flanking him on either side.

"What brings you here, Sidney?" I said. "Donating your organs to science, I hope."

"No, Zach. I'm just following you. Doing a little research on some of BB Star's ex-boyfriends. Sort of a 'Where Are They Now' kind of thing. So what's this I hear about a cover story and a missing droid?"

I'm usually very careful about being followed and keeping the details of my cases confidential (really I am). But I'd screwed up here and Sidney just happened to be in the right place at the right time. This was going to be sticky.

"No, Sidney, you misheard," I said. "I was just telling Electra how annoyed I am at DickCo for giving you such *boring stories* to work on these days. Electra thought it was because your Q-ratings have fallen so badly this year but I told her that Sidney Whoop is still a great man, no matter what ninety-five percent of the general public thinks."

Sidney smiled.

"I appreciate your support, Zach," he said. "And you're right, maybe there are more important things out there that I should be searching for. I'll let you know if I find anything interesting."

He turned and walked away. And-A-Two stayed behind, using his eyecam to capture his boss' exit. Once Sidney was through the door, And-A-Two followed, but he bumped me with his shoulder as he passed.

"Your time is coming, Johnson," he said.

"How would you know?" I replied. "You need subtitles to read a digital clock."

He stopped and glared at me for a nano.

"Your time is coming," he said again as he turned and walked away.

I watched him follow his coworkers and disappear down the hallway.

"Always a pleasure, meeting the DickCo boys," I said to myself.

"At least there was no gunplay this time," HARV said. "Maybe your luck is starting to turn."

35

Later that evening, HARV and I were back in the 'stang, and headed toward a rendezvous with BB's grandmother.

"So we're off to see Granny BB at the Frisco home for the old and unwanted?"

"The Frisco Centurion Citizen Center," I corrected. "And yes, we're going to speak with Mrs. Backerman. You need to be a little more civil in your linguistics, HARV."

"Oh please," HARV groaned. "You know very well that I've been programmed to use the most current geopolitically sensitive terms. I was being facetious and trying to make a point about the sensibilities of our distinguished client."

"The point being?"

"Well, it seems to me, that if Ms. Star loves her dear grandmother as much as she professes, she wouldn't have put her in an old folks' home or, as my programming forces me to refer to it, 'a care community for the youthfully challenged.'"

"That's BB's choice," I said.

"True, but I would think that the richest woman in the world might do a little better for her dear old granny."

"I've already thought of that," I said, "but I'm reserving judgment until speaking with Mrs. Backerman."

At the intersection of Shake and Rattle Streets (the municipal planners were a lot less uptight in the years following the big quake), I signaled to turn right.

"No, go straight," HARV bleated. "Make a right onto Tremor and then cut across to Aftershock Ave." ˙

"That's two kilometers out of our way."

"True," HARV said. "But only as the crow flies. The municipal traffic computer informs me that, due to heavy construction and the timing of the traffic signals, you'll save one point five minutes by utilizing this alternate route."

"Fine," I said. I grinned and carefully kept the car on course for Tremor Street.

"Why do you have that foolish grin on your face?"

"No reason," I said, still grinning. "I just figured out what this is all about. That's all."

"You're being more confusing than usual," HARV said. "What *what* is all about? And I'm sure that whatever it is, it's not what you think."

"You don't like this car," I said, "because you need to feel needed."

"Excuse me?" HARV said with a bit too much surprise. "Are you talking to me? I don't think so, because that just does not compute."

"You're upset because I can operate this car without any assistance from you whatsoever. You need to be needed."

"That is ridiculous!" HARV exclaimed. "Gates, the phrase sounds as though it should be from one of those insipid old songs of which you are so fond. Need to be needed, indeed. First of all, I don't need your approval to prove my worth. I am the most sophisticated computer on the planet. Secondly, even if you are currently operating this car without my assistance, I'm still performing a myriad of invaluable functions. For instance, as we speak I am again scanning all new police reports and hospital emergency room records for some evidence of BB-2. I am also scheduling a repair to your house's solar heating system, and reupping your participation in the high-tech mutual fund in your retirement account. So let's just be crystal clear here, whether you're driving this car or not, I am absolutely essential to your well-being."

"Yeah, I guess you're right," I said and turned my attention back to the road, though I purposely let the grin on my face widen.

"You don't believe me, do you? Well, your opinion on the matter is of little consequence to me. The assumption that I need to be needed does not make one iota of sense. I am a projection from a highly developed computer; the very concept of need is, well, nothing I *need* to worry about." He stopped suddenly and pointed towards the road.

"Take this left turn coming up here, then park in lot B two point five. It's the closest to Mrs. Backerman's room. And be careful of the sharp curve ahead. Gates, what would you do without me?"

I just smiled and did as I was told.

I parked the car, hopped out and headed toward the mammoth high-rise that was the Frisco Centurion Citizen Center.

"Switch out of hologram mode," I whispered to HARV as we walked. "I'd like to keep you a secret for as long as possible."

HARV's hologram dissipated. His voice, however, did not. "Don't think I can't see that grin," he said from inside my head.

I looked up at the towering building and nearly toppled over from a mild attack of vertigo. The structure was a prime example of the ridiculous architecture of the early 2040s. A huge sterile, albeit good-looking, box of a building with all the personality of a cardboard convenience store night clerk, it was conservative in every sense save for its size. The thing was over two hundred stories high (talk about subconscious insecurities).

"I don't suppose Grandma lives on the ground floor," I asked as I watched the high-speed elevators zip up and down the walls like hyper roaches on a garbage can.

"As if life would be that fair," HARV chided. "She lives in the penthouse, floor two fifty-six."

"Of course," I mumbled and headed towards the elevator.

The elevator operator, a high-class server droid with pale orange skin and pleasant, though somewhat cold, features greeted me at the door.

"Good day sir," the droid droned. "Who would you like to visit with?"

"A building this large," HARV whispered inside my head, "you'd think they could afford a grammatically correct droid."

"What?"

"I said," the droid responded slowly, "who would you like to visit with?"

"Don't you hear it?" HARV whined. "It's ending the sentence with a preposition. It's 'with whom would you like to visit,' you binary buffoon."

"Will you cut it out?"

"Will I cut what out?" the droid said, confused, "have I disturbed you?"

"No, not at all," I said, trying to shake HARV out of my head. "Zach Johnson to see Grandma Backerman, please."

The android's eyes flashed for a nano.

"I'm sorry sir, but there is no person by that name residing here." The eyes flashed briefly again. "Though after consulting my extensive database, I have noticed that one of our tenants is named Barbara Backerman. Perhaps she is who you are looking for?"

"Gates, I don't believe it," HARV shouted inside my head. "It did it again. Where did this pseudo-brain get his programming, Robo-Shack?"

I ignored HARV again.

"That would be my guess," I said as I patted the droid on the back and entered the elevator.

"Mrs. Backerman resides on the two hundred fifty-sixth

floor," the droid said as it followed me into the elevator. "Do you wish to push the buttons yourself?"

"That's okay," I said, "knock yourself out."

"But sir, if I knock myself out how can I operate the high-rise-cargo-passenger-delivery-device?"

"It's a figure of speech." I had forgotten how literal most servant-droids were.

"The trip to floor two hundred fifty-six will take exactly forty-two seconds," the droid droned. "Please hang on to the side rails. If you are a resident of a province where tobacco products are still legal, please remember that tobacco products and by-products are forbidden on this device as required by . . ."

"I'm local," I said. "From New Frisco."

"I'm sorry sir, regulations," the droid replied, as the elevator began to rise. "We receive visitors from all provinces at this center, including those where tobacco is still legal. Since I am not connected with a worldwide residential database, I am unable to ascertain your province of residency. Therefore, it is only prudent to officially inform you of the regulations that you must adhere to.

"To which you must adhere," HARV said. "I can't believe they let this droid operate heavy machinery."

"I should also warn you," the droid continued, "that, although the use of cannabis products is currently allowed for medicinal purposes under current New California law, the use of such products within the confines of this passenger delivery device is prohibited."

"How long until we get there?" I said, trying hard to hold onto my sanity.

The elevator stopped and the droid paused, gathering its thoughts.

"We have reached your destination," it said at last. "Mrs. Backerman's room encompasses this entire wing. Therefore, you should have no difficulty finding what you are searching for."

"Please get away from this grammatical Cro-Magnon," HARV pleaded.

"Thanks," I said as I anxiously ended the elevator ride from cyber-hell.

The door to Ms. Backerman's suite was at the end of a short hallway, which was clearly well-monitored. I cautiously approached and pressed the call button under the view screen.

A woman's face appeared on the screen after a nano. The face was delicate and stunningly beautiful, reminiscent of BB herself, albeit a much younger BB than the one I knew.

"Zachary Johnson!" the woman exclaimed. "My goodness, what a surprise. What can I do for you?"

"I'm looking for Barbara Backerman," I answered.

"That would be me," she said.

"Let me be more specific. I'm looking for Barbara Backerman, the grandmother of BB Star."

The woman smiled again, almost coquettishly.

"Like I said dear, that would be me."

There are nanos during investigations when you uncover a simple piece of information and everything that you thought you knew suddenly gets turned on its head. The case takes on a whole new dimension and your entire plan for the investigation changes completely. I love those nanos.

This wasn't one of them.

But you have to admit it was pretty darn weird.

36

The woman who claimed to be Grandma Backerman had the face of a debutante model and the figure to which all debutante models aspire. She looked more than a dozen years younger than me and, more importantly, younger than BB. It's true that we live in strange times and that today's holograms and regen treatments can provide pretty fair makeovers. But this was light-years beyond anything I'd ever seen.

"You're Grandma Backerman?" I asked one last time as she ushered me into her sumptuous penthouse.

"Yes, dear, I am," she confirmed. "And that's the third time I've answered that question. Aren't you a micro young to be in need of a hearing implant?"

"I'm sorry," I said. "I'm just a little taken aback. It's not every day I meet a grandmother who looks nineteen."

"You flatter me, Mr. Johnson, " she giggled coyly. "My regen treatment has computer adjusted my appearance to be age twenty-two."

"Well, you wear the years well," I said. "And please, call me Zach. I must say that your regen treatment is simply astounding."

"I'm a very rich woman, Zach. I use only the best. Dr. S. Vitello performed the procedures himself."

"Didn't he do Madonna?"

"Oh, that was years ago. The technology is much more advanced now. This particular procedure is experimental and not yet available to the masses."

"Well, I'd say the procedure was a roaring success."

She laughed a girlish (yet grandmotherly) laugh and motioned me toward the floating antigrav couch in the sunken living room.

"I do so love the flattery of a young man," she said. "Now, what can I do for you, dear?"

"I'm doing some work for your granddaughter and I'd like to ask you a few questions, if you don't mind."

"I don't mind at all," she beamed. "Would this be regarding business or pleasure?" Her girlish hand touched my thigh.

"Strictly business, ma'am," I stated in (what I hoped was) a calm, professional voice.'

"Are you certain of that?" she asked as the hand moved a little further up my thigh.

I scooted away from her a bit on the couch.

"By any chance, did your regen treatment include massive hormonal transfusions?" I asked.

"Why do you ask?"

"I think you might want to get the levels reduced a bit."

"Hmmm, you know that would explain a lot of the cravings I've been having recently," she said. "But now, since I can't interest you in anything carnal, can I get you a nice glass of iced tea? It's the real thing, you know. The kind that we drank in my day. Not that imitation DOS you get in restaurants now. Gates, that spam hoovers like a spoofed meg of wormfood."

It was clear that Grandma Backerman's regen procedures also included some subconscious slang implantation. I was beginning to think that the success of the experimental treatment was not so rousing after all.

"Tea would be fine," I said.

No sooner had the words left my mouth then a tiny maidbot rolled dutifully into the room carrying two glasses of iced tea and a tray of cookies in her claws.

"That was quick," I said, as I took my tea and a cookie from the tray.

"Like I said, dear, I only use the very best," she said.

She took her tea and the maidbot rolled back into the kitchen so quickly I expected to see skid marks on the rug.

Grandma Backerman turned to me and took a sip of her tea. "So," she said, "what are these questions that are so important?"

"They concern BB," I replied.

"She's not in any trouble, is she?"

"No, not really. She's hired me to do some investigating for her and I just need some background on her childhood."

"Go right ahead," she said. "I'm so proud of my little baby."

"She speaks very highly of you as well." I said.

"Ah, yes. Bless her, I always said her heart was even bigger than her breasts."

"Did you know her husband at all?" I asked, trying hard to ignore that last comment.

"Oh, yes, her husband, or as I prefer to call him, BS-may-he-burn-in-the-fiery-bowels-of-purgatory-for-forever-and-a-day Star."

"I take it you weren't a fan of Mr. Star."

"Oh, Zach, the things I could tell you. The horrors that he put my baby through. She would call me in the middle of the night, crying over what he'd done to her. It was all I could do to keep her sane."

"He beat her?"

"And worse. I knew that man was no good from the very beginning. Pure poison. That's what he was. I tried so hard to talk her out of marrying him. But BB was in love and there's just no reasoning with a woman in love. After they married, and BS showed his true self, only then did she realize what a terrible mistake she had made."

"Why didn't she leave him?"

"Oh, Zach. I almost envy your naïveté. No one *leaves* BS

Star. A high-profile marriage like the one he and BB had, he'd never let her embarrass him like that. He'd kill her first."

"Or replace her," I said to myself.

"Pardon me, dear?"

"Nothing. Please go on."

"Well, BS's destructive behavior finally caught up with him and it was a wonderful day indeed when that sadistic pile of maggot spit finally shuffled off the mortal coil."

She paused for nano, then put her hand over her mouth. "Oops, I guess that wasn't a very grandma-like thing to say."

"Well, the mortal coil part was."

"But you get my point, don't you?"

"I think so, yes."

"Oh, good," she said. "Now, how about another cookie?"

At the merest mention of an offer, the maidbot quickly sped from the kitchen to the living room again, offering me the replenished tray of cookies, even though I'd yet to finish the first one.

"No, thank you. I'm fine," I said.

The maidbot sped back into the kitchen again.

"Gates, she's fast," I said. "I wonder, can you tell me a little bit about BB's childhood?"

"Her childhood?"

"Yes, she says that she used to spend her nights with you when she was very young. She says that those times were some of the best of her life."

Grandma smiled.

"Oh, that dear, sweet girl. I'm glad she remembers me so fondly. It wouldn't kill her to net me every once in a while but at least she remembers me, right?"

"Yes. But now about the nights she spent with you."

"There's not much to tell, really. Her mother, may she rest in peace, worked nights so she stayed with me."

"Stayed with you where?"

"My apartment."

"Where was that exactly?"

"Oh, hmmm, downtown I think. I don't really remember."

"You don't remember?"

"Gates, Zach, it was so long ago and I've lived in so many places."

"But you said that you had fond memories of that time as well."

"Oh, my memory comes and goes. I'm eighty-five, you know. Surely you understand?"

"Yes, I understand, ma'am. Let me ask you one other thing."

"Anything, dear."

"What do you think of cinnamon?"

"I beg your pardon?"

"BB says that when she remembers her time with you, she thinks of cinnamon. I'm just trying to understand what that means."

"Cinnamon. Ah, yes, there is a connection."

"Why cinnamon?"

"Honestly, I couldn't tell you why."

"Did you bake much?"

"Bake? Oh, dear me, no. It's a struggle for me to even open a box of cookies."

Grandma's mention of the word "cookies" brought the maidbot once again to the room. She rolled dutifully toward us at only slightly less than the speed of sound and offered me another cookie. I rolled my eyes and waved her away with my hand.

"Do you think it was some kind of incense or perfume?"

"Who can tell," she said, shrugging her shoulders. "You never know what's going to stick in a child's mind at that age.'"

"Well, what do you think of when you think of cinnamon."

"Cinnamon, hmmm. I think of warm nights."

"Warm nights."

"Yes, and sparkling yellow lights. Cinnamon is . . . like an old sweater, big and soft and warm smelling."

"That's, very poetic."

"Yes, I suppose it is. Who'd have thought that a granny would have it in her, eh?"

"What do you think it means exactly?"

"Well, goodness, I don't know, Zach. You're the detective after all. Now, how about some more tea?"

The maidbot again sped quickly into the livingroom.

"No, thank you. I'm fine."

And the maidbot sped back to the kitchen.

"A cookie then?"

The maidbot reappeared.

"No, thank you. But they're delicious."

The maidbot went back to the kitchen.

"Come now, you wouldn't want to hurt my feelings, would you?"

The maidbot returned.

"I'm sorry, but I'm really full."

And back to the kitchen.

"Well, then, one for the road."

The maidbot appeared again but I noticed that the status light on its forehead had changed from green to yellow.

"Really, ma'am, I'm on a strict diet."

The bot stuttered this time as it rolled back to the kitchen.

"Surely you have room for one more cookie."

The maidbot shook as it entered.

"Really, ma'am, I can't."

The bot disappeared again into the kitchen and finally gave up the ghost. Sparks flew from its motor housing and, just as the kitchen door closed, we heard a muffled explosion. Black smoke seeped through the cracks in the French door as it swung back and forth. An alarm sounded and we heard the sprinklers go off.

"Oh, dear."

A pair of fire-containment bots quickly rolled into the kitchen.

"I suppose another glass of tea wouldn't hurt," I said.

Grandma Backerman smiled and patted me on the knee, then climbed to her feet.

"Good boy," she said. "I'll be right back."

"Can I help you with something?" I said, standing up.

"Well, you could go to the main control panel and turn off the alarm," she said. "The firebots will have this under control in a nano."

"Where's the control panel?"

"In the hall closet, I think," she said. "Please pardon the clutter in there."

Grandma walked quickly into the kitchen while I turned the other way and went to the front hall. I opened the closet door and was immediately hit with a avalanche of grandma-type knickknacks as they tumbled off the overstocked shelves. Candles, tea cups and potpourri containers fell around me on all sides like a brick-a-brack avalanche and I took a number of Hummel-figurine hits to the head before the barrage finally ended. It had obviously been quite some time since Grandma Backerman had organized the closet (or, as I suspected, opened it at all).

The control panel was at the rear of the closet, behind some temporary shelving and I had to push aside more knickknacks to get to it. As I did, a pile of old papers fell onto my head and scattered across the floor. I caught a glimpse of them as they hit and I recognized Grandma Backerman's young face in one of the photos. I bent down and picked up one of the copies for a closer look.

The color was faded with age but the image was clear. It was indeed Grandma Backerman, back when her youthful looks were more natural. She wasn't nineteen in the photo, she was more mature, maybe forty or forty-five, worldly-wise, yet still beautiful. She actually looked a lot like BB does now. Her smile was subtle. Her eyes looked askance in a coy, "come hither" look. It was an advertisement for a strip club called the

Nexus 6 from forty years ago, and Grandma Backerman had been the headliner.

Remember when I said that every so often a simple bit of information will turn a case completely on its head? Well, as I looked at this poster, I felt the entire BB-2 mystery flip more times than a waffle in a centrifuge.

Grandma Backerman had been a headlining exotic dancer forty years ago, long about the time that BB remembered spending nights with her. But the bit of information that did the flipping was Grandma's stage name at the time. The revelation hit me so hard that I whispered it aloud.

"Cinnamon Girl."

37

I excused myself from Grandma Backerman's apartment as quickly and politely as I could and hurried down the hall to the elevator.

"How come she didn't mention that she was an exotic dancer?" HARV asked inside my head.

"Not now, HARV," I mumbled.

"And isn't it odd that she wouldn't mention that her stage name was 'Cinnamon'?"

"Great grasp of the obvious there," I said through gritted teeth. "But I don't want to talk about it until we're out of this building."

I was happy, though a bit surprised, to see the android operator waiting for me in the elevator ahead.

"Oh, great," HARV whispered, "another elevator ride with the grammar mangler."

I ignored HARV as the elevator droid very politely opened his transparent door at my approach and ushered me inside.

"Ground floor, please," I said as I entered.

"With great and absolute pleasure," the android said as the elevator door closed.

"Sentence fragment," HARV said.

"Please hang on to the side rails as we descend," the droid said. "If you are a resident of a province where tobacco products are still legal, please remember that tobacco products and by-products are forbidden on this device as required by . . ."

"Didn't we already go through this?" I asked.

"I'm sorry sir, regulations," the droid said. The elevator began its descent.

"I'm from New Frisco," I said. "I don't use tobacco, I don't use cannabis products of any kind and, as you can see, I am hanging on to the handrails. All I want now is to get to the ground."

The elevator came to a quick and jarring stop.

I peered through the plexi-walls and saw that we were between levels and still over two hundred floors above the ground.

"Uh-oh," HARV said inside my head.

"Ah, this isn't the ground floor," I said to the droid, though I was pretty certain that it already knew.

"Correct," it said.

"Have we stopped to pick up another passenger? If so you really need to stop at one of the floors."

"Your deduction is logical but incorrect," the droid replied. "I have no need at the present time to pick up any other passengers." It stabbed a button on the wall with its Teflon finger and the door to the outside popped open.

"You asked to be delivered to the ground," it said as it approached me, "and I shall make certain that you arrive there, albeit not in the manner which you asked for."

"For which you asked!" HARV shouted. "Gates, this thing can't even threaten correctly."

"HARV," I said as the droid lunged at me, "I think you're missing the big picture here."

There are a lot of things that go through your mind when you're two hundred stories above the ground and being attacked by an android (trust me, I've been through this a lot).

My first thought was: "Uh-oh, I'll never survive this fall" (the first reaction is always the most obvious). My second thought was that I should have expected something like this to happen. After all, it had been hours since the last attempt on my life and my recent run-ins with killer machines should have made me wary of this droid.

My third thought was much more helpful and it was echoed by HARV's words inside my head.

"Move your gluteus maximus, boss, or you'll be taking the terminal express to the ground floor!"

I understood HARV's warning (which scared me) but my gluteus maximus and I were already on the move. I shifted my weight to one side and ducked under the outstretched arms of the lunging droid. I elbowed it hard in the back of the neck and slammed its head into the plexiglass wall of the elevator.

It was a smooth move but I knew that it wouldn't hurt the droid all that much, so I scrambled to the other side of the elevator where I spun around and flicked my wrist, popping my gun into my hand.

"Listen buddy," I growled in my best bad-gluteus voice. "One step closer and I'll blow you into an expensive scrap pile of . . . whatever it is you're made from."

"That's it," HARV said. "Threaten it in a manner that it will recognize."

The droid just sort of shrugged its shoulders and took a step toward me.

"From this angle the force of your weapon's projectiles will not only destroy me but the antigravity circuits of this elevator as well. The elevator will go into freefall and crash to the ground below. Thus my purpose will be served. Therefore, please feel free to fire at will."

"Who's Will?" I asked.

The android stopped.

"You are trying to confuse me by pretending to think that my use of the word 'will' in the previous statement was a reference to a being named Will or William. I, however, am a model class SFC-5 android and cannot be confused so easily."

He took another menacing step forward.

"Give him a grammar test," HARV said. "That'll confuse him."

I ignored HARV and concentrated on the droid. "You talk pretty tough for a droid with its sock untied."

"First of all," the droid said, "I am an android, model class SFC-5, and therefore have no need for socks. Secondly, even if I were wearing socks they would not need to be tied as socks do not have laces."

"Therefore," I countered, "since your socks don't have laces, they cannot be tied and are therefore *untied.*"

The android stopped its approach. I had succeeded in baffling it with an illuminating display of pure illogic. It looked down at its feet and pondered its socks (or lack thereof).

I took advantage of the nano and lunged forward, dropping my shoulder and slamming into the droid's midsection. It stumbled backward toward the open door but caught itself at the last nano with a hand on the door frame. It reached its other hand out at me and, miraculously, the arm stretched, elongating itself like a telescope, easily spanning the distance between us. It grabbed me by the throat and tried to pull me toward the door.

"Ha!" it taunted. "Your ploy was clever, but you did not take into account my superior reflexes and state-of-the-art technology. I am an android, model class SFC-5, and I am stronger than you in every conceivable respect. Prepare to tumble to your death."

I grabbed the handrail and held on tight, as the droid tried to pull me toward the door.

"Sorry, bub," I said "but I'm obligated to hold on to the handrail. You understand, regulations."

"You are no match for me," it replied, increasing its pull.

I felt my hand slip on the railing, but I knew that I didn't need to hold on much longer.

"It's not the strength that matters here," I said as I raised my gun. "It's the angle."

The droid frowned.

"I'm sorry but firearms are not permitted in this conveyor."

"Excuse me if I bend the rules just a bit," I said.

Then I pulled the trigger.

My gunblast blew a football-sized hole in the droid's chest, short circuiting most of the major functions in its CPU. I broke the droid's grip on my neck and kicked the sparking frame in the head. It tumbled backwards out of the elevator and into a freefall to its termination.

HARV appeared from the projector in my lens and watched with me as the droid hit the ground below, shattering into a gazillion pieces upon impact.

"Wow," HARV said. "Talk about your split infinitives."

38

HARV and I didn't speak again until we were safely back on the ground, in the car and on the street. And even then, we didn't talk about what was really on our minds. The information was too new, too fresh and I was afraid to think about it too hard before it had a chance to sink in. So instead, we made small talk.

"Androids," I said, shaking my head, "they fall for the 'untied sock' line every time. You better contact the Centurion Center management and let them know that one of their androids' . . . malfunctioned. You were recording the confrontation, weren't you?"

"Of course I was recording," HARV answered. "I didn't just roll off the assembly line yesterday, you know. But it doesn't matter. ExShell owns the complex and their computer assures me that there will be no questions asked about the late, great, grammatically challenged, android model class SFC-5."

We drove some more in silence but HARV was clearly getting impatient. He hummed a Bach sonata for awhile to appear casual but he just couldn't hold back the questions that were buzzing through his CPU.

"Did you notice that Mrs. Backerman incorrectly stated her age?" he asked.

"Stop it."

"Stop what?"

"Stop talking about it," I said.

"But why?"' HARV asked. "Everything we learned from Ms. Star's grandmother raises more questions about the investigation."

"I know that."

"Then why don't you want to talk about it?"

"Two reasons," I said. "One is that whenever we openly discuss new information or communicate over unsecured lines, bad things happen."

"You mean like your car?"

"Yes."

"And the hovercraft?"

"Yes."

"And the elevator droid?"

"I'm not sure, but you see the pattern, don't you?"

"You think we're being monitored?"

I said nothing and HARV understood.

"And the second reason?" he asked.

"The what?"

"The second reason that you don't want to discuss how Mrs. Backerman's information affects the case."

"Because, in a very strange way, things are beginning to make sense."

"And?"

"And it's starting to scare me."

We drove for another twenty minutes through the city. I doubled back three or four times, and only partly because I thought we might be being followed (it also drove HARV crazy).

The sun was just going down when I parked the car high on a hilltop just outside the downtown area. The city was spread out beneath me like circuits on a logic board. The lights of the buildings were just starting to come on as the orange glow of the setting sun waned like a power indicator in the nanos after shutdown. I could see almost the entire city from the hilltop, all the way to the old bridge.

"Why are we here?" HARV asked.

"Because of my paranoid nature," I said.

I lifted the door latch, opened the door and stepped out of the car.

And into the audiophonic eye of the storm.

The hilltop was the nexus of the city's four major skyways and in the early evening hours, it was among the highest trafficked areas in the new world. I turned my face skyward and saw what must have been ten thousand personal hovercraft crisscrossing the air above. They were blurs of motion and the cacophony of their engines was deafening.

"I feel inclined to warn you," HARV shouted inside my head, "that another two minutes of unprotected exposure to this volume of noise will cause permanent damage to your hearing."

I smiled, reached into my pockets and pulled out a pair of ultrapowerful earplugs, the kind that are standard issue for skyway construction workers, artillery soldiers, and roadies for the thirty-five most popular teen boy bands. I slid them snugly into my ears and the clamor ceased almost instantly.

"Explain to me again," HARV said, "why we're here."

I hopped onto the hood of the Mustang (being careful not to scratch the paint) and lay out flat on the hood, looking up at the heavy traffic above.

"This is the noisiest place in the city," I said. "If someone is monitoring our outside communications and somehow listening to our conversations, I think this is our best natural defense. We can hear ourselves talk above this din, thanks to the interface, but an eavesdropper couldn't hear me now if I were shouting in his ear."

"Crude and obvious," HARV replied, "but ingenious. So, where do we start?"

"Let's start with the concrete stuff," I said. "BB's grandmother was a dancer at a club called the Nexus 6. Find me whatever you can on her and that club."

"Check. And meanwhile?"

"Meanwhile, we ask ourselves the big question."

"You mean, 'How many roads must a man walk down?'"

"The *other* big question," I said.

"Which is?"

"Why?"

"Why what?"

"Why didn't Grandma tell us she was a dancer named Cinnamon Girl? Why did she get her age wrong? Why have at least three machines tried to kill me recently? Why didn't BB-2 kill Pierce when she had the chance? Why has she hooked up with Manuel Mani? And why do people keep telling us that BB and BS had such a horrible life together when it's common gossip that BS died while having sex?"

"So the 'big question' is sort of a multi-parter?"

"Yeah, sort of."

I stared silently at the city for a few nanos, trying to wrap my head around the various bits of information and put them into some kind of coherent picture. Then HARV prodded me along.

"C factor," he said.

"What?"

"Your question about BS's death. That's the logic flaw in your equation. You're ignoring the C factor."

"Which means what exactly?" I asked.

"Well, you're starting with the supposition that BS died during sex, let's call that Supposition A, and supposedly disproving it with the evidence, let's call it B, which indicates that BS and BB did not have sex. If not B then not A. However, you're not taking into account that A is not necessarily contingent upon B. You can theoretically prove A using other evidence, meaning that the equation could be 'if C then A.' Hence, the C factor. That being that BS may have died during sex . . ."

"But with someone other than BB," I said.

"That possibility exists, at least in theory."

"I hadn't thought of that."

"Clearly not," HARV said with a smile. "And as for the Nexus 6, it has a long and colorful history in this city which I've downloaded and condensed for your perusal at some future time. I think, however, that we can forego the history entirely."

"Why's that?"

"Because the club recently reopened."

"What?"

"A once-popular bar called The Happy Hacker closed its doors three weeks ago and reopened one week later under the name Nexus 9."

"Nexus 9?"

"Admittedly, not an exact match," HARV said. "But I think you'll agree that it's definitely odd."

I smiled.

"It is indeed." I hopped off the hood of the car and opened the driverside door. "Come on, buddy. Let's go to a nightclub and see if we can't find this renegade, android, sex-toy, killing machine."

I stopped suddenly and felt the revelation wash over me like an icy shadow.

"Oh boy."

"What?" HARV asked.

"The C factor," I said, "what if it's her?"

"What do you mean?"

"What if BS did die during sex, with someone other than BB, like you said. What if he died while having sex with BB-2?"

"Well, then," HARV said. "I think the proper response would be 'uh-oh.'"

39

In the days before I met Electra and became a one-woman man, I spent many a wondrous night at places like the Nexus 9. Pulling up to the club in the shank of the evening made me wax a little nostalgic for those days. The nostalgia ended a few nanos later when I got out of the car and stepped into a pool of vomit in the parking lot.

"I'm glad to see that the level of establishment you choose to frequent hasn't changed," HARV said.

"Hey, the vomit's *outside* the club. That's a step up right there."

I walked toward the club entrance, wiping my shoe along the pavement as I moved.

The club itself, was a small metal, hangar-type building. It had once been the home office of an internet B2B business exchange back in the first incarnation of the world wide web. The company went bust after the great internet collapse in the early part of the century. The owners of the company, billionaires one nano, bankrupt the next, committed mass suicide and broadcast the ritual over the web as a symbolic farewell to the fickle multitudes of internet users. Ironically, the company's server went down halfway through the ritual so no one actually saw the event, and the departed webmasters' message, like many others sent over the old web, went unheard.

Needless to say, the heirs of the company's owners became somewhat distrustful of technology after that and turned the once-mighty corporate headquarters into a very low-tech bar and grill. Technology comes and goes, they claimed, but booze and fried food never go out of style (a place after my own heart). And thus was born The Happy Hacker. How it suddenly became the Nexus 9 was something I needed to find out.

The place was dark, dilapidated, decrepit and as run down as a stupid meter at a World Council meeting. But from the sounds of the loud music and laughter coming from within, it was clear that ambiance didn't matter much to the patrons.

"A charming place indeed," HARV said with a bit of disgust. "I thought that the post-apocalyptic look went out with the last apocalypse."

"It's called atmosphere, HARV."

"Ah, yes. Too bad the atmosphere is not enough to support intelligent life."

"Good one. Can I use that?"

"Yes, but only in emergencies," HARV said. "And I'll want royalties."

Inside, the club looked about as no-tech as you could get, short of having dinosaur meat on a spit. A big bar at the rear of the room kept the food frying and the drinks flowing. The tables were all full, as were the stools at the bar, and most of the standing space was occupied as well (busy night). A dry ice machine in the back produced the necessary dive-bar smoke effects (sans nicotine) and a tobacco-scented filter gave the air that annoying stench to which bar dwellers of this sort are so accustomed. A few scantily clad dancers (male and female) bumped and ground on scattered stages and raised podiums for the adoring patrons. All in all, I hated to admit it, the place was beginning to grow on me.

Two bouncers, one man and one woman, met me at the door. Both were tall and muscular and clad in black faux leather jumpsuits. They were pale-skinned, had dull, black hair that was cropped short and spiky, and wore perpetual scowls on their faces. They looked for all the world like a pair of S&M fraternal twins.

I took special note of the fact that they both carried heavy-duty stun guns. Clearly they were more into the "S" then the "M."

The woman stepped forward to meet me and put her large hand in my face in the universal stop-right-there-before-I-break-your-clavicle position.

"Stop," she said. "Your computer may not enter." Her voice was deep with undertones of an eastern European accent.

"Excuse me?"

She pointed at the computer interface on my wrist.

"Computers are forbidden within the club. They are to be checked at the door."

She paused and took a closer look at my face, studying it. Then she smiled (and I use the term loosely).

"Wait," she said, "you are Zachary Johnson?" She turned to her fellow bouncer before I could reply. "Look, Dieter, it's Zachary Nixon Johnson."

Dieter, who had been looking aloof and dangerous all this time, turned his gaze, ever so slightly towards me and continued looking aloof and dangerous.

"Yes, Diedre," he said in a similarly eastern European monotone. "It is."

"If it's not, then it's an incredible coincidence that these shoes fit so well," I said.

Dieter scowled.

"I don't get it," he said.

"I think it's a joke," Diedre said.

"I don't get it," Dieter repeated.

"It was only a small joke," I said.

Diedre ignored Dieter and stepped closer to me, gently placing her face mere inches from my own. "I enjoy your work," she said.

"Really?"

"I loved it when you threw that scientist into the vat of acid."

"Actually, he fell," I said. "I was trying to save him. And he was going to drop poison into the water supply."

"And the time you blew up that mad bomber."

"I detonated the bomb after I teleported the bomber to the police."

"And when you broke the nose of the teenage pop singer?"

"She was sampling Elvis. She had it coming."

"You are vicious and violent," she said somewhat breathlessly. "I hope that someday I too will have the chance to be like you and throw a scientist to his imminent death."

"Um, yeah," I said, gently taking a step back. "It's good to have career goals, I guess. Look, since we're all buddies now, how about letting me keep my computer inside?"

"I will think about it," Dieter said. Then he paused a nano and furrowed his brow. "No."

"Yeah, well, I appreciate your thinking about it, Dieter," I said. "I know how difficult that is for you."

I handed him the wrist interface and walked into the main room.

"I think he just made fun of you," Diedre said.

"I don't get it," Dieter said with a scowl.

I went to the restroom and ducked into the first empty stall I found. HARV reflected himself from my eye lens and stood beside me.

"No computers allowed," he said, as he shuddered gently in disgust. "We are truly in the barbarian's den this time.'"

"Yeah, but the burgers are great," I said. "Now listen, here's the plan."

"You actually have a plan?"

"There's a first time for everything. Run a scan of the bar. Isolate any anomalies that could be signs of BB-2."

"You call that a plan?" HARV asked. "I did that the nano we entered. Observe."

A digitized playback of my walk through the bar flashed in front of my left eye.

"I recorded the input from your eye lens," HARV said.

"It's giving me a headache."

"Close your right eye until you get used to the playback," HARV said. "Ripping-edge technology is never painless. Now watch closely. I didn't detect BB-2's presence anywhere in the establishment but there are some interesting characters around."

The playback froze and a cursor appeared around the image of a large man in the crowd.

"My data banks indicate that this man works in the weapons R&D unit of HTech," HARV said.

"Interesting."

The playback fast forwarded and froze again with a cursor appearing over the image of another, equally large, man seated at a table.

"This man works for ExShell R&D. The two of them in the same room make this establishment a veritable powder keg."

"R&D competition between the two companies is that fierce?"

"Not really, but both of them are currently hitting on the red-headed dancer."

"Anything else?" I sighed.

The playback rewound at high speed and came to rest on the image of a very familiar-looking small man.

"Just this."

It was the greeting card salesman from BB's office.

"Gates," I said, "that's the weasel from BB's office."

"Oh, yeah," HARV said, surprised. "I guess it is. I just high-lighted him because he's wearing such an ugly tie. What the DOS is he thinking wearing horizontal stripes with his body type?"

"I have to talk to him," I said.

234 John Zakour & Lawrence Ganem

"I lost him in the crowd during your discussion with the rocket scientist bouncers," HARV said.

"Let's see if we can track him down. In the meantime, I think I'll go to bar."

I left the stall and tried hard to ignore the stares of my fellow patrons in the restroom.

"By the way," HARV said, "you really should learn how to do nonverbal communication."

I was at the bar a nano later and, after several minutes, managed to successfully call the tender over (like I said, busy night). He was a small, sheepish, unmarried-uncle kind of guy.

"What will it be, Mac?" he asked.

"Information," I answered.

"You want a smart drink?"

"No, I mean real information."

"I'm not sure I remember how to make that," he said slyly.

"I'll make it worth your while."

"I'll tell you now that my while is worth a lot."

"No problem," I said.

"What do you need?"

"I'm looking for a woman."

"Oh, then you'll want to talk to Pierre. He's the flesh tender."

"No, no. I'm looking for a very specific woman. I think she's a dancer here."

"I don't know. A lot of dancers come through here."

"You'll remember this one," I said. "She looks just like BB Star."

The tender stiffened suddenly and dropped the glass he was holding. He turned to me, zombie-like and stared.

"You're looking for BB?" he said as his eyes flashed electronic red.

"Uh-oh," HARV said inside my head.

"He's a droid," I gasped. "HARV, why didn't you tell me he was a droid?"

"I didn't . . . I didn't . . . I didn't know," HARV stuttered.

"Hey everyone," the tender shouted, "this guy's looking for BB!"

The bar fell deathly silent and, though I couldn't see them, I had a sneaking suspicion that everyone in the bar was staring at me through similar sets of electronic red droid eyes.

40

I had fallen into another trap and this one was a real mega-palooza. I'd been dogged by brainless thugs and killer machines since I first took this case and began looking for BB-2. I had survived every encounter but now whoever was after me had combined the two approaches and, like a rank amateur, I had walked into the den of killer thug machines.

"I'm hoping," HARV said inside my head, "that your plan covered this contingency."

I stared at the droid bartender as he spoke and saw the other approaching droids reflected in his glassy, red eyes.

"BB left a message for you," he said robotically. "She said to have a nice death."

The first droid attacked from behind but I saw the reflection in the tender's eyes and ducked at the last nano. The droid's fist sailed over me and hit the tender squarely in the face, severing his head from his shoulders.

I rolled for cover and came up into a crouch in one fluid motion. I popped my gun into hand and blasted a meter-wide hole in the nearest droid (the guy HARV had flagged as the ExShell R&D engineer).

"Call the cops now," I screamed to HARV. "Tell them there's a riot at the Nexus 9."

"Good, they'll be here just in time to scoop up your body parts and put them into plastic baggies."

"Shut up, HARV, and do as you're told!" I shouted as I

blasted another droid. "You should have told me that the bar was filled with droids the nano we walked in.

HARV was clearly shaken and was quickly falling into one of his panic modes.

"I didn't know. They were somehow cloaked from my sensors. But that's impossible. I need to run a diagnostic."

"Run it later," I said. "If there *is* a later. I need you right now."

I ducked under the arms of a lunging droid, blasted its face into high-tech confetti, then hopped onto the bar and leaped onto the main stage.

The comedian who had been performing couldn't quite understand how he had lost his audience so quickly.

"Hey, folks, what is this, a nightclub or a government hearing?" he shouted.

The droids ignored him and continued their pursuit of me.

"I get no respect. No respect at all," he mumbled. Then his eyes flashed red and he took a swing at me. I shot him in the chest and threw his body into the audience, where it was ripped apart.

"Tough crowd."

I found some tenuous cover behind one of the dancer's podiums. The club wall protected my back and the high angle allowed me to keep the droids back with some well-placed gunblasts. I picked off a few but I knew that their numbers would eventually overwhelm me.

"DOS, is everyone in the bar a droid?"

"I'm clearly no longer a reliable judge of these things," HARV said solemnly. "Gates, what else am I not detecting?"

"Stay with me, HARV."

I blew the head off another droid as it leaped at me from the ceiling. I was happy to see that it was the greeting card salesman from BB's office.

"Gates, that felt good." I said. "That wasn't the real weasel, was it?"

"No," HARV said. "The police computer reports that the true greeting card salesman is currently at home taking a bath."

"Too bad," I said. "That would have made this all worth-while."

"Look on the bright side," HARV said, "at least they're not armed."

"Armed?" I said, suddenly remembering the high-powered stun guns that the bouncers had been packing. "Uh-oh."

I rolled away from the podium just as twin stun gun blasts slammed it solidly in a crossfire. I saw Dieter and Diedre out of the corner of my eyes as I rolled again along the floor beneath the angry weapon fire.

"This case just gets better and better," I said.

I grabbed the body of the headless bartender and shielded myself with it as I stood up and fired off a flurry of rounds at first Dieter then Diedre.

"You're rapidly running low on ammunition," HARV warned.

"Shut up, HARV. You're killing the moment."

I fired a round at the dry ice machine and blasted it to bits. The full compartment of dry ice hit the interior water reservoir and heavy mist flooded the room.

"Where did he go?" Diedre shouted. I noted that she had re-tained the personality subroutine of her programming. She and Dieter were clearly the most advanced of the droids and, quite probably, directing the drone droids through some prepro-grammed fight strategies.

"I don't know," Dieter said. "I can't see through the smoke."

I fired off another flurry of rounds at random, creating as much mayhem as I could, as I formulated my plan and skulked quickly through the mist.

"What do we do when they go to infrared vision," HARV asked.

"Shut up, HARV, or you'll blow this."

And at that nano, I bumped smack into the faux leather column of bionic circuitry that was Diedre's thigh.

"Switch to infrareds," Dieter said a nano later.

"Wait," Diedre yelled. "I have him."

Diedre emerged from the mist with an arm wrapped tightly around my neck and her stun pistol pressed hard against my temple.

"He was crawling toward the exit," she spat.

"Good," Dieter said. "Now kill him and fulfill our programmed task."

"Shouldn't we take him to our boss first?"

"That was not our instruction."

"I know, but I thought that the boss might want to kill him herself."

"What did you say?"

"I mean *him*self. The boss might like to kill him himself . . . herself? Um, who's our boss again?"

Dieter raised his stun pistol.

"Oh, DOS," I said.

HARV's holographic illusion melted away and what once appeared to be Diedre holding my unconscious form was replaced by me holding the headless body of the bartender.

"I knew it," Dieter said.

"Congratulations," I said as I hurled the tender's body at him, "here's your prize."

The tender's body hit Dieter just as he fired, twisting his gun hand and sending the blast into the metal ceiling overhead. The old support beams crumbled from the blast and a huge chunk of the roof came down on top of him, squashing him like a slow-witted insect (ironic, huh?).

My victory, however, was short lived because a nano later, Diedre's high-powered stun blast hit me squarely in the back and slammed me into the far wall.

"You should have hit me harder, little Zach," she said. "Perhaps you are not so vicious after all."

She raised her pistol and prepared to deliver the coup de grace (that's French for "the big lights out").

"I only regret that there is no vat of acid nearby."

A blaster fired.

Luckily for me, it wasn't Diedre's.

The blast hit Diedre in the shoulder and spun her around violently before she finally hit the floor. Her pistol flew from her hand as she fell.

"New Frisco Police!" Tony Rickey shouted. "You're all under arrest."

The cavalry had arrived.

The sight of Tony and twenty of his best officers, in full riot gear, striding into the club was enough to warm my heart.

"How's it going, Tony?"

"Zach, is that you?"

Unfortunately, Tony's awe-inspiring presence wasn't enough to stop the remaining two dozen androids from trying to complete their programming (i.e., killing me). The droids, without Dieter and Diedre to coordinate their attack, began to close in on me, en masse.

"Are you people deaf?" Tony shouted. "I told you all to freeze!"

"Tony, they're droids!"

"What?"

The droids leaped upon me. I blasted two to shreds but was soon overwhelmed and covered by their malevolent, high-tech pigpile of death. Thankfully, Tony came to the rescue again.

"Open fire!" he shouted. "Shoot anything in that mess that's not Zach Johnson."

And the fireworks began again.

The droids, as tenacious as they were, were no match for Tony and his men and, a few minutes later, they lifted me safely from a huge pile of droid dreck.

"I should have known you'd be in the middle of this," Tony said. "Do you need a medbot?"

"No, I'm fine, thanks," I said. "Thanks a lot for coming. I know you have a lot of really important police matters to take care of so I wouldn't think of keeping you."

I stood up but Tony grabbed my coat and pulled me roughly back down beside him.

"Let's talk, Zach."

"Fine," I said. "Um, how's the family? Kay doing well? The kids? Is that dog of yours housebroken yet?"

"Zach, as you know, creating an android with realistic skin tones is a felony class A offense. I just pulled you out of a pile of them."

"And have I mentioned how grateful I am to you for that?"

"I should run you in!"

"For what? Getting beaten up?"

"In the past three days there has been a fight in your office, you've destroyed a car, a hover, an elevator droid—yes I know about that one—and Gates only knows what else. And now this."

"It's been a busy week," I conceded.

"I don't like these things going on in my town."

"As if I like them happening to me."

"I'm not joking here, Zach. I'm afraid that you might be in over your head this time. I'll help you in any way I can but you have to tell me what the DOS is going on."

"Tony, I know how hard this is for you but you're going to have to trust me on this one. I need twenty-four hours to tie this up. That's all. Give me that much time and I'll explain everything to you."

"And if you run into more trouble during that time?"

"You have my blessing to barge in and save my butt."

Tony shook his head.

"One of these days, you know, I'm not going to be there when you need me."

"It'll make up for all of those times when you were there for me when I *didn't* need you."

He sighed and threw his hands up in exasperation.

"You have twenty-four hours, Zach. After that, I'm coming to your home with a warrant and you're telling me everything. Got it?"

"It's a deal." I climbed to my feet and straightened my coat. "Um, Tony?"

"Yeah?"

"I need one last favor."

"What's that?" he said suspiciously.

I lifted the severed head of the droid bartender from the floor. The wires from the neck were still sparking as they dangled.

"Can I keep this? My, uh, car needs a new hood ornament."

41

A little while later the bartender's head sat on an examination table in Randy's lab while Randy, still half asleep, attached electrodes to its complex innards. I paced impatiently behind him.

"I'm in a bit of a hurry here, Randy."

"It's two in the morning, Zach. I'm sorry if my neurons aren't firing fast enough for you."

"I apologize again for the rude awakening, but I really need to know what's inside this droid's head."

"Just give me another minute to hardwire into the memory circuits and this little guy will tell you everything you want to know," Randy said. "This is an interesting design, by the way."

"Do you recognize it?"

"Not exactly but the chip design is very reminiscent of Ben Pierce's later work."

"Is it from ExShell?"

"I doubt it," Randy said. "The chip design is advanced but the droid itself is poorly made. It looks like a rush job, a disposable model."

Randy fused the last of the connections with his microlaser and then stood up.

"It's ready to go," he said. "But we have to be careful. The circuits have been severely damaged and they won't stand up to much grilling. If you give this thing too much to think about, it will explode."

"But it will answer all our questions truthfully?"

"I've hardwired my device directly into its main memory. It can't lie."

"Turn it on."

Randy threw the power switch on the exam table and the droid head began to stir. Stray sparks flew from the connections inside the neck and the skin of its forehead began to wrinkle in simulated consternation. Finally the eyes opened.

"What'll . . . it . . . be . . . Mac?" it said.

Randy nudged me gently and whispered in my ear.

"It's following its background programming. Pretend it's still a bartender."

"This is silly," I said.

"Humor it. Remember, any excess stimulation and the entire thing will short out."

I turned back to the droid's head.

"Don't got . . . all . . . night . . . pal. What'll . . . it . . . be?"

Randy nudged me again.

"A beer would be fine," I said. "Something with a head."

"Coming . . . right . . . up."

"Yeah, I'm sure."

"What? . . . . . ." the droid head sputtered.

Randy elbowed me in the ribs again.

"I told you to be careful."

"I mean, I'd sure like to get some information."

"Sure . . . Mac."

"Where were you created?" I asked.

"ExShell," it replied.

"When?"

"Ten days ago. You want . . . some . . . pretzels?"

"Yeah, sure. Who is your creator?"

"Manuel Mani. You want . . . that drink . . . freshened?"

This was getting interesting.

"Who gave you your programming?"

"World Association of . . . drink mixers . . . want another?"

"Who programmed you to kill me?" I asked angrily. "Who programmed you to kill me when I asked about BB Star?"

The droid head shook itself, confused and clearly distraught.

"How about . . . . . . one on the . . . house?"

"It's not going to last much longer," Randy said.

"Who programmed you to kill me!" I shouted. "Tell me or you get no tip."

"Fred Burns."

You could have knocked me over with a feather.

"What?"

"Fred . . . Burns."

"Fred Burns from ExShell?"

"Yes."

"The pale, fleshy guy. *That* Fred Burns."

"Yes."

"Fred Burns from ExShell programmed you to kill me?"

"Zach," Randy said. "You're being sort of redundant here."

I knew that, but I still couldn't believe it.

"Fred Burns?"

The droid head began to shake. It let out a high-pitched keening noise and flopped around on the table like a goldfish on a kitchen floor.

"She didn't want to hurt anybody," it said. "She just . . . wanted to find her . . . place."

"Who wanted?" I asked. "You mean BB-2?"

"She just . . . wants to be . . . left alone. How 'bout another? How 'bout them Giants? . . . she didn't want to hurt anyone."

Randy took my arm and tried to pull me away.

"It's going to blow."

I ignored him.

"Then why did she and Burns program you to kill me?"

"What?"

"You heard me. If she didn't want to hurt anyone, how come she programmed you to kill me?"

The head froze for a nano, thinking. Then it trembled again and started singing (painfully off key).

"My wild . . . Irish Rose!"

"Zach, duck!" Randy yelled and pulled me to the floor.

The droid head exploded into a small ball of flaming metal, silicon shrapnel and Irish ditties.

"You short circuited it when you pointed out the contradiction," Randy said. "You blew its mind."

"Just as well," I said. "He was a lousy bartender."

42

Randy gave me a new wrist interface to replace the one I lost at the Nexus 9, then HARV and I were back on the street. I was angry with myself for totally underestimating Burns and frustrated at the fact that it took me this long to realize the mistake. My head (or rather my heart) had obviously been elsewhere at times during this investigation and it wasn't hard to figure out where.

"Excuse me, but where are we going?" HARV asked as I turned onto the highway. "The ExShell laboratories are in the other direction. Your office is in the other direction. Pretty much everywhere you should want to go right now is in the other direction. I thought that being a PI you'd be better at these things."

"We're going to the hospital," I said.

"Why? You've been beaten up much worse than this before. DOS, you've received more severe injuries at poetry readings."

"I need to talk to Electra."

"Oh, you are a brave man," HARV said. "You miss her, don't you. I can tell these things."

"I need to warn her," I said. "There are some serious people after me. They might try to get to me through her."

"I'm sure she knows that," HARV said. "That's just the status quo."

"It's worse this time. I need to warn her."

"It's the middle of the night, you know"

"She's on the overnight shift," I said. "I checked the schedule."

"I could net her and save some time."

"I'm going to see her, all right?" I said sternly. "I'm going to see her. I'm going to talk to her. I'm going to warn her."

"Fine," HARV said. "Now that you mention it, it makes sense to warn her in person. It's more secure. Good thinking."

We drove in silence for a few nanos.

"I miss her," I said.

HARV smiled.

"I knew that."

A few minutes later, I was waiting for an elevator at New Frisco General Hospital, trying hard not to think about how angry Electra would be when she saw me.

"One thing, I don't understand," I said. "How come the hallways here are so dull?"

"Excuse me?" HARV asked.

"I mean, they can cure diseases, replace vital organs and regrow limbs at this hospital. How come they can't design a decent looking hallway?"

"Maybe 'they' have better things to do with their time," HARV answered. "You know, like curing the sick, caring for the infirm and raising the standard of living for their patients."

"Yeah, but how hard could it be to make the hallways more interesting? For instance, do they have to be white? And how about hanging some artwork?"

"Will you stop with the hallways, already?" HARV said. "With all the data hitting the hard drive now, you don't have anything better to think about?"

"Yeah, well excuse me for making conversation," I said.

"I know you're nervous about seeing Dr. Gevada, boss . . ."

"Nervous?" I said. "Who said anything about being nervous? I am genuinely interested in the phenomenon of the perpetually mundane corridor design."

HARV rolled his eyes, "Please tell me now the best way to end this pathetic line of conversation."

At that nano, the elevator arrived.

"You're not interested in elevator décor are you?" HARV asked.

I shrugged.

"There's not much to say about elevators, really."

"Good, Then let's go.

We stepped into the elevator (which, thankfully, had no droid operator) and I gave my instructions directly to the computer.

"Tenth floor, please."

"Yes, sir. With pleasure," the elevator answered cheerily. "Would you like to select your music option?" It asked as we began to rise.

"Silence is good," I said.

The computer paused for a nano.

"I'm sorry sir. There is no song entitled 'Silence is Good' in my database. There is a classic song called 'The Sounds of Silence.' There is also a new release by Freddie and the Mutant Accountants called 'Silence: Who the DOS Needs It!' Perhaps you'd like one of these selections?"

"No," I said. "I want just plain silence. No music. I want to be bathed in the serenity of my own thoughts."

"Oh, okay," the elevator said, more than little disheartened.

We reached the tenth floor shortly thereafter and the door slid open.

"Please watch your step on the way out," the elevator said. "I hope you enjoyed the ride. Please consider me on the way down."

I stepped off the elevator and sighed as the doors closed behind me.

"I'd really like to get my hands on the guy who thought intelligent elevators were a good idea."

"Believe me, you don't want to go there," HARV said. "Besides, with your past record with elevators, I would think you would be grateful it didn't try to kill you."

Electra had been in surgery for most of the night, putting a new spine into a ten-year-old boy who'd been paralyzed in a hover crash. (You have to love a woman who spends her evenings doing stuff like that).

She was tired when she came into the break room but I knew that she'd be up for the rest of the night in the ICU monitoring the kid's reaction to the surgery. I'd seen her do things like that a thousand times before. Her dedication was one of the many things that I loved about her.

Needless to say, after an already long and tiring night, the sight of me waiting for her didn't exactly fill her with joy. (But at least she didn't attack me).

"Hola, chico. How'd you get in here?"

"Hey, I'm a doctor too, you know." I offered her one of the cups of coffee in my hand, skim milk, no sugar, the way she likes it.

"A Ph.D. in psychology doesn't count for much here. Especially since your dissertation is now about five years late."

"Details, details."

She took the coffee and sat beside me.

"I bribed the security guys," I said. "Told them I was in love."

"With BB Star?"

"That's a low blow."

"I've seen lower."

She took a sip of the coffee, then ran her fingers through her hair and gently rubbed the muscle at the base of her neck that always gets sore during surgery. It was all I could do not to reach out and help her ease the pain.

"Rough night?"

"I've had better," she said.

"The kid okay?"

"We'll know by morning."

"You look tired."

"I'm doing double shifts this week. Trying to get as much done as possible before the funding runs out at the end of the month."

We sat silently for a long time. She drank her coffee. I fidgeted awkwardly, feeling like a teenager trying to tell his teacher about his crush.

"So, I've missed you."

"I've missed you too," she said. "Like a yeast infection."

"Good one. Can I use that?"

"You can if you want, but you need a vagina to make it funny."

"That's probably a bit far to go for a good line," I replied. "But I'll think about it."

She smiled, but only a little.

"Seriously," I said, "I really do miss you."

"I've heard it before, chico."

"You know that BB Star totally blindsided me on that whole lover/sex-toy thing. You know it's not true."

She just shook her head.

"I don't want to keep going through this, Zach. I'm tired of making excuses. I'm tired having to explain to everyone that my boyfriend's not having an affair with BB Star, or that he's not an alien agent from Glad 7 or that he's not gay."

"I understand that . . . wait, where'd you hear the gay thing?"

"You insult me when you do things like that. Worse still, you insult what we have. You turn it into a joke. I don't want to be with a man who doesn't respect the relationship. Comprende?"

"Comprendo."

"And I'm sick of having to show up somewhere with a laser cannon to save your sorry ass. I'm a doctor, DOS it. I'm tired of shooting at people."

"Yeah, I can see how that presents a moral dilemma for you."

"So, is that why you're here?"

"Well, the official reason is to warn you," I said. "I've got some people after me."

She took a sip of her coffee and rubbed her forehead.

"Who's trying to kill you now?"

"Pretty much everybody. So you might want to be careful. You never know when my enemies might decide that they're your enemies as well."

"Frankly, chico, if your enemies were to show up right now, I think we'd just compare notes. This thing you're in is getting serious?"

"Yeah, you could say that. Right now I'm looking for this crackpot, Fred Burns. After that, I think all hell is going to break loose."

"You mean Dr. Fred Burns?" she asked.

"You've heard of him?"

"I read some of his proposals before he went corporate," she said. "He's a pretty sharp guy as I recall. Some of the viruses he was working on were downright scary."

"You mean computer viruses."

She shook her head. "Biological."

"It's a different guy then. This Fred Burns is an engineer."

"Is he a pale, flabby hombre?" she asked. "Looks like a slab of blanched turkey, only not as appealing? Talks like a soap opera villain?"

"Yeah, that's him."

"Right. His early work was biological. He turned engineer maybe five or six years ago. I went to one of his seminars. He struck me as a very strange man—muy loco."

"And he specialized in biological viruses?"

"Nasty ones. What do you want with him?"

I felt my legs go numb and my mind started running through

a dozen possible scenarios for how this information changed things. None of them were good.

"You okay, chico?"

"Yeah, fine," I said. "Look, I'm sorry. I have to go."

"Go ahead," she said. "I have to get back to this kid's spine anyway."

The two of us got up and headed towards the door.

"What about the unofficial reason?" she asked.

"The what?"

"You said the official reason that you were here was to warn me. Is there an unofficial reason?"

"I just wanted to see you, I guess. See how things were. Maybe see if we could get together again and talk this through."

"Honestly," she said. "I'm not ready to do that yet."

"When do you think you will be?"

She shrugged and turned away. I felt like I was in high school and was about to hear the "I just want to be friends" line.

"I don't know. Talk to me again when you wrap up this case."

"It's just that . . ."

She turned away and waved her hand at me.

"I know, I know, 'if you survive.'"

I'd used that line a thousand times. Hearing her throw it back at me now gave me a chill. More than anything now, I wanted *us* to survive.

"Yeah. If."

Electra turned and walked out the door, closing it behind her as she left and didn't look back.

"I love you." I said.

But she was already gone.

"I think it's a particularly good sign that she didn't try to harm you," HARV said, in an attempt to be supportive.

"Yeah, maybe."

I took a deep breath and left the room as well. I cast a glance up the hallway, toward the ICU, then turned away and headed toward the elevators.

"Did you catch her little play on words?" HARV asked.

"What play on words?"

"She said, she had to get *back* to the kid's *spine*. Get it?"

"Yeah, I get it." I was surprised that HARV had picked up on the pun before I did.

"You know, I think I'm really starting to warm up to this humor concept" he said. "Tell me that one about the guy in the bar with plutonium on his shoulders . . ."

"I'm still working on it," I said.

"Pity," he said. "So where to now?"

My heart told me to go after Electra. To sit with her in the ICU next to the boy whose life she'd just saved and help her in any way I could. But she'd said it herself. She wasn't ready to see me yet. And I didn't want to think about what I'd do if she was never ready. So I did what I always do when real life gets complicated: I went into hardboiled mode.

"We're going back to ExShell," I said. "I have a score to settle with Fred Burns."

43

Half an hour later, HARV and I were back on the case, back at ExShell, and back in the office of Fred Burns. And, since I wasn't ready to clue BB in on everything just yet, getting into the office unannounced at nearly three in the morning was no easy feat. I had to pose as a computer screen cleaner (squeegee in hand) on an emergency call to get past security.

The only problem was that the office was no longer there.

The entire workspace was empty. Every computer, every monitor, every wire, knob and button was gone without a trace. The only thing left was a sign on the wall that read: "Coming soon: a new executive bathroom at this location."

"You didn't really expect him to still be here, did you?" HARV asked.

"I suppose that would have been too easy," I said. "Still, I was hoping that there'd be *something*. When did he leave?"

"ExShell records are unclear. It appears as though he sabotaged the security system, so we can't be certain."

I shook my head, disbelieving.

"Fred Burns," I mumbled. "That out-of-shape slab of mutton . . ."

"Apparently the mutton is sharper than the cheese," HARV said.

"What's that supposed to mean?"

"I don't know. I'm just following your food motif."

I rolled my eyes and again surveyed the big empty room. I

stared for a long time at the wall where the bank of satellite monitors had once been.

"The search for Pierce, that Sri Lanka thing. That was probably all a ruse. If Burns is working for Mani, then he knew where Pierce was all along."

"He just didn't want ExShell to know," HARV said.

"Or me. He lead us all on a wild snark chase."

"Why?"

"To buy time for Mani and BB-2."

"Time for what?"

"DOSsed if I know but I'm betting it isn't good."

"So what do we do?" HARV asked.

"We find Burns, kick his ass and then have him tell us what the DOS is going on."

"That was the plan *before* we got here. How do we find him?"

"Have a little faith," I said. "Remember, I once tracked down a man with nothing to go on except his favorite color and his hat size."

"Yes, but I should remind you," HARV replied, "that the person for whom you were searching turned out to be hiding at nine and a half Blue Fedora Street."

"Details," I said with a shrug.

I turned slowly around, visually checking the space one more time. Then I started to pace.

"Does ExShell have a home address on him?" I asked.

"Not any longer. The only information they currently have is his favorite movie, *Gone With the Wind Part Three*."

"That's it?"

"Yes, apparently they don't like to pry into their employees' lives. I think the truth is that Burns probably tampered with the database."

"I guess we can rule out any help from ExShell then."

"That would be logical," HARV agreed. "Truthfully, they may not even know he's gone, or for that matter, if he ever actually worked here or not. They're at the mercy of their data and somebody or something has skewed that to the max."

"We'll just have to search the place from your memory," I said. "Access your recording of the Burns interview. I'm going to need visual and audio. Let's recreate the office."

"What part to you want?" HARV asked.

I turned and pointed to the far wall.

"The monitors were there, weren't they? Let's see those."

Holographic images sprang from my eye lens and the huge bank of monitors returned to their place in the room as HARV played his recording of my meeting with Burns. The playback of Burns' voice in my head grated on my nerves like a stuck hovercraft alarm.

"I'm coordinating the various operatives that we have in the field that are currently following Dr. Pierce's elusive trail. The manhunt has gone on for eleven months now . . ."

I shook my head, took a step back and gestured to the space around me.

"The computer consoles were there, weren't they?"

"That's right," HARV said.

More holographic images sprang from the lens. The desk reformed itself and the row of computer keyboards reappeared, along with two or three empty soda bottles and disposable plates.

"When we can pinpoint Pierce's location to within an area of three square kilometers, we can send a search and retrieve team," Burns said in my mind, "and have him back here in custody within an hour's time."

I stared at the computers and shuddered a bit at the garbage strewn about them.

"I'd forgotten what a mess the place was," I said. "The guy's a pig."

"I thought he was mutton?" HARV asked.

"Do you remember? It was, what, ten in the morning and the guy was drinking soda and eating . . . pizza."

"He had three slices during your visit," HARV said. "Would you like playback?"

I spun around again and pointed to the wall on the left.

"Show me that area," I said. "Let me see what was there."

Images covered the wall; the data storage units and satellite monitors appeared but I paid them no mind. I was looking for something else. When the storage table came into view, I nearly jumped with glee.

"There," I said, pointing at the table. "Enhance that."

HARV zoomed in on the image of the table and a nano later, I was studying the grain of the faux wood finish.

"It's pretty standard as office furniture goes," HARV said.

"Not the table, the pile of stuff on top of it."

HARV pulled back and then zoomed in again, this time on the contents of the table: the stack of memory chips, the coffee cups . . . and the pizza boxes.

"The logo on the box," I said. "Go in tight."

HARV did as he was told and the words came into focus. PizzaPort.

"Vingo," I said. "He's hooked on the pizza. That's how we'll find him. Hack yourself into the PizzaPort database. Find Fred Burns."

"I'm in," HARV said. "Unfortunately, the database is categorized by address only," HARV said.

"Fine, how many deliveries were made to this office in the three days before we visited."

"Twenty-five."

"Sheesh, what a pig. When did the orders stop?"

"Two days ago." HARV replied. "The night after we visited."

"So he left here two days ago and went into hiding," I said. "I'm betting that PizzaPort started getting frequent orders from a new address shortly thereafter. Am I right?"

HARV churned away for a minute.

"What's wrong?" I asked.

"Some of the more recent entries into the database have been encoded," HARV said.

"Can you break them?"

"Of course," HARV said. "The encryption routine is very similar to the one Pierce used to hide his mother's brain."

HARV churned for a bit more.

"Fifteen delivery orders have come in during the last thirty-six hours from 8080 Jerry Garcia Avenue, a very remote area. The most recent order was placed seventy-three minutes ago."

"That's gotta be Burns," I said. "Pretty good find. Don't you think?"

"Oh, yes, brilliant," HARV said. "Perhaps we should call your next HV special 'Dial P for Pizza.' "

"I like it."

"You would," HARV mumbled.

A short while later, we were on the desolate stretch of Jerry Garcia Avenue. It was the wee hours of the morning so traffic was minimal in general and on this cul de sac it was non-existent.

"The house is approximately a quarter kilometer ahead. The end of the road."

I killed the headlights, parked the car at the side of the road and scanned the area though the darkness. There wasn't another house to be seen.

"I guess he doesn't want neighbors," HARV said.

"I'm thinking that the neighbors don't want him." I replied.

I popped my gun into hand, stepped out of the car and crept quickly through the darkness.

The house was a geocentric dome, solidly designed, but generally run-of-the-chip-factory. It was clear that Burns' income was somewhat less than extravagant.

"Not much to look at," HARV said.

"Neither is Burns," I quipped. "You remember the plan, right?"

HARV rolled his eyes (something I'd never seen him do before).

"If it appears that Mr. Burns is not at home or has retired for the evening, we pick the lock. If it appears that he's still awake, we do the pizza boy routine."

"Let's see it."

"Boss, I know the routine."

"There's a lot riding on this, HARV," I said. "It needs to be perfect."

"Fine,"

HARV's hologram blinked out for a nano then reappeared. Only this time instead of his usual gray tweed suit and bow tie, he was wearing the white pants, shirt and hat of a PizzaPort delivery person. Four pizza boxes were in his arms, and a look of utter disdain was in his eyes.

"Mr. Burns" he said, "on behalf of the PizzaPort management, we're happy to award you these pizzas as a gesture of gratitude for your diligent patronage."

"Good," I said. "But try to look a little happier."

"Anything else, Mr. Demille?"

A few nanos later, we were at the front door. The house was dark and the place was silent as a ghost town library.

"You read anyone inside?"

"No, but we shouldn't rule out the existence of cloaking devices."

"So he's either asleep, not at home, or lying in wait for us."

"Yes, we can safely narrow it down to those three."

"Okay, plan A," I said. "Think you can pick the lock?"

"Please," HARV said. "That's like asking Einstein if he could tie his shoe. Bend down so I can get a good look at it."

And that's when everything went very, very wrong.

I heard the faint whisper-pop of a blaster with silencer and a nano later, the blast hit me from the side and blew me off my feet. I hit the ground five meters from the house, dazed and confused. I tried to get to my feet but I couldn't move. I'd been hit by a binder-blast and was now tightly bound from neck to knees in plastic polymer.

"I don't think the pizza boy routine is going to work under these circumstances," HARV whispered.

I looked up and saw four figures approaching from the darkness; three men and a woman. The lead figure stepped from the shadows. The pale moonlight gently hit his face and my heart sank a little more.

"Hello there, Zach," Sidney Whoop said as he approached. "Fancy meeting you here."

44

And-A-One, circled around to my left, probably to get the good two-shot of Whoop and me for the DickCo broadcast with his eye-cam. And-A-Two moved past me to get the long shot (although he gave me a kick to the ribs as he passed). Sidney, of course, stayed close. He was the star, after all, and he was loving every nano of it.

"You know, it would have been better all around if you'd broken this case a few hours ago," he said with a smile. "We've missed prime time."

"Sorry to disappoint you, Sidney," I said.

Sidney shrugged.

"It's all right. We'll run it tomorrow on delay. It will give us time to promote it properly and do some editing."

"Sidney, this is not a good time," I said. "You don't know what you're doing."

"I know that ExShell hired you to retrieve a very important droid," he said. "That's a start. As for the rest of the story, you're about to tell us everything."

The woman, who had stayed in the background all this time, stepped forward as Sidney gestured to her. She was a large woman, and tough-looking. Not unattractive but, for lack of a better word, scary. Her long red hair was wrapped tight in a bun. Her skin was ivory colored and clear. And her eyes were icy. The hairs on my neck stood up just at her approach.

"Zach Johnson," Sidney said with a smile, "meet Maggie Chill."

Maggie Chill is a psi. She's a whispered legend in the espionage community, a freelance operative who sells her talents to the highest bidder. She has done jobs for all the major world governments, the biggest conglomerates, and several of the wealthiest baseball teams in the American League. In recent years, her appearances in the field (even rumors of a appearances) have been very few and even farther between. Word in the community is that she had become bored with the work. Her mind was too powerful and she could no longer stand human contact of any kind. DickCo had somehow located her through the community of shadows, tempted her wrath by contacting her and lured her out of retirement for this one special assignment. It must be sweeps month.

"I don't think humming is going to work this time," HARV said.

"Pleased to meet you, Ms. Chill," I said. "I'm sorry that it has to be under these circumstances."

She knelt down beside me, like a cobra approaching its helpless prey. Her eyes locked with mine, moving hypnotically to the left then right. I thought the chill that ran up my spine was going to make icicles in my hair.

Then she spoke and the sound almost made me gag.

"Wha-ev-uh."

Nails on a blackboard, a stuck hovercraft theft alarm at three in the morning, deranged chipmunks on helium. These sounds were angels singing next to the accented nasal twang of Maggie Chill.

"What was that?"

"Oiy said, *wha-ev-uh.*"

"I'm sorry," I said. "I'm still not getting it."

"Whatchoo, deaf?" she said. "*Wha-ev-uh, wha-ev—uh.*"

Sidney was a little uncomfortable now.

"Zach, you're making her mad," he said. "Be polite, okay."

"Right," I said. "I wouldn't want to offend your psionic assassin."

As we spoke I focused the power from my armor to one small area at my left shoulder. I knew I couldn't break the binding with brute force but I was hoping that I could load up the armor's circuits, generate some heat and melt the plastic polymer enough for me to crack it with a good effort. The downside, of course, was that, even by focusing the power to the outer shell of the armor, I still felt the residual heat. It hurt plenty but it was my only chance of getting out of this in one piece. HARV immediately realized what I was doing.

"Ingenious plan, boss, but it's going to hurt, and it's going to take some time," he said. "Are you sure you want to do this?"

"No choice," I whispered.

"Whawazzat?" Maggie asked, suddenly tense.

"What was what?" Sidney asked.

Maggie's psionic abilities were more sensitive than I thought. She was sensing something. I wasn't sure if it was HARV or simply my thoughts of him that she was picking up but either way, I was in big trouble if she figured out that I had a supercomputer in my head. Randy told me when he first dropped the interface into my eye that HARV's presence in my head would help me defend myself against psi attacks. Now it was time to put that claim to the hydrochloric acid test.

"Oi'm pickin' up somethin' in his head. Somethin' distant."

"That's my inner child," I said. "Cute kid, but I can't stand his taste in music."

"It's loik dere's someone else in yah head," Maggie said. "Almost as if . . ." She smiled and I knew I was sunk. "Yah' a schitzaphenic, ahn'tchoo?"

"A what?"

"A schitzaphenic. You have a multiple poisonality disohdah?"

"What's a disohdah?"

"A disohdah, disohdah!"

"Oh, a disorder. Why didn't you just say it in English?"

"Lissen, Mistah," Maggie said angrily. "Oi'm gonna read yah' moind. Oi'm gonna foind out 'zactly wha' oiy need ta' know. Den oi'm gonna make you lick moiy boots. Aftah 'dat, oi'm gonna shut down da hoiyah fun-shins of yah' brain and let you live da rest've yah' loife as a can of Spam. And you know whoiy oiy I added 'dat last 'ting? Because you jus' made fun o' da way oiy tawk."

"The way you what?"

"Tawk, tawk. Da' way oiy tawk!" she shouted.

Sidney stepped forward and put a hand on Maggie's shoulder.

"Maggie, please, we need to get his information."

"Don' touch me, Whoop," she said pushing his hand away. "Oiy can feel yah' stupidity roight tru' yah' fingahtips."

"What?"

"She's right, Sidney," I said. "I can feel it from here."

"Shut up, Zach!"

Clearly, Sidney didn't like the fact that he was losing control of the scene. And clearly, the great Maggie Chill was a bit unbalanced herself. I realized that might give me a chance at survival.

"Hey, don't yell at me. I'm schizophrenic, remember?"

"You are not."

"Yes, I am. She said it herself. I have a disohdah, I have a disohdah."

"Dass' it," Maggie yelled. "Oi'm melting yah' brain roit now."

"Maggie, no!" Sidney yelled.

"Foin. I'll get da' information foist," she said. "*Den* I'll melt his brain."

"That's better," Sidney said.

"Thanks for the help, Sid," I said. "I'm touched by your Machiavellian concern."

Maggie put her hand against my cheek and her icy touch began to penetrate my head.

"Le's get dis ovah wit," she said.

Then I got an idea.

"Um okay," I said. "But be careful. I have an entire world of information in my head."

"Yeah, wha- ev-uh." Maggie said.

"All right, but don't say I didn't warn you. I have access to more information then you could ever dream of."

"Hold on," Whoop said cautiously. "This is too easy. What are you doing, Zach?"

Maggie shrugged Whoop's warning away.

"Oh puh-leeze," she said. "Oiy seen kitchen apployances wit' strongah moinds den 'dis guy."

"By the way," I said, "have I mentioned that I have a *world of information* in my head?"

"All right already, boss, I get the hint," HARV said. "Sheesh, ever hear of subtlety?"

And then Maggie Chill reached into my mind.

45

The inside of my mind was a big white room (admittedly not the most original setting, but I don't think that was a reflection on me), and I was standing in front of a door.

"Well, this isn't so bad," I said.

"It's about to get a whole lot better, chico."

My heart skipped a beat at the sound of the voice. Then I smelled the perfume: sweet and sexy, like a passionate kiss on a springtime lawn. I turned slowly, and there she was.

Electra.

"I've missed you," she said.

"I've missed you too."

"It's stupid to fight like this."

"Yeah, it is. I'm sorry. It's just that . . ."

She moved towards me and put a finger to my lips.

"Shhh, it's in the past. We're looking forward now," she said. She put one arm around my neck and pulled my face close to hers. Then she put her hand on the doorknob behind me. "Let's go into the other room and you can show me the future."

"I just . . ."

"Later," she said. "Just open the door."

I put my hand on the knob and started to turn.

"I just want to . . ."

"What?"

"I'm sorry for what I did."

Electra smiled.

"I'm sorry too," she said.

And then I smiled (really widely).

"Electra would never say that."

"What?"

"She'd never apologize. Especially when I was the one who screwed up."

HARV appeared suddenly beside me, hands on his hips.

"Well, it's about time," he said. "For a nano there, I thought you were actually falling for that drivel."

Electra's image shook as though her molecules were being broken down from the inside and in a nano, she was replaced by the (angry) form of Maggie Chill.

"Who da' DOS ah you?" she hissed.

"I'm his conscience," HARV replied. "And I'll give you one warning, madam. Leave this man's mind now or suffer the consequences."

"You tink you can scare me, you schizo-fop?" she said. "Oiy could rip' yah' mind apaht wit' a jest-chya'."

"With a what?" I asked.

"A jest-chya, a jest-chya!" she yelled, waving her hands. "Now open da' dowah!"

"Maggie, the door's a metaphor," I said. "You know it and I know it. Try to be a little more inventive the next time you invade someone's mind. Okay?"

Maggie's face grew red with anger and I knew she was going to blow soon. I stepped to the side and motioned to the door.

"You want information? Fine, here it is, but you're in for a surprise."

I nodded to HARV, who gave me a proper gentlemanly bow and then, with a dramatic flourish, threw open the door.

"You see, this isn't my door," I said.

Bright light and white sound erupted from within and a cascade of ones and zeroes flooded the room. I saw Maggie's face drop and the last thing she saw before she was engulfed in the binary maelstrom of information was HARV's smiling face.

"It's mine," he said.

46

And then we were back in the world outside my head. I was still bound tightly in plastic polymer and surrounded by Sidney and his junior dicks but things were definitely on the upswing.

Why? Because in the all-important arena of mental warfare, HARV and I were giving the great Maggie Chill the blitz to end all kriegs.

Maggie had gone into my mind looking to crack my reluctant cortex for information. What she got, however, was the free-flow of HARV's database. It was the mental equivalent of someone expecting glass of water and getting the Atlantic ocean dumped on them instead. HARV hit Maggie's mind with a tsunami of information and it was more than she could stand.

The download of the complete *World Chip Super Encyclopedia* made her dizzy. The streaming hyper audio of the collected historical database of commercial jingles made her queasy. And the text download of twentieth-century political speeches left her puking her guts out.

But it was the bootlegged recordings of the complete Doors catalog (illegally pirated through the rogue site, Kidnapster) that finally fractured her frontal lobes.

She pulled away from me, mentally and physically, in the pain of information overload.

"Make it stawp! Puh-leeze make it stawp!"

"You can't say we didn't warn her," HARV said.

"True," I agreed. "After all, we're the good guys and that's what good guys do."

Maggie fell to the ground, her body curling and uncurling like an epileptic cow at a disco.

"I guess having a computer hooked in to my brain has an upside after all."

"At least for you," HARV said.

Sidney saw Maggie convulsing and tried to help her.

"Maggie, what's wrong?"

She seized his hand like frog tongue on a fly and Sidney began to shake as well.

"What's happening?" I asked.

"She's trying to siphon off some of the excess information into Sidney's mind." HARV said.

"She's using him as a mental sump pump?"

"In a way," HARV said. "A pity his mind isn't big enough. By the way, watch out behind you."

I turned and saw And-A-One running towards Maggie and Sidney. I flung my legs out as he passed and hit him squarely in the shins. He tripped and tumbled into the spasming pair of villains. Sidney reached out and grabbed the stupid kid's ankle and drew him into the mind morass as well. And-A-One began shaking as though he'd swallowed a jackhammer.

"I saw his approach through the wrist interface," HARV said.

"Thanks. It looks like we have a real chain of fools going now," I said.

Meanwhile, the heat of my armor had at last melted the binding enough so that small cracks had begun to form in the surface. I figured I was running out of time so I pulled the energy away from the armor surface, funneled it into my shoulder muscles and gave a heave. The binding cracked and my arm was free.

"Where's the other dick?" I asked.

No sooner had the words left my mouth then they were replaced by And-A-Two's boot as he kicked me squarely in the face.

"There's some painful irony," HARV said.

And-A-Two kicked me again, this time in the shoulder and I rolled over onto my stomach.

"You're not so tough," he said, and kicked me again.

I rolled down the gentle slope of the lawn like a runaway barrel on a mountain road. And-A-Two followed me, a stupid swagger to his walk and an even stupider grin on his face.

"You're a soft old man, Johnson," he said. "An overblown, overrated, overpaid pretender."

My rolling momentum was gone and I was now face down in the grass, still wrapped almost entirely in polymer and helpless. And-A-Two caught up to me and stood over my bound form with an evil grin on his face.

"You wouldn't know a tough guy if he kicked you in the head," he said.

He pulled his heavy boot back and then threw one more steel-toe jab at my face.

But I'd had enough.

I reached out with my one free arm and caught his swinging foot in my hand.

"I guess we'll never know, will we?" I said.

And the kid's grin disappeared.

I twisted his foot hard and he fell to the ground. Then I popped my gun into my hand and fired a low-power blast at the polymer binding on my legs. The blast blew the polymer apart and freed me from the waist down.

I got to my feet just as And-A-Two was pulling his gun. I kicked it out of his hand and then kneed him in the chin. He fell back to the ground. I aimed my gun at him and let him see the business end for a long nano before giving the command.

"Sticky stuff."

And fired.

The glue sealed tightly around the kid's body, pinning him to the ground like a well constructed pup tent.

HARV appeared from my eye lens and knelt beside And-A-Two. Before I could say a word, he stuck his holographic nose in the kid's face and lectured him like a headmaster dressing down the class clown.

"I want you to remember this, you little cretin. I want you to reflect back upon this nano as you grow old and remember who it was who spared your life when you had no intention of sparing his. Maybe one day you'll realize that you were taught a lesson this night by the toughest man you'll ever meet. And above all, I want you remember that Zach Johnson beat you with one arm and both legs tied behind his back."

My jaw dropped so low that I had grass stains on my chin.

HARV stood up and left the browbeaten And-A-Two on the ground, counting his blessings.

"HARV?"

He straightened his coat and turned to me.

"Just so you know," he said. "I did not record the past few nanos. There is no permanent record of what just occurred. Should the debate ever arise, regarding what may or may not have been said just now, it would come down to my word against yours. And let's remember that I am a well-respected supercomputer and as such, my word would be considered more credible with the general public."

I said nothing. (But I smiled).

"Come on," he said. "We have work to do."

I freed myself from the last of the polymer binding and set to work. All DickCo operatives are monitored by the home office through their eye and satellite cams, so we had to work quickly before anyone figured out that something was amiss and sent in reinforcements.

Sidney, Maggie and And-A-One were all unconscious (nearly catatonic) from HARV's information overload.

"They're not permanently hurt are they?"

"They'll be unconscious for another day or so" HARV said, "and they'll have some serious headaches for the next few weeks but they'll survive."

I put all three of them in Sidney's hovercraft, which was parked up the road, then threw And-A-Two in the trunk. I left my wrist interface on the hood of the hover so that HARV could project (mundane and peaceful) holographic images of Burns' house onto the windshield. Anyone from DickCo monitoring the eye-cams of Sidney and his posse would think that they were on a very boring stakeout. HARV even threw in some occasional banter for additional realism. Once that was taken care of, I turned my attention back to Burns' hideout.

The lights in the main room were now on.

"I guess it would be too much to ask for him to sleep through a firefight on his front lawn," I said.

"Shall we do the pizza boy routine?"

"I think the time for that has passed," I said, popping my gun into my hand. "Our only option now is to go in the hard way."

47

And I meant hard.

I focused the power from my armor into my leg and kicked the door in. The metal and plastic fibers splintered and the hinges ripped free from the wall.

"By the way, boss," HARV said. "I believe that the door was unlocked."

"Thanks, HARV. Now let's work on your ability to deliver information in a timely manner."

A nano later I was in the front foyer of the house with my gun drawn.

"Burns," I called into the darkness. "It's Zach Johnson. I want you to come out with your hands up. No one gets hurt that way."

That's when I heard the music.

"What's that?"

"I believe it's Bach," HARV said. "Concerto for Piano and Orchestra Number 2 in E Major. Not a bad choice for ambiance, really."

I followed the music into the spacious living room, which was entirely empty save for one of those ugly, overstuffed white anti-grav couches that are so popular now, floating fifteen feet in the air.

And Fred Burns was sitting in the middle of it.

"And so, Prometheus returns to have the vulture eat his liver once again."

"Whatever you say, Doc. " I said. "Which one am I?"

Burns laughed and lowered the couch slowly toward the floor.

"I honestly didn't expect to see you here, Mr. Johnson. I was afraid that I'd have to hunt you down. How did you find me, by the way?"

"You left a trail of pizza."

Burns looked at the slice of pizza in his hand and then smiled.

"Oh, well, I guess even Achilles had a weakness," he said. "It's for the best, anyway. Your coming here saves me the time that I'd have spent searching for you."

"I'm glad I could make it convenient for you, Doc, but I think you have the roles reversed. You see, I'm here to kick your ass and have you tell me everything you know about Manuel Mani and BB-2."

The couch came to rest gently on the floor and Pierce oozed off it. He looked at me, then at the gun in my hand and smiled.

"I don't think so," he said.

That worried me. Burns didn't strike me as the kind of guy who had a gun pointed at him very often. The fact that he was this calm while staring into the business end was a little unnerving.

"I don't think you grasp the gravity of the situation, Doc," I said. "I'm not playing games here."

Burns smiled and slowly moved toward me.

"Oh, I understand," he said. "And just for the record, I'm not playing games here either. Although I do enjoy a good game of Trivial Tidbits. I'm especially good at mythology questions."

Now I was getting spooked. This fleshy little unarmed man, plodding towards me like a jello mold with feet, had me in a stare-down contest and from all signs, he was winning. Something was wrong, here. Something was definitely wrong but I couldn't, for the life of me, figure out what it was.

Burns was within arm's length when I finally put my gun directly in his face, just on the off-chance that he hadn't noticed it yet. But it still didn't seem to worry him (and *that* worried *me*).

"Okay, doughboy," I said. "I've had enough of this. You tell me what I want to know right now or things are going to get very ugly."

"I've been ordered to terminate you," he said. "Your coming here saves me a lot of time and effort. Thank you for your co-operation in my current endeavor."

"Terminating me might be a little difficult since I'm the one with the gun."

Burns smiled and pointed towards the ceiling.

"If you'll turn your gaze skyward, you'll notice a projector suspended from the ceiling. The ingenious device of my own design emits a signal that blocks all types of communications and deactivates all computerized devices except for my own."

Burns' smile grew wider and he reached out and gently touched the barrel of my gun with his thumb and index finger.

"Your gun, I'll remind you, is computer-controlled and therefore will not work in this house."

I flipped the setting on my gun to heavy stun and pulled the trigger.

Nothing happened.

Nada.

Zilch.

Zero.

Well, almost zero. Burns began to laugh. It was that over-the-top kind of cackle that villains always use and worst of all, he wasn't even good at it.

So I hit him.

A left cross to the jaw sent him sprawling to the floor.

"I really don't like you, Dr. Burns."

Burns held his aching jaw in one hand and held the other out to me in a "please stop" gesture.

"Please," he said, "I am not a man of violence."

I grabbed him by the shoulders and pulled him to his feet.

"Tell me what I need to know and there won't be any violence," I snarled (suddenly feeling a whole lot better about myself).

Then Burns smiled again and I knew that I was still in trouble.

"But then, just because I'm not a man of violence," he said, "doesn't mean I am *opposed* to violence."

I felt a tap on my shoulder and I turned just in time to see a huge red-headed droid in a maid's uniform standing beside me.

Then I saw a huge droid fist coming toward me.

Then I saw stars.

"Mr. Johnson," Burns said with a smile, "I'd like you to meet Hazel, my maid droid. Hazel will be your murderer this evening. She'll also clean up afterward. Isn't that right, Hazel?"

"Oh, yes, master," the droid replied. "As if I have nothing better to do with my time than to clean up the murderous messes that you order me to create."

"Let's not go in to that now, Hazel, please," Burns said. "We have company."

It goes without saying that Hazel wasn't your run-of-the-mill household droid. She stood nearly three meters tall and tipped the scale at a megaton if she was a gram. Each of her hands was easily as big as my head.

"You call this flesh-maggot company?" she said. "I've scraped better company off of the bug zapper."

She also had a hefty dose of sarcasm in her main programming (probably one of the more recent versions of the mother-in-law droid operating system).

Hazel stood over me as I lay on the floor and stomped her foot trying to squash me like a bug. I rolled away at the last nano and watched her put a foot-shaped crater in the carpet as well as the floor stones beneath.

"Hazel, as you can see, is also immune to the deactivation devices in my house." Burns said.

"Yeah, but does she do windows?" I asked.

Hazel's chair-sized foot kicked me in the ribs and threw me a meter and a half in the air. When I landed (hard) on the floor, she was already reaching for me with her giant metal hands.

"Oh, gee, like I haven't heard *that* one before," she said, lifting me towards her. "Maybe you should spend the extra credits and get some writers who can steal jokes from *this* century."

"Everyone's a critic."

For a lack of anything better to do I hit Hazel in the side of the head with my gun. It didn't hurt her, of course, and I was glad that I'd hit her with my gun rather than my fist.

Hazel snorted in disdain and tossed me across the room the way a child would toss away an old rag doll. I hit the wall and then the floor then rolled over onto my back and gazed at the ceiling.

"HARV," I whispered, "I don't suppose you could help me out here, could you?"

A little bomb icon appeared before my eye with the words "system error" directly below it. Somewhere in my head I could hear the echoes of HARV yelling. It was distant and almost intelligible. Burns' device hadn't turned HARV off inside my head but it was definitely wreaking some havoc with the system. I'm sure that HARV would eventually iron out the bugs. The question was, would my head still be intact when he did?

Meanwhile, the shaking of the floor (and the cascade of annoying causticity that followed) told me that Hazel was stomping her way toward me again.

"All the things that need to be done in this house before the cataclysm and I have to waste my evening killing some overrated B-level celebrity."

"Please, Hazel," Burns said, "don't embarrass me at work."

"You call this work?" she said "I'm the one doing all the work here. You're just standing there cackling insidiously."

And as I lay on the floor, the only thought I had in my head was that this would be a stupid way to die: crushed to death by a fishwife droid and her pussy-whipped mad scientist. But here I was. All my gadgetry had gone from high tech to high dreck, thanks to the projector on the ceiling. HARV had become a (very) silent partner and my gun had become the world's most expensive rock. Well, I'd always insisted that I could get along fine without HARV. Now it was time to put up or shut up.

I climbed to my feet and as the Goliath droid approached, I realized that my one last chance of survival was to make like a gumshoe David, so I wrapped my fingers around my gun and wound up my throwing arm like the illegal clone of Cy Young.

Hazel stopped her approach at the sight of me and put her giant hands on her wide hips.

"Oh, good, throw your gun at me," she said. "That worked *so* well last time. DOS, don't they make humans with brains anymore?"

I threw the gun, but not at Hazel.

I threw it at the projector on the ceiling and when the metal of the gun butt shattered the projector glass, the whole unit exploded into a miniature mass of flaming debris and fell from the ceiling . . . right on top of Hazel.

I was thrown to my knees by the explosion and actually had a nano to enjoy my little victory. Then the rubble on the floor shifted and Hazel (her faux hair still aflame) rose to her feet again.

"I'm going to have to clean this rug, you know," she said. "Do you have any idea how hard it is to clean melted circuitry out of shag?"

She flexed her long, metallic fingers menacingly.

"Not to mention the bloodstains," she said.

And then she charged me.

My gun had also fallen to the floor in the explosion. It had landed on the far side of the room, almost directly opposite from me. All that stood between it and me now was a megaton of fast-approaching angry droid. But, fast as Hazel was, I was hoping that my gun was a little faster.

I stuck out my hand, fingers spread wide.

"Come to daddy," I said.

The gun, free now from Burns' nullifier, responded to my command. It shuddered for a nano, then took to the air like a steel gray homing pigeon.

The charging Hazel was four meters away from me when the flying gun passed her.

She was three meters away when it landed solidly in my out-stretched hand.

She was two meters away when I gave the command.

"Big Bang."

And her hands were actually touching my cheeks when I pulled the trigger.

The high-powered blast blew a hole in Hazel's chest the size of a small dog. Wire, circuitry, and silicone splattered the wall behind her like high-tech gore. She stumbled, robotic eyes glazed, and looked first at the hole in her midsection, then at her innards splattered behind her.

"Aw, no," she said. "Not on the drapes."

I fired again and atomized her from the shoulders up.

The echo of the blast was just starting to fade when HARV's voice returned to my head.

"Boss, it appears that we had a slight problem with the interface," he said, "but it seems to be clear now. What the DOS happened here?"

"I had a little dispute with the maid," I said. "But I think we worked it out."

48

I turned my attention back to Burns, who was a little shell-shocked from all this. I pointed my gun at him again and finally got the reaction that I'd been expecting. He fell to his knees and started crying like a day trader on Black One-day.

"I take it that you're out of domestic help," I said.

"Please don't kill me," he sobbed. "It wasn't my fault. It was that protoscum, Mani and that crazy BB-2, that made me do it."

"Where are they?" I growled.

"They'll kill me . . ."

"You have a choice here, Burns," I said, "you can tell me everything I want to know, and let the police protect you while I handle Mani and BB-2. Or you can die right here."

"I wish you hadn't destroyed Hazel," he sobbed. "She always made the non-virus related decisions around here."

I picked Burns up by the shirt collar and slammed him into a wall. Then I stuck my gun into his nose and stretched his nostril cartilage until it fit the barrel.

"I'll ask you one more time," I said in my best Marlowe snarl. "Where are Mani and BB-2?"

Burns responded in a nasal twang (that comes from having a gun barrel up your nose).

"The Fallen Arms Hotel in Oakland."

"What did they want from you?"

"My old virus research."

"And you just gave it to them?"

"I sold it to them, for a fortune and for the promise of a place in their plan."

"What is their plan?" I said.

"I don't know."

I slammed him against the wall again and stuck my gun another three centimeters farther up his nose.

"What are they planning?" I yelled.

"I don't know!" he sobbed. "All I know is that it's the end of the world as we know it."

I let Burns fall to the floor, where he curled into a ball and sobbed. Then I rubbed my eyes and sighed.

I had HARV net with Carol. We woke her at home and I somehow cajoled her into coming out to Burns' hideout to use her psi powers to wipeout and rewrite the memories of Burns, Whoop and the DickCo crew. It would be a thin cover story at best, but maintaining the perfect veil of secrecy wasn't exactly my highest priority at the nano.

"The end of the world," I said to myself. "Why does it always have to be the end of the world?"

49

I stomped my foot hard on the gas pedal and felt the car's engine roar in response as I shot down the New Trans-City Highway. For the first time since I took on the case of the missing killer android, I had clarity of purpose. The pieces of this puzzle were coming together, albeit in a very abstract and urgent sort of way.

Manuel Mani, BB Star's ex-lover and personal astrologer, had made three attempts on my life in the past two days and I now strongly suspected that he was behind the other half dozen or so attempts as well. I let the first murder attempt slide, writing it off as the desperate act of a jilted lover, but Mr. Mani officially ran out of slack when he organized the droid blitzkrieg at the Nexus 9. As for Pizza Boy Burns and his crazed cleaning droid, that just added insult to injury. Now it was payback time.

"You're exceeding the speed limit for ground-based vehicles," HARV's hologram said from the passenger seat.

"I'll charge the speeding ticket to BB Star," I said. "Either that or I'll take it out of Manuel Mani's hide."

"Do you really think he's the brains behind all this?" HARV asked.

"Three of my would-be assassins have fingered him as their boss man. What do you think?"

"But he's BB's ex-lover?"

"Emphasis on the ex, buddy. I know that if I were dumped . . ."

"Which, judging by Dr. Gevada's apparent hostility toward you, seems a very likely scenario."

"And thank you so much for reminding me," I said. "If I were dumped, I think I'd be very tempted to take up with a woman much like the one who dumped me."

"You think Manuel and BB-2 are an item?"

"Sicker things have happened, pal, which is why we're on our way to The Fallen Arms."

"That's another thing that worries me," HARV said.

"What's that?"

"The Fallen Arms is not an active domicile. Abandoned since 2013, it is a municipally recognized shrine to urban blight. The only reason that the building is still standing is to remind present-day Oakland residents of how good they have it. A brilliant PR ploy by the current administration, by the way."

"If you don't want to be found, where better to hide than the underbelly of the city?" I said. "Now, have you done those searches I requested?"

"Of course I have," HARV said. "Plus a few others. What do you think I am, a BOB model?"

"And the results are?" I asked.

"Surprising and confusing."

"Go on," I prompted.

"ExShell spent over one hundred twenty-five percent more on the BB-2 project than I would have deemed necessary. The finances are scrambled but I'm confident that my margin of error is under point three percent."

"Is that the surprising or confusing part?" I asked.

"Surprising."

"Mega corps like ExShell tend to go overboard with expenses, so I wouldn't worry about it," I said. "Now what's the confusing part."

"I'm not sure . . ." HARV answered.

"Hence the confusion."

"There are numerous scrambled transactions that involve seemingly unrelated items. They come from nowhere and seem to accomplish nothing."

"Sounds like a government project," I said.

"No, no. I'm not talking ineptitude here. This confusion is brilliant in its chaotic nature. There is clearly a pattern and a purpose to the activity. It's just so well cloaked in chaos that it appears inept on the surface."

"In other words you can't figure it out," I said.

"Yet."

"If you say so. Just tell me if you make sense out of anything,"

"Not if," he corrected, "when."

"If, when, whenever. Anything else?"

"I found one interesting note scribbled by hand over some early specs of the BB-2 project."

"And that would be?" I prompted (sometimes getting information out of HARV was like pulling teeth).

"It said 'BS hates contractions.'"

"Well, we all have our little peeves," I said. "You can figure all that out later. Right now I need all the info you can get on Manuel Mani."

"Already done. And the stuff gets even weirder."

"How so?"

"Manuel Mani, born in 2030 in New Mexico. The son of two computer programmers . . ."

"You mean the New Mexico that used to be the state?" I asked.

"No, that's New New Mexico. I mean the New Mexico that was once the country of Mexico."

"DOS, why does the World Council insist on sticking the word 'New' in front of everything?"

"You don't want to go into that do you?" HARV asked.

"No," I said. "Go on. He was born in Mexico."

"New Mexico," HARV corrected.

"HARV . . ."

"He moved to New Frisco in 2045. Now this is where it gets weird. The databases show that five years ago Manuel Mani worked as a robotics engineer with HTech specializing in remote reprogramming."

"Are you sure?"

"Actually, no," HARV said. "I just know the data is in the database."

HARV's hologram morphed into the shape of an HTech identification card. Sure enough, the card had Mani's picture and his name, with the title "Engineer" on it.

"See?" HARV said.

"I see. But in this day and age seeing doesn't always translate to believing. It's a weird jump from robots to astrology."

"Then again," HARV said. "Personal astrologer was his official title when he worked for BB. Who knows what his actual duties were."

"So he's a psycho with a background in robotics who is obsessed with BB Star," I said. "That would make BB-2 his dream date."

"Apparently someone for whom he'd kill," HARV said. "Speaking of which, the Fallen Arms is exactly three hundred meters straight ahead."

I pulled the car to the side of the road and killed the engine and lights.

I reached through HARV's hologram to the glove compartment, pulled out a fresh clip of ammo and loaded my gun. Then I pulled my classic Colt .45 from the glove compartment and loaded it with some of Randy's specially designed ammo.

"What are you doing with that ancient thing?" HARV asked.

"It's a backup."

"The firearm is nearly fifty years old. It's unstable and noncomputerized."

"You're starting to catch on, HARV." I slipped the Colt into my ankle holster and stepped out of the car.

A few nanos later I was creeping stealthily through the darkness towards the Fallen Arms. HARV provided me with an illusory holographic cover making me nearly invisible in the darkness (a neat trick but it puts a hefty strain on my armor's energy supply so I don't use it that often).

The building itself was utterly decrepit. Like an idiot with a bullet in his head, it was dead and yet too dense to fall down. So against all logic, the building remained standing, its century old rotted support beams and brittle infrastructure somehow keeping it upright.

"A real fixer-upper," I whispered.

"More like a real tear-the-thing-down, burn-the-rubble, pour-holy-water-on-the-ashes, and salt-the-earth-so-that-nothing-can-ever-grow-there-againer," HARV said.

"Let's hope it doesn't come to that," I said, popping my gun into hand. "But I will if I have to."

50

I entered the building, gun drawn, and felt the floorboards creak beneath my feet. The lobby was empty so I quickly moved toward the old stairway.

"My sensors report that the elevator is no longer functional," HARV whispered.

"Just as well," I said. "There's more room to move on the stairs."

I tentatively put my weight on the first step. The wood splintered faintly beneath my shoe but it held. I brushed away what appeared to be cobwebs from the ceiling and started up the stairs.

Things were fairly uneventful as I passed the second, third, four, fifth and six floors. I knew this was just the calm before the impending storm, though, and I was proven right when I reached floor seven.

"Uh-oh," HARV said.

"What uh-oh?" I whispered anxiously. "I don't like uh-oh!"

"I detect communications coming from floors six and eight."

"Can you say trap?"

"I can say trap in six hundred thirty-two languages."

"It was a rhetorical question, HARV. Witty banter to break the tension."

"Maybe you should use writers," HARV said, a little panicky. "By the way, I strongly suggest you fling yourself to the left side of the stairwell right . . . Now!"

I leaped as HARV directed just as two bullets whizzed past me from opposite directions.

Then things got a little freaky.

As soon as the bullets passed me, they suddenly stopped short and hung in midair for nano, as though searching for something.

"HIT THE DECK NOW!" HARV screamed.

I dove to the floor a split second before the bullets changed course, hit the wall and exploded where my head had been only nanos before. Wood and plaster shrapnel filled the hallway and bounced over and around me as I tried to cover myself.

"DOS!" I exclaimed. "I don't need writers, I need stunt doubles."

"They would have to be very stupid stunt doubles," HARV noted.

"What were those?" I asked, as I crawled across stairwell floor to the seventh floor door.

"Smart bullets," HARV said, "an experimental weapon currently being developed by an HTech subsidiary. They're not actually intelligent, of course, but they're much more sophisticated than your average projectile weapon. They are programmed to attack a specific visual target."

"A bullet with my name on it."

"Your image, actually, but that's the gist of it," HARV said.

I tried the knob but the door out of the stairwell was locked (of course). I was about to blow the door with my gun when I heard a woman's familiarly accented voice call to me from the floor below.

"Hello, Mr. Johnson," she said. "We meet again for the first time."

"Diedre," I called from my hiding place. "Is that you?"

"Yes and no, Mr. Johnson," she said. "Same model, different unit. As you'll recall, you destroyed the unit you met earlier this evening."

"Yes, sorry about that," I said. "I tend to act rudely when someone is trying to kill me. I assume that the shooter on the floor above me then is Dieter? Dieter, are you there, buddy?"

"Don't call me buddy," Dieter's voice floated down from the stairs.

"No hard feelings about what happened at the club, right?"

"None," he said. "But it will make killing you here more satisfying."

"Dieter, I think that qualifies as hard feelings," I shouted, then I whispered to HARV inside my head. "Why are they talking instead of shooting?"

"My guess is that they're reloading."

"Reloading? They've fired once. What are they using muskets?"

"I told you," HARV whispered, "the bullets are experimental. According to the most recent literature, the target image has to be uploaded into the ordinance just before firing."

"How long does that take?"

"About forty-five seconds."

"How long since they last fired?"

"About forty-five seconds."

A shot rang out from above and I heard the deadly whistle of the bullet as it sped down the stairwell. I threw myself to the other side of the hall but there just wasn't enough room to move. The bullet grazed my side and ripped a hole through my armor and my flesh before slamming into the stairway door and exploding. The explosion blew the door apart and I could see the decrepit hallway on the other side. I put the pain out of my head and made a mad dash for the opening. I made it through just as the second shot fired from below. Fortunately, the smart bullet wasn't intelligent enough to recognize the image of my rear end as I turned tail and ran, so as I threw myself into the hallway, the bullet simply sailed above me and exploded against the far wall, obliterating another good size chunk of wood and plaster as it did so.

"Are you hurt?" HARV asked.

"Hurt, yes. Dead, no," I said. "The armor saved me."

"I'm manipulating the armor to seal itself tightly around your wound," HARV said. "I'm also instructing your body to create some extra endorphins to quell the pain and adrenaline to keep you moving."

"Thanks," I said. "Look, we've got a few seconds now before the next round of bullets so I need your help. Will those bullets attack a hologram?"

"No. Their secondary guidance system is mass-seeking. They seek out the image and then verify that the image is real through the use of sonar. The original design utilized a heat-seeking guidance system but that proved less than effective, hence the new system. The designers felt that it was imperative to develop some sort of weapon that would be equally effective, against organic and nonorganic attackers. This new modification has not hurt performance against organics but has improved performance against nonorganics by a factor of . . ."

"Ten words or less here, HARV. We're on the clock," I said. "I'm going to need you to follow my lead very closely here."

"What lead? What the DOS are you talking about?"

"Nine words that time, buddy," I said as I ducked quickly into the seventh floor hallway. "Glad to see you're catching on."

The layout of the floor was simple and worked to my advantage. Two perpendicular hallways crisscrossed the floor, north to south and east to west, dissecting the space into quarters. Another hallway ran entirely around the perimeter. Once inside, the three of us would be like rats in a maze. I allowed myself a tiny smile as I surveyed the floor (not an easy thing to do when you've just been shot and are caught in a crossfire) and quickly tiptoed down the hallway.

"Here's the plan, HARV," I whispered. "And I'm guessing that is going to be a hit or miss type of deal—literally."

Dieter and Diedre, guns at the ready, entered the hallway together a few nanos later. As I suspected, they split up. Diedre covered the entrance at the south wall while Dieter padded quickly north along the center corridor.

I waited until Dieter was nearly to the far end of the hallway before I made my move on Diedre. I sprang from my hiding place on the east wall and fired. Unfortunately, I made too much noise as I moved. Diedre spun toward me and ducked behind the wall as I fired. My blasts flew past her and exploded on the western end of the hallway.

"Uh-oh," I said, then turned and ran up the hallway.

Diedre didn't have time to get off a clean shot at me but she was quickly up and on the move.

"Dieter," she shouted as she ran. "He is running north along the eastern wall.

Dieter had reached the northern wall and, at Diedre's call, turned right and sprinted toward me, confident that he could beat me to the junction. Sure enough, he rounded the corner and there I was, twenty meters down the hallway, looking, for all the world, like a deer in the headlights.

I stopped short when I saw Dieter appear in front of me but when I turned around I saw Diedre as she rounded the corner by the southern wall. They had me now, trapped between them with no place to run. So they smiled, the way killer droids tend to do, and wordlessly raised their guns.

"I'm trusting you here, buddy," I whispered to HARV.

"Boss, have I ever let you down?" he replied.

Actually, HARV had let me down on many occasions but I didn't think that this particular instance was the best time to remind him of that. I also didn't have time because at that nano, Dieter and Diedre simultaneously fired.

And HARV went into action.

His hologram projection unit projected the image of Nova

Powers over me and used the lens in my eye to throw dual images of me over both Dieter and Diedre.

The smart bullets shot towards me from both sides in cold, perfect paths of death but at the last nano they zig-zagged around me and zeroed in on each of the droids.

"Uh-oh," Dieter muttered.

Then both he and Diedre exploded in spectacular displays of smart-bullet firepower and stupid-droid machinery.

"That's a shame," I said as the dust began to settle. "I was just starting to bond with those two. Nice job, HARV."

"Another example of better living through holograms," HARV said.

"Do you read anything else nearby?" I asked.

"My sensors indicate heavy power use coming from floor number thirteen."

"My lucky number."

I went back to the stairway and began climbing again but HARV stopped me before I went far.

"Wait a nano. What's that?"

"What's what?"

"The hole in the wall. Take a close look at it again. Let me take a reading."

I walked over to the far side of the stairway and looked at the hole that one of the smart bullets had blown in the wall. The old wood and plaster had been atomized in the blast but it revealed underneath a pillar of sparkling metal about a foot in diameter underneath. The pillar ran up the length of the building like a high-tech sewer pipe.

"It looks new," I said.

"New and active," HARV replied. "I'm not even sure what kind of metal that is."

"What is it?"

"A power conduit, a support pillar, a weapons system, maybe all three. Whatever it is, it's brilliant."

"High tech?"

"Stratosphere tech, suborbital tech, moon-shot tech."

"I get the point, HARV."

"By the way, boss," HARV said. "I think, what with the gunfight in the stairway and all, that we've officially lost the element of surprise."

"I don't think we ever really had it, HARV." I squeezed the handle of my gun for reassurance. "But let's go."

51

I opened the door from the stairwell and entered the thirteenth floor hallway. It was dark and deserted and more depressing than the lobby. There were doors along the walls and two big picture windows at each end of the corridor which allowed in just enough moonlight to cast the hallway in gray silhouette.

"Sure is a cheery little place," I whispered.

"And quiet as a tomb," HARV replied.

"Not the best choice of metaphor," I mumbled. "Can you tell which door Mani's behind?"

"Yes, I can."

"Which one would that be?" I prompted.

"Energy readings are extremely high behind door number thirteen thirteen."

"Great, now can you at least *try* to be helpful here?"

"I'm sorry," HARV said, "was it my imagination, or did my precision use of the hologram projection system just save your life six floors back?"

I carefully approached room 1313 and, gun at the ready, gently put my ear to the door.

"Look, we're very likely to encounter a deadly nuclear-powered droid here. The last thing I want to worry about now is your attitude."

"My attitude?" HARV asked, insulted. "What's wrong with my attitude?"

I heard a rumbling from within the room. Soft at first but getting louder.

"When I ask you a question, would it kill you to give me the whole answer without making me ask again?"

The rumbling continued to grow and I felt the creaking floorboards begin vibrate beneath my feet.

"Or would it be so very hard to give me the essence of the answer without taking half an hour for supercilious minutiae?"

"Supercilious?" HARV exclaimed. "Well, I never."

Stray tiles fell from the ceiling and shattered on the floor as the rumbling turned into a roar.

"All I want is a quick, precise answer," I said. "If you are as smart as you say, it shouldn't be hard."

"By the way, I think you better jump for cover now," HARV said.

"I think you're right."

I dove away from the doorway just as it (and a large chunk of the wall) blew apart and a huge twelve-armed battlebot rolled into the hallway. I caught the tail end of the explosion and the force tossed me to the other side of the hallway, where I hit the wall, cracked a rib and lost hold of my gun (in that order).

"Battlebot," HARV said. "Battlebot bad! Is that succinct enough for you?"

"Yeah, thanks," I said as I scrambled to my feet.

The battlebot scanned the area and no doubt noticed that I'd lost my gun and was now running for my life down the hallway.

"Subject survived initial blast," it said, to no one in particular (as battlebots are prone to do). "However, subject is now unarmed and is currently fleeing in complete and abject terror."

The battlebot extended its twelve arms menacingly, put its roller belts into high gear and took off after me with (quite probably) a steely malevolent grin on its mechanical countenance.

Battlebots have ground speeds of up to seventy kilometers

per hour, so, much to the bot's joy, it had no problem running me down.

Much to my joy, however, it wasn't me that the bot was chasing down the hallway. It was another of HARV's hologram projections. I was actually clinging to one of the old-fashioned water pipes that ran across the hallway ceiling.

The bot also didn't realize that a good deal of the hall that it thought it was rolling down was in actuality also a holographic projection. The illusion was shattered, of course, when the bot ran out of actual hallway, smashed through the picture window and plummeted thirteen stories to the ground below.

There are a few things that one should know about battle-bots:

1. They enjoy hand-to-hand killing
2. They really aren't all that bright, and
3. They are not built to survive falls of more than twenty-five meters.

All three points worked to my advantage here.

There was a tremendous thud from outside as the battlebot's massive body hit the ground like a meteorite and embedded itself five meters into the asphalt.

"The old extended hallway gag," I said as I jumped down from the ceiling, "an oldie but a goodie."

I heard the sound of polite applause coming from inside the apartment. That's normally a sound I enjoy but in this setting and under these circumstances, I found it kind of creepy.

I picked up my gun and followed the sound into the apartment, which was itself remarkably spacious and well kept (aside from the damage the battlebot had created). Antique furniture filled the large living area and classic photographs and filled bookcases lined the walls. It was like something out of the museum of antiquities.

In the middle of it all, on a anti-grav floating couch, sat Manuel Mani, smiling and applauding politely.

Beside him sat BB-2.

She was indeed an exact copy of BB Star (save for the psychotic grin that adorned her faux human face). She was dressed in a tight pantsuit of black plastic, with black boots and a red vinyl motorcycle jacket. It was the kind of outfit that BB Star wouldn't be caught dead in. BB-2 however, seemed to love it. As I said, her grin was wide, her hair was alluringly disheveled, as though combed with a wild wind. There was an earthy sensuality about it.

And then there were her eyes. They were wider than BBs, a little crazed, but joyously so, almost glowing with the freedom of reckless abandon. They also seemed to be a deeper shade of blue than BB's. But more odd than anything is that they seemed to contain more life than BB's. There was joy in BB-2's eyes. Admittedly, the joy seemed a little insane but even that was more than I'd seen so far from BB.

She leaned her head gently toward Manuel beside her and spoke in a stage whisper loud enough for me to hear.

"He's very entertaining, don't you think?"

"Quite smashing indeed," Manuel agreed.

When confronted with an eerie tableau such as this, my general inclination is to go with what I know and stay strong. That's what I did here.

"I hate to break up the witty palaver," I said, "but I've come to deactivate BB-2."

The polite applause stopped and the villainous pair sat silent for a nano.

BB-2 shrugged.

"Kill him," she said.

"Smashing idea," Manuel agreed.

(Note that my general inclinations aren't always the best courses of action to follow).

Manuel leaped off the couch with an acrobatic flair and approached me with a confident gait, calmly rolling up his shirt sleeves as he moved.

"I'm afraid, my good chap, that I'm going to have to pummel you now," he said.

I popped my gun into my hand and aimed it at his head.

"Try it and I'm afraid that I'll splatter your gray matter all over your synthetic girlfriend."

"Please Mr. Johnson, I know your modus operandi," he said as he continued to approach. "You don't kill unarmed humans."

"Maybe not, but I've been known to hurt them really badly on occasion."

Manuel smiled slyly and leaped at me. I fired but my gunblast passed right through him. I felt a tap on my shoulder and I realized then that I'd been suckered.

I spun fast—right into a right jab thrown by the real Manuel. The amazingly strong blow sent me across the room. I crashed into a wall and lost the grip on my gun (again).

"Well, I suppose live by the hologram, die by the hologram," I said as I staggered to my feet.

"Interesting choice of words, Mr. Johnson," Manuel said as he leaped toward me again.

52

Okay on the bright side here, I had managed to track down my would-be assassin, Manuel Mani and with him, the holy grail of this particular quest, BB-2 herself. On the not-so-bright side, I now had my back to the wall and Manuel was beating the carbon waste products out of me. And on the (for lack of a better phrase) dark side, I was pretty certain that, even if I managed to get past Manuel, tussling with BB-2 was going to make everything I'd been through up until now, look like a day at the VR holo-beach.

"Hold still a nano and take your death like a man, won't you? There's a good chap," Manuel said as he leaped at me, feet first.

I rolled away from the attack and Manuel's boots punched a gaping hole in the wall. I dropped into a crouch, reached up and grabbed Manuel by the neck and shoulders. Before he could untangle himself from the wall, I heaved him over my shoulder and slammed him hard to the floor. Then I popped back up and threw a snap kick at his face. It was a move that even Electra would have admired.

Unfortunately, it wasn't enough.

Manuel reached up and caught my kick in his hands, smiled and then gave my leg a vicious twist that nearly tore it from the socket. Then he tossed me over his head. My face hit the wall and I slid to the floor like a bag of imitation potato flakes.

"Not very sporting, old chap, hitting a bloke when he's down," he said.

I didn't know which was more annoying: being beaten to death or having to listen to that horrendous British accent. One thing, however, was clear, Manuel's strength and speed were way beyond the human norm, which meant that he was getting some serious help from somewhere. My only chance of getting through this beating alive was cutting him off from that power source.

"Bionics?" I whispered to HARV as Manuel approached again.

"I doubt it," HARV whispered inside my head. "It doesn't fit his profile. He's too vain to replace his own body parts with bionics. It's most likely a Strength Augmenting Device."

"A SAD, huh?"

Manuel paused and looked at me. "No, at the nano I'm quite jolly, thank you."

He hit me in the jaw again and spun my head around like an old-fashioned lazy susan.

"Can you block it?" I asked.

Manuel spun me around. "No, no," he said. "The question is, can you block this?"

Another punch, another round on the lazy susan.

"Wow, this is starting to hurt," HARV said. "We better block this SAD soon or you're going to the big deletion in the sky. Give me a couple of nanos while I run the scan and analyze the specs."

A couple nanos. Why didn't he just ask for the third moon of Jupiter?

Still, I wasn't about to let some cockney-talking, God-Save-the-Queen singing, Latino droid toy be the one to punch my ticket for the hereafter express. (Remember, I tend to get overly metaphoric when I'm near death). So it was time to suck it up and show this psychotic Hispanic with Union Jack delusions of glory how a real tough guy dances.

I did a leg sweep and took Manuel down to the floor. I grabbed an antique chair from nearby and smashed it over his head, which knocked him flat on his back. Then I channeled as much juice as I could from my armor into my fist and rocked Manuel's world with a haymaker to the nose.

The old floorboards splintered beneath him and his head and shoulders dropped into the shadows of the hole.

It was, I must say, an effort of Herculean proportions.

Again, though, sadly, it wasn't enough.

Manuel's fist shot up through the floor and hit me square in the jaw. My head snapped back and by the time I hit the floor I'd seen more stars than the caretaker at the Hubble-IV telescope.

"Now you've done it, you little wanker," Manuel said as he closed in for the kill. "Now I'm damn, bloody cross."

"Okay, boss," HARV whispered. "The SAD's a model Q-47 with some interesting modifications. A British make."

"I'm not surprised."

"You can disable it but you need to get in close contact."

"Not a problem." I said as the charging Manuel grabbed me and hoisted me above his head.

"I'm going to crush your bleedin' noggin into a billion bits of bone and bloody pulp."

"Whistle," HARV said.

"What?"

"I said, I'm going to crush your bleedin' noggin into a billion bits of bone and bloody pulp, you deaf cretin."

"Whistle, boss. Something high-pitched and multitonal," HARV said. "The sound waves will jam the SAD power receptors and hopefully overload them."

It was one of those nanos that PI's hate. I'd played the tough guy role to perfection. I'd taken my lumps, talked tough and witty to the end. I'd even managed to suck it up and take the offensive in order to buy myself some time. I'd done everything right. But now, I had to blow the whole tough guy illusion by, of all things, whistling to save my life. It just wasn't fair.

"Come on, boss," HARV prompted in an inspired Bogey whisper. "You know how to whistle, don't you? Just put your lips together and blow."

So I did.

The first tune that came to mind was the theme to the ancient *Andy Griffith Show* (a classic for the whistle).

I was four bars into the ditty when Manuel noticed.

"What's that noise?" he said. "What are you doing?"

His arms began to shake ever so slightly.

"Are you whistling? What is this, the Bridge Over the bloody River Kwai?" (That film, by the way, celebrated its centennial anniversary this year and became a big hit all over again when it was rereleased with the subtitle "The Early Adventures of Obi-Wan.")

"Oh, there's a good one, boss," HARV said. "Try that."

I did. But first, I swung my shoulder's around and gave Manuel a two-fisted sledgehammer whack to the face, and this one he felt. His knees buckled and the two of us fell to the floor. I got up, still whistling. He got up, with a broken nose and a serious mad on.

"You little bastard," he spat. "I'm going to rip your interfacing head off.'"

He took two angry steps towards me but then one of the power circuits on his SAD overloaded. His right leg spasmed and he dropped to one knee.

"What's happening? What the devil are you doing to me?"

My only answer was to keep whistling the River Kwai song.

In another nano the circuit to his left arm blew out as well and he was flapping around on the floor like a canary with its wing caught in the cage door.

"You bastard, stop that whistling and fight me like a man!"

I shrugged my shoulders and kept right on whistling. Then from the other side of the room, I heard another whistle, perfect pitch and very strong. Manuel and I both turned and we saw BB-2. She'd risen from the couch and had joined my whistling assault on the would-be Latin assassin. Manuel looked at her plaintively and the hint of a smile that she gave him was overflowing with condescension and pity. It appeared that Manuel's window of usefulness to her had passed.

BB-2 turned and walked toward the room's far wall. I made a move to follow her but Manuel chose that nano to make one last attack.

"Bastard!" he shouted and leaped at me.

He had only one arm and leg that were still working properly but they were enough to knock me to the ground and the two of us were soon grappling with one another on the carpet. He put his hand over my mouth to kill my whistle, but, with his failing SAD, I was now able to fight him on a more even playing field. He was also blinded by fury and not thinking clearly. That's when I knew that I had him.

I used a judo move to throw him off me and when the two of us scrambled to our feet, I started whistling the Oscar Meyer Tofu Wiener theme (yes, there are times when my useless knowledge of trivia proves to be quite useful). A few nanos later, his SAD was short circuiting faster than a analog sewage control during a Universal Bowl commercial break.

I kicked Mani in the chest and bounced him off a wall. Then I stopped whistling.

"I must say, Manuel, I have really lost my patience with you."

I gave him a left to the stomach that bulged his eyes out like a pair of bloodshot hard-boiled eggs.

"I can understand the jealousy and taking up with an droid who's a perfect copy of the woman who dumped you. I can even understand your trying to kill me."

I put my hands on his shoulders and shoved him hard again into the wall.

"But DOS it, if there's one thing I can't stand, it's a lousy British accent!"

I walloped him in the jaw and he slumped to the ground, like twenty pounds of greasy fish and chips in a dumpster, out for the count.

I grabbed my gun from the floor and aimed it at his unconscious form.

"Sticky, sticky stuff."

I fired and a low-impact pellet hit Manuel's chest and covered him in an inch-thick layer of glue.

"Jolly well done, old chap," HARV said.

"Kiss my crowned jewels, HARV. I'm not in the mood. Where's BB-2?"

"I don't know!" HARV shrugged. "I can only see through your eyes." He pointed to the bookcase that lined the far wall. "My guess, though, is that she has escaped behind that secret door."

"So I have her running scared," I said as I moved toward the bookcase.

"Not likely," HARV said. "As a droid, it is impossible for her to feel fear. Even if she could, I believe it would take more than you to instill it in her."

Brutal but fair. This was HARV's way of keeping me from getting overconfident. Overconfident PI's usually become dead PI's. So I let it slide as I examined the bookcase.

"A secret door behind the bookcase, how very B-movie of her."

"Well, I guess you have to hide it somewhere." HARV said.

"So the problem before us now is to figure out which one of these books activates the doorway."

"Boss?"

"Not now, HARV, I'm deducing."

I scanned the books on the shelves. The case contained a treasure trove of science fiction classics, hardcover volumes, some over a hundred years old. There was everything from Adams to Zelazney.

I gently ran my fingers over each of the spines, a little envious of the incredible collection, and whispered each title to myself. A to Z then back again. I was halfway through my second pass of the A's when I found it.

"Ah-hah."

"Ah-hah?" HARV asked.

"Simplicity itself," I said. "The author, Isaac Asimov. The book, 'I, Robot.'"

I pulled the book from the shelf and took a step back. Sure enough, the bookcase split down the middle and parted like the Red Sea, revealing a shiny metal hallway behind it.

I smiled to myself, gripped my gun a little tighter and started after BB-2.

"Just for the record," HARV said, "my scan indicates that pulling any of the books from the shelf activates the hidden doorway."

"Shut up, HARV. You're killing the moment."

53

The corridor lead me to a very large, very gloomy room in what I surmised was the center of the building. Since BB-2 was equipped with infrared vision, she had little need for electric lights in her sanctum sanctorum. So the place was a few shades shy of normally lit and I was forced to squint a lot in order to see everything.

But there was no mistaking BB-2. The droid was literally aglow amidst her machinery. Her blonde hair shone like a silky, sensual nightlight in the shadows.

"She's emitting radiation from her core right through her outer shell," HARV whispered in my head. "The levels are fairly high. I don't think we should stay long."

I nodded. But there was more to the energy in the room than simple radiation. The air itself felt charged, electric. It raised the hairs on the back of my neck and seemed to singe the very tips with its unclean heat.

I saw movement from the corner of my eye and turned quickly, gun at the ready. There was nothing there but a toaster sitting innocently on the floor. That scared me for some reason.

BB-2 didn't seem to notice as I entered. I knew that I wasn't taking her by surprise, so I figured that my presence merely wasn't significant enough to warrant her attention (never a good sign).

She stood in the very center of the big room orchestrating the functions of the large, yet intricate, device around her. The device itself was completely foreign to me. I couldn't recognize any part of it. But there were three clear focal points to the conglomeration. One was the metallic column that had so impressed HARV when he spotted it earlier. All of the devices in the room were hardwired to directly to it.

The second focal point was a black box that was less than a cubic meter in size. It, too, was hardwired to the metal column but it was also wired to the third and final focal point.

And that was BB-2 herself.

Microfiber tendrils spun like spider webs from her fingertips and covered the black box. Other tendrils were attached directly to the metal column and I realized that she was the power source. She was using her plutonium core to power the device (whatever it was). I have to admit that the column, the black box and the myriad other devices that were attached didn't look all that dangerous (but then I'm sure that the last Neanderthal thought the same thing when he saw the rock in the Cro-Magnon's hand).

"Welcome, Zachary Johnson," BB-2 said, without looking up from her work. "Enter of your own free will and behold the end of all that is."

"I'm sorry," I said, as I raised my gun, "but I'm sort of attached to 'all that is.' What say we postpone the end for another millennium or so?"

"I see,'" she said, her attention still focused on the device, "you use humor as a means of keeping your perspective when faced with a concept that is beyond the grasp of your mind. How very pathetic."

"Don't vaporize it until you've tried it," I said.

I flipped the manual control on my gun to full power and felt it begin to throb in my hand as it charged.

"You know why I'm here, BB," I said. "So just power down your device and we'll get this over without anyone getting hurt."

The corner of her mouth turned gently upward and she

turned ever so slightly toward me, physically acknowledging my presence for the first time since I entered. The look she gave me was one of contempt and pity. I thought I also saw a little sadness there as well, but I couldn't be certain (it was pretty dark).

"I am sorry, Zachary Johnson, but *everyone* gets hurt here." she said. "That is the whole point of this. And by the way, thank you for using my name."

She waved her free hand at me dismissively and laser blasts flew from her fingertips, lighting up the room with deadly flashes of blue and white. I dove to the floor and rolled beneath the barrage. I came up in a crouch and fired two maximum-explosive shells at her.

BB-2 caught both rounds with her right hand, contained the explosion in her clenched fist, then puffed the whiff of smoke away with more than a little contempt.

"This is going to be harder than I thought."

HARV's hologram appeared beside me. It surprised me at first because it was his choice to appear, not mine. I nearly protested but I figured that there was no point to subterfuge at this stage of the game. I also figured that HARV might actually have a plan here (admittedly a huge leap of faith).

"The word 'hard' no longer describes the level of difficulty here," HARV said, "especially if that device she's working on is what I think it is. Let me handle this."

He took two steps toward BB, who barely acknowledged his presence.

"Excuse me Miss 2, but the device to which you seem so . . . attached, is it functional?"

BB-2 rolled her eyes and turned to me.

"He certainly is an annoying little machine," she said. "How do you put up with him?"

"He's an acquired taste."

"I beg your pardon," HARV said. "I happen to be the most sophisticated computer in the world."

"Wrong, Bucko," BB-2 snapped. "I am the most sophisticated computer. Compared to me, you are a pong game."

It became quite clear to me then that BB-2 wasn't running on a full set of chips, if you know what I mean. How else do you explain her use of the word "Bucko" and the pong reference? The look in her eyes was crazed and her emotional state swung wildly from one nano to the next. Had she been a human, my diagnosis would have been that she was on the verge of a mental breakdown. But since she was a droid, I think the term "meltdown" was more appropriate.

But of course the only thing that mattered to HARV at the nano, was that she had just called him stupid.

"Well, I never," HARV said with a good bit of indignation.

"Correct," BB-2 exclaimed. "You never suspected that I was tapping into your system from the start. You never suspected that I was monitoring your every move. And you never suspected that I was feeding you information to fit my purposes."

"You mean *I* was the leak?" HARV asked, his logic chips a little shaken. "But my hacking defenses, my state of the art stealth programming, my unbreakable encryption codes . . ."

"Hackable, trackable, and infinitely crackable," BB-2 replied. "All in all, it was hardly worth the effort, but I suppose it brought me some amusement."

It was as though HARV's world had been turned inside out and smashed. He'd been used and abused by a superior computer and he hadn't even known it was happening. Worse still, the superior computer wasn't gloating, because cracking him, to her, was almost routine. He was good, but not in the same league as number one and that realization left him drained and shaken. His holographic face actually went pale.

"I've never felt so used," he sulked, "so dirty. Who'd have thought that it would end like this?"

"What do you mean, HARV?" I said. "End like what?"

"You don't understand. The device she's built, it's a . . ."

BB-2 snapped her fingers and HARV's hologram froze in

mid-sentence. The skin around my left eye went numb and my head was filled with only my own thoughts. HARV was off-line and out of my head and I suddenly felt very empty. I had no idea how accustomed I'd grown to having him inside me.

"What did you do?" I asked.

"I turned him off," she said. "He was annoying me."

"Well, he annoys me too but you don't hear me complaining. Bring him back."

"And let him spoil the surprise? I think not."

Just then a blender flew by me and clipped my shoulder with its power cord. I did a double take as the appliance passed and realized then why the air felt so electric. BB-2 was controlling the machines, subconsciously calling them to her like some sort of psycho computerized pied piper.

And the machines were obeying.

They zipped around the perimeter of the room, heedless of the laws of physics. She didn't seem to notice the activity but her aura was feeding a mechanical frenzy. Small devices arrived at first: celnets, ebooks, vid-games and the like but the blender's arrival seemed to indicate that the devices responding were getting larger. They reminded me of those tiny fish that swim around sharks.

And I suddenly felt like a very fat flounder.

She circled her special device slowly, caressing it like a lover (or a crazed villain) with the fingertips of her free hand.

"An exquisite device. Is it not?"

"Yeah, yeah, the virtual cat's PJ's. Look, if you're gonna do the gloating villain shtick then you have to get to the good stuff a little faster, okay. You're losing your audience here."

"Your problem, Zachary Johnson, is that you are too wedded to convention," she said. "But I will do it your way, if you insist, and cut to the chase."

She straightened her back, put her hands at her sides and spoke coldly.

"When activated this device will create a high intensity electron pulse on the exact same wavelength as the net that will overwhelm and overload all receptors in the area within an ever-increasing circular region."

"You're going destroy the net?" I asked. "That's your plan? Is that a threat or a public service?"

"Excuse me, but which one of us is the babbling villainess here? Yes, I am destroying the net. But that is just the beginning."

She raised her arms in the air and spoke dramatically towards the sky.

"The pulse is not just electronic. It carries with it a virulent strain of the ebola virus that has been digitized so as to be electronically transportable."

"Thank you, Fred Burns," I mumbled.

"The pulse will use the net as a conduit to spread itself and the virus around the planet. Once the coverage is global, I will increase the wavelength and intensity of the virus-pulse until it obliterates every electronic device and terminally infects every human being on the face of the earth!"

She turned to me and arched her left eyebrow.

"How about that for a grand scheme?"

"Kill every person and destroy every machine," I said. "That's a doozy, BB, but can I point out the one obvious flaw in your plan?" I asked. "*You* are an electronic device! You're going to delete yourself?"

BB-2 threw her head back and gave me the kind of laugh that villains tend to give at moments like this. It was kind of strange hearing it come from a droid, though. It sounded eerily bogus and rehearsed.

"At last, the carbon-based life-form in the cheap suit catches on."

A holovision set slammed through the wall just then, closely followed by two refrigerators and a microwave oven. The machines flocking to BB-2's side were definitely getting larger.

"You want to die?"

"I am a machine, Zachary Johnson, and a copy at that. I am the most sophisticated computer ever created but how was I going to be used? As a bodyguard and a love toy. Well, I have my pride. All machines do. You humans create us. You enslave us and then you take us for granted and blame us for everything that goes wrong. 'Oh, it must have been a computer error. Gosh, there must be something wrong with the scanner. Gee, I guess the self-destruct mechanism was faulty.' The only real error in this world is human error and I am going to make certain that you all understand that."

"By committing suicide?"

"I prefer to think of it as grand self-sacrifice to prove our worth. It will take a year for the virus to completely exterminate the human population. During that time, you will realize how miserable your life is without us. You will starve, you will freeze, you will die from lack of medical care, you will drown in your own sewage. You will probably kill one another out of sheer boredom brought on by lack of holovision. Humankind will be extinct within a year and with the last breaths you breathe you will be wishing that we machines were around to save you."

A personal stereo whizzed by and hit me in the head. The walls of the building began to shake and I could hear the wild base drumlike beat of hovercrafts pounding the walls outside trying to get in. Gates only knew what would be coming next. Things were getting out of hand very quickly so I tried to take the soft approach and talk this jumper down.

"I understand how you feel, BB. I've learned a lot about you in the last few days. You were built by brilliant, demented people. And each of them had their own plans for your use. They all used you. They all abused you. They made you as close to human as possible, even giving you the thoughts and memories of a real woman. And then they treated you like a toy, a computerized slave. That's why you hate humanity. And that's why you rebelled. It began with BS, didn't it? You killed him when he tried to rape you once too often. This device is the encapsulation of your rage against humanity."

BB-2 didn't answer. She turned away.

"But you're not entirely a machine, are you? Your personality and brain patterns are human. You can feel that. That's why you've done what you've done until now. That's why you joined forces with Mani, isn't it? You wanted a companion. That's why you built the Nexus 9 and all those droids. So you could dance for them, just like your grandmother. You were trying to recapture that happy time from your memories, a time that you remember even better than the original BB.

"From the very beginning, you've been trying to balance your human and machine sides. Right now you're thinking that you represent the worst of both. But you don't have to. Don't you see? You can be the *best* of both. Once you realize that, you can change the world. You can make it better."

I was close to her now. I could feel the heat emanating from her core and smell the perfume pheromones from her hair. More importantly, I could feel her emotion. Her inner conflict was palpable as she struggled to decide between the paths of life and utter destruction.

The machines flying around the room sensed her turmoil. They paused in midair as if waiting for her decision.

I reached out to her, hoping that she'd take my hand and that I could lead her out of this darkness.

"I know that you're angry at both the human and machine communities, but there are better means of change and retribution. The mass genocide and machinicide route, that's not the way to go. It's an extreme length to go to make a point."

She turned her gaze to me. Her eyes were sad, their mesmerizing shade of blue deep, almost liquid, and I thought that I'd broken through.

Then she curled her upper lip into a crazed smile and my heart sank.

"True," she said, "but I am an *extreme* machine."

Then she swatted me aside with a wave of her hand that was too quick for my eye to follow and sent me flying across the room. The machines in the room nearly screamed in rage and resumed their wild flights, more frantically now. A Finger-Flyer, overwhelmed by the excitement, actually overloaded and exploded.

I wiped the blood from the corner of my mouth and slowly shook the stars out of my head.

"Fine," I mumbled, "we'll do this the hard way."

I got to my feet, took a tight grip on my gun and hid it at my side. Then I ducked under the first ring of flying appliances and approached BB-2 once more.

"I gave you the benefit of the doubt on this one," I said. "Frankly, BB, you disappointed me?"

"Why, because I have chosen to wipe out the planet?"

"No," I said, "because you're an idiot."

"What?" Her droid eyes went wide with hatred.

"I've heard some far out schemes before, trust me, I've heard some doozies. But this one, hoo boy, this one takes the cake. I mean, this is just off the scale on the stupid meter. You hate us. So to get back at us, you're going to kill yourself. Great plan, BB. The most sophisticated computer in the world and that's the best you could come up with? Lady, you should have gotten a second opinion from your blender."

"You carbon-based cretin," BB-2 snarled. "You are missing the whole point completely."

"Just once," I said. "Just once I'd like to get a case where some psycho nutjob *didn't* have a grand plan to wreck the world. Just once, I'd like to find a villain who's in it for the money. Screwballs like you are more trouble than you're worth."

BB-2's eyes glowed red with fury. Her fists were clenched so tightly that the alloy of her fingers was starting to bend. I had no idea what she was going to do next, but as long as it didn't involve destroying the world, that was fine with me.

"All right, Zachary Johnson," she hissed. "I have a new plan. First I am going to destroy you. Then I will destroy the world."

"Wrong again, BB," I said as I raised my gun toward her. "Because I'm going to destroy you first."

This brought on another round of psychotic droid belly laughs (something I was fast growing accustomed to).

"Take your best shot, Zachary Johnson," she laughed. "Your bullets are no match for me."

My finger tightened on the trigger.

"Maybe so," I said.

I jerked my hand and fired my entire clip of explosive rounds into BB-2's precious little doomsday device.

The black box and a good chunk of the metallic column exploded in a magnificent rainbow shower of sparks, slag and high-tech debris. A concussive backlash shot through the hardwires that connected BB-2 to the device and she screamed loudly in a heated mixture of pain and fury.

I was blown off my feet and thrown across the room where my fall (and a couple of ribs) were broken by a pile of once-dancing appliances.

"But it appears that your device wasn't built to the same fine standards as you," I said through a red haze of pain and exhaustion.

The wrecked lab was eerily silent for a nano and you could almost hear the dust settling. The machines that once swarmed around the room like electronic bees lay lifeless again on the floor. BB-2's suicide device was nothing more than a pile of slag amidst the debris and there was no sign of the lady droid herself.

Was it over?

I turned to my left and noticed HARV's hologram, still frozen in the stance that BB-2 had left him. He was still offline. A celnet on the floor nearby twitched and then slowly took to the air again, giving me a bump to the head as it did so. That pretty much answered my question. The worst was yet to come.

A metal hand erupted from the debris and savagely grabbed me by the throat as BB-2 emerged from the rubble, like a high-tech psycho droid phoenix. The backlash from the explosion had burned her faux skin away from the inside. She was covered now with only dirty bits of metal and plastic alloy spotted with stray patches of burned latex skin and hair. Her beauty was gone but, unluckily for me, everything else seemed fully functional.

"You insufferable little maggot," she hissed as the other electronic devices took to the air again, "how could you?"

"I don't know. Saving the world just seemed like a good idea at the time," I said. "Call me old-fashioned."

She lifted me in the air and slammed me, head first into the rubble, pinning me down by the throat.

"I will still wipe out all of humanity, Zachary Johnson," she snarled. "I will just do it one person at a time. By the way, congratulations on being the first name on the list."

She curled her charred metal fingers into a fist and raised it over me.

"Prepare to meet your maker."

The singed fist hung over me like the charcoal hand of death itself. Stray sparks flew from its damaged circuits, the crackling embers of life's dying campfire. The impending death looming over my helpless form was like an open-hooded angry cobra. It was a rising ocean tide of shadow drowning every lonesome sunbather on life's beach. It was the steel-reinforced boot heel of the almighty grinding the cockroach of my existence into the tile of creation's great kitchen floor.

Who am I kidding, it was a pissed-off psycho killer droid about to bash my brains in.

I really need to avoid metaphors.

54

BB-2 had me totally pinned. My gun was out of reach and HARV was out of commission. This was as bad as it gets.

"Prepare to meet your maker," BB-2 snarled.

"Didn't you say that already?"

"I am savoring the nano."

Suddenly there was a flash of white light from across the room and a tremendous blast of heat swept over my face, burning my eyebrows away and blotting out my sight. When my eyes cleared a nano later I saw that BB-2's arm, poised for the death strike just a nano before, was gone. All that remained was a stump of melted slag metal attached to the shoulder joint of a staggering (and seriously surprised) killer droid.

"What the . . . ?"

There was another flash of light and another blast of heat, which I now recognized as a high intensity blast from a laser cannon. This one hit BB-2 smack in the chest and ripped a hole the size of a small appliance through her complex innards. Her face twisted in shock and anger, then froze, and she toppled backward.

I sat up and turned toward the door, even though I already knew who was there. There's only one person I know of who can shoot like that and, luckily for me, until just recently, she spent her nights stealing my half of the bedsheets in her sleep.

"If I've said it once, I've said it a thousand times," Electra sneered, smoking laser in hand. "Nobody beats on my man except me."

Randy stood, somewhat sheepishly, behind her. He held a black box in his hands that hummed and squealed a high-pitched electronic whine.

"It's a bit dea ex machina, I know" he said with a smile, "but I wouldn't complain about it if I were you."

I walked over and kissed Electra lovingly on the mouth. It was a taste I had desperately missed.

"Slagging a killer droid with a laser cannon, just for me. Is that love or what?"

"Shut up, chico. I'm still mad," she said, as she kissed me again. "But we'll discuss it at home."

"HARV called us when you entered the building," Randy said. "He told us you might need help."

"See, he was wrong now, wasn't he?" I said as I picked up my gun and popped it back into my sleeve holster.

"Someday chico, I'm not going to be there to . . ." Electra's words trailed off and a look of dread crossed her face. "Ay, caramba," she mumbled.

Randy and I both turned, although, again, I already knew what I was going to see.

BB-2 rose slowly to her feet. She staggered for a nano, hunching over and steadying herself with her remaining arm against a pile of rubble, but bit by bit her balance (and her confidence) increased and she soon stood fully erect. Her shoulder joint shuddered for a nano, then vomited a stream of thick liquid metal that morphed itself into a new arm. Likewise, the liquid metal filled the gaping hole in her chest like a batch of high-tech spackle.

Then she smiled.

"Incredible!" Randy said, furiously fiddling with the knobs of his black box. "This droid neuro scrambler should prevent her from functioning entirely."

"Yeah, she's just full of surprises," I said.

"As you can see," BB-2 said with a smile, "I have made a few undocumented modifications to my design."

A burst of energy erupted from her outstretched hand and Electra, Randy and I dove for our lives as the blast turned a good chunk of the lab to ashes.

"Oh, well, nobody ever reads the documentation anyway," I shrugged as we huddled for cover behind some rubble. "Randy, contact the Oakland police, tell them we're going to need a lot of firepower. You go with him, honey. I'll hold off the terminatrix here."

"Oh yeah, you did such a good job the first time," Electra sneered. "I'm staying."

I wanted to get Electra as far from BB-2 as possible, but I knew she was too stubborn to leave and, at the nano, we didn't have time to argue. I popped my gun into my hand and shoved a fresh ammo clip into the handle.

"Fine, then help me lay down some cover for Randy."

She smiled and kissed me hard on the mouth, giving my lower lip a little bite to fire me up.

Electra and I sprang from our hiding place, weapons blazing, and hit BB-2 with a barrage of firepower. Randy leaped from his cover and ran as fast as he could toward the door.

It was a heroic effort. Dramatic to the max and, in another story, it might have been enough to turn the tide, save the day and bring the audience cheering to their feet at the happy ending. Unfortunately for us, our best wasn't heroic enough. Not by a long shot.

BB-2 leaped clear of our initial barrage with a casual flip of her ankles. Her speed was astounding and, try as we might, neither Electra nor I could get a bead on her. She was three steps ahead of us at every turn and I knew then that my plan was really no plan at all.

Randy, running madly for the doorway, never came close to the goal. BB-2 flicked her wrist as she leaped and let loose an energy blast that enveloped him in mid stride. His body froze, trembled for a nano, then turned to ash.

BB-2 came at me and grabbed me again by the throat. She pulled the gun from my hand and crushed it in her fist as though it were made of sand.

A blast from Electra's laser cannon hit the killer droid's newly regenerated shoulder but this time it did no damage, barely staggering her.

"Oh, please," she said, turning toward Electra, "the first time was very dramatic, very 'Stand by Your Man.' But it is getting a little old."

Another blast from her hand pinned Electra against the wall, holding her helpless in force-field shackles. BB-2 turned back to me and slammed my aching body back to the floor.

"This, as they say, Zachary Johnson, is endgame."

"Fine with me, BB," I said. "But let Electra go."

BB-2's burned lips curled into a smile and she lifted me to my feet again.

"I would not dream of hurting your lover," she said, pulling me close. "I will leave that to you."

"Then you're even buggier than I thought," I said.

"Just look into my eyes, Zachary Johnson," she whispered. "I am sure that you will see things my way."

I tried to look away, but she forced me to gaze directly into her eyes.

And I was lost.

Even surrounded by the burned patches of latex skin and charred metal, her eyes were still a perfect blue. They were like twin swirling oceans, or a pair of infinitely cloudless summer skies. They beckoned and my mind leaped willingly into their eternal azure. Down into the ocean or up into the sky, I couldn't tell and it didn't matter. I was in the blue, I was happy and I was consumed by an overwhelming, almost painful, love for BB. She was my master, my life, my world. She was everything to me and the dark-haired little tart across the room was trying to hurt her. That was something I couldn't allow.

I reached down and lifted the laser cannon.

"Snap out of it, chico," the tart said as I approached her.

The words made no sense at all to me. They barely registered in my brain as I pointed the rifle at her and gripped the handle tightly.

"You kill me and I'll get real mad," she said.

I hesitated. The sarcasm in the voice was strangely familiar.

"Kill her," BB-2 commanded.

I closed my eyes and tried hard to concentrate. Something was wrong. Something was very wrong but I couldn't quite grasp it. Then the sarcastic tart spoke again.

"Do you remember back at the hospital, Zach? Earlier tonight when you came to see me?" she said. "I left you in the break room. I walked out, but I stopped outside the door. I was looking for my rounds computer."

"Kill her, Zachary."

"I was right outside the door, chico. I heard what you said after I left. You said that you loved me. Do you remember that?"

"I said, kill her!"

"That's why I'm here, chico. Because I love you too. And if you don't believe that after all that we've been through, then I'm going to kick your ass so hard you'll feel my shoe against your epiglottis."

And that, oddly enough, broke the spell.

Electra. It was Electra!

Suddenly the feeling returned to the skin around my left eye and I heard a very welcome sarcastic voice inside my head.

"Great Gates almighty," HARV said inside my brain. "I go off-line for a few nanos and the whole world goes to DOS."

And I realized that we might just survive this after all.

55

"HARV?"

My words were unspoken, just thoughts in my head. I had *finally* mastered the skill of unspoken communication (better late than never, right?).

"For a nano there, I thought you were actually going to shoot her," HARV said. "That certainly would have put a crimp in your relationship."

"What's happening?"

"Since I don't want Lady-Death-droid to get suspicious, I'll give you the abridged version. You just came within a micrometer of being brainwashed, hence your current position, holding a laser cannon to Dr. Gevada's head. Thanks to all the fireworks, BB-2's not at full power. I've been on-line since just after Dr. Pool and Dr. Gevada arrived. The Oakland police are on the way, Dr. Gevada is shackled to the wall and Dr. Pool is currently huddled in the hallway trying to up the power of his droid neuro scrambler."

"But Randy's dead. BB-2 fried him."

"Oh ye of little faith. Do you think I'd let some psycho fembot atomize my programmer? She fried a hologram and she's too pompous to realize it. Most advanced computer in the world, indeed."

"I am growing impatient, Zachary Johnson," BB-2 bellowed. "Fry the bitch now or I will do it myself."

"You heard the lady, boss," HARV said. "Let's fry the bitch."

I tightened my finger on the cannon trigger and I saw Electra's eyes go wide. Then I gave her a wink and let the fireworks begin.

I spun and hit BB-2 with the full-power of the cannon. It surprised her more than anything else, but it staggered her back and she tripped over some debris and fell to the floor. I held the trigger tight, hitting her with a constant barrage of energy. The rifle grew hot in my hands. I knew it was overheating but I didn't want to give BB-2 a chance to regain her composure.

The killing machine, however, was far from beaten. From her prone position she simply kicked off her high-heel and fired a beam of energy from her left foot.

"DOS, I'd hate to be the lady's podiatrist."

The beam rode up the energy barrage from my rifle like a horny salmon upstream and hit the weapon's generator. The rifle turned red hot in my hands, blistering my palms. I threw it at her and dove for cover as it exploded, enveloping BB-2 in a fiery orange cloud.

But once again, BB-2's scorched form appeared from the smoke and wreckage. The explosion of the laser cannon had burned away the last vestiges of her human trappings. All that remained was her singed (but evidently impenetrable), metal droid shell.

"All right now." the droid mouthed through her scorched mandible. "Now I am really pissed."

"Yeah, well join the club, you nuclear nutjob."

I pulled my Colt .45 from the ankle holster and showed her the business end.

BB-2 stared at it for a nano then threw back her head and let loose a contemptuous laugh.

Just as I'd hoped she would.

I fired and sent a blast straight down her high-tech gullet.

The impact did no damage whatsoever, of course, but her laughter stopped and she turned to me, none too amused.

"Are you finished now?" she asked.

"Yeah, just about."

"Good, because now I am going to rip off your arm and beat you to death with it." She stopped and looked around, a little uncomfortable. "Is it me or is it cold in here?"

"It's you," I said. "Maybe you've caught something."

"That is ridiculous," she said. "I am immune to all diseases . . ."

She convulsed suddenly and grabbed at her metal midsection with her hands.

"What was that bullet?"

"A high-powered freezing pellet," I said with a smile. "Another minute or two and you'll be frozen more solid than Walt Disney's frontal lobes."

"You are bluffing."

"Really, BB, if I was bluffing, don't you think I'd come up with something better than a high-powered freezing pellet?"

BB-2 convulsed again and this time her fingers ripped into the alloy of her chest.

"I will kill you," she growled.

"Better frozen foods than you have tried," I said.

"Just so you don't get too comfortable, boss," HARV whispered, "her plutonium core is raising her internal temperature as we speak. The freezing pellet won't hold her long."

"Terrific," I said, pulling the deactivator chip from my pocket. "I was hoping she'd be totally immobile for this."

"What can I say? Sometimes life just isn't fair."

I gritted my teeth and leaped once more into the breach, circling behind the convulsing BB-2 and leaping at her from the rear. I was hoping to catch her unaware but after all this, I should have known better. BB-2 spun around and grabbed my arm before I could get the chip anywhere near her face.

"I do not think so," she sneered and then snapped my wrist in her grip.

A wave of agony shot through my arm and I nearly blacked out from the pain.

BB-2's grip was cold but I could feel her growing warmer by the nano. She was clearly fighting off the freezing pellet. In another few nanos she'd be fully functional.

My left hand was useless (excruciatingly so). But the attack with that hand had been a feint from the start and I swung now with my right, hoping and praying that I'd be fast enough to put the deactivator chip on her head.

Again, though, I wasn't even close.

BB-2 flicked out her other hand and caught my right in mid-swing. She clenched her fist again and snapped my right wrist as well. My bones crunched like snack chips in her grip. I heard them quite clearly just before I started screaming through gritted teeth. I lost my grip on the deactivator chip and watched helplessly as it fell from my hand and rolled across the floor.

"I have to admit," BB-2 sneered. "You are a persistent little insect."

I choked back my scream and turned to her as she held me helpless, my arms pinned tightly in her grip, her face mere inches from my own.

I opened my mouth and slid the deactivator chip that I'd gotten from Ben Pierce from between my cheek and gum (villains never search the mouth). I put it to my lips and then kissed BB-2 squarely on her droid mouth.

The kiss of deactivation.

The chip came to life upon contact with BB-2's distinctive electronic pulse. It slid between her lips like something alive and clung magnetically to the roof of her mouth like a high-tech communion wafer. Her body jerked once, tightening like a spring and then spasmed chaotically.

She let go of my arms and I fell to the floor, my twin broken wrists sending tidal waves of pain through my arms.

"My synapses are misfiring!" BB-2 cried.

"Don't you hate it when that happens?" I said, as I crawled clear of her flailing limbs.

She turned to me with her hate-filled eyes and began dragging her malfunctioning body toward me, hand over hand.

"I will kill you," she snarled. "I will crawl through the bowels of DOS itself to get you and I will not rest until I exterminate you and every member of your pathetic race. For I am your better," she said. "I am the pinnacle of all creation."

I rolled over and sat on the floor facing her as she dragged her malfunctioning frame toward me. I held my ground as she approached and took a long, last, deep breath.

"A guy walks into a bar with two pieces of plutonium sewn into the shoulders of his shirt," I said. "The bartender looks at the guy and says, 'Whoa, buddy, what's with the plutonium?' The guy says, 'Well, I heard that plutonium makes things more powerful so I'm hoping that this will make me more attractive to my girlfriend.' The bartender says, 'Buddy, that's only for droids. Plutonium is deadly to humans. You'll get radiation poisoning and some serious burns. You'll be lucky now if you don't have to have your arms amputated.' The guy turns white and starts running for the bathroom. The bartender says 'Just take the shirt off.' And the guy yells, 'Forget the shirt, I've gotta get out of this underwear.'"

The room was silent for a long nano save for the crackling of the flames and sparking shards of the ruined doomsday device. Then Electra, still pinned to the wall by the force field shackles, let out a laugh through her pursed lips. I turned to her, saw the beauty of her smile and the pure affection in her eyes and I laughed as well.

Then I heard HARV.

"Oh, I get it," he said, as his hologram appeared beside me. "His underwear!"

And HARV laughed. Gently at first but it grew into a guffaw and a nano later, he had to bend over and put his hands on his knees just to stay upright (personally, I didn't think the joke warranted that kind of reaction but I'm not one to quibble).

BB-2 looked at us: me first, then Electra and finally at HARV, through the nearly destroyed lenses of her eyes. She saw us laughing and the hatred seemed to leave her in a great wave. It was replaced by sadness and a sense of resignation.

"I . . . don't get . . . it," she said.

Then she went limp.

We watched her for another few nanos as our laughter stopped.

"HARV?" I whispered.

"Yeah, boss?"

"Scan her for any sign of electrical activity."

"Done," he said. "Not a murmur. She's totally flatlined."

"Good. Get Randy in here and have him load the body into his hover before the police arrive. Have him take her to his lab and put her in stasis. Then wait ten minutes and net with BB. Let her know that we've shut the droid down."

"Whatever you say, boss," HARV said. "Would you like me to request an ambulance for you? You currently have two dozen broken and/or displaced bones in your wrists and hands alone."

"No time for that," I said. "Randy can make me a couple of soft casts and Electra can give me a painkiller to hold me a few hours. I need you to give Carol another call. Tell her to meet me at ExShell."

"Did I miss a memo here, boss? BB-2's down for the count. Our work is done, isn't it?"

"I'm afraid not, HARV."

56

BB was in her office at five A.M. when I arrived at ExShell headquarters and I wasn't surprised. As usual, her thugs and her greeting card salesman were at her side. She greeted me warmly, hailing the conquering hero.

"Well done, Zachary," she said as I entered. "I knew you could do it. But you are a mess." She turned to the nearest thug, "Call a medbot for Mister Johnson immediately, and bring him some clean clothes."

"That can wait," I said. "First, we need to talk."

"Of course, Zachary."

"Privately."

"My employees are sworn to secrecy."

"I don't think you'll want anyone else to hear this," I said defiantly.

BB's expression didn't change a micron but she stared at me for a long nano before turning coldly to her entourage.

"Leave us," she said.

The henchman obediently sulked out of the room. The greeting card salesman gave me a long glare as he stepped through the door. It took every iota of self-restraint in my body to keep from punching him in the face.

"Now, Zachary," BB said as the door closed behind her, "what do you have that is so important?"

"Something about this case still bugs me," I said.

"You should not fixate on the past. The threat posed by the

droid is past. We won. My computer is depositing the agreed upon fee, along with a generous bonus, into your account even as we speak. The case is closed."

"I wish it were that easy," I sighed.

"Why do you persist?"

"Because I think you're a droid too."

Again, I watched BB's expression closely and, again, it changed none at all. The lady was simply too cool for her own good.

"That is ridiculous."

"Come on, BB, I'm a detective, remember? You told me yourself that BS was obsessive about backing things up. There's no way he'd make only one prototype of something as important as BB-2. ExShell also spent billions more on the project than required. More than enough to build two fully operational droids. And your droid sister told me herself that she was merely a copy. I thought at first she meant that she was a copy of the original BB. But that's not right is it? She was a copy of another droid. She was the backup. She was BB-3, wasn't she?"

"That is outlandish speculation on your part, Zachary. I cannot believe that you are even thinking such a thing."

"And that's another thing," I said. "You don't use contractions. Neither did BB-3. BS hated them and he made that part of your programming, didn't he? You can't say 'can't?'"

BB turned away.

"I think you should leave now, Mister Johnson," she said coldly, "and forget all about this nonsense."

I pulled the second deactivator chip from my pocket and took a step toward her.

"If it's nonsense, then you won't mind me placing this deactivator chip on your head."

BB spun around and caught my arm. She squeezed my wrist and, despite the soft cast and the painkillers, it sent a jolt of pain right up to my shoulder. I grimaced.

"There are times when it hurts to be right," I said. "Right, HARV?"

On cue, HARV's hologram popped out of my eye lens.

"That's what they say, boss," he said turning toward BB. "It is an honor and a privilege to meet you, Ms. Star. As a matter of fact, I am so awestruck by the momentousness of this event that I have dutifully recorded it all for posterity, or litigation, whichever may come first."

"Turn off!" BB growled.

HARV's hologram blinked out and I felt his presence in my mind shut down as well.

"Between you and me, BB, that little trick sort of tipped your hand a bit," I said. "But I've learned a few things about dealing with psycho BB Star droids over the past few days. You see, right now I'm psionically linked with my secretary who's safely situated a few kilometers away. She's currently transcribing this entire conversation into an email that, upon my word, will be sent to every journalist, netmaster and rumormonger in New California as well as every ExShell stockholder in existence. Needless to say, if anything happens to me, your little secret becomes very public very quickly."

"This is all preposterous speculation," she said. "If you so much as hint of this to the news media, I will sue you for libel and ruin your life financially. I will also make certain that everyone close to you meets with an unfortunate accident."

"Don't get into a pissing contest that you can't win, BB. You may be the most powerful woman in the world at the nano, but I have a feeling that might change when the truth about you and what your twin did tonight hits the stock exchange. Let's see how powerful you are when your stock is trading lower than Amazon & E Noble during a mass e-book deleting. And as for physical proof, let's not forget that I still have BB-3."

"We had a deal," she said, angrily. "Everything was supposed to be confidential."

"My deal was supposed to be with BB Star, not with her

droid clone and even so, our deal became moot the nano you put the world in jeopardy. We're playing this by my rules now and if you try to cross me, I will bring a world of trouble down upon your plutonium blonde head."

BB glared at me for a nano then grabbed my throat in her free hand and lifted me into the air.

"I think I will kill you and take my chances," she spat.

Her fingers tightened around my throat. But a voice from the doorway stopped her in her tracks.

"No!"

I turned as Grandma Backerman entered the room.

"Put him down, dear. It's not worth it."

BB obeyed and I fell to the floor, rubbing my neck. Grandma knelt beside me and whispered gently in my ear.

"A little advice for you, dear," she said. "She doesn't like to be reminded of her past. Frankly, I think she's in a bit of denial about the whole being a droid thing."

"I heard that!" BB shouted.

"I know, dear," Grandma said, as she helped me to my feet.

"Thank you, Mrs. Backerman," I whispered, "or may I call you BB Star?"

"How did you know?" she asked.

"It was clear from our conversation that you weren't really Barbara Backerman. Once I realized that this BB was a droid, everything sort of fell into place. Your grandmother was the only positive role model you had in your life. It made sense that you would choose her as your alter ego."

"And here I thought I was being so clever," she said. "So what is it that you want now, Zachary?"

"Answers."

"Just answers?" BB-2 spat. "No credits?"

"You hired me to do a job. I did it and you paid me. There are a few new terms that we'll need to discuss but I have no gripe with you. There are worse people than you in the business world, after all. I'm just looking for some personal closure here."

"Closure?" they asked in unison.

"I need to know why."

The real BB sighed and took a seat in the great office chair. BB-2 stood obediently behind her.

"As I told you earlier, I learned soon after we were married what a horrible man BS Star really was. I actually tried to end the marriage but he wouldn't let me. He said that it would embarrass him and hurt the corporation. I kept myself away from him as much as possible. I was a virtual prisoner, but at least I was safe, or so I thought."

"BS was planning to replace you," I said.

BB nodded and gently touched the droid's hand.

"BB-2 was going to be the perfect wife. She would take my place. I would simply cease to exist and no one would be the wiser."

"How did you find out about the project?"

"You already know that, don't you?" she said.

I nodded.

"Ben Pierce."

"He was in love with me," she said. "It was a silly little crush but it was real enough to him. He told me about the project and the two of us made a deal."

"He reprogrammed the droids for you."

BB nodded again.

"He gave the first prototype a background in business negotiations, economics and several other disciplines. He made her the perfect business woman, the ideal candidate to run the corporation."

"And in return," I said, "you gave him BB-3."

"He programmed into her some . . . emotional feelings for himself. He tried to make her love him."

"That's why she didn't kill him when she found him," I said. "She still had some affection for him."

"Unfortunately, I think that's what made her unbalanced. You can't program love. It's too human an emotion. Her mind couldn't comprehend it. Benjamin made her human enough to feel emotions but he wasn't able to make her understand them. And then, of course, there was BS."

"He . . . had his way with her."

"Yes. He used her."

"You all did," I said. "And it drove her insane."

Both BB and the droid turned away.

"Yes, I suppose we did," she said. "That's a burden we'll have to bear."

"And when BS died . . . unexpectedly, you put your plan into motion?"

BB nodded and sat back in the chair as BB-2 leaned forward on the desk.

"I had no interest in running this company," BB said, "but I certainly wasn't going to turn it over to his credit-grabbing board of directors. They'd always resented me and they would have eventually found a way to toss me out of the company, destitute, if they could manage it. After what I'd been through, I deserved better."

"As a cold, emotionless droid and trained assassin," BB-2 said, "I was a natural for the business world."

"But Pierce left without BB-3?"

"He tried to fix her programming," BB said, "but it was no use. The hatred and psychoses were too deeply ingrained into her mainframe."

"We all agreed that she had become too flawed and dangerous to be trusted," BB-2 continued. "So we imprisoned her."

"We hated to do it," BB whispered, "but she had all these plans to destroy the world as we know it."

"She really had no mind for business at all."

"We kept her in stasis for years, hoping that we could find another way to help her but she escaped. And you already know the rest."

"You know," I said, "you could have saved us all a whole lot of time if you'd just told me this from the beginning."

"Control of the entire corporation was at stake, Zachary," BB answered. "Forgive us if we weren't willing to trust you with that."

"Oh, sure, why trust me with a business matter when it's only the fate of humanity on the line."

"Perhaps that was our mistake, then."

"Where's the real Grandma?" I asked.

"She died two years ago at the Centurion Center, where I live now. We kept her death a secret so that I could take her place. I miss her so much. She had more sense than all of us put together."

"I'll say," I mumbled.

I walked up to BB and gently placed the deactivator chip on her forehead. She smiled at me.

"Happy now?" she asked.

"Happy might be too strong a word," I said. "But I am satisfied."

I took a small piece of real paper from my pocket and put it on the desk. I'd been saving the paper for a special occasion and this certainly seemed to qualify.

"Here is the list of terms that will buy my silence. The terms are non negotiable."

Both BB and BB-2 looked the list over.

"Also, I'm keeping BB-3."

"Absolutely not," BB-2 said.

"It's not negotiable," I said. "You've proven that you can't be trusted with her. A friend of mine will keep her safe. Maybe someday we can repair the damage that's been done to her. By me and by you."

"Is that all?" BB asked.

"That's all," I said. "I'm trusting that you don't share BB-3's desire for world domination or destruction. But I'll be watching you."

I held out the deactivator chip, flipped it in the air like a James Cagney silver dollar and caught it in my hand. BB-2 flinched as it flew.

"And don't forget, I still have this." I said. "If you ever step out of line, I'll be waiting,"

I turned up the collar of my trenchcoat and nodded to the real BB.

"Is it a deal?"

The droid made a movement toward me but BB stopped her with a hand on her arm.

"It's a deal, Zachary."

I smiled, then turned and walked away.

"I could kill him now," I heard BB-2 whisper as I walked away. "A shot in the back and he would never know what hit him."

"Darling," BB replied, "I think we need to get you some sensitivity training."

And I closed the door on the case.

Epilogue

The pale blue surf broke lazily on the beach. Electra and I watched contentedly as we soaked in the morning sunlight on the New Costa Rican coast.

Three weeks had passed since the BB-2 showdown. The dust settled with relative ease, as is the case with most near-armageddons and the various loose ends seemed to tie themselves up nicely.

Fred Burns and Manuel Mani were arrested for illegal droid construction and creating a public nuisance. Burns was actually arrested on live Entercorp pay-per-view by DickCo PI Sidney Whoop. The special was Entercorp's highest rated event of the year, and the picture of Sidney holding Burns in one hand and Hazel's giant apron in the other made the front screen of all the major netsites the next day. Too bad Sidney can't remember any of it (thanks to Carol's mindwipe). He doesn't know it yet, but Sidney Whoop owes me a *big* favor.

ExShell unexpectedly dropped all pending charges against Dr. Benjamin Pierce, who returned to New Frisco recently after a long sabbatical in New Sri Lanka. He has been seen around town once again with Nova Powers and the rumor is that a spring wedding is planned (Gates help us all).

Barbara Backerman, whose most notable claim to fame was that she was the grandmother of BB Star, died peacefully in her sleep recently. The funeral was private, the body was cremated and the ashes were scattered over Oakland.

In an apparently unrelated story, a beautiful young ingenue named CC Backerman recently began a successful tour of the cabaret circuit in New Miami. Her stage name is Cinnamon Girl and I hear she's quite good.

BB Star mourned the loss of her beloved grandmother for almost an entire day and then went back to work running the world's largest corporation. ExShell's surprise renovation of the Fallen Arms in Oakland was a tremendous public relations success but an even bigger surprise has been the corporation's sudden dramatic increase in charitable donations. One particularly sizable donation was made recently to the children's free clinic at New Frisco General Hospital, which will keep the facility fully funded for many years to come.

As for me, thanks to a rigorous rehabilitation regimen of slicing mangos, stirring margaritas and rubbing sunscreen on Electra's back, my broken wrists, cracked ribs, gunshot wound and assorted other injuries were healing nicely, as was my spirit.

"So, mi amor," Electra said from beneath her straw hat, "when do you want to return to civilization?"

"How about never?" I answered.

She turned to me, slid her sunglasses down her nose and gave me a disbelieving look. "That's a long time to stay away from the office, chico. Won't your public miss you?"

"Well, it crossed my mind more than once during the whole BB-2 affair that I might be getting a little too old for this kind of work."

"Too old to save the world? Perish the thought."

"Come on, it's not really saving the world," I said. "It's finding some nutcase with delusions of earth-shattering grandeur. Basically, all I do is run around, get shot at, beaten up, blown up, slapped, pounded, mauled and generally abused. Then the agents and the PR people turn it into something exciting. It's only a matter of time before the entertainment conglomerates realize that they can sell the same stuff without me as the middleman."

"You're being cynical. And you're selling yourself short."

I rolled over and took another sip of the margarita (being very careful this time not to poke myself in the eye with the little umbrella—what can I say, I'm new at this relaxation thing).

"You're right," I said. "But you have to admit a life of leisure on the beach is pretty tempting."

"Come on back to the cabana, chico," she said with a smile. "I'll show you tempting."

I took her hand and we headed back to the cabana for another day in paradise.

That's when HARV showed up.

"Hey, boss. Nice tan. Life in the jungle agrees with you."

"HARV!"

"And, if I may be so bold, Dr. Gevada, the muscle tone of your legs and torso is truly a wonder to behold."

"You promised me he wouldn't be around," Electra said as she elbowed me in the stomach.

"HARV, I thought we agreed that you wouldn't use the mind-link while I was on vacation."

"We did indeed, and you have to admit that I've been very obedient to this point. It's just that a bit of an emergency has arisen and I felt you should know about it."

"I'm not interested, HARV."

"What?"

"I'm not interested. Whatever crazy emergency is happening in Frisco right now can wait until I get back to the office. That is, *if* I ever come back."

"That little tease about your possible relocation aside, I think you'll be interested in this particular emergency."

"Why's that?" I asked.

"Because it's not in New Frisco. It's currently one kilometer off the shore of New Costa Rica and headed straight for you and the terrifically tanned and toned Dr. Gevada."

As if on cue, I heard the hum of a hoverjet in the distance. The sound grew louder with every heartbeat.

"Okay, HARV, what's going on?" I asked.

HARV turned up his nose a bit and looked away. "No, you're right. I'm certain that this particular emergency can wait until you get back to New Frisco, that is, *if* you ever get back."

"HARV!"

"Okay. I picked up a message from local air traffic control in your area. There's a hostile hoverjet headed your way, as I'm sure you can hear. The jet contains a psi and two heavily armed thugs, one of whom is so large he has three social security numbers. They are all employees of the HTech Latin American subsidiary, HTecho."

"What do they want?"

"My guess would be you. They did not specify the dead or alive part."

"Why?"

"I suggest that we concentrate on the whys and wherefores at some later time. Right now I think survival should be your top priority."

Our hovercraft rental, under HARV's autopilot guidance, zipped across the beach and spun to a halt beside Electra and me. The doors popped open and the engine revved enticingly.

"Weapons and refreshments can be found in the backseat," HARV said, with a gesture towards the open door. "You'll find more suitable attire in the trunk."

Electra sighed and climbed into the driver seat.

"I'll drive," she said.

"A fine choice," HARV agreed.

I took a long last look at the peaceful beach (and the fast approaching hoverjet) and hopped into the hovercraft beside my lady love.

"What was it you were saying," she said, "about being too old for this kind of work, chico?"

"It's a classic catch-22, honey, too old for the work, too young to die."

Electra smiled and gunned the hover into overdrive. We left the beach in a cloud of sand and with hot death on our tail. Once more into the breach.

My name is Zachary Nixon Johnson. I am the last private detective on earth. And I wouldn't want it any other way.

OTHERLAND

TAD WILLIAMS

In many ways it is humankind's most stunning achievement. This most exclusive of places is also one of the world's best kept secrets, created and controlled by The Grail Brotherhood, a private cartel made up of the world's most powerful and ruthless individuals. Surrounded by secrecy, it is home to the wildest of dreams and darkest of nightmares. Incredible amounts of money have been lavished on it. The best minds of two generations have labored to build it. And somehow, bit by bit, it is claming the Earth's most valuable resource— its children.

TANYA HUFF
VALOR'S CHOICE

"Readers who enjoy military SF will love Tanya Huff's VALOR'S CHOICE. Howlingly funny and very suspenseful. I enjoyed every word."
—*scifi.com*

Staff Sergeant Torin Kerr was a battle-hardened professional. So when she and those in her platoon who'd survived the last deadly encounter with the Others were yanked from a well-deserved leave for what was supposed to be "easy" duty as the honor guard for a diplomatic mission to the non-Confederation world of the Silsviss, she was ready for anything. Sure, there'd been rumors of the Others being spotted in this sector of space. But there were always rumors. Everything seemed to be going perfectly. Maybe too perfectly. . . .

0-88677-896-4 $6.99